BELLADONNA

BELLADONNA

ANBARA SALAM

WHEELER PUBLISHING
A part of Gale, a Cengage Company

GALE
A Cengage Company

Copyright © 2020 by Anbara Salam.
Wheeler Publishing, a part of Gale, a Cengage Company.

ALL RIGHTS RESERVED

Wheeler Publishing Large Print Hardcover.
The text of this Large Print edition is unabridged.
Other aspects of the book may vary from the original edition.
Set in 16 pt. Plantin.

**LIBRARY OF CONGRESS CIP DATA ON FILE.
CATALOGUING IN PUBLICATION FOR THIS BOOK
IS AVAILABLE FROM THE LIBRARY OF CONGRESS**

ISBN-13: 978-1-4328-8141-2 (hardcover alk. paper)

Published by arrangement with Berkley, an imprint of Penguin Publishing Group, a division of Penguin Random House LLC.

Printed in Mexico
Print Number: 01   Print Year: 2020

For Maria, Photeini, and Rebecca

■ ■ ■ ■

I
CONNECTICUT

■ ■ ■ ■

1.

JUNE 1956

It was Isabella who invented the game Dead Nun. Before she moved to St. Cyrus, we had simply played Nun. Decked out in white pillowcases, we knelt between the beds in Flora McDonald's spare room until someone guessed which nun we were aping. It was easy enough; Sister Josephine was a characteristically heavy breather, and Sister Mary Benedict blinked in long, slow strokes, like a dairy cow. But when Isabella joined our sleepovers, she insisted on the morbid finale. And so Flora moved the beds apart until four girls at a time could lie side by side on the floor. That's when the challenge began: the last girl silent won. The last girl silent was always Isabella.

My job was to count Mississippis. Partly because pretending to be dead was a terrible jinx, but mostly because I was never actually invited to join. Instead, my place was by the window, where I perched on the sill with what I hoped passed for easygoing cool. Since Flora had once been a Girl Scout, her job was to make sure nobody cheated. Flora claimed she could judge best by standing in front of the door, but I knew it was strictly preventative, since Mrs. Mc-Donald was the kind of mom who covered Kleenex boxes in ruffled quilts for modesty. And even though Flora made me say Hail Marys with her after each sleepover, and even though watching girls lying still and being quiet wasn't much of a Friday night, I appreciated that the game gave me a chance to be close to Isabella. To observe how she wrinkled her nose when Sophie Le-Baron giggled and spluttered. To cheer her when she rose victorious from the floor, red-faced and clammy, her pulse beating in the hollow of her throat.

When Isabella arrived at our high school that year, I never dared to hope we would be friends. The rumors of her malaria had awarded her an irrevocable celebrity even before she enrolled.

On her first day, she'd turned up wearing old sneakers, as if school regulations were already of no consequence to her. She possessed heavy, quirky good looks — straight, dark eyebrows, full lips — and we immediately recognized her potential for womanly beauty. Her hair was long and black with a wealthy sheen to it, and though the rest of us had been wearing our hair in pageboys, I decided then to grow mine out. She had a low voice and moved with a careless confidence we studied with reverence. Mrs. Stockley, the dance teacher, was always telling us to sit like ladies, to cross our ankles like ladies, and occasionally she made us practice gliding up and down the gym with hardback copies of *The Adventures of Tom Sawyer* balanced on our heads. But Isabella gnawed her fingernails and crouched on the cafeteria bench with her knees pulled to her chest. She was perpetually jiggling her foot during classes, and as she passed through the corridors, she whistled, like a boy. Around her right wrist was a band of pale skin she said was a tan mark from the hospital bracelet. I realized later it couldn't have been, because surely nobody wears their hospital bracelet to the beach.

Isabella's robust constitution took on a mythic quality. Girls began minimizing their coughs and colds, keeping Isabella in the corner of their vision as they stoically refused to complain about strep throat or sinus infections. There was a sudden mad fashion for charity work. Talent shows and

11

bake sales and raffles to auction sunset cruises and Calder mobiles. And all the proceeds going to the African Trust for Tropical Diseases. Never mind that Isabella wasn't actually *in* Africa when she got malaria. The rumor alone was enough to sustain our guilty frenzy of conspicuous altruism.

And over the course of the year, Isabella's infamy had only grown. Samantha Bleath said she'd seen Isabella diving from the top board at St. Cyrus Country Club. Eleanor Robinson said that while drinking a milkshake at the Creamery, she'd seen Isabella pass by, check to see that no one was watching, and kick Mr. Anderson's Scottish terrier. Flora reported that Isabella's father brought her back a new charm for her bracelet from every country in Europe. I covertly appraised Isabella that year during Mass: the raw fingernails, the charm bracelet tinkling above her not-a-hospital-band tan line. But I understood my role as second-tier acquaintance. I would be allowed close to Isabella at sleepovers, at lacrosse, and during games of Dead Nun. It seemed selfish to wish for more.

But then a rumor spread around high school that we were playing Dead Nun, and our game was busted. The nuns got the wrong idea and thought girls were giving each other sacraments. The whole grade was called into an assembly. With rheumy eyes, Sister Marie Carmel warbled on about the sinfulness of mocking the last rites while we muffled yawns and stared at the gilded list of prefects inscribed on the far wall. Flora was sitting straight upright, the tips of her ears turning pink. Sophie LeBaron was picking at a thread on her kilt, and Eleanor Robinson was studying the back of her Bible with unusual concentration. Three rows in front of me, Isabella turned and caught my eye. Slowly, she crossed herself and then mimed a knife through her heart.

My pulse shot into my eardrums. I didn't care that everyone would see. I was glad everyone would see. Isabella. Acknowledging in front of the whole school that we were allies. That we shared a secret. From the teachers' bench at the front, Sister Mary Florence flinched and her lips grew tight. She tapped her wristwatch, mouthing, "Corridor," with a menacing arch in her eyebrows.

After the closing prayer, Isabella and I waited in the corridor while girls filed by us into classrooms. As they passed, they whispered and nudged each other, looking at us, or conspicuously not looking at us. Isabella

13

chewed her fingernail and began trying to balance on the edge of the banister, as if she weren't in trouble at all. My ears were hot. It was the first time I had ever been sent into the corridor.

"Demerit," Sister Mary Florence said, appearing from the auditorium. "Both of you." She took out the little leather book she used to record the names of delinquent girls.

I'd expected worse. A lecture. A Bible reading at the least.

Sister Mary Florence flicked through the book to find a blank page. "And detention until four p.m. in the library."

Isabella's mouth fell open. "But I can't!" She turned to me, as if I had any say in the matter. "I have a dress fitting today." Her expression was so stricken it prompted something inside me, a bubble of inspiration.

"It was my fault," I said.

Sister Mary Florence snapped her book shut and stared at me. I don't know that she'd ever looked at me properly before. "I beg your pardon?"

"It was my fault," I said, more loudly now, pressing my fingernails into my palms. "I dared her. Before school."

Sister Mary Florence sighed. "Fine. Report to the library after class. Miss Crowley, you are dismissed."

Isabella shot me a wild look that was part horror and part relief.

"You can call your mother from the office," Sister Mary Florence said, beginning to turn. "And explain why you'll be late home."

I didn't move.

Sister Mary Florence frowned over her shoulder. "Come along."

I struggled against the prickling in my eyeballs. If I cried now, it would ruin the bravado I had conjured. And Isabella was gazing at me as if I were a fighter pilot about to board a jet. I swallowed to keep my voice steady. "My mom won't be there."

Sister Mary Florence raised an eyebrow. "She won't?"

I shook my head. That the truth sounded like a lie made me feel even guiltier somehow. I pressed my nails harder into my palms.

"Fine. After lunch, please ask —" Then Sister Mary Florence stopped and focused on my face. "Ryan, isn't it?"

I nodded.

"Bridget Ryan?"

I nodded again.

She adjusted her glasses on her nose. "Walk with me, Miss Ryan." As we turned the corner I looked back at Isabella, who was staring after us. The door swung again and again on its hinges, revealing stutters of her astonished face.

"Tell me," Sister Mary Florence said quietly. "How is your sister?"

"Rhona? She's good," I said, before recognizing the opportunity. "I mean, not good, but . . ." I trailed off.

Sister Mary Florence stopped in front of the staircase to the teachers' lounge. "On this occasion, I'm willing to rescind your demerit, Miss Ryan."

I held my breath.

"I understand at the moment you must have" — she coughed — "pressures at home."

I tried to look suitably pressured.

"But you must still report for detention. Let it be a lesson to you." She put her hand on the banister post and twisted it under her palm. "And one more word of advice, Miss Ryan," she said. "Guard yourself against bad influences."

When she continued to stare at me, I gave her a humble, slow nod. Only when she closed the door to the teachers' lounge did I realize that by "bad influences," she meant Isabella.

■ ■ ■ ■

After detention I swung open the library doors with so much enthusiasm that the cafeteria windows bounced in their frames. I blinked into the afternoon, surprised by how improbably bright it was — I had almost convinced myself it would be nighttime. The bitter, sickly scent of dill pickles was leaching from a vent in the wall, and I took a deep breath, reveling in my new appreciation of liberty.

"Briddie," Isabella said, leaping off the railing by the tennis courts.

"You waited?" My voice came out high and hoarse. "For me?"

She shrugged. "I finished early."

"Oh."

"Anyway" — Isabella snapped her gum, which wasn't allowed on school property, although I didn't say so — "you really didn't have to cover," she said. "They never woulda made me."

"Oh."

"But it was amazing, Briddie. You're such a hero."

"Thanks," I said. My cheeks burned. I tried not to stare at her as we walked together past the tennis court where Miss

Frobisher was yelling at Catherine McLoughlin.

"What'd she make you do? Lines?"

"Flagellation," I said.

Isabella's mouth hung open, gum and all. Then she smacked me hard on the arm. "Jeez, Briddie."

I cleared my throat. "You don't think they'll count it against me, will they? For the academy applications?" Although I had tried to pass it off as a casual question, the two hours I'd spent copying out 1 Corinthians had given me plenty of time to picture in feverish detail the tribunal where Sister Mary Florence's little book would be placed on a set of weighing scales, and my blackened name would be struck off the list of nominations.

Isabella blew a halfhearted bubble that deflated with a squeak. "Course not."

"You're sure?" I held my breath, willing to be persuaded.

"The academy isn't going to reject you just because of one lousy detention."

"OK."

"Anyway." Isabella spat out her gum and, with deft precision, poked it into a join in the railing. "Silent nuns would practically be *pleased* about our game. It's practically a compliment."

"Sure," I said.

As we stopped at the crosswalk, Minty Walsh shouted, "Izzy!" from the tennis court.

Isabella turned and gave her a dainty little wave.

I straightened my posture. There I was, casually walking side by side with Isabella. Where other people would see! I checked my outfit. Was there any chalk dust on my kilt? I had Rhona's silver acorn pin on my blazer and I took confidence from that, knowing Flora had coveted it since middle school.

We crossed the road and walked along the path that joined Main Street. I felt for the "emergency" dollar bill in the pocket of my kilt. "You want to go to the diner?"

"Not hungry," Isabella said.

"OK."

As we turned the corner onto Main Street, Isabella pointed to the fountain that was meant to commemorate John Everett Jr.'s faithful Labrador. With an exaggerated sigh, she slumped onto the edge of the fountain.

I sat next to her and rubbed my Abercrombies together until they squeaked.

"I'm so beat," she said, throwing her arms behind her and leaning on them, rolling her head from side to side. It was a strangely adult gesture. I had seen my father stretching his neck in the same way. It made Isabella seem even older, more mature, than she had previously. My stomach scrunched. Isabella was so sophisticated; why would she ever want to be friends with me? Rhona's pin seemed childish and stupid. I wished I could take it off and put it in my pocket without her noticing.

"It has been super hot lately," I said, regretting the weak comment even before I finished saying it.

"Yeah. And I get beat so easily now, you know." She tugged down on the skin under her eyes.

This was new. Isabella was not a whiner. If anything, she wore her endurance like a blue ribbon. I nodded sagely and pulled the compassionate lip twist people always adopted when they talked about Rhona.

Isabella looped a lock of hair around her finger. "So listen. It actually wasn't a dress fitting." A penny in the fountain was shining, and it threw a silver fleck onto her face. I watched it wobbling from her cheek to her lashes.

"I had a doctor's appointment."

I gave her as neutral a nod as I could manage. "OK."

Isabella sat forward and rested her chin

on her kneecap. "Sorry I didn't say. I mean, I woulda said, but —" She licked her lips. "Sorry."

A plume of warmth surged through my spine. "Don't worry."

The fountain bubbled. The silver fleck quivered under the line of her eyebrow.

"So did the doctor give you the OK for your motorcycle license?"

Isabella snorted. She kicked her heels against the fountain. "God, Briddie, it's so *boring* being sick. I mean, I'm not really sick anymore. But still. I'm so bored waiting to get normal again. You know? Last summer I was practically a shut-in. I swear I'll go crazy if I have to spend any more time indoors."

"Could you at least read?" I tilted my head back, closed my eyes, and let the sunlight beat against my eyelids. I hoped that was the right way to act. Taking it for granted instead of making sympathetic gurgles.

"Oh no. I didn't even know where I was most of the time. I was like a rag doll."

I opened my eyes and glanced at her.

She was staring at me with an odd flush in her cheeks, all the fidgeting abandoned. "My mom had to clean me. Even when I was well again. She had to *wipe* me." She said it with a hardness in her expression, as if challenging me to console her.

I knew she was being real then. That we would be friends. Because there's nothing glamorous about a mom lowering her teenage daughter into the tub.

"My mom can't even wipe the kitchen clean," I said.

Isabella tipped her head back and laughed. The sound of her laughter filled my chest. I swallowed the guilty squirm for being cruel about Mama.

"Anyway." She licked her lips. "Don't tell, will you?"

I felt the frown on my face.

"It's just, I don't want the girls whispering and stuff," she said, shifting on the edge of the basin.

"I won't tell."

"Promise?"

"Promise."

Isabella shuffled closer to me. "In that case," she said, "I have a secret for you."

"Oh?" My stomach lurched. It was a secret about when she had malaria, I was sure of it. Sophie LeBaron would be so jealous.

Isabella leaned toward me and pressed her hand to my ear. Her breath was hot and smelled of bubble gum, artificial and buttery. "You're the prettiest girl in school," she said.

I blinked.

She pulled back and, with a groan, jumped down from the basin.

Speckles of water from the fountain flicked against the back of my neck. What was the right thing to say? It was a lie. Not just a small, white lie either. It was a lie so untruthful it was almost insulting. Isabella took a long stride toward a crispy-looking leaf. Was it a test? Was I supposed to deny it? If I said thank you, would that make me bigheaded?

"Not after you moved here," I heard myself saying instead.

Isabella stamped on the leaf and turned to me with a smile. "Briddie," she said, "you're ridiculous." She held out her hand.

Pulse rushing into my temples, I stepped forward and took her hand in mine.

And there she was, holding my hand.

Isabella.

2.

JUNE

On Monday morning I pushed Flora Mc-
Donald to the front of the line for Mass. All
year I had found it distracting to sit behind
Isabella, studying the line of her nose,
searching out the tiny beauty spot behind
her right ear. So when I nudged Flora into
the first pew, I made a special effort to flutter my eyelashes during prayers. To smile at
Flora with mischievous cheer, to show how
much fun I was, how interesting. At the end
of service I squeezed past Flora to stand
behind Isabella, and before I knew what I
was doing, I reached out and touched the
back of her shoulder.

She turned and her eyes loosely focused
on mine. "Oh, hi."

My confidence faltered. "Um. Did you
have a good weekend?"

Isabella shrugged. "Republican Club benefit."

The Republican Club benefit was a lavish

affair hosted by Mrs. Quincy, a widow with such celebrated Yankee pedigree that her skeleton was probably made from strips of the *Mayflower*. The attendees had to wear red masquerade masks, and there was a silent auction at midnight.

"Who won the boat?" I said. There was always a boat.

On the other side of Isabella, Sophie Le-Baron turned and scrutinized me. "Were you there?"

I examined her. Was she being cruel, or was she really so dreamy she couldn't remember the guest list? She began to chew absently on her lip, and I came down on the side of dreamy. "Not this year," I said in the end.

We shuffled out of chapel and I fell into step beside Isabella. "Are you going to camp over vacation?" I crossed my fingers in my kilt pocket. If Isabella was staying in St. Cyrus, I would at least have a chance to court her friendship. Maybe she'd invite me to the country club. I'd have to buy a new bathing suit.

Isabella shook her head. "No, no camp for me."

A rush of glitter soared through my body. "Really?"

"We'll be in Bristol, at the summerhouse."

And all my hopefulness shrank back. I pictured a whitewashed cottage, windows blown open onto hillocks of dune grass. In the distance, a Dalmatian running across yellow sand. "So you won't be here?" I said, my voice dangerously close to breaking.

"No, Briddie, we'll be in Bristol." Isabella rolled her eyes. "Bristol, *Rhode Island.*"

On the other side of her, Sophie giggled. She pushed her arm through Isabella's with such careless familiarity that I felt ashamed of my delusions of competing with her. Sophie LeBaron wasn't the richest girl in our grade, but her particular kind of richness afforded her a flimsy glamour, like a gold butterscotch wrapper. Her house had a downstairs ballroom with special carpet laid in strips so their house-maids could roll it back for dancing. Her parents threw infamous parties: at Thanksgiving, Mrs. LeBaron hid an emerald ring inside a pecan pie for a guest to find. But the most anticipated event was their Labor Day fireworks display, which my parents were never invited to. Flora said Mr. and Mrs. LeBaron ordered coolers of lobster specially delivered from Maine. And a woman from the conservatoire played a harp in a ball gown. Sophie's family was from Texas, and since she had been the "different" girl before Isabella enrolled, it was pure social economy they should be best friends.

Sophie began talking about a cousin with a boat, or a cousin's cousin with two boats, and I fell halfway into a daydream where I took a bus to Rhode Island and strolled along a pier at sunset. Isabella would chance upon me as my hat blew into the water. Or maybe I'd be lounging on a candlelit patio, surrounded by amorphous, elegant friends.

"Will you be going to camp, Bridget?" Sophie said, with such articulation that it was clear she was taxed by her own politeness.

"No," I said.

Isabella laughed. "Briddie doesn't have any interests." My cheeks filled with blood; my shoulder knocked against the handle of a locker. Isabella gave me a theatrical wink. "Like me." She tapped her yearbook.

Sophie frowned at Isabella. "You have interests."

"I'm *interested* in getting out of St. Cyrus for the summer," Isabella said with a toss of her wrist, her charm bracelet jingling.

They laughed and began to talk between themselves about the Fourth of July, about the correct lotions for lightening freckles. And as Sophie and Isabella filed into the library, I hung back. I pulled my yearbook

27

from my satchel. It still had the glorious fresh yearbook smell, like a new plastic tablecloth. I flicked it open to our junior class photos, and true enough, there were only two girls with blank spaces where clubs and activities should be: under Isabella's photograph, it simply read "Izzy," and under mine, "Bridge." Even Sophie was a member of the Riding Club. I closed the book with a snap. Was that all I had to offer Isabella? Nothing?

That week I watched Isabella as she sunbathed on the tennis court during recess, as she doodled in the margins of her textbook during religious education. And in the evenings after school I sat on my bed and dreamed up scenarios for coaxing her friendship. It had shimmered before me, the day of detention. The promise of acceptance into a realm of hearty constitutions and fearless stunts at the country club. But now a long, Isabella-less summer vacation was looming ahead. Me and Rhona would lay out in the backyard on an old sheet Mama had darned too many times to be usable. Me and Flora would go to the community pool and paddle in the shallow end, since Flora was afraid whenever she couldn't touch the bottom. And by fall, Isabella would have forgotten we were ever close to being close.

And so, on Thursday morning, our final proper school day before vacation, I took destiny into my own hands. As the girls ran out for tennis, I faked an untied shoelace and lingered in the locker room. My heart crashing through my skull, I slipped my hand into Isabella's satchel and withdrew the cool, jangling chain of her charm bracelet. My fingers were numb, my heartbeat splashing against my eardrums. If anyone was to come in now, I'd be done for. I threaded the bracelet through the grate at the top of my locker and then ran onto the court, squiggles of white vapor creeping over my vision.

After tennis, I scratched myself across the ribs racing to change back into my uniform. Only as I was leaving the locker room did I risk a peek at Isabella. She was sitting on the bench and had begun to rummage through her satchel, pulling out barrettes and pens and tossing them onto the floor. Giddy, almost tearful, I ran straight home after school, convincing myself all the way that I could hear a telltale tinkling inside my bag. At home I locked my bedroom door, pulled the curtains, and withdrew the bracelet. With shaking hands, I examined the charms for clues to decipher Isabella's magic: the ballet slipper, the butterfly, the heart-shaped locket with the tiny, stiff key.

Friday was a half day on account of the summer vacation, and everyone was antsy, undoing their top blouse buttons as a concession to recklessness. Roll call was a scrimmage of girls inscribing yearbooks and exchanging bags of peppermint hearts from the drugstore. Isabella was in high demand, signing autographs and writing the address of her summerhouse on slips of paper for urgent vacation missives. Patiently, I waited until she was released from the melee and stopped at the drinking fountain.

I approached her as casually as I could manage. "Hi. So, did you leave a bracelet behind in the locker room?"

Isabella wiped her mouth with the back of her hand. "Yeah," she said slowly.

"It's just, I found one, and I wasn't sure if it's yours or not," I said airily, as if I hadn't traced its contours until the silver got warm.

With a yelp, she reached out and hugged me, her yearbook jabbing me in the chin. "I musta looked everywhere. Where was it?"

I licked my lips. "Between the slats in the bench."

Isabella raised her eyebrows. "Jeez. Close

call. Thanks, Briddie." Her eyes traveled over the line of my pockets, her interest slipping.

"Oh, I don't have it on me," I said. "I took it home in the end, for safekeeping." Now was the moment for my triumph. "I'll meet you tomorrow so I can give it to you," I said. "Maybe at the park?"

Isabella chewed her thumbnail. "Tomorrow? Tomorrow is the club mixer."

"Oh." I had forgotten about the monthly St. Cyrus Country Club Mixer. The other girls were always restless on the Friday before, forsaking lunch for slices of grapefruit packed into their satchels while I drank my cafeteria milk. Members were allowed to bring their dogs, and even from the bench on the other side of the street, I could hear a symphony of barking that lasted long into the evening. "Sunday, then, after church?"

Isabella screwed up her nose. "I'll just come over tomorrow and pick it up."

"Come over?" I blinked at her.

"Yeah."

"To my house?"

Isabella rolled her eyes. "Yes, Briddie."

My gut was tight. I tried to place Isabella in my house. It was like setting a chess queen on a game of tic-tac-toe. "Why don't

I just meet you somewhere? The Creamery?"

"But I don't know when the mixer will be done." Isabella batted me on the shoulder with her yearbook. "Leave the bracelet with your mom if you'll be out."

"OK," I said. My stomach was churning. Isabella wanted to come over; she *offered* to come over. Her willingness was surely a good sign. But then why did she mention Mama especially? I observed her as she scribbled in Minty Walsh's yearbook. Only Flora had ever been to my house. What if Isabella was just coming to investigate? Or worse, what if she was an envoy from the rest of the class? Isabella caught my eye and gestured for my yearbook. I watched over her shoulder as she wrote, *Briddie saves the day again! See you soon, love Isabella.* I stared at her inscription, at our names nestled there together. I allowed myself the luxury of hope.

On Saturday after lunch, I rearranged my bedroom with a curatorial fervor. My mermaid night-light I pulled out and wedged into a drawer between my jeans, along with a goofy photo of me and Rhona in matching Easter bonnets. Then I began a deliberate messening, selecting tokens of slovenliness that might indeed prove I was a real person. A tube of Mama's Rose Sunset lipstick, discarded just so under my mirror. I draped a white cashmere sweater from Granny by the window seat even though it was far too hot to be out of the closet. I stood by my vanity and assessed. It could have been worse. At least I didn't have cross-stitched Bible quotes framed above my bed like Flora. I positioned Isabella's bracelet on my dresser at a nonchalant angle and then, for the final touch, pulled a book about Italy from my shelf and cracked the spine, laying it on the bed. When the door-bell rang, I flew down the stairs, yelling, "I'll get it, Mama."

Isabella was on my doorstep.

"Hey." She was wearing white slacks and a white T-shirt with an oversize tweed jacket.

"Aren't you hot?"

She raised her eyebrows. "Not really. Gonna invite me in?"

"Oh." I stood aside.

Isabella pulled one hand out of her pocket and pointed to a picture on the wall. "Oh my God, baby Briddie!"

I froze. I'd been so worried about my bedroom, I'd forgotten to doctor the evidence of my awkwardness in the rest of my house. In the photo, Rhona was precious and pigtailed, and I was pressing my fist to my eye, a spit bubble forming. "It's terrible, don't look," I said.

Isabella smiled. "It's adorable. My mom lost a bunch of my baby pictures in the move, so you'll just have to imagine me small and ugly."

I scrabbled for the right response. "I hardly have to imagine," I said.

She stuck her tongue out at me. "Is that your parents?" She gestured to a photo hanging over the telephone and began to walk down the corridor. There was an anticipatory clench in my stomach.

"Isabella? Sorry, it's just, my mom — do you mind — is it OK if you take your shoes off?" I said, all in one breath.

"Sure." She leaned against the banister, still staring at a picture of Mama and Dad in a rowboat on Lake Quinsigamond. As she handed me her sneakers I noticed her left sock had a ladder in it through which I could see the staggered line of her heel. Isabella shrugged off her jacket, too, and as I hung it up, I fumbled under the collar for the make. But an embroidered name tag had been sewn over the label: Ralph De-Laney. Of course. Ralph. What other allure could persuade someone to wear tweed in June? I gave it a tentative sniff. It was sour, like a dusty rug that had been lying in the sun. Isabella was climbing the stairs, whistling, and as she reached the top landing she turned. "Which one's yours?"

I pointed to the door on the right and she let herself in. "Cool."

The bed screeched, and I came in to see her bouncing on her elbows. As I'd hoped, she'd picked up my *Treasures of Italy* book and had opened it straight to the photos in the middle. "Oh my God. Look at that." She held it toward me, tapping a photograph of a woman drinking espresso in front of a cathedral.

I wasn't sure if I was supposed to be impressed or scornful so I settled for a neutral "I know."

Isabella sighed. "It's divine," she said with uncharacteristic wistfulness.

I perched on the edge of my dresser and then on the corner of the bed. Then back on the dresser. "So you'll apply?"

Isabella frowned at me over the top of the book.

"For the academy. I mean, your parents will let you apply?"

Isabella snorted. "They couldn't stop me."

A treacly sort of happiness flooded my chest. "Me too," I said. "I've been hoping for it since sophomore year. Though my grades are kind of . . ." I trailed off.

Isabella looked up at me, her eyes bright, conspiratorial. "Me too," she said.

"So you like art history?" I stared at the carpet. It felt somehow exposing to be asking her directly.

Isabella rolled over onto her back. "I guess." She smiled up at me. "And what's *not* to like about adventuring in Europe? Jailbreak!"

I nodded. "I can't wait to get out of St. Cyrus." As I said it, I probed the idea, pushing myself to the town boundary, then to the coast, across the ocean. It was an elastic sort of feeling, projecting myself away from home. Pliant, precarious. I wasn't sure that I liked it.

"A whole year away from Rotary Club luncheons," Isabella said dreamily.

I had never been inconvenienced by a Rotary Club luncheon so it was hard to summon the right kind of relief. "It would be cool."

"It would be everything," Isabella said, fixing her eyes on me. "Just think, Briddie. We'd have a whole year, just for us!"

"We would?"

She laughed. "Of course."

"But —" I licked my lips. "But what about Sophie?"

Isabella scoffed. "Sophie will be married to Matty before they've cut the cake at her cotillion."

"Right," I said, although I didn't know who Matty was. "So." I swallowed. "You'd go without her?"

"But you're going, right?"

I crossed my fingers behind my back to avert a jinx. "I mean, I want to."

"Then I'll go with you," she said, shrugging, as if the matter was settled. "You just have to swear that we'll stick together so we can have fun — never mind the nuns." And she laughed.

"OK," I said. My cheeks were tingling. "I swear."

She smiled. "It'll be glorious, Briddie."

Me and Isabella, juddering on bicycles through an orange grove, sitting at the end of a pier, dangling our legs into the sea. And then my heart plunged. "But, Ralph, he's not — I mean, doesn't he want to get married?" I pinched my nails into my palms.

Isabella sat up and twirled her hair around her wrist before letting it fall. "His trust is all tied up 'til he's twenty-one, so, you know."

I nodded, although I didn't really know. The important thing was that he wasn't trying to claim her. I saw Ralph and Sophie falling aside like two bowling pins. "You should probably take this." I handed over the bracelet.

Isabella let out a breath. "Briddie, you're my champion." She thrust her wrist toward me, and when I stared at it, she shook her arm. "Help, please."

I focused so hard on clipping her bracelet that I grew light-headed.

"My parents woulda given me the lecture of a lifetime if I lost this again," Isabella said, waving her wrist so the charms clacked together. With a bounce, she leaped off the bed and opened my closet. She flicked through my dresses in such a perfunctory way, I knew she wasn't admiring them.

"How did yours meet?" she said. I was concentrating so closely on the shuffle of my darned cardigans that I didn't catch her meaning. "Your parents."

"Oh." There was a tightening in my throat. I could feel the conversation brewing before us. "The war," I said eventually. Although that wasn't strictly true. Or true in any part.

"Neato." Isabella pulled out my straw boater and admired herself in the mirror on the inside of the closet door. "Was your dad in the army?"

"No." I pretended to adjust a plastic tray

on my dresser. "He was working. In England."

"That's so cool." Isabella took off the hat and put it on the wrong hook. "I wish my parents had a cool story of how they met. Something romantic. But they knew each other their whole life. It was practically an arranged marriage."

I made a noncommittal noise.

"And it wasn't a big deal? Her being from Arabia and all?"

Woodenly, I repeated the phrase Dad had made us practice. "My parents were married legally in the United Kingdom and my mom's naturalization was approved in 1947," I said.

Isabella rolled her eyes. "I knew that," she said.

I didn't think she really did know that.

"I mean, didn't your dad's parents throw an absolute fit?"

"Not really. Granny — my grandmother — she likes my mom. I guess it wasn't a big deal."

"That's neato," she said again. "My grandmom is an old bat." Isabella turned around and caught sight of Dubs, my stuffed bear, on the shelf above my bed. She picked him up with a swoop. "And who's this?"

I winced. Why hadn't I thought to hide

him? "Some toy."

"Yes, but aren't you going to introduce me?"

Just then, Mama knocked on the floor with the broom. Isabella turned to me, her eyebrows high on her face.

"That means it's suppertime."

Isabella laughed, tossing Dubs on the bed. I laughed too, though it had never struck me as funny before.

I swallowed. "Will you stay for dinner?" I wasn't entirely sure I wanted her to stay for dinner. Things were going so well, it seemed like gambling to ask for more. "You don't have to, I mean, maybe you have —"

"No, I'd love to stay," Isabella said, picking up *Treasures of Italy* again.

My heart bopped in my chest. "You don't need to ask your mom?"

"She's still at the club."

I ran downstairs, two steps at a time. "Mama, I have my friend here can she stay for dinner?" I said breathlessly, bursting into the kitchen.

Mama was sailing between the fridge and the oven, a half smile on her face. I evaluated her through Isabella's eyes. Her apron was clean; her navy blouse was conservative, unobjectionable. Though she never wore mascara, her eyelashes were enviably dark. She would pass, I decided. Through the door into the backyard I could see the back of Dad's head on a lawn chair, where they had evidently been sitting for some time, since the ashtray was full.

"Of course, Budgie. I'll just set an extra place."

"Her name's Isabella."

"OK, Budgie. Sounds great." Mama opened the oven door. "Go get your sister."

I ran back up the stairs. "Mom says it's OK," I yelled to Isabella, who nodded behind *Treasures of Italy.* I stuck my head through into Rhona's room. It was thick with a sort of nap-time stuffiness. "Supper, Rhony."

She sat up groggily from her bed. "Is someone here?"

"Yes, my friend Isabella," I said.

"Sophie's friend?" Rhona said, rubbing her face.

I shrugged.

"I'll be down in a minute." She reached for a sweater on her ottoman.

"Your hair is all messed up from the pillow," I said, unable to help myself.

Rhona's face appeared through the neck hole in her sweater and she shot me a frigid look. "Don't worry. Her Majesty won't be inconvenienced by my uncombed hair."

"Thank you." I tried to apologize with an extra-wide smile. Still, I left before she stood up, so I didn't have to see the knobs of her spine moving through her sweater. Something about Rhona's back always made me feel kind of odd. Like she was really a fish and that was her fin.

Mama had made lasagna. It was the special way I liked it, with bread crumbs on the top to make it extra crispy. Isabella sat next to me and the table jiggled every time she kicked the leg, although thankfully Dad didn't tell her to stop.

While we waited for Rhona to come downstairs, Mama set out her saucer of carrots and another of buttered bread. "Rhony is on a special diet," she said to Isabella with a deliberate breeziness.

I held my breath, staring down at the tablecloth.

But Isabella just nodded. "Sure."

Rhona came to take her usual place opposite me, and as promised, her hair was combed and pinned back with a green bow.

"Your hair looks *lovely,* darling," said Mama. "How lovely you all look."

Rhona gave Mama a stiff smile. "Hi," she said to Isabella; then, sitting down, she flipped the bread over to check it hadn't been buttered on both sides. When Mama went to refill my milk glass, I watched as Rhona scraped a thin layer of butter off the slice with her knife and wiped it into the napkin. She caught me watching and let her knife fall on the side. I didn't say anything.

As we ate, Dad lectured us about the dangers of fireworks even though nobody asked. Then we got onto lightning, and then he told us about a storm from when he was a boy and how the hailstones were as big as eggs. Isabella said she'd once read about a storm in Hawaii that sucked up a bunch of frogs, carried them over to another side of the island, and rained them down again.

"Raining cats and frogs, eh?" Dad said, overloudly, to Rhona.

Rhona gave him a blank smile and crunched another small mouthful of carrot. She took a gulp of water, and I could see the movement of the water through her throat as she swallowed. I turned my attention back to my lasagna, hoovering it up at great speed.

"Would you like some more lasagna, Isabella?" Mama said.

Isabella shook her head. "Thanks, Mrs. Ryan, but I'm full to burst."

"More for you, Budgie?"

Everyone else had put down their forks. "Yes, please, Mama," I said.

"Young ladies," Dad said, standing up and tipping an imaginary hat to us. He went into the kitchen and I heard the rustle as he picked up a newspaper.

"Is it true you have a private tutor?" Isabella said to Rhona. A jolt of panic rattled through my eardrums. I definitely had never told her that.

"Yes," Rhona said icily. "Is it true you have a horse?"

"Yes," Isabella said.

"But she doesn't ride it," I added, although that made it worse.

"Pebbles. He's more like a big gerbil," Isabella said, kicking the table leg again. "Strictly for petting."

"Rather an extravagant kind of gerbil," Rhona said.

"Yeah. And I *also* had a private tutor, so I guess I win the brat contest," Isabella said with an audacious smile.

Rhona shot me a look that was a blend of question mark and amusement.

Mama came back and put down my plate with an extra square of lasagna on it. She kissed me on the top of my head, and I tried my best not to squirm away.

Isabella leaned over and grabbed hold of my wrist, pulling my watch toward her. "Say, I should probably jet off. Sorry, Mrs.

Ryan." She looked at me. "I'm supposed to meet Ralph."

"Oh."

I walked her to the front door, handing back her shoes, her coat. My face was throbbing. Of course she wasn't going to stay and hang out with me. Of course she was rushing off to see Ralph. If I hadn't had her bracelet, she would never even have come. And now she was leaving. Leaving for the whole summer. Next year I'd have to go back to staring at her from behind during class, hoping that the force of my interest alone would be enough to charm her. Like being watched by a sentient potato.

"Are you coming to Sophie's birthday next Saturday?" Isabella adjusted the cuffs on Ralph's jacket.

I swallowed. "I don't know." But I did know, as I hadn't even been invited.

Isabella frowned at me. "You *have* to come."

"Maybe." I tried to look indecisive.

She flicked her hair over her shoulder. "I insist," she said. "I'll remind her to remind you."

"You will?" A gate swung open in a meadow, a staircase appeared in the chute of a waterfall, a woman in a scarlet dress reached into the audience and ushered me onstage.

"Sure." She shrugged. "Don't think any more of it."

3.

JULY

It began raining on the way to the LeBarons' house, and Mama was driving so slowly I even saw the mailman pass us by. She was wearing the wide-brimmed hat normally reserved for Mass, and a blue neckerchief. I inspected her out of my peripheral vision, suspicious about how much she had fixed herself up just to give me a ride. But it wasn't every day we got to drive up to the door of the LeBaron mansion, so I appreciated her need for preparedness.

We drove past the iron gates at the front of their property and down a long, straight gravel driveway. Mama pulled up on the left of the house. White roses bloomed over the doorway and a silver balloon tied to the front porch bounced under the raindrops, reflecting lozenges of light into the car.

Mama snapped opened her purse, took out her compact mirror, and reapplied her lipstick. I realized then she was going to come in with me and tried to climb out of the car as quickly as possible.

"Bye, Mama," I said, gathering Sophie's gift from under my seat.

"One second, Budgie." She rubbed her index finger over the front of her teeth.

But I had already slammed the door. "I don't think there are many grown-ups there, Mama," I said through the window.

"Sweetheart, it's rude if I don't thank her for inviting you."

I cursed myself for not expecting this — Rhona was usually so good at predicting when we would have to discreetly detach ourselves from Mama in advance.

"OK," I called over my shoulder, taking long steps toward the front door. If I put as much distance as possible between us, maybe it wouldn't seem like we were there together. I heard Mama's car door slamming behind me as I reached the porch. The door was propped open and a white ribbon was tied around the knocker. I paused and took a breath. I pictured myself on horseback, charging across a drawbridge and into a watchtower. The fortress that would unlock Isabella.

The front hallway was decorated in fern green wallpaper, and something about the dim light and the smell of wood polish lent it the worn grandeur of a museum. A huge oak staircase on the right disappeared off onto a second landing. Loitering at the base of the staircase, I looked over a narrow table boasting photos of Sophie in various stages of childhood dorkery — milk-toothed on horseback, diapered and gripping the threadbare ears of an ornamental tiger-skin rug. A door on my left opened and I caught the smell of broiled salmon.

"Afternoon, miss." An older black lady wearing an apron approached me. "Can I take that for you?" She gestured to the gift.

"Thank you," I said, looking up at her. "It's from Bridget," I added.

"Oh yes, there's the card." She smiled appreciatively at my drawing of a birthday cake. I had copied it from one of Mama's cookbooks. It was supposed to be a wedding cake, but I didn't think Sophie would mind having her birthday treats promoted.

"Would you like some ice tea?" she said. Before I could answer, Mama came behind me and rested her hand on my shoulder. Suddenly glad she was with me, I nodded at the maid.

"Thank you," I said.

I saw her look from Mama to me. "Mrs. LeBaron and the other ladies are in the garden."

We walked in single file down the corridor, past four or five doorways. On the right, an open door revealed a cavernous wood-paneled room with a real glass chandelier. I craned my head, hoping for a glimpse of the famous carpet.

"Don't dawdle, Budgie," Mama said, pressing me forward.

We came into a large kitchen with a stainless steel refrigerator and marble counter-tops. I touched them in case they were painted Formica, but the surface was cool under my palms. On the right was a winding staircase leading down, and I tried to peer into the gloom in case the LeBaron basement was superior in some way I'd never thought basements could be.

Through the back door I could see ladies in pastel day dresses milling around beside a kidney-shaped pool. There was a banner hanging from one side of the garden to the other: Sophie's Sweet Seventeen. I stepped out, searching among the crepe de chine for Isabella. The garden was the size of a hockey field, lined with urns of purple heliotrope. At the back was an imitation Greek pool house, where mothers I recognized from the clothing drives and charity fairs at school were sheltering under the awning, smoking and patting hairdos fluffy with drizzle. It was easy to spot Mrs. LeBaron. She was wearing a peach silk dress stained with raindrops, giving instructions to three young men in dinner jackets wrestling with a patio umbrella.

There weren't any girls from school in the garden, and I had an irrational moment of panic that I might have come on the wrong day. Mrs. LeBaron stared at me a moment, then waved me toward her. Her fingernails were painted with dark lacquer.

"Bridget, honey, how nice," she said, kissing the air around my head. A heavy gold ring clinked against her champagne flute.

"Thank you for having me," I said.

A raindrop fell into the bowl of Mrs. LeBaron's glass and she frowned up at the darkening clouds. A strong, sweet gust of wet grass and warm clay rose from the earth. "Why don't you go upstairs and see the girls? Sophie *will* take her time getting ready."

"My mother is here," I said, glancing behind me at Mama, who was lingering in the kitchen, admiring, or pretending to admire, a refrigerator magnet in the shape of a banana.

"We can take care of your momma," she said. "Why don't you go on and join the girls upstairs?"

I gestured for Mama to step into the garden, and she followed, wobbling as her heels sank into the grass. "Bye," I said, hurrying past her, deliberately not looking behind me. I didn't want to watch Mama try to make conversation. I didn't want to spark that feeling I got sometimes, watching her try. It was a queasy and pitiful feeling, like finding a drowned butterfly in a baby pool. I started up the oak staircase, following the sound of chatter to the first landing and toward a room on the right. I passed an oil portrait of Mrs. LeBaron, chinoiserie vases filled with white roses, a taxidermied bear cub holding an ashtray. Softly, I knocked on Sophie's door, then poked my head around. The room was large, with canary yellow wallpaper. Isabella was hunched over on a window seat, wearing a mint green dress with a sweetheart collar, the tan lines from her bathing suit pale against her neck. Sophie was in peach silk, like her mother. She was curling her eyelashes with concentration at a Perspex vanity. The twins, Alison and Meredith Graham, were in sky blue tulle, kneeling on a sheepskin rug, and Alison was brushing Meredith's hair. I surveyed the room for chandeliers, seams in the carpet that indicated it might be rolled back. Sophie's bedspread was decked in ruffles, and in pride of place in the center, I was relieved to see a teddy bear with a red heart patched onto its stomach. On the walls were mawkish illustrations of rosy-cheeked girls skiing somewhere wholesome, perhaps Canada. The air in the room was dry and cool, and it took a moment before I realized that the machine in the window ruffling Isabella's dress was an electric air-conditioning unit.

"Hello," I said from the doorway.

Eleanor looked up at me. Her dress was so close to the shade of the wallpaper that I hadn't registered her. She sat cross-legged on the floor with a book spread out on her knee. *Rookie,* I thought. Even I knew better than to bring a book to a party.

"Bridget's here, at last!" Eleanor shouted, as if they had all been waiting for me. I could have hugged her then, book or no book.

Sophie gave me a smile in the mirror. "Welcome." As I went over, she planted a kiss on my cheek.

"Happy birthday!" I said.

"Thanks." Sophie tossed her hand as if birthdays were nothing but a tiresome facade.

There was a moment of silence while everyone surveyed my outfit. I smoothed down my dress with my palms. Rhona had generously called it "dove," although it was apparent now that it was closer to pigeon.

"Briddie." Isabella patted the window seat, and I obeyed. She was breathing on the window and doodling in the steam. "You're late," she said, with the hint of a pout.

"Sorry," I said.

Alison and Meredith abandoned their hairdressing and joined Sophie at the mirror, licking their fingers and smudging down their eyebrows. I saw then they were all carrying velvet cases heavy with lipstick and rouge. Eleanor joined the girls at the back and began fixing her earrings. My cheeks grew hot. I hadn't known to arrive in a state of strategic undress.

"Would you like some hairspray?" Sophie said, catching my eye in the mirror. Even as I was shaking my head, I knew I should have said yes.

"It smells heavenly. It's Oriental Pearl."

Meredith nudged Alison in the ribs, then giggled, covering her teeth. They both looked at me.

Heat prickled over my breastbone. Were they laughing because I didn't use hairspray? Because I *didn't* smell heavenly? Rhona had let me use her Youth-Dew;

54

maybe that was the wrong kind of perfume?

"Oriental Pearl. Like you," Meredith said eventually.

I looked to Sophie for help, but she dropped her eyes to the carpet.

"I've never been to the Orient," I said stiffly.

Alison wrinkled her nose, like I was spoiling their fun. "The other one, then," she said, shrugging.

Meredith giggled again. "Maybe the spray would make half of you invisible."

I opened my mouth and closed it. I had the sense the insult was moving too fast for me to catch hold of it. My stomach lurched as if I were jumping down a playground slide.

"You know" — I put my face against the window — "I think Matty just lit up a cigar," I said. Although I wasn't sure that Matty was even there. Or which one he would be. Through the condensation all I could see of the boys was a hazy prep school rubric: pasty faces floating above piped jackets.

"No," Sophie gasped. "Did my mom see?"

"She's sharing it," I said.

Isabella burst out laughing.

Sophie looked from me to Isabella. "Bridge. You monster."

Isabella squeezed my arm. I smiled at her, though my face was tight.

"What a shame about the weather," I said, trying to approximate the right tone of mature refinement.

Sophie sighed and, nudging Alison out of the way, took a seat on the edge of her bed. "This whole party was my mom's idea. I *told* her we should have rented the club. Whoever heard of a sweet seventeen anyway?"

"Your cotillion party is all that matters, right, Soph?" Isabella said. She tapped her ring finger meaningfully.

Sophie smiled at her with performative bashfulness. "Don't jinx it, Izzy. Just because *your* mom wants to lock you away 'til you're twenty-one."

Isabella chewed her fingernail. "Let her try."

"Is your mom here?" Alison said to me.

I nodded.

Alison and Meredith exchanged a glance. "Can we see her?"

I licked my lips. "I don't think she could stay long." I crossed my fingers under my skirt, hoping against every last hope that Mama had already left.

"Ignore her, Bridge." Sophie leaned over and squeezed my hand. The move was so fluid, so assured, I suddenly realized they must have been talking about me before I came in.

Sophie was still holding my wrist. "Anyway, I swear you couldn't tell." She gave me an exaggerated wink.

"Tell?"

Sophie licked her lips. "You know —" She started to laugh and then stopped. The room was poised with the hush of deliberate listening. A fizzy sort of anticipation bubbled in my gut.

"You know," Sophie said again. "Your mom. It's not like she's . . ." Sophie mouthed, "Obvious." She gave me a winning smile. "Not like Ali Baba or anything." And she picked up the laugh from where she had abandoned it before.

Isabella stretched out her foot and kicked Sophie's shin. "You are such a dunce — Maria Montez is Dominican," she said.

I was so filled with gratitude I could have floated out of my seat.

Sophie waved her hand. "Come on — you know what I mean about Bridge. Like, if you didn't *know,* you wouldn't know, you know?"

Eleanor rooted around in her velvet purse. "I have some new lipstick," she said loudly. "Bridge, you want to try?"

Isabella let out such a gruesome groan we all turned to look at her. She slumped against the window. "Jeez, you are such a pill. I'm sick of messing around with makeup. Let's play a game. Or are we just going to be stuck inside all afternoon being bored to death?"

The danger of Isabella's boredom was palpable, and we looked between each other in an agitation of despair. Meredith shot me a terrified, collusive grimace, and my stomach relaxed. I forgave her jibe in a rush. Perhaps it was quite funny? Perhaps being compared to an Oriental Pearl was flattering? I bunched my hands into fists. Maybe Sophie was trying to be nice to me. To point out no one could tell. Why did I have to take everything so seriously?

"Izzy's right," Sophie said. "Let's go down. I think we kept the boys waiting long enough." And she raised her eyebrows at Isabella.

There was a twinge in my gut. Was Ralph downstairs? Would I have to speak to him? To be nice to him? I steeled myself. I'd have to summon my most enthusiastic laugh for the inevitable, rowdy teasing boys always employed when trying to prove to themselves that girls were entertained by them.

The lamps in the room flickered twice and

went out. We all shrieked although we weren't afraid. It was almost blue in the room. The clouds had darkened outside and the heavy sound of rain was clattering against the windows. With the air conditioner off, the room grew syrupy with the smell of vanilla hand lotion.

"Miss Sophie?" a woman's voice called up the stairs.

"Sarah?" Sophie groped for the door handle.

"The power's gone out, miss. Just stay put. I'll bring up some candles."

We whispered and clutched each other — the unexpected drama was a thrilling disaster. Sophie's maid brought up two lit candles and passed one to Sophie. "Mind you don't trip on the way down the stairs," she said, gesturing for us to follow her.

Giggling and shushing one another, we fell behind Sarah, and every few steps she called out, "Mind the edge of the carpet," or "Railing on the left," even though we could just about see anyway. Sophie was holding her candle low next to her bodice, and an apricot loop of light glowed around her. Isabella ran to her side and pushed her arm through Sophie's. I followed at the back, behind Eleanor. The bottom of Mrs. LeBaron's portrait came into view, and the vases; then the beady eyes of the taxidermied bear cub loomed out of the shadows, and when Eleanor crashed into its ashtray we all yelped.

Downstairs was now filled with guests. It was muggy and close with damp silk as women filed through the corridor. Gold candlesticks had been placed on the sideboards, and through the murky light I took nervous, shallow glances for Mama but couldn't spot her. I lingered at the bottom of the staircase. Through the windowpane on the front door I could see that our car was gone from the driveway. So that was one thing to be grateful for. There were more guests than I'd realized, maybe thirty adults. Mrs. Quincy was checking her reflection in the hallway mirror, adjusting an oddly whimsical pair of earrings shaped like mallards. Mr. Robinson, the fire chief, was humoring Father Brennan as he delivered a long, monotone speech about the renovation at St. Christopher's. The sideboard was now stacked with a tasteful display of arthritic, formal gifts: a rosary, a silver carriage clock, a bottle of wine to be set aside. It was clear that Sophie's birthday was merely the excuse and not the occasion. It was noisy in the crowded space, and people began filing into the ballroom, where I could hear Mrs. LeBaron calling for Sophie. The girls were nowhere to be seen. My belly was heavy. I turned and went back into the kitchen so I could pretend to search for a drink. Somehow, it would be much lonelier to be standing on the edge of the crowd. In the kitchen, pails of ice were being loaded onto the counters by hassled-looking men in white waistcoats making dashes into the rain to retrieve platters of sodden fairy cakes. The kitchen floor was streaked with grass and crushed ice. I stood by a table of punch and took a glass, watching the orange slice bobbing dolefully in the liquid.

Isabella tapped me on the elbow. "Briddie, there you are. Come, we're playing sardines."

"What?"

"Come on." She looked over her shoulder and motioned for Alison and Meredith. "I got Briddie."

"Where's Eleanor?" Alison said.

"Reading?" I offered.

Isabella snorted. "Briddie, you're awful."

"What about Sophie?" Alison said.

"The president of the Rotary Club is giving a speech." Isabella stuck out her tongue and crossed her eyes. "It'll be ages — I'll go out of my mind. Come on, we did it last year at my sweet sixteen."

I had the strange sense I was rolling backward. Of course Isabella had birthdays before she moved to St. Cyrus. She had friends even before Sophie. I pictured a row of girls in peach silk dresses marching in a procession along Main Street.

Isabella ushered us past the table of punch and through a swinging door into a deep pantry. A chink of light through the hinge shone on rows of canned tomatoes. It smelled like sawdust, and there was a baited mousetrap in the corner. "Count to fifty," Isabella said. "That way we can all have a chance before the power comes back." Isabella slipped out the door and it squeaked shut behind her.

Meredith cleared her throat. "Do you think she's really hiding?"

"What?"

"Last time we played sardines, Izzy was in Ralph's car all along."

The sides of my face tingled. "Why?"

Alison and Meredith giggled. "Bridge!" Alison squeezed my arm. "You're so bad."

I didn't understand what was so controversial about that, but at least they were laughing with me now instead of just in my direction.

"Do you think it's been fifty counts already?" Meredith said.

"Let's wait twenty more."

There was a pointed silence, so I assumed my customary role and counted Mississippis. Then we swung the door open. Whispering, the twins turned right and slunk between two waiters carrying trays of highball glasses.

I was unexpectedly nervous. I started toward the big oak staircase and then stopped. Isabella only wanted fifty counts, so she couldn't have gone too far. Instead, I crossed the kitchen and approached the basement stairs. I felt out for the steps with one foot and slowly descended, my heartbeat tinny in my ears. On the left was a utility room, with a narrow window that peeped over the top of the lawn, allowing gloomy light to mark out the shape of a washer and an old bathtub. The room was stuffy, the air damp. It was harder to hear the rain down there, although the gutters on the side of the building gurgled with water.

"Isabella?" I whispered. I waited and listened. A woven wicker mat lay across the top of the bathtub, and two folded sweaters had been moved from the mat onto the floor. I rolled the mat back from the edge of the tub. And there she was!

Isabella grinned. "Quickly," she said, shuffling over.

I climbed into the bathtub. We just about fit, although we had to nestle down under pleats of her mint green silk. Isabella shook out the mat and shifted it about until it covered us. It was utterly black and unbearably hot inside the tub. Our breath stewed in the confined space. Beads of sweat pearled on my skin. The heat of Isabella's body pressed all along the right side of my own. As my eyes grew accustomed to the darkness, I saw her face was painted with darts of faint light through the weave of the wicker.

Footsteps clattered down the stairs and the staircase jogged about. I hoped it hadn't shaken so heavily when I came down it.

"Izzy?" Alison's voice.

Slowly, Isabella's fingers crept to the bodice of my dress. She started tickling. I squirmed but clamped my mouth shut. I would not cry out and lose the game. She tickled harder, scrabbling beneath my underarm. I buckled against her once, twice, snorted out my nose. I put my left hand on her shoulder to push her away. The glint of her smile was visible even through the gloom. She grabbed hold of my hand.

"Izzy?" Alison came into the utility room and flicked the light switch, but the power was still out. My heart was beating wildly. I could feel the drum of Isabella's pulse against my shoulder. She took hold of my ring finger and brought it to her mouth. I felt the dampness of her breath against my fingers, and then the hot softness of her tongue against the tip of the one she held. She closed her teeth and bit it gently. A squirm went through my body, like a guitar string. It caught under the curl of my toes and traveled through my core and into my throat. My pulse surged so rapidly, my temples grew tight. I said nothing. I willed myself not to make a sound. It would lose us the game. She would not make me a loser. But I was concentrating so fiercely my whole body trembled.

The staircase thumped again. Now I heard Eleanor's voice. "Did you check the kitchen?"

"Yes," said Meredith and Alison at the same time.

"Where's Bridget?"

"I haven't seen her."

"I'm getting creeped out now."

"Ugh! Is that a spiderweb?"

"Do you think she's in the washer?"

"I felt something on my neck for sure."

"Is there another room down here?"

Isabella inched closer to me, and now her mouth was by the corner of mine. I could feel the humid exchange of our breath. The quake traveled into the tips of my fingers. My heartbeat must be so hard she would surely notice it.

Isabella inched closer.

The backs of my knees were shaking.

And then she bit the corner of my mouth. I may have gasped, but I don't think so. I would not give the game away.

Then her tongue was liquid inside my bottom lip. And her mouth was moving for mine. Her pulse was beating through her lips and in the arc of her neck, where her heartbeat fluttered. I let my tongue curve up and meet the slightness of hers. And the guitar string was plucked again, harder, deeper, through the center of my body from the hollow of my throat right to the join between my legs. I felt I might be passing out. My brain unspooled. Her body tensed and then gave, a yielding, an accord. And Isabella made a noise, just a slight noise. And at that, I began to unwind.

With a judder and a whir, the lights flicked back on. A record player stuttered back to life, and there was a cheer from upstairs, followed by the chime of clinking glasses.

Laughing, Isabella sat up and pushed the mat aside. "Hurray! Come on, Briddie." She clambered out of the tub and fluffed out her dress, combing down her hair with her fingers.

I sat up, dazed, my lips swollen, prickling. Isabella began climbing up the staircase. The hairs on my arms were standing upright. Everything in my body was alert, listening. I climbed out and followed up the staircase, my ears ringing.

In the kitchen, the waiters were blowing out candles and the air was tickly with smoke. My eyes stung. Mrs. Riordan was talking to Mrs. Quincy about the Catholic League; someone in another room was playing a violin. My brain felt full of bouncing putty. I leaned on the edge of the drinks table.

"Bridge, where were you?" Sophie said, gripping me by the shoulder. Her cheeks were pink. "I was looking for all y'all." She smiled, but her mouth was twitching. "My mom gave this toast." She picked up a glass of champagne from the table.

"Sorry," I said. "Isabella —" I swallowed.

"Ugh. Izzy. I should have known. Where is she?"

I pointed to where Isabella was standing, behind the door of the ballroom. She was talking to a young man, presumably Ralph. His features were puffy, bland, given shape only by the bulb of a snub nose.

"Sometimes, I swear —" Sophie shook her head. She let out a breath and sipped from her glass. "Well, you know what Izzy's like. The thing is not to let her wind you up."

"OK," I said.

But I was unwound completely.

■ ■ ■ ■

II
ONE YEAR LATER

ITALY

■ ■ ■ ■

4.

AUGUST 1957

I traveled to the academy a week before the start of term. It was my first Italian train journey and I pushed the window right down to the quick for my introduction to Europe. After leaving Milan we jostled between hills lined with crumbling stone walls, silver olive trees crouching in the scorched grass. We passed through fields of blazing sunflowers, women wearing faded head scarves yawning by the tracks. Somewhere outside Colonna, three boys on the roof of a shed waved to the train, then pelted the carriages with mulberries, shrieking. I closed the window after that.

I was the only person leaving the train at La Pentola. It was two thirty p.m., and the station was empty, the ticket office shuttered. The ground was spotted with gummy tree sap, tiny flies squirming in the mastic. By the front entrance a wooden signpost that read ACCADEMIA pointed to the hills above. And true enough, high up over the lake, the bell tower of the academy was poking out from behind sunburnt leaves. I could have broken into a jig. My new home! I corrected myself: *our* new home. Isabella might even have arrived already.

I stood under the awning at the front of the station, hoping for a taxi. But after twenty minutes of loitering and peering down the overgrown, rutted lane, I decided to walk. Clutching my suitcase and hatbox, I followed the lane between lines of fruit trees cast in nets. The fields were thrumming with cicadas in jouncing waves of noise, the air gritty with toasted grass. After half an hour, the path joined a hill alongside La Pentola Lake. I was squelchy and molten with afternoon heat — it was like being pressed in the center of a grilled cheese sandwich. At last, at the top of the hill I spotted a black-and-white marble staircase. On the right, a large wooden cross was nailed into the earth, its paint blistered from heat.

The wind ruffled through a eucalyptus tree, rallying a squall of brittle leaves that skittered against my hat. The breeze was chalky with hot dust and vaguely skunky from oregano roasting in the hedgerows. I took a deep breath. Isabella and I would have Italy to ourselves for a whole year! My opportunity was finally at hand — we'd study side by side and drink red wine at wobbly roadside tables. We'd stay up talking long into the night, reading Italian poetry, debating Renaissance art. Together. Always together.

The two-story building at the top of the stairs was the academy proper, a sun-bleached ochre square with a mossy terra-cotta roof. To the left of the academy was a chapel with a rough stone bell tower, gray-brown and much uglier than I had antici-pated. Farther left, the landscape rose to sparse woodland. I hoisted my cases up the steps toward the grand front door, and on my right the cypress trees thinned out, sunlight flashing on the lake. Finally, I got close enough to read a tarnished panel fixed to the stone: ACCADEMIA DI BELLE ARTI DI PENTILA. I nearly cheered out loud. By the door was a discolored pull cord, and when I yanked on it, a bell echoed inside the building.

Almost immediately, the door opened to a tiny bird of a woman. She was very small and very old. Her face was round as a peach and marked with deep lines.

"Welcome, welcome," she said, standing aside.

I took off my hat and stepped past her, trying in that step to demonstrate my studiousness, my respectable upbringing, my right to be an academy scholar.

She patted my arm and shuffled behind a desk. The room was dark and faintly musty with the lingering scent of damp plaster. There were two bucket chairs on the right, worn through to the weave at the back, with shiny patches on the arms. Over the desk was a cheap-looking clock that filled the room with its deliberate tick.

"Here," she said, opening a ledger near the telephone and tapping it with some urgency.

It was a pencil-lined visitors' book. I scanned the page for Isabella's name, but there was only one other entry from August, and it was a "Greta Sniegowska." I wrote my address and name carefully, although my hand was sweaty and left a crescent-shaped mark on the paper.

"OK," she said, smiling and showing the stumps of three teeth. She crossed to a door on the far side of the room. "Come, come." She motioned. We climbed up a dark, narrow staircase that opened out onto a bright landing.

"Santa Teresa," the old woman said, crossing herself before an alcove where a faded tapestry of St. Teresa of Pentila hung. St. Teresa's red hair cascaded down her back, a golden arrow parted her lips, another pierced her heart. Her hands were folded over her chest in pious contemplation. I crossed myself politely and pretended to gaze upon it appreciatively.

"Galleria." The old woman gestured in front of us to where the marble landing became corridors with shuttered windows overlooking a central courtyard. The academy was a square building. The top floor contained bedrooms for the students, and on the ground floor there were classrooms, a refectory, and a library. I knew this much from my welcome folder.

The old woman turned to me. "Donna Maria," she said, pointing at herself.

"Donna Maria," I repeated, giving her a curtsy and cursing my stupidity.

But Donna Maria smiled and patted my arm. "Good," she said.

She took a right along the corridor, and I glanced out onto the courtyard. It was paved with honey-colored stone, and in the center was a stunted palm with a circular bench around its base. The upper-floor corridors projected over the courtyard, creating an arched cloister gallery below. On the far side of the courtyard was the convent itself:

the church with its ugly bell tower, and a single-story, narrow building, which contained the nuns' cells. Behind that was another complex of cabins whose purpose I didn't know. The tips of the Blue Mountains framed the landscape, and to the right, ribbons of fruit trees stretched out as far as I could see. Just then, a figure in a white dress and mantle opened the convent gate and crossed into the sunlight.

"Wow," I said, gripping a window frame.

Donna Maria paused and raised her head to look out into the courtyard. Her face twitched as she surveyed the scene, and, clearly not able to imagine I'd exclaim over the sight of something as mundane as a nun, she frowned at me. I tried not to blush — it was stupid of me to yell out like that. But a real Italian nun! It was like spotting a zebra or an elephant in the wild.

We followed the shape of the building, traveling parallel to the lake. Lined up on our right were neat little bedrooms. Through the windows on the far side, sunlight glittered on the water. I crossed my fingers over the handle of my suitcase and wished my room would have a lakeside view. But we reached the corner of the building, and as we turned away from the water I cursed my luck.

Donna Maria took me two doors down and unhooked a key from a ring in her pocket. The room was larger than any of those we had passed and had brown floor tiles and two single beds, one on either side of the window. It smelled like cider vinegar and beeswax. The window looked out onto the Blue Mountains, and stretching out below was an apple orchard.

"Grazie," I said.

She put the key on an oak dresser behind the door and waved good-bye at the doorway. Her slim tread echoed along the corridor.

I tested both beds and settled on the left-hand one, for no other reason than that the two screws at the joist were pleasingly symmetrical. Hopefully, my roommate wouldn't think I'd been selfish enough to choose the better one. We could swap, I decided generously, so she could see for herself how thoughtful I'd been.

On the dresser was an envelope with my name written in blue ink. As I picked it up, a pamphlet about the "Quickening Miracles of Santa Teresa" skittered to the floor. With it had fallen a postcard reproduction of the *Mona Lisa,* and I turned it over to find Isabella's cramped writing.

You've arrived early, haven't you? Send the nuns my love! Paris is splendid, I've drunk buckets of champagne, and guess what? Ralphy asked me & I said yes! It was terribly romantic. He says you have to swear to protect me from all the Italian lotharios.

Ciao! Izzy xx

5.

AUGUST

I sat for a while on the bed, staring at the orchard below my window. Ripe apples dropped to the earth with dull thuds. Bumblebees stumbled frowsy girdles around the trees. Isabella had been talking about her French vacation for months, and I knew of course that when Ralph met her in Paris, there was a risk he'd ask her to marry him. My skin felt suddenly saggy and limp on my body. Ralph had known to seize his opportunity; maybe he was smarter than I'd realized. It was meant to be *our* year, I thought sullenly. Our year of freedom. Isabella wasn't supposed to spend it yoked to Ralph.

I stared at the bland expression of the *Mona Lisa.* Why would she have chosen to send me this postcard? Perhaps the image was so cliché it had come back around to being fashionable? Or perhaps she really thought I was so dull and unimaginative that I'd appreciate such a stale keepsake. I read through her message again and noticed it was postmarked three weeks ago. A spark of hope twinkled in my chest. Isabella often got carried away. She could easily have changed her mind after three weeks of listening to Ralph's theories about federal income tax rates. Probably, most likely, almost certainly, she got wrapped up in the moment. And by the time she arrived, they'd have had some foolish squabble and called it off. She'd be poking fun at Ralph's Yale cufflinks and complaining about his loud, boorish friends with names like Peanut and Stoaty. Probably, most certainly, there was nothing for me to worry about.

I rummaged for my toiletry bag and followed the corridor down to the bathroom at the end of the hallway. It was so large it was almost industrial, as if you'd wash sheep in there. On the right were three ancient tubs stippled with verdigris under the faucets, and on the left three sinks and three cubicles with toilets. The unshuttered window at the back of the room looked onto the sharp contour of the Blue Mountains, so anybody for miles around would be able to see us bathing. Peering out, I thought of those boys by the train tracks, lining up to throw mulberries at the glass. I washed my face and hands at one of the basins, and the door swung open to reveal a blond girl.

"Oh hi," she said, her eyes alarmed. "Please tell me you're a student."

For a wild moment, I imagined telling her that I was the headmistress, a new chambermaid, faking a French accent, affecting a lisp. I grappled with the urge like a big billowing sail until it collapsed. "Yes, I just arrived."

"Thank goodness!" She gripped my hand. It was Greta of the visitors' book. She had a creamy complexion and the hale prettiness of a cherub. "I'm so glad to see you. I've been here for a week already and I'm going out of my gourd."

"No one else has arrived yet?"

She shook her head, leaning against the edge of the basin. "It's just been me and Donna Maria. And the silent sisters. If they count. I suppose they don't. Do they?" She laughed in a teetering, unsteady way.

"Where have you traveled from?" I had practiced the phrase on the train, deciding it was exactly the right tone of elegant curiosity with which to quiz my new classmates.

"Oh, hardly far," Greta said, slouching against the sink. Her backside was ample and shapely, and her curves spilled over the rim of the basin. "I was in Venice with Bobby, my fiancé."

I braced myself for the phoniness I'd need for the next part of the conversation. "How exciting! May I see?" I gestured toward the diamond on her left hand.

"Please." She yanked the ring from her finger and handed it over with so much enthusiasm I realized I'd misjudged her. As I held up the stone, I thought, *She'll be one of those girls who stretches out her angora sweater by sitting with her knees inside it, and gives her last cigarette away to a veteran at a tram stop.*

"Lovely," I said.

"Try it on, if you like," she said, gripping the edge of the basin. "Unless — you're not engaged, are you?" She scanned my hand in a panic. Her eyes were green like a cat's, her lashes blond.

"No." I smiled and slipped on the ring. I held out my hand. "How pretty." I took it off as quickly as seemed polite and gave it back to her. "Do you have any photos?"

"Of Venice?" Her eyes widened. "Oh, hundreds. And postcards, too. It's simply divine. Have you been?"

I'd been referring to her fiancé but was relieved she'd misunderstood me. I shook my head.

"You must come to my room and let me show you my album. It's exactly as nice as everyone says it is," she said with a sigh. "Even so, it doesn't really make up for being away." She looked over to the window and back at me. "I think I'm homesick already. I've been bawling my eyes out." She swallowed. "I promised Mom I wouldn't. But even *she* was bawling her eyes out when it came time to say good-bye. I bet there are moms all over America worried to death about their little girls being so far away." She smiled, but her lips were twitching. "Was your mom awful sappy about it?"

Startled, I opened and shut my mouth. "No," I said.

She frowned.

"I mean —" The day I had left to board the *United States,* Granny had taken Rhona for an anemia test and Mama had been distracted on the drive, looking again and again at her watch. "My mom has this big party to plan." I licked my lips. "She's kind of preoccupied with entertaining." I searched for possible reasons to celebrate and settled on the annual LeBaron extravaganza. "Labor Day."

Greta smiled, rolling her eyes. "Oh boy, my mom is just the same. We always have a cookout, and this year my brothers insist on catching all the fish themselves." She shook her head. "It'll be mayhem — all wet Labradors and piles of sailing gear on the dining table —" She broke off, shrugging. "But I don't need to tell *you,* I'm sure."

I gave her a smile but my chest was tight. "Yes," I said. "I know exactly what you mean."

Before supper, Greta insisted on touring me around the downstairs landmarks: the whitewashed classrooms, the mail cubby, the Mariani frescoes of golden apples across the library ceiling. Then back in my room, she fell into ecstasies over the view of the swollen afternoon light falling in spokes through the apple trees. At six, we washed our hands and faces and Greta brushed her hair. She offered to brush mine, but I knew it would make it frizzy more than neaten it up, so I pinned it behind my head with the tortoiseshell hairpin Rhona had given to me. Or rather, Mama had given to me and written, *Love from Rhona,* on the card.

We sat about in my room with our neat hair and washed hands and waited until the peals of a bell rang through the building.

"Suppertime," Greta said, leaping from the mattress of the other bed.

The refectory was a large room with

wood-paneled walls and two long banquet-style tables with benches. We lingered on the threshold as the nuns filed in from the door on the left wall. In their white habits and scarves the sisters all looked identical at first, but as I let my eyes settle on them I began to pick out the details. Not all the nuns were old, as I'd expected. Some were older even than Donna Maria, with gummy mouths and lined faces. But there were young nuns, too. I figured at least five nuns were under thirty, although it was difficult to guess their actual ages without hairstyles or clothes to give them away. Most of the sisters appeared to be Italian, tan and freckled from outdoor work. One nun walked with a limp; one had such rosy coloring I would have sworn she was wearing rouge if I didn't know any better. There were even two black nuns.

"Before you came, I was by myself on this whole table; it was dreadful," Greta whispered.

"Are we supposed to talk in here?" I whispered back.

She shrugged. "How would I know?"

This struck us as terribly funny and I had to look away from her so as not to catch the giggles. A pale nun with a long nose served us a jug of what I took to be apple juice, and two small glasses, like the kind you might use to gargle mouthwash.

"This is the famous hard cider," Greta said, sticking the tip of her tongue out as she poured.

"I don't know," I said nervously. "I mean, are we allowed?" The only alcohol I had ever tasted before was champagne, since dawdling by the catering table was a convenient form of social camouflage at St. Cyrus events.

Greta smiled. "It's positively encouraged. Look, even the sisters are drinking it."

And true enough, the sisters were pouring themselves glasses and sipping it as if it were pink lemonade instead of liquor.

Greta held up her glass to mine. "Cheers," she said, and we clinked.

The cider was bitter, with a loose silt swirling in the bottom of the glass. It was flat, ice-cold, and terribly strong. My eyes watered.

The long-nosed nun returned with two plates of buttered pasta with slivers of garlic and tiny clams. Donna Maria rang a bell and said a short grace in Italian. Then all around came the clink of forks against plates and the clatter of hollow shells tapping against the china.

I watched a young nun with a pointed

chin slurp noodles from her fork. "Have you ever seen a nun eat before?" I said.

Greta put down her fork. "I guess not." She paled.

"You don't think we're supposed to wait for another sitting?" I said.

We looked around us hopelessly.

"Maybe it doesn't count because it's not term yet?" Greta said.

"Maybe."

"I'm so glad you're here," Greta said seriously. "It's like being chaperoned by ghosts." She lowered her voice. "They don't even really look at you."

"The others will be here before too long," I said. Isabella would probably be late, I decided. Just to keep me waiting, as usual. I focused on prying a tiny clam from its shell, but it kept slipping through the tines of my fork. It was queer, though, how the sisters were in the room with us, but still separate. All year we'd be running parallel.

"Do you think the other girls will all speak Italian?" Greta said, suddenly.

I dabbed the butter from my mouth with my napkin.

"I mean, it's not a requirement, so . . ." She trailed off. She was looking down at her plate, but there was tension through her neck.

"I'm sure we don't need to worry," I said. "I know Isabella can't speak a word."

"Is she another student?" Greta frowned, fumbling in the pocket of her dress.

"Yes, she's a friend from high school." After a moment, I added, "My best friend." As I said this, I tested it in my mouth. It was a new era, after all, and I was poised to take over as best friend, confidante, champion.

"Hello there — oh dear." Greta yanked a single pearl earring from her pocket. She grimaced. "I've been searching for this everywhere."

I waited silently so we could return to the matter of Isabella.

"Wait." She twirled the stud between her fingers. "You have a friend coming? Oh, but you must both be awfully smart," she said with some alarm.

"Well." I hesitated. I wished with a palpable ache that Isabella was there to laugh off the question, to put Greta at ease without talking us down. "Our school always has two academy places," I said carefully. "This year, we were the most eager. I don't know about the best," I finished with an apologetic shrug. I had tried to talk myself into guilt about our placement, despite our B grades. But it was hard to feel anything else but blessed — it was something closer to a miracle.

Greta smiled. "The other girl who was supposed to come with me, Maggie Asquith, her mom got squirrely about it, and so I ended up coming alone."

"That's bad luck."

"Tell me about it," Greta said. "She has to take etiquette classes in DC instead! I already had such mournful letters from her. Did you know there are twenty-nine different types of spoons?" Greta began to rattle off a taxonomy of spoons and I stared at the backs of the sisters' heads. If Isabella were here, I thought, she'd be pointing out how noisily the nuns were eating, she'd be kicking the bench, poking fun at the middle-aged nun who had dropped a clam inside her wimple and was now searching for it with some consternation.

"And she already learned the pinwheel fold before her coming-out," Greta finished, staring at me with an incredulous expression.

I supplied her with a sympathetic smile.

Greta was still twirling the earring. "What luck to have your best friend with you. And here I thought you were an orphan like me."

"Promise, we'll look after you," I said, trying for a reassuring smile. It hadn't occurred to me before how difficult it must be for the others, to come to the academy alone.

A different nun, one with beady brown eyes and heavy jowls, collected the pasta plates and left us with a silver platter piled with fruits. Red grapes and rough-skinned ginger apples and egg-size violet plums, cloudy, as if they were breathed with condensation.

Greta and I attacked the fruit plate, and my tongue was soon raw; the apples were tart and coarse. Even if we did have to take meals in silence, I decided it wouldn't be so bad. In the far left of the room one of the nuns cut an apple in half and passed a section to her sister, who accepted it without even acknowledging the gesture. It must be quite relaxing, I thought, to be so close to someone you can forsake all the petty transactions of offer and reward.

6.

AUGUST

Over the next few days, yet more students arrived, and the academy class of 1958 was nearly complete. Nancy was a tall, pale girl from LA who wore her hair in twin auburn braids. There were two girls from New York City — Bunny and Barbie — who'd met on the *United States* and spent a week together in Milan before coming up to the academy. Patricia was a mousy-haired girl from Chicago, Katherine a tall, striking brunette from Boston who spoke with an English-sounding accent. Sally was from Florida, blond down even to the hairs on her legs, and deeply tan. There was a curly-haired girl, Betty, from Dallas, who spoke with the same chewy friendliness as Sophie LeBaron. Ruth, from Michigan, I took against straightaway. She had the vague shadow of a mustache and the dour self-righteousness of the unreasonably pious. There were two Marys — Mary Leonard, whose father was a professor at Princeton, and Mary Babbage, from Washington, DC. And there were Joy and Joan, whom I couldn't tell apart, and Sylvia, from Seattle, who had blond-red hair and a manic, lilting laugh that you could hear through the walls.

The upper corridor was now suffering under the collective enthusiasm of so many young women. Tubes of toothpaste squeezed out underneath the mirrors, face powder caking the tiles, sponges abandoned at the bottom of the bathtubs, limp stockings hanging to dry over the banisters. The corridor was hazy with hairspray and magnolia hand lotion and cigarette smoke and Dior perfume. It was noisy with running water and slippers clacking over marble and coughing and the humming of half-remembered jingles and "Will you just pull this zipper?" or "Have you got a needle?" or "Did I leave my grammar book here?" Our main entertainment was lining up in the corridor and watching the sisters coming and going from the chapel, debating which was the oldest or the youngest nun, the prettiest, the tallest. Barbie and Bunny developed a short-lived game that involved whistling like a cuckoo from windows on opposite sides of the corridor until one of the sisters looked up — and then hiding below the frame. I suspect Ruth gave them a scolding for it, because one afternoon both of them appeared from Ruth's bedroom with chastised expressions.

I lay in my rickety bed each night and hoped the next day would bring Isabella. We would get up early to go to the market in La Pentola on Saturdays, I decided. We'd collage signs for each other's doors, as Bunny and Barbie had done. I tried to relish the solitude of my room in case it was my last evening before my roommate arrived. The only time I'd ever shared a room had been at Camp Waramaug the summer after seventh grade, and I wasn't keen to repeat the experience. What if my roommate snored, or spoke in her sleep? What if she suffered from head colds and I had to listen to her turning and sniffing, accruing jars of allergy pills and sinus compresses? One of the truly liberating things about my life at the academy so far was my release from the regimens of the sickbed. And what if she wanted to stay up late chatting? We could set out a system of rules, I decided. A timetable. And a penalty scheme for indiscretions. Of course, I hardly dared to hope, but there was always a chance my roommate might be Isabella.

■ ■ ■ ■

The weekend before term precipitated a scurrying panic as girls sorted their papers and notes and arranged their bags and their outfits. As if the clothes we'd been wearing so far would no longer be glamorous enough for the scrutiny of the same group of people once we were sitting side by side in class-rooms instead of in each other's bedrooms. Greta and I retreated to my room so she could instruct me in the art of French braids. I sat on my bed, and Greta knelt in front of me on a towel on the floor. She combed out her hair so it was full like a cloud. "Now gather more from the left and cross it over."

I brushed it again, until her ears grew pink at the shell. I bit my tongue in concentra-tion. Greta's hair was so fine it kept slip-ping through my grip. It was like combing the locks of my old china doll. "Am I pull-ing?" I said, my eyes watering in sympathy. Having my own hair brushed by another person was close to a phobia — even Mama tugged at my curls and yanked my scalp.

"Not at all," she said, raising the hand mirror on her lap to catch my eye in the reflection. "You're a natural! I can't believe you don't have any sisters," she said. "Brothers are such bad luck, aren't they?"

Startled, I paused in the middle of braiding. "Oh." My pulse swirled through my eardrums. She didn't think I had a sister? Had I said something to suggest that? I cleared my throat. "I don't have any brothers actually," I said, deliberately leaving the first part of her sentence unattended. Now would be a good moment. I could mention Mama's curly hair, or say that Rhona's was fine due to illness. It was a casual opportunity to hint at complications to come. "How did you learn to French braid?" I said eventually, stalling for time. Greta had taken a breath to reply when the door opened. Standing in the corridor was Isabella. Her hair was faintly tousled, and she had the rumpled and rosy-cheeked air of someone who has been sitting on the prow of a ferry.

"Ciao," she said, in a careless sort of way, letting the door slam behind her and climbing onto the chair under the window.

I stared at her, trying not to tweak Greta's hair. "You're here?"

My heart began a pathetic flutter, like a butterfly trapped in a matchbox. She was here! I was itching to go to her. But the bunny softness of Greta's sweater was firmly tucked between my legs, my fingers in her hair. I would've had to swing one leg over Greta's head to get out, or else she'd need to wriggle. But she didn't wriggle.

Isabella looked from me to Greta, giving me a small-mouthed smile and raising her eyebrows in an ironic gesture I couldn't interpret. "Did you miss me?"

"It's you," I croaked. I had a ridiculous urge to cry.

"Hi, I'm Greta." She reached out to shake Isabella's hand.

"Isabella Crowley, how do you do?" As she leaned toward Greta, a lock of hair fell across her face, and she swept it back with a toss.

Greta clapped. "But you're the famous Isabella — I've heard all about you!"

Isabella smiled. "Don't believe any of the rumors Briddie has been telling you."

Greta glanced at me over her shoulder. "She never told me how gorgeous you are."

Isabella wrinkled her nose dismissively. But she did look gorgeous. Her skin was tan and glowed with a wealthy polish. Her brows and hair were lightened from the sun. "Oh no, I'm a dreadful mess." Isabella tugged at the worn boatneck that was still somehow chic on her. She took a tress of hair between her fingers and examined it. "I've been going totally wild in France. I was on the coast, and *all* the women were bathing nude." I knew she composed this declaration to see if Greta would react with ladylike shock.

But Greta looked down at her arm and said, "Good for you! If I go out in the sun I turn red as a cherry. It's hideous. If I had your coloring, I'd never wear my bathing suit."

Isabella laughed as if Greta had said something witty. But it meant Greta had passed the test. "While you're hairdressing, do you think you could cut mine?" she said to Greta, drawing a strand away from her head.

"No, really? But it's so beautiful!" Greta hobbled toward her on her knees. She put her fingers through Isabella's mane and lifted it so all the hues of brown and gold caught in the sunlight.

"Just a trim. To neaten it up for the holy sisters. Please? You'd be such a darling."

"You're sure?"

"Positive." Isabella beamed at her.

Greta stood up stiffly, holding on to the bedside table. She groaned, rubbing her knees where they were pitted from the weave of the towel. She limped out of the door, and it swung shut behind her.

Isabella and I were alone for the first time

in months. The last time I had seen her was a hasty farewell at St. Cyrus's Fourth of July parade, Ralph watching with the closest to bemusement his bland features would allow.

Isabella pouted. "Aren't you going to welcome me?"

I agonized; I wanted to show her how truly happy I was to see her, but now that she'd asked me to celebrate her arrival, anything I did would seem phony. I embraced her, and she patted my back with a sort of perfunctory acknowledgment. I was on the verge of tears. I'd ruined our meeting in Italy. I should have been downstairs to meet her at the door. I should have knocked Greta over and cheered. I searched for a prop to smooth over my thoughtlessness. And there, flashing on her finger, was as good a distraction as any.

"*What* is that meteorite?" I said, feigning astonishment.

Isabella grinned, sticking a dart of tongue between her teeth. She held up her hand and raised her eyebrows.

"Oh my goodness!" I fell to the side of the chair, gathering her hand in mine. "He asked you? Why didn't you tell me? Wow, it's beautiful!"

Her eyes crinkled in disappointment. "But

didn't you get my *carte postale*?"

I shook my head.

"What a shame. Well, anyway. Yes! Ralphy asked me in Paris! It was his grandmother's. He went all the way to Nantucket to ask Auntie Kathleen for it. Isn't it gorgeous?"

"Marvelous," I said, still pretending to be entranced by the dim spittle of the ring.

"It's kinda old-fashioned. I'll have it swapped when we get back to the States."

"I'm so happy for you," I said. But there was a ripple in my throat, a lurch of desperation. She was still engaged. They hadn't fallen out. My lip wobbled. I let it travel over my face in the hopes Isabella would read it as sentiment.

"And you'll be a bridesmaid?" Her voice was soft and real.

"Really?" Despite myself, I almost forgot my distress — she wanted me by her side on her wedding day.

She laughed. "Of course, Briddie." She kissed me roughly on my forehead. "You know you're my favorite."

My stomach squeezed. "Of course, of course." I breathed in the Isabella smell. Soir de Paris and cigarette smoke and something else, maybe traces of Ralph's cologne. "I've missed you," I said quietly.

Her face softened. "I've missed you,

Briddie. There's so much to catch up on." She folded her legs over the arm of the chair. "But listen — before Goldilocks comes back, you won't tell anyone, will you?"

"About?"

She rolled her eyes. "The engagement."

I tried to settle my expression to cover the eager leap in my gut. "You're not sure?"

She smiled. "It's not that." She twisted the ring from her finger and pinched the stone. "You know how serious Mom is about school. And if Ralphy gets married before twenty-one, then his trust fund — Well, I'm sure you're the same." I nodded, although I had no idea. Rhona had alluded to some kind of "arrangement" for after Granny died, but no one thought to involve me in those discussions and I never offered.

"I don't *want* to keep it a secret," she said. "But I mean, you know that girl Sylvia Carrol?"

I nodded.

"Her mother was on the Gardening Committee with Mom."

"She was?" My mouth was dry. "I thought she's from Seattle."

"Apparently her mom grew up in Aspen. Mom practically called everyone in her phone book when she saw the class list."

A door shut against me somewhere, and I was crouching down behind it, peering through a keyhole. I tried to keep my voice steady. "I didn't realize you two were already friends."

"We're not," Isabella said. "The point is — you just never know who's going to blab. And me and Ralphy can't say anything 'til after graduation, so . . ." She trailed off.

The leap in my stomach gathered itself into a garland. She didn't want anyone to know. She couldn't be *that* certain. And here we had almost a year for her to change her mind. "Of course," I said. "I won't say a word."

"Thanks, Briddie." She pressed her cheek against mine. She squeezed the ring into the top pocket of her jeans, as if it was a loose button and not a diamond. "I only wore the ring for you. So you could see it."

The door opened and Greta came back in, holding her scissors aloft like a trophy. "Sorry, girls, I couldn't find them anywhere — Oh, but what's wrong?" She stopped, her face falling at the sight of our tearful embrace.

"We're just being silly," Isabella said, wiping her damp eyes like an actress.

That night I lay alone in my single bed. Isabella wasn't to share with me after all.

She had a room on the east side of the building, overlooking the lake. Although it was a single, her room was far nicer than mine. It had an antique trunk at the foot of the bed, and on the wall next to her closet was a Mariani fresco panel of a wasp burrowing into an apple. So I didn't even suggest she abandon it to join me in mine. I lay awake long after the curfew bells had rung. I heard Isabella's voice again in my head. *"You know you're my favorite,"* I heard her saying. *"I only wore the ring so you could see it."*

7.
AUGUST

The first morning of term, we assumed our usual positions in the corridor to watch the sisters waiting to enter chapel. They were lined up two by two, and when one of the nuns at the back stifled a yawn, her partner caught it from her moments later.

"What's the point of going to Matins if they can't say anything?" Sylvia asked suddenly.

We stared at her.

"I mean" — she folded her arms — "why not just pray in their bedrooms or something?"

"Sibbs!" Katherine nudged her. "You are such a heathen."

Sylvia blushed. "I just don't understand," she said, looking down into the courtyard. "What's the use?"

We turned back to watch the sisters. But Sylvia's question bothered me. What *was* the use in their silence? It must make it easier to be holy, I decided, if you have no other option.

Just before ten, we congregated at the top of the stairs for the opening ceremony. Everyone was swinging satchels or clutching notepads or nibbling pencils or adjusting ponytails. The bells rang and we all pulled our shoulders back. Even though we were already quiet, Ruth whispered, "Shh!"

We walked down the dark stairs and into the downstairs corridor. Donna Maria was standing by a pair of glass doors open onto the courtyard. Silently, we filed out into the sun. None of us had been permitted into the courtyard until then, and we took the privilege seriously.

Standing on the left was Mrs. Fortescue, the academy coordinator. Her silver hair was coiffed into a pageboy and she wore a navy sheath dress with matching jacket. A thrill went through the girls. We'd all met her in New York during our interviews and followed her florid signatures on our slips and brochures. It was like being presented to a respectable minor celebrity: a Rockefeller widow or an aging De Beers model. Standing behind her was a youngish priest in a black cassock, a white-haired woman wearing bright red lipstick, and an older man with graying sideburns and the dappled nose of a secret drinker.

"Two lines, two lines, please." Mrs. Fortescue pointed in front of the palm tree, her handbag wobbling in the crook of her elbow. We arranged ourselves with the taller girls at the back, like a class photograph.

The priest stepped forward. "Good morning," he said. "I am Father Gavanto. Welcome to the Accademia di Belle Arti di Pentila." He ran his fingers through his hair with the twitchy, flustered gestures of seminary school. He gestured to Mrs. Fortescue. "We are lucky to have Signora Fortescue visit us today. Please applaud."

We all applauded with genteel restraint.

Mrs. Fortescue stepped forward. "Ladies. I've had the pleasure of interviewing you at the beginning of your journey, and I'm delighted to welcome you here, at one of the most picturesque locales in Italy."

Now that she had given us permission, we conspicuously took in the surroundings. The upper floor of the building was decorated with sun-bleached Mariani frescoes of golden leaves and green apples. A brittle swallow's nest dangling from the eaves above the library shed feathers onto the flagstones.

Mrs. Fortescue gestured to the white-haired woman. "This is Signora Moretti."

The woman grinned and waved. "And this is Signor Patrizi." She gestured to the older man, who bowed.

"You have all been particularly selected for this program as a result of your academic scholarship and excellent deportment as ambassadors for the United States of America. Over the next nine months, you will have to work hard and devote your utmost attention to your studies. And this time next year, you will join our esteemed alumni as a Pentilan scholar. Welcome, class of 1958."

Greta began spontaneously to clap, and when none of us joined in, she buried her face in Sally's shoulder, a blush spreading over her collarbone. We tittered at her affectionately.

"I will shortly read your class assignments. But first, some administrative matters. Should you have had any difficulty with your checks, I will be in the library between one and two this afternoon. If you have not signed your slips, please return those to me before the end of the day.

"Now." She took a breath. "A reminder of our rules. The Innocent Sisters of Pentila are our hosts, and we are grateful for their hospitality. Please remember to conduct yourselves with decorum at all times. In particular, you are expressly prohibited from trying to engage the sisters in conversation. The liaison for this year is —" She looked around and Signora Moretti filled in.

"Sister Teresa."

Mrs. Fortescue nodded. "You may talk with Sister Teresa only when necessary, ladies. Any housekeeping matters should be referred to Donna Maria."

We nodded solemnly.

"Breakfast is at seven a.m., and lunch is served at noon. Vespers is at four p.m. sharp. Supper is at six. You have permission to leave the premises to visit La Pentola, but make sure to be back by the ten p.m. curfew or you will incur a demerit. Three and you will be expelled from the academy.

"I remind you of the honor code you have all signed. We expect exemplary behavior from our scholars." She raised an icy eyebrow. "No overnight visitors. The telephone is available for one hour a day. No smoking in the refectory. And *absolutely* no smoking in the chapel." Katherine giggled at the back, and Mrs. Fortescue searched out her face in the crowd. "You laugh, my dear, but it has happened. Attendance at classes is mandatory unless you are taken ill. We insist upon good conduct — no cursing, modest dress, and no bikini suits in the courtyard."

Apparently recent alumni of the academy

had been rather wayward. I looked at Ruth and saw the line of her mouth setting in determination to shame the bikini-wearing, cursing, chapel-smoking girls of years past.

"I wish you luck." Mrs. Fortescue smiled, and her face powder broke into fissures around her mouth. "If you do not need to attend my administration hours, I look forward to awarding you your certificates in May at graduation."

She unfolded a piece of paper from her handbag and began to read our names. We were divided apparently at random, and we split off and filed in the direction of the classrooms. I scurried at once, not wanting Isabella to see me linger for her. I was assigned to the room Masaccio, which I knew to be on the left-hand side of the building.

The classroom was small and musty with the scent of stale pencil shavings. It was equipped with eight desks with inbuilt inkwells, and a set of glass doors at the far end opened onto the courtyard. A shelf along the left wall held the usual classroom detritus — glass jars filled with pencils, a pile of hardback Bibles, a busted plastic globe dangling from its hinge. On the wall was a framed painting of St. Teresa addressing a crowded marketplace following a "quickening." She was raised on a dais overlooking a rabble of sailors and bearded Turks, so I supposed it to be somewhere in Sicily. A ray of light from a parted cloud outlined her garb with an aura, and a seam of gold ran from her lips. Over the course of the nine months, I came to know that painting so well I could have drawn it myself with my eyes closed.

Greta and Sally were already sitting at desks in the front row. Greta looked around expectantly as I entered. "Bridget, phew! I'm so glad!"

"Come, grab this one." Sally slapped her palm on the desk next to her.

I hesitated, wanting to leave room for Isabella. "I'm too nervous to sit up front," I said, taking a bench in the middle.

Greta gestured to a chalkboard propped against the window. "Do you think when —"

The door opened and Signora Moretti entered. *"Buongiorno."*

She began to speak rapidly in Italian. Greta turned around and glanced at me in panic. I feared for a moment I'd gone into the wrong room.

Signora Moretti sighed theatrically and put her finger to her lips. "We will not speak English here. Only Italian. For today only, I make an exception. And then —" She mimed a throat being cut. "Let us begin." She pointed to herself. *"Mi chiamo Elena Moretti, e —"*

At that moment, the door opened and Isabella pinched my arm before sliding behind the desk next to Sally. I smelled a bitter gust of cigarette smoke on her clothes as she passed.

I stared at the back of her head, stunned. Why would she sit there and not next to me? My stomach swiveled. Did she do it deliberately? Was I being punished? Or worse — perhaps she had taken the seat without even thinking of me at all. I surveyed Sally. Was there something especially appealing about her I had underestimated? She was terribly blond. I chewed the end of my pen. That wasn't fair. It wasn't fair if it was because she was a blonde. Blondness was something I had no hope of achieving.

"Mi chiamo . . . ," Elena prompted again, looking pointedly at Isabella.

Isabella crossed her legs. *"Mi chiamo Bella,"* she said.

Elena cheered.

Sally and Greta turned to look at Isabella and grinned.

I felt a queasy premonition. Isabella had such a certain kind of boldness, it was hard to tell how the other girls would take to her. How much she would be hated, or loved.

8.

AUGUST

And so our year at the academy began. In the mornings Isabella and I sat side by side in the refectory, drinking milky coffees from heavy bowls, dipping soft rolls into the froth. Then Italian lessons, according to our three levels. Only Nancy and Ruth were in the top set. They spent their mornings reading the *Inferno* under the tutelage of Signor Patrizi, a retired lecturer from the University of Milan. He traveled to the academy every day on a battered scooter, and we could predict his arrival by the desperate coughing of its exhaust as it battled up the hill. Katherine, Sylvia, Bunny, Barbie, Joan, and the two Marys were composing letters of complaint with Signor Moretti, Elena's husband. Greta, myself, Patricia, Sally, Joy, Betty, and Isabella, meanwhile, were still struggling to conjugate basic verbs and spent our mornings loudly declaring the meal to be delicious, or the operator to be unavailable.

Italian lessons were followed by a light midmorning lunch of miniature ham sandwiches left for us in the refectory. We served ourselves, leaving our plates on a tray for an unseen sister to clean up later. Then we had a two-hour break. Usually, Isabella and I retreated to our rooms for clammy, restless siestas. Or else we stripped down to our slips and sprawled out on the twin beds in my room, smoking and reading novels. Some of the girls climbed down to the lake and snuck in a quick dip, turning up to our afternoon lectures with damp hair and sunburned noses.

The afternoon lectures were delivered by Signor Patrizi and took place in the lecture room off the lobby. Although thankfully they were conducted in English, he spoke with a pronounced accent that made his words so rounded you could slip off the end of them. Combined with the dim light and the whir of the projector, the lectures were deliciously soporific. The far window faced out onto the lake and I let his words roll over me, stupefied into a half doze on Isabella's shoulder as sparrows wheeled over the water.

Lectures finished just before four p.m., at which point we joined Vespers in the chapel.

We were all supposed to attend, even Nancy, who was Episcopalian. Then we had an hour free to rest or to wash and change before supper. Supper was two courses and fruit, with the obligatory pitchers of hard cider. The meals were simple and glittering with salt. After supper, we were free to do whatever we wanted until curfew, at ten p.m. — which meant hanging around our bedrooms or the common room, which was tucked into the southeast corner of the upstairs corridor.

Isabella wanted to be thorough about exploring the academy, so I helped her chart our new home. We startled a brood of gray-feathered chickens in a coop at the end of the orchard. We discovered that the back left alcove of the chapel was a gruesome ossuary cabinet with twelve shelves of bones arranged in order of size, as slender and brittle as ivory combs. My favorite place by far was the kitchen. The room was cavernous and cool, stocked with a paint box of treasures: lemons in straw, scarlet-speckled borlotti beans. The first time Isabella and I dared to peek past the heavy kitchen doors, there was a diminutive, elderly nun standing on a stool to chop onions at the counter. The nun looked up and gestured for us to enter. Her cheeks were slack, and one of her eyes was white with a cataract. I followed in after Isabella, desperate to open the doors to the larder and investigate the alchemical substances within. The nun motioned for Isabella to approach, then clamped her hand over Isabella's and forced the handle of her knife into Isabella's palm.

"No fair," she gasped, as the nun gestured for her to take over slicing.

As the nun climbed down from the stool, I stared around. Hanging from nails on the right-hand wall were puckered red chili peppers and bulbs of hirsute garlic. At the back on the left was a dark cubby containing waxed rounds of provolone, gleaming behind a net screen. At home, Mama bought cheese that came in slices, and somehow I'd thought the blocks would be square. The sister pointed at a deep iron saucepan on top of a silverware cabinet. I used the stool to climb up and retrieve it for her. It was sticky up there, the top of the cabinet lined with yellowing newspaper academy girls must have left behind, since the section underneath the pan boldly advertised the figure-trimming benefits of Caspar's girdles. As a reward for our labors, the nun pressed upon us a handful of striped green tomatoes. They smelled gloriously of dirt and geraniums and tasted so sweet my eyes watered. Isabella was eyeing mine greedily, so I gave the rest of my handful to her.

Although we were permitted to go to La Pentola, our options for entertainment were slim. It was a tiny village, with a post office that opened only on Thursdays, attached to a kiosk selling dusty bottles of Cinzano and Coke. There was a drab harbor with several chipped rowboats, a whitewashed church, a defunct drinking fountain, and two taverns. The academy girls favored the *enoteca,* run by Signora Bassi, a middle-aged woman with curly black hair. It was supposedly a wine bar, although I rarely saw people making a fuss over the choice of vintage. Instead, Isabella and I went there to drink her cheapest, wateriest red wine. Katherine and Sylvia were regulars, and we sat all together outside at a table near the harbor, listening to the glug of water against the dock, swatting away mosquitoes. The locals stuck to the other *taverna* after term had begun. I suppose after many years they had tired of schoolgirls using them as test subjects for their verb endings.

By the time we walked back up to the academy, the first stars had come out, dimpling silver studs in the lake. The stone path pulsed heat underfoot, and owls fluttered in the chestnut trees along the hill.

Isabella and I strolled arm in arm through the shadows, taking deep breaths of warm air dusky with herbs. Sometimes as we walked, Isabella whistled, or else we dreamed up histories for the silent sisters. They had been tragically widowed, disgraced movie stars. They were lost princesses, heirs to castles in Monaco. They had once been academy girls, just like us.

9.

SEPTEMBER

The second Saturday of term, Greta and I rose early and passed the time before breakfast playing cards in the common room. When one of the sisters came in to shake the rugs out of the window, we put down our hands and assumed a polite silence. It seemed rude to carry on chatting while one of the sisters was there, as if we were deliberately excluding her. Greta and I had taken armchairs on either side of the fireplace, and over her shoulder I watched the lake turning a champagne color as the morning grew hotter and hazier. When Isabella woke up maybe I could convince her to go down to the water — I had a new bikini and I was anxious for its Italian debut. After graduation, Granny had insisted on fitting me out with a new wardrobe for "touring," as she called it. My academy closet was decked out in gloriously bland linen dresses and cotton T-shirts. The bikini itself had been Granny's suggestion, "for sailing parties." I didn't know what kind of cruises she expected me to attend in a convent, but I was grateful anyway.

Greta dealt me a hand. "I refuse to be 'old maid' again," she said seriously. I snapped out of my daydream and stared at her for a second, misunderstanding.

Nancy knocked on the door. "Good morning," she said. "So. Donna Maria was just saying there are trails all around where we can go hiking." She put one hand on the doorknob. "Would you two like to come with me?"

"Um . . . now?" Greta looked at me, startled.

"Just us two?" I said.

Nancy shrugged. "You want to ask Bella?"

"Yes," I said, beaming. It was glorious to be so carelessly acknowledged as a pair, inseparable.

Greta was gnawing on the corner of a playing card. "Is it a long hike?"

"Not so long. Two hours, maybe three. I'll meet you downstairs after lunch," Nancy said.

Greta sat up in the armchair. "But won't it be terribly hot?"

Nancy wrinkled her nose. "It won't be so bad. Doesn't it get hot in Delaware?"

Greta pursed her lips into a little bow, as if she were trying not to cry. "Yes, but then we go sailing."

"Let's do it at four," I said, to break Nancy's gaze from Greta. "It'll be cooler then."

"OK," Nancy said. "Sounds swell."

After lunch, Greta came to my room and lit a cigarette by the window. She'd changed into linen pants and a white cotton T-shirt and tied her hair back in a ponytail with a white ribbon. She looked as dainty as a novelty candy.

"Do you do lots of hiking in Connecticut?" she said.

I shook my head. "Isabella doesn't enjoy hiking."

Greta tapped me playfully on my arm. "I mean your family, silly."

"Oh." I pressed my fingernails into my palms and tried to suppress a blush. "Not really. We only go hiking to find a good picnic spot." I conjured a false memory, of Mama, Dad, and Rhona, sitting on a tartan picnic blanket peeling oranges and tossing pith into the grass.

Greta laughed. "Your mom sounds way too glamorous to be fighting off midges. Unless — are you sporty types?" She ran her finger over the filter of her cigarette. "As soon as my brothers stop talking about regattas, they start talking about skiing." She smiled, but I could see the thought of home had wounded her. She cleared her throat. "Where does your family go skiing?"

"We don't. Not exactly." I swallowed. I watched the sunlight striking the faint, downy hair on her brow. My stomach filled with static as I deliberated how to begin. Mama was afraid to learn because she didn't even see snow until she was married? Rhona was prone to breaking bones because of poor health? My eyes burned. It had been nice, for a while, to be anonymous, unremarkable.

"Oh, Bridge," she said. "I'm sorry, I didn't mean to make you homesick."

I bit the inside of my cheek. I didn't deserve her sympathy. I could feel it swelling before us: sly questions, subtle inferences, pointed looks during dinner-table discussions about desegregation.

"Do you want to call them now?" She looked at her wristwatch. "It's breakfast time on the East Coast. I'll wait with you if you like. You'll feel much better once you hear your mom's voice, and if you're feeling tearful, Donna Maria will let —"

"My mom won't be there," I said.

Greta's head twitched. "Is she" — she

blinked at me doubtfully — "at work?"

A thick, sticky trepidation coated my insides. Now was the moment to explain Rhona's appointments. And how she needed special attention but it was OK because of Mama's nursing career. And, no, Mama wasn't a nurse in Connecticut but she had been in England, but no, she wasn't English, and their two weddings and Granny's tolerance and no, I know I don't look it and yes, of course we go to Mass, and my slight but undeniable irregularity. I grasped for a neutral place, a safe space, where my family could dwell until I could bear to retrieve them.

"She's at the summerhouse," I heard myself saying.

"Oh." Greta's face relaxed.

I saw Mama standing by the window of a whitewashed cottage. Sandy footprints on a nautical-striped rug. A bundle of sunshine yellow sweet corn abandoned on a marble countertop.

"They don't have a phone there or —"

I shook my head.

Greta brushed the curls out of my face. "Oh, Bridge, let's not talk about home anymore," she said, reaching to hug me. "It'll only make us blue, and we're supposed to be here for an adventure."

We waited for Nancy by the side door of the academy. The tread in the center of the step was worn down to a stub, and I realized the front door with the bell must only be used for visitors. Isabella was flicking her lighter on and off, experimentally holding it to a dry leaf and blowing away the charred embers. Nancy appeared from round the front of the building, wearing a gray men's shirt, jeans, and sturdy-looking boots.

Isabella nudged me. "Does she expect us to climb the mountains into Switzerland? It's like Pippi Longstocking goes camping."

I hushed her but rubbed my tennis shoes together self-consciously. Would there be much sport at the academy? Part of the social purpose of art history was its decidedly indoors quality, ruling out moments of jollity that inspired casual games of tennis.

"Hello," Nancy said. "Let's go, shall we? Sister Teresa will show us the way."

We all nodded. Nancy walked down the stone steps with brisk purpose. We crossed the hill and turned left, away from the lake and toward the convent. We followed a well-worn path past the orchard and around the front of the chapel, where white pigeons were roosting in the mesh of the bell tower. Nancy began to climb the slope and we trailed behind, dodging stinging nettles. The grass was coarse and golden and smelled rich as buttered popcorn. Crickets sang in the weeds, and my ankles itched, tickled by bristly wildflowers. I wished I'd worn proper pants and not my capris.

"It's so hot," said Isabella, pouting. "This was a dreadful idea, Briddie."

My pulse shot into my throat. I balled my fists. Greta's breath was heavy, her cheeks pink with concentration as she searched for safe places to tread. It *had* been a dreadful idea. Why had I agreed to it?

Ahead of us a nun standing by the convent gate turned, and I saw she was one of the black nuns I'd noticed in the refectory. Nancy waved, and to my surprise, the nun raised her hand and gave her a thumbs-up. I'd not realized before, but the sister was quite beautiful. Her skin was dark brown, with freckles under her eyes. She had a high forehead and fine cheekbones. Her jaw was sharp like the bottom of a heart.

Nancy and the sister began talking in rapid Italian; then Nancy waved at us. "Hurry up, slowpokes," she yelled.

Isabella groaned and broke into a trot. Greta and I followed, loping over uneven hillocks.

"This is Sister Teresa," Nancy said as we approached. "The speaking liaison."

"How do you do," we murmured politely.

"Where would you like to tour today? The lake's beautiful, but perhaps you'd rather visit where our founder originated?" Sister Teresa said.

All three of us blinked at the sister.

Nancy grinned. "Wow. Your English is swell!"

Sister Teresa smiled. Her front two teeth were larger than the others, which gave her a vaguely rabbity look. "As is your Italian. You must've studied for many years."

"Gee, thanks." Nancy blushed.

"But how on earth did you learn English?" said Greta. "You don't even get to speak Italian, do you?" She clapped her hand over her mouth. "Oh, I'm sorry."

Sister Teresa was still smiling. "Don't apologize. I learned English in my infancy."

Isabella stared at her. "Jeez — how long have you *been* here?"

Nancy frowned. "Look. Never mind that for now. We have plenty of time to get to know each other." She folded her arms. "So. Lake or shrine?"

Given the heat, I had no interest in climbing the hill, but it seemed impolite to say so in front of a nun. And since Sister Teresa was looking at me, I said, "The shrine, I guess?"

"Great. Lead the way, Sister," Nancy said, pointing up into the distance.

Sister Teresa walked ahead of us. She was slim and tall, even taller than Nancy. What I had taken for a habit was merely a white tunic over linen pants. She was wearing heavy black boots, scuffed at the toes. Nancy took a few long strides and joined her. They wove through the deep grass, and Sister Teresa spoke to her, pointing into the apple trees down below.

"Do you think they can *all* speak English?" Greta was whispering. "Like, secretly?" The color in her face was hectic. "Can they understand our phone calls?"

"I don't know — maybe." I shrugged.

"Could they read our *mail*?" she said, her voice strangled.

Isabella pushed her arm through mine. "Is she afraid they might read the thrilling secrets about her pony?" she muttered.

We followed Nancy and Sister Teresa over a stile and farther uphill, away from the orchard. From above, the apple trees looked puny, stunted even. Then I realized they must be cut deliberately short, to make

126

picking the fruit easier for the nuns. Even up on the hill there was the odd apple tree, leaves already blotchy with ginger freckles. Smaller fruit lay concealed in the grass, sodden and browning, attracting wasps. Every now and again, Isabella or I slid on the peel of disintegrating fruit or stamped straight into a crust of mushy caramel pulp.

Sister Teresa brought us to a stone ledge, which we clambered over one by one. The path became narrow, passing through blackberry hedges studded with blind stars where berries had already been plucked. I took a deep breath of the air, coppery and sweet with rotten fruit, like old pennies dipped in honey. Isabella tipped her head back so the sunlight caught her face. She opened her eyes and found me staring at her. She smiled.

"OK, maybe not such a dreadful idea," she said, lacing her fingers through mine. I traced the outlines of her ragged thumbnail, my stomach jittering. We walked along the bramble path, swinging our arms. Isabella began whistling tunelessly. The light ruffled through blousy dog roses and towering pine trees, swallows fluttering in alarm from the branches as we passed. After half an hour we approached another crumbling wall dotted with stringy weeds.

"Shall we visit the spring?" Nancy said, pointing farther uphill to the left.

"Um." Greta swallowed. "Is it a detour from the shrine?"

"A short one." Sister Teresa wiped her forehead with her sleeve. I felt vindicated that even she was sweating, and she must have to climb up the hill all the time.

"Thanks, but we'll wait here for you guys," Isabella said. "Us indoors pets aren't used to being let off the leash."

"We shan't be long," Sister Teresa said, giving her a thumbs-up. Where had she learned that? Perhaps the bikini-wearing chapel-smoking alumni had tutored her.

Isabella and I balanced on the uneven slate wall and Greta sat heavily on the ground, wiping her grass-stained hands carelessly on her linen pants. "We should've brought a picnic," she said, smiling at me. "Next time you can be our expert picnic adviser."

I laughed. "My true calling."

Greta twirled a hollow piece of grass between her fingers. "How long will your mom stay at your summerhouse?"

A jolt of electricity ran from the base of my spine to my skull. "What?"

"Is that where the big Labor Day party is?"

Isabella stared at her. "Um. No."

Greta grinned. "I love that you're such good friends you even talk for each other," she said.

Isabella shot me a look as if Greta was an idiot dog scrounging for scraps that you had to humor because the owner was watching.

Greta had noticed the look. Her voice took on a pleading, explanatory tone. "Poor Bridge was feeling awful homesick, and *I* said she should just call and speak to her mom, but of course her mom's not there."

"Oh?" Isabella's eyes moved over my face, a question in the tilt of her eyebrows.

"Because. Because she's at the summerhouse," I supplied woodenly. I radiated a silent plea for Isabella's mercy. My lip twitched.

Isabella's eyes flicked to and fro as if she were tracing something onto a map. "Sure," she said eventually. She turned to Greta and said brightly, "It's such a great house."

I wanted to cry.

"Anyway." I swallowed. "Let's not talk about home anymore."

Greta reached forward and put a paw on my ankle. "I know just how you feel, Bridge. Is your family coming for Christmas, at least?"

"What?" My mouth hung open, but she

seemed not to have noticed my tone. She had picked another stem of grass and was occupied tying it into a bow.

"For the vacation."

I yanked a piece of grass myself and tried to snap it in half, but it was so springy it merely bounced between my fingers. "No."

"Izzy, are yours?"

"God no," said Isabella, fumbling in her pockets and pulling out a pack of Lucky Strikes. "They'll be in Colorado with my grandmom." Isabella lit a cigarette. "I didn't even invite them here anyway. I pretty much *want* to get away from them."

Greta's eyebrows shot up. "Oh, Izzy, what a dreadful thing to say." Her tone was mocking, but her expression was fearful, as if Isabella's disdain might be contagious.

The dim sound of a bell tolled in the distance. Greta sat up on her knees and began threading a daisy through the knot of grass. Suddenly she dropped her arrangement and turned to me. "Bridge! You should write and ask your parents to come for the vacation," she said, beaming. "Mom and Pops are meeting me in Florence." Greta clapped her hands. "We could all go out for dinners together — it would be so much fun."

I winced, not daring to look at Isabella. I

flashed to an image of my family arriving at the grand wooden door of the academy. Mama conspicuously overdressed with that long chain of pearls that went out of style a hundred years ago. All the girls' eyes switching between her and Dad. Convoluted explanations about Egyptian Christians. Sylvia measuring Rhona's tiny wrists with a perplexed kind of envy. Rhona sleeping in the bed next to mine. Listening to Rhona rise in the night, the sound of her soft footsteps as she paced back and forth across the tiles.

"No," I said finally, my eyes prickling. "They won't. They have — we also — they can't, this year." My stomach was tight.

Isabella tapped the ash of her cigarette in a crevice between the stones. "Briddie hasn't told you?" she said. "Her parents throw this simply lavish party each Christmas. It's famous in St. Cyrus. With big platters of lobster and a woman harpist wearing ermine fur." Isabella batted her eyelashes prettily. "It's divine. The event of the season. The whole of St. Cyrus would be devastated if it were canceled."

Greta's eyes widened. "How dreamy. But you poor thing, you're missing out?" She put her hand to her face. The diamond on her finger caught a shard of sunlight and pierced my eye.

I tried to smile but it snagged at the edge of my mouth. "It's fine," I said.

"It's simply *killing* Briddie to miss out," Isabella said. "She adores her family. *I* try not to talk about home so it doesn't make her sore," Isabella said in an artificial voice.

I let out a deep breath. It was a nice swerve — a marvelous swerve. I wanted to kiss Isabella's hand.

"Oh, Bridge," Greta sighed. "You're just as bad as I am. Izzy, you'll have to take extra-good care of Bridget over Christmas, then."

"I will." She smiled. "We'll have the best time, just the two of us." She saluted me with her cigarette. I was dazzled by my sudden reprieve. I felt light, airy. Isabella had saved me. I wanted to bundle her up and hoist her on my shoulders.

Nancy and Sister Teresa reappeared at the crest of the hill and began waving. Groaning, we climbed toward them over steep ground pitted where rabbits had burrowed into the earth and flung desiccated droppings that crumbled under my soles. The air was close and coarse, with a bitter, powdery taste, like brick dust. Sweat collected with my sunscreen and stung the corners of my eyes. Sister Teresa and Nancy were talking rapidly, Nancy gesticulating in stiff waves as if she were flagging down a taxicab.

Panting, Isabella leaned on my arm as we struggled through sand-colored burrs and dodged ankle-turning divots. "Thanks," I whispered to her. "For covering."

Isabella squeezed my wrist. "We can't let the busybodies spoil our year of freedom," she said.

Finally, we reached the top of the hill. It was mostly bare, scattered with prickly, sunburnt shrubs. Below us, fields of chapped grass and spindly wildflowers stretched out toward the Blue Mountains.

"This way," Sister Teresa called, pointing to our right. Hidden behind a cypress tree was a whitewashed arch, where an oil painting of the saint was propped against the wood, faded and cracked from the sun. Candle stubs dribbled with fossilized wax sheltered in its arch, and around the shrine loose stones and pieces of flint had been piled to protect the candles from the wind.

As Sister Teresa approached the shrine, the rest of us hung back. She touched the top of the arch, crossed herself, then dropped to her knees in front of the shrine, her lips moving in prayer. I watched the fragile skin on the tops of her eyelids fluttering. When she opened her eyes, her gaze met mine directly, and she smiled. I looked away in embarrassment.

Then we each approached the shrine and made the sign of the cross. I took time to linger at the monument as if I were lost in contemplation, although really I was unmoved. How could one be sure St. Teresa had ever lived there? What if we were all observing a moment of reverence at a place of no significance to the real St. Teresa — her chicken coop, or her woodshed? Isabella was examining her cuticles. She looked up and, catching my eye, mimed a yawn.

10.

SEPTEMBER

Our first term at the academy stretched its back into the last of the summer. The apple leaves in the orchard crimped around the edges, and scarlet berries of mountain ash trees smoldered in the hedgerows. White daisies glazed the hills, and each day as the sun rose, their petals filled the air with the smell of toasting sage. We were conscious that the warm days of the year were numbered, and girls sunbathed down by the lake in a frenzy of oil and lotions that baked greasy blotches onto the hot stones.

We had begun to split off into cliques. Girls coupled up and claimed their own territories in the common room. Katherine switched rooms to be nearer to Sylvia, and Joan only had sore feelings about it for an afternoon. Of course, Isabella was beloved. She entertained us by mimicking the darting movements of Donna Maria and became a hero after she picked the lock on the correspondence box so we didn't have to sign out paper each time. And we were unbreakable, a pair. Girls would catch my eye during her hijinks, shaking their heads indulgently. "How do you control her?" Sylvia would say. I relished the assumed intimacy of being her ballast, the only one who could fathom her quirks.

I spent less time with Greta, as she spent more time with Sally from Florida. They brought out a silliness in each other and were always giggling and sharing jokes no one else understood. Joy grew terribly homesick, and one morning she was just gone. Her roommate, Mary L., said she had been crying at night and decided she wanted to go back to the States.

This disconcerted me a great deal. I couldn't believe Joy wouldn't be willing to at least stay until Christmas vacation, when she was due to meet her parents in Switzerland for a week of skiing. It hadn't occurred to me that girls would find their independence distressing. Finally, I was Bridget, alone. At home, I was "Rhona-um-Bridget" or sometimes, "Rhona-Rex-Bridget." And Rex had been put down four years ago. How could anyone find autonomy so taxing?

But homesickness had spread through our ranks like a cough. Girls began to complain about mundane parts of life at the academy: Italian soap didn't lather as well as American soap; there were too many soccer matches on Italian radio. A rumor began that Italian milk was more fattening than American milk, and girls took to spooning the froth out of their morning coffees. Others submitted to maudlin reminiscences about their mothers' cookies or their sisters' cotillions, until their voices grew thick with emotion.

"I don't get it," Isabella said, perched on her windowsill, smoking a cigarette. She stuck her legs out under her nightdress and scratched at the scab of a mosquito bite on her right knee. "I mean, I miss Ralphy and all that" — she wrinkled her nose — "but I'm not bawling myself to sleep at night. To hear Barbie howling, you'd think she was in Alcatraz instead of . . ." She waved her hand toward the flinty strike of moonlight on water.

I pictured the carpet powder Mama sprinkled over the hallways before she vacuumed. The ceramic fish stuck to the tiles in our bathroom from when we were babies, which no one had ever thought to pry off. I pictured the dejected mealtimes when Dad cracked bad jokes and Mama fussed and Rhona sipped her water. There would be nobody there to ask for second helpings now.

I lit one of Isabella's cigarettes and crossed to stand next to her with my back against the window frame. I was suddenly irritable about the unexpected swell of guilt for not being there. I turned to see Isabella watching me with an amused expression.

"You're not homesick at all, are you?" she said, pointing her index finger at me while a ribbon of smoke wound out of the window and down into the night. On the other side of the building, the bells for Compline began to ring.

"Honestly? No," I said.

She turned to face me with a mischievous smile. I let her observe me while I smoked. I had no idea why the admission pleased her. And I hadn't even been trying, so it was a real victory, solid and bright as a gold coin.

"You know, Italy's good for you, Briddie," Isabella said.

"What?" My cheeks grew hot. "What do you mean?"

Isabella chewed her lip. "I dunno. You're less sarcastic here."

I leaned back against the window, feeling petulant. I'd never thought of myself as sarcastic. It sounded mean and bitter, a quality befitting a homely schoolmistress.

"Don't be sore," she said, her tone on the verge of exasperation. "I just mean, it's good. You should loosen up more. Relax."

I stared at the painted wasp on the fresco panel on her wall. The tips of my ears were burning. "I am relaxed," I said, hearing a sullenness in my voice.

"Well, if you relax *more,* it'll be easier," Isabella said, "making friends."

I felt like I'd been slapped. "I do have friends."

"Other than me." Isabella rolled her eyes.

I opened my mouth and closed it again. That wasn't fair to say. I had made friends with Greta before Isabella even arrived. Nancy often knocked on my door to say hello in passing. I pressed my nails into my palms. I'd have to focus on being less sarcastic. More relaxed. I should laugh more, I decided.

"Anyway," she said, stretching, "I'm sure it's just a matter of time before the girls all love you."

The knot in my throat loosened, and all my truculence fell away. "They already love you," I said quickly.

Isabella laughed. "Course they do. I'm adorable." She leaped off the sill, stabbed her cigarette against the stone, and threw it out the window into the grounds. She began to brush her hair at the mirror.

I turned to smoke the last of my cigarette with my elbows propped against the sill. "I can't believe anyone isn't happy here," I said. "All those girls crying over their beaus. Seems like a waste." The evening was cool and the breeze tawny with damp earth. I heard her laughing.

"Isn't Patricia the worst?"

I nodded, swallowing the last of the smoke as my eyes smarted. I pressed the butt onto the ashy mark left by Isabella's cigarette on the flagstones and tossed the rest of the cigarette into the night as she had done. Although I never did such a thing in my own bedroom. I now had a special clay pot filled with sand by the window for my smoked filters.

"It's like she finds reasons to be upset." Isabella mimicked an interaction, playing both roles. "Patricia, would you like a stick of gum?" She held out her own hairbrush and pretended to wipe her eyes over it. "Oh, but Charles loves gum." And she faux sobbed into the folds of her nightdress.

I laughed, not even out of duty, but because I agreed with her, and it was a relief not to have to make false cooing noises of sympathy and understanding.

I lay in my own bed that night thinking over Greta and Bobby, and Patricia and Charles, and Isabella and Ralph. I was strong-hearted and cruel in my youthful algebra of love. How foolish and wasteful to allow the joy of the academy to be eaten away with tears for a beau. Not like me, I thought. I was so modern, so independent. I didn't miss anyone. I had everything I needed, right there at the academy.

The next evening, Katherine knocked on my door as I was dressing for dinner. I was trying to set my curls into waves, but one section insisted on kinking at the back of my head and my arms were shamefully tired from rolling the same spot over and over.

"Come in," I said, giving up and pulling my hair into a ponytail.

Katherine stuck her face through the door. "Bridge? Do you have any bobby pins?"

I swiveled my whole body toward her, since I couldn't turn my head without losing control of the ponytail. "Help yourself," I said, gesturing to the plate by my mirror.

Katherine came in and scooped up a generous handful that I tried not to mind about. She sat heavily on the right-hand bed and began threading the pins together.

I watched her in the mirror, unnerved.

Was she waiting for something? Was I sup-posed to offer to help her with her hair?

"Everything all right?"

"Yeah," Katherine said, in a tone that implied she might be persuaded otherwise.

I licked my lips. "Are you sure?" I tried my best to sound relaxed. "Is there anything troubling you?"

Katherine sighed. "Not really."

"OK," I said. "But I'm always here if you need a friend." Did that sound inviting enough?

Katherine threw the pins down on the bedspread and I heard a couple clatter on the tiles. "Ugh, Bridge, I'm fed up."

I let go of the ponytail. My heart began hammering. Was I in trouble? Had I done something? Said something? I cast about for any possible infractions. At lunch, Isa-bella had made a joke and I'd laughed, dropping a mushy mouthful of sandwich on my sleeve. But everyone had been laughing.

"How come?" I said warily.

"Joan's upset because I didn't save her a seat this morning."

"Oh." A great wave of relief roared over my head and swallowed me up. I composed my face and nodded earnestly at her in the mirror.

"And Sibbs gets so mad when Joan gets

upset. But Joan stormed off, and I *had* to go after her. And I didn't mean to forget her this morning — I just forgot."

I picked up the hairbrush again and commenced attacking my ponytail. "Sylvia only minds because she's supposed to be your best friend," I said. "And as for Joan, make it a point to remember tomorrow and she'll forgive you."

Katherine nodded seriously. "Thanks, Bridge. You're probably right."

I smiled at her in the mirror.

Katherine sighed and stood up. "I better brush my hair too."

Before she reached the door, I seized my moment. "Say — do you and Sibbs want to have a picnic with me and Isabella later? I bought a bottle of that plum wine from the market." I congratulated myself on how casual my suggestion had sounded, the sort of thing a real person might say.

"Sounds swell," she said, absently tapping the door handle.

"Down by the spa?"

"Great!" Katherine licked her lips. "But you won't tell Sibbs I said anything — will you?"

I turned to her. "Never."

"It's just, she gets real sensitive."

"I won't say a word. Not even to Isabella," I said.

"Bridge, you're a doll." She blew me a kiss.

I evaluated myself in the mirror as she closed the door. I could make friends just fine.

Supper that evening was a buttery mushroom risotto and I ate every last mouthful and then some of Patricia's, feeling in some odd equation that it was compensation for my failed hairdressing experiment. After supper, Isabella and I waited for Katherine and Sylvia at the side door. We sat next to each other on the step, listening to the shuddering throb of cicadas.

"Do you have a light?" said Isabella, tapping a cigarette out of her pack.

I felt my pockets and shook my head.

"Damn." She clenched her cigarette in the corner of her mouth and stood up to rummage better through her pockets.

My belly was so full of risotto that I was annoyed by her movements, as if she needed to be still so I could concentrate on being uncomfortable. "Katherine will have a light," I said.

"Hey, look." Isabella kicked her leg behind her and caught me at the soft part of my arm. Over my shoulder I squinted into the dark orchard, where the red glow from the tip of a cigarette was burning.

"Hullo?" she called into the darkness, and strode off toward the smoker. I contemplated unpacking the blanket from my basket so I could sit on it instead of on the rough stone, but I could barely move.

Isabella came back toward me. "It's the nun," she hissed.

I stared up at her blankly.

"The nun — smoking. It's that nun — the African one," she said.

"You mean Sister Teresa," I said, not understanding why Isabella was so surprised. I had often seen her and the sister with the bright blue eyes smoking before — they usually sat on the stone bench under the apple trees.

"Do you think I can ask her for a light?"

"Of course."

Isabella hovered. "Will you come?"

Slowly, I levered myself off the step and dusted my behind. We crunched under the trees.

"Buonasera," Isabella called out.

"Buonasera," Sister Teresa said.

"Can I borrow your lighter?" Isabella waved her cigarette.

Sister Teresa grimaced. "Sorry," she said. "I used up my matches, but here —" She held out her hand for Isabella's cigarette, then put it to her lips and drew on it using the coals from her own cigarette until it smoldered. She handed it back to Isabella.

Isabella stared at it as if it had been transformed into a magician's wand.

"Thank you, Sister," I said, as Isabella stood there in silence. "Come on," I said, leading Isabella by the arm. I called, *"Buona-notte,"* behind us. Sister Teresa gave us a bemused half wave.

"What's up with you?" I said.

Isabella shrugged me off. "Nothing."

As we approached the side door, I saw Katherine and Sylvia had finally arrived. Sylvia was holding my basket and looking about her.

"There you are," she said. "Ready?"

I nodded.

"Sorry for the holdup," Katherine said. "My zipper got stuck. Thought Sibbs would have to cut me out!"

We walked down the path under the pine trees, and the herbal smell of resin filled the air as we crushed pine needles underfoot. Sylvia had brought a flashlight and it cast crooked shapes against the boughs. Katherine was making a "Wooo" sound, and Sylvia dropped the circle of light to the earth and swatted her.

"Maybe we'll see the ghost," Katherine said.

"*Please* don't, Kitty. It's creepy enough as it is!"

"What ghost?" I said.

"A blazing nun who appears in the window of the spa, and you can tell she's about to appear from the smell of incense," Katherine said, wiggling her fingers dramatically.

Sylvia tapped her with the flashlight. "Don't, I swear I'll cry."

"Sibbs, you are such a scaredy-cat." Katherine put her arm around her shoulders.

"We can go back to the chapel and I'll pour some holy water in my pockets," I said.

They both looked at me and laughed. I gulped against a sudden tightness in my throat. Was that sarcasm? I glanced at Isabella, but her face was drawn and concentrated. "Are you all right?" I said.

"Fine," she said.

"You seem kind of quiet."

"Christ, Briddie, give me a break for five minutes, will you?" she snapped.

My cheeks tingled. Had the others heard her speak to me that way? I searched for anything to divert attention from her jibe. "Have you two spent much time with Sister Teresa?" I called to Katherine and Sylvia.

"Who?" Sylvia wrinkled her nose.

"The speaking nun," I said.

Katherine squinted, raising her hand to just below her shoulder. "Is she the short one?"

"That's Sister Benedict."

"Oh." Sylvia smiled. "Isn't she the one that fetches the mail?"

"Maybe," I said. "I suppose being speaking liaison comes with all sorts of jobs. You should say hi. She's a doll." I cleared my throat. "Right?" I raised my voice to Isabella. "She's a doll, right?"

Isabella shrugged.

The path ended at a rocky outcrop, and we clambered down it one by one, using well-worn grooves in the rocks carved by students over the years. The back of the abandoned spa looked quite ominous in the gloom. The south side of the building was blackened and the tiles ruffled from fire damage. Bats were swooping in and out of a cavity in the roof. Sylvia began walking so quickly she was almost jogging. Finally, we came to a wide ledge that looked out onto the bowl of the lake. It was too dark to see much, but lights blinked on the opposite shore from the litter of houses in the cove of Brancorsi, one of only two villages on the lake. The breeze blew dank and mossy across the water.

Isabella and Sylvia ran ahead to toss pebbles into the lake, straining to catch the faint plunk as they broke the water. I unpacked the blanket and laid out two paper bags of biscotti and a bottle of plum wine.

"Oh, cookies!" Sylvia said. She picked one up. "It's stale," she said, with such horror that Isabella laughed.

"They're supposed to be hard," I said. "But then that's what the wine is for." Isabella was looking at me. "For dipping." My face flushed.

Isabella leaped onto the blanket. "Briddie, you're a genius."

My chest relaxed. She'd forgiven me for whatever I had done earlier.

Isabella seized Nancy's penknife and, with a swift tweak, uncorked the wine. "Cheers!" She took a slug straight from the bottle and a scarlet drop rolled from the corner of her mouth and down her neck before she caught it. She passed the bottle to Sylvia. "You don't mind, do you?" she said, in an interrogative tone. "Briddie and I don't bother much about etiquette," she said.

I was gratified — was that true? Were we too modern to bother with social decorum?

Sylvia smiled. "Not at all." She accepted the bottle and took a dainty sip, then handed it to me.

The wine was sweet and thick, like cough syrup. The sugar spiraled into my brain. I wished I had thought to bring a bottle of water. We crunched the cookies and sipped the wine until our lips were stained violet.

"Such a good idea," Katherine said, with her mouth full. "Of course Bridge is a natural host."

A rush of joy bubbled inside me. "Hmm?"

Katherine motioned for the bottle of wine and took a deep drink. Sylvia filled in for her. "Greta told us all about your mom's famous parties."

"Oh." My cheeks prickled.

"Say, where is your summerhouse?" Katherine said.

I froze.

Isabella leaned forward. "Bristol, Rhode Island."

"Get out!" Katherine reached forward and grabbed my leg. "We have a place in Newport!"

My heart leaped under my tongue.

"Were you there this year? Did you come for the Summer Sail? Oh my *God*, were you there when the coast guard found Dickie Baron's yawl?" Her grip was fierce on my leg. "It was *so* dramatic," she said to Sylvia.

I shot Isabella a horrified glance. "No," I said.

Isabella sighed. "We were dragged to this stuffy Republican Club event in St. Cyrus," she said. "We missed all the fun."

"It's a silent auction," I supplied weakly. "There was a boat."

"Me and Briddie's houses are practically next door to each other in Bristol," Isabella said.

Katherine grinned. "This is *such* good luck! Oh, and we can go to the America's Cup next year together! When are you going there next summer?"

"I'm not sure," I said. I felt dizzy.

"Or" — Katherine clasped her hands — "even better, you can invite me to your famous Labor Day party."

"Maybe," I said. "I'm not sure that we're doing it next year, though." My lip was wobbling. "My mom says it's too much work."

Katherine's face fell. "Oh, too bad. Though I suppose she has Thanksgiving and Christmas to plan."

"You can come to mine for Labor Day." Isabella patted Katherine on the shoulder.

"What about me?" Sylvia said mournfully.

"You too, darling." Isabella reached over and pinched her cheek.

Sylvia smiled. "Quite right. So anyway, if

you three are all done with your New England association" — she hoisted her bag onto her lap and pulled out a miniature red book with gold-edged pages — "I thought we could have a poetry recital."

"But we're not supposed to take the red-bound ones out of the library, are we?" I said.

Sylvia shot me a quizzical look.

"I mean, not that it matters," I added.

Isabella groaned. "Poetry? Sibbs, honestly, I didn't take you for one of those. Tell you what. I'll give you a recital myself." She straightened her shoulders, took a deep breath, and in a suitably theatrical voice yelled, "Candy is dandy, but —" until we shushed her.

"Trust me." Sylvia opened the pages onto a bookmark fashioned from cigarette foil. "You'll enjoy this. It's from our patron saint herself." She cleared her throat. "My beloved approaches me like a thief in the night. In the hours of darkness, my love lies beside me, his golden shaft a ray of sun that pierces my body, filling me with —"

Isabella and Katherine were howling with laughter and Sylvia caught the giggles from them so bad she had to stop reading.

"It *doesn't* say that —" Isabella grabbed the book from Sylvia's hand, wiping her eyes. She gestured for the flashlight and squinted at the page. "I can't believe it! Good for old lady Pentila." Isabella rose to her knees. "Filling me with waves of light. He is my beloved, and as his consuming love fills me" — she began wheezing with laughter — "I quicken with growing anticipation —"

While the other three moaned with laughter, coughing and dabbing their eyes, I fixed a sort of incredulous expression on my face, as if I couldn't believe what I was hearing.

Isabella broke off to take a deep swig from the bottle. Sylvia clutched my knee.

"Oh, poor Bridge — look at your face," she shrieked. "Oh, Bridge, you're so disapproving — don't be disappointed in us."

I shook my head, figuring that "disapproving" was better than admitting I didn't follow their joke.

"Don't be mad," Sylvia said, holding her hand out for the book. "We have to have *some* fun here with no boys." Katherine passed her the wine and Sylvia wiped the rim of the bottle before taking an unsteady sip.

"If you say so," I said, hoping it sounded like a tease.

"Speaking of boys, have I told you Patrick sent me the most darling letter?" Sylvia said dreamily. She began talking about Patrick's job and how he had flown in an airplane on two separate occasions. Katherine was unattached, but her sister was a volunteer nurse with a VA hospital and had just married a neurologist from Rhode Island.

"I miss her, though, now she lives in Providence," Katherine said with a sigh. "Her room is empty and it's terrible to look at. Me and Mom just start blubbering whenever we go in there."

Sylvia reached over and took her hand. "You should make a special date, once a month, just for the two of you. Me and Bonnie make it a point to go to the stables every third Saturday. That way we get a whole day of sister time."

Katherine took a sip from the bottle and turned to me. "How about you, Bridge?"

I was watching a brown moth flutter around the mouth of the flashlight. "How about me, what?"

"Anything! Everything. Sisters. Brothers. Do you have a beau? Some lacrosse player crying for you into his supper club at Yale?"

I blushed. "No."

Sylvia shook a cigarette from her pack. "And are your siblings married?" She broke off. "Gee, Bridge — do you even have siblings? Or are you an only child like Bella?"

They watched me, poised with polite inquisitiveness.

"Yeah," I said. My heart began a hollow pound.

Katherine squinted. "Yes to which? Siblings or only child?"

A roaring flush ran through my body. I pressed my fingernails into my palms. "Sorry?"

Katherine laughed. "Bridge, you are such a dreamer. Do you have any siblings or is it just you?"

I swallowed, pressing my fingernails harder into the flesh. "Just me," I said at last.

Sylvia sighed. "That's too bad. Although at least you don't have to share your wardrobe."

Katherine nudged her, and they started talking about garden party attire. I looked off into the bowl of the lake. My cheeks were burning. I could feel Isabella staring at me. I couldn't bear to catch her eye. What was she thinking? Was she disappointed in me? Was she ashamed of my omission? *Was* it really an omission? At the academy it certainly felt like I was my own individual — liberated, independent, finally.

"So aren't your parents dying to marry

you off?" Katherine said, frowning.

"It hasn't been raised," I said stiffly. I looked down to see Isabella's hand on my arm. She shot me a dazzling smile.

"Briddie's mom is just as strict as mine," Isabella said breathlessly. "No dating until after graduation. And her trust is all tied up until she's twenty-one. Isn't that right?"

After a moment, I nodded.

"Gee, that's rum luck," Sylvia said, the smoke from her cigarette billowing above the flashlight. "A no-dating rule? You may as well be a nun!"

Katherine laughed. "I'm sure your mom already has her mind set on the right suitor for you." She winked at me conspiratorially. "I know what Irish Catholics are like."

I opened my mouth and shut it again. Was it as easy as that? A convenient omission, a convenient vagueness. And there it was: total, glorious mediocrity. Meddling Catholic aunties and summer regattas. Boarding school hijinks and garden party silk. I was woozy with relief, exhilarated, askew. My eyes prickled.

"Do you think the nuns ever regret it?" Sylvia was saying. "Missing out on having a family?"

Katherine pinched her on the shoulder. "Darling Sibbs, you can tell you didn't go to a Catholic prep school. I think those gals knew what they were letting themselves in for."

"I suppose they're all so ancient it doesn't matter anyhow," Sylvia said.

Isabella leaned back on the blanket to cross her legs. "But some of the nuns are practically our age, like Sister Teresa."

Sylvia blinked. "Which one is she?"

Katherine nudged her. "Heavens, what's wrong with you, Sibbs? She's the one that fetches the mail, remember?"

"Oh, right." Sylvia tapped herself on the head. "Gosh, how awful it sounds. Having just one year where you can speak. You'd have to fit everything you ever wanted to say into it!"

Katherine laughed. "You'd never stop talking."

Isabella chewed her fingernail. "And then to be cooped up here the rest of your life. What a waste."

Sylvia grimaced. "Lord save us from a lifetime at all-girls' school."

Isabella crossed herself ironically. "And at least we're free to leave."

I stared at her. "I think she's lucky," I said. "I wish we never had to leave."

11.

SEPTEMBER

The first signs of fall appeared in late September — yellow grass, crumpled mushrooms unfurling in mossy clefts along the hillside path. And so our sunbathing took on a frantic quality — Sylvia even complained she couldn't wear her bikini in the courtyard. On weekend afternoons, Isabella and I followed the orchard path down and then north along the border of the lake, where we had discovered a stream that bubbled over a jutting outcrop. It wasn't a waterfall exactly, but a thin trickle that shattered onto the rocks by the shoreline, prompting a cloud of condensation that caught the sunlight in rainbows.

Isabella and I went there as often as we could and spread our towels in the haze of smashed droplets. We were close enough to the lake that pulses of coolness from the water mitigated the heat of the day still burning on our backs. The air smelled sharply of ozone, like a faraway thunderstorm.

Isabella perched happily, swinging her legs over the rocks. Water from the falls beaded on her skin.

"This is heavenly," she sighed, tipping her head back.

I made a murmur of agreement, although I couldn't get my words straight. The afternoon heat spun in my brain and made me dozy and stupid. I was dimly aware that the pebbles under my towel were sharp and uncomfortable, but I was loath to move.

Standing up with difficulty, I hopped over to the shoreline rocks, which were furry with lichen. I stepped onto the unsteady, slimy stones just under the lake's edge and launched myself in the rest of the way. The water was warmer at the surface and icy at the bottom. It smelled dank and green, like crushed plants, and as I treaded water my feet kicked through the mulchy softness of underwater weeds.

I swam backward toward the center of the lake and looked up at the tufty birds' nests huddled into cracks in the rock, the fruit trees at the top of the hill, and between the boughs, the cloaked figures of the sisters, startlingly white.

There was a loud splash, and Isabella's

face bobbed toward me, the tips of her ears parting her wet hair.

"It's so cold at the bottom," she said. "I keep thinking something might reach up and grab me."

I shuddered. "Don't say that." I looked down into the depths of the water, and although it was clear, the weeds and silt at the bottom made it impossible to see much farther than my own kicking feet.

Isabella took a deep breath, dove under the water, then clasped the arch of my right foot and yanked it downward. I yelped.

She broke the surface spluttering and laughing. I kicked out at her. "You beast," I said.

"I think you mean the beast of the lake." She paddled around me in a circle to face the spa. "This would make a super flick. *The Beast of the Lake,* with the creepy old hospital and all us innocent young girls."

I had a sudden moment of daring.

"I hear the beast of the lake needs a virgin sacrifice," I said, and I allowed myself to sink lower into the water. I popped the catch of my bikini top and pulled the halter over my head, then kicked up toward the surface. I held it aloft, spitting water. "But what will tempt him from his slumber?"

Isabella shrieked with laughter; she could

barely keep her head above the water. Bobbing down as she concentrated, she wriggled out of her own halter and we both peeled off our shorts. She was laughing so much she was gargling water.

"You're no use," I said, flicking the straps in her direction. "I said a *virgin sacrifice.*"

She squealed, swimming toward me with wide eyes and trying to kick me under the water, blowing froth from her lips. "I think *you're* the beast of the lake," she cried between giggles, gripping my arm. Her fingertips were already wrinkled on my wrist. I thought of how if our bodies were to touch, they would slip over each other, like seals.

Isabella sighed and, in one motion, pushed back toward the rocks. With a groan, she levered herself out of the water onto her elbows and threw her wet bikini toward her bag. Her hair was sticking to her back, her buttocks tan as the rest of her. She hadn't been bluffing about nude bathing. There were no marks on her skin from her swimsuit, and her skin was a chestnut color, darker on her forearms and her shins. She folded her arms over her breasts and shook her hair so drops of water scattered and fell upon the hot stones.

I watched her from the lake, suddenly

vertiginous. As if I were seeing her from a terrible distance, or her image was a miniature projection from a movie reel. She turned to the side, and I saw the faint lines of stretch marks on the top of her thighs and the black hair between her legs. She leaned over and threw her towel over her head, rubbing so vigorously her skin trembled.

I was immediately aware of my own nakedness. Compared to her, I was one of those pale grubs that worms to the surface of the soil to find rain. I tried to scramble back into my shorts, but they had loosened in the water and become so voluminous it was even more difficult to wriggle into them. The halter I merely hung around my neck. I kicked over to the rocks and pulled myself up with a great deal of difficulty. I was so weightless in the water that the heaviness of my limbs was a disappointing hindrance. I dragged myself backward over a sharp rock, scraping my thighs. I tried to attach the hooks of my top, although my fingers were numb and clumsy with cold. Finally they caught. I scraped the suit around and pulled the wet fabric over my breasts and around my neck.

Isabella was lying out on her back, naked in the sun, with the towel over her face. I glanced quickly at the curve of her body and the water still glistening on the line of her belly. Turning away, I unpinned my hair from the bun and combed through it with my fingers.

"You look nice with your hair like that." Isabella's voice. She evidently was still able to see me from the shade of the towel.

My cheeks prickled. "Thank you," I said. "You look nice too." After a moment, my pulse jousting into my throat, I said, "You're always beautiful, though. To me."

Isabella laughed. "Darling Briddie," she said, blowing me a wet kiss. "Thank God we're here together."

12.

SEPTEMBER

The following Saturday, I was sitting at the chair under the window in my room trying to write a letter to Rhona. I kept pausing, as if there was something clogged in the nib of my pen. It felt poisonous to write to her when I had tossed her aside so easily. But I forced myself to continue as a kind of penance. After all, she would never find out I had sidestepped the finer details of my background. I had already taken pains to briefly reference my absentminded cousin Rhona, outfitting her with a pet Dalmatian and an interest in rowing, so there was no danger in leaving a letter for her in Donna Maria's tray.

I tapped the lid of the pen against my teeth. I knew Rhona didn't care much for Cosmati mosaics, so I searched for idle details to offer her. I described the girls' outfits and jewelry, how Sally's father was a gynecologist and how she didn't seem to be the least bit embarrassed by it. How Patricia was a twin but they weren't at all identical, and in fact her twin had buckteeth and a low hairline. I told her of how Elena had once come to Italian lessons wearing mismatched earrings.

With her characteristic clatter of elbow on doorknob, Isabella pushed open my door, tossing her straw hat onto the second bed.

"Briddie, I've got a treat!" she said.

"You scared me —"

"Sister Teresa is going to take us to the spa," she said, bouncing on the mattress.

I flapped the letter in the air to dry the ink. "Oh," I said. "You want to hang out with the nuns?"

Isabella frowned. "She's not *really* a nun."

"Of course she is." I folded the letter in half. "Nancy said —"

Isabella cut me off. "Fine — technically, she's a nun." She waved her hand. "But she's the speaking liaison. So she gets to go all over the place. Wherever she likes."

"She does?" I pictured Sister Teresa browsing the aisles of a department store, idly perusing a pile of woolen berets. I stifled a giggle.

"Yeah. I got talking to her out in the yard —" She pointed out into the orchard, where I knew for a fact she never went.

"What were you doing out there?"

"Just walking." She tossed her hat in the air and caught it. "What do you say? Come on and forget about your boring letter."

"OK," I said reluctantly. I pictured Rhona's reaction to me knocking off her letter to go out with Isabella — tutting and pursing her lips in her best impersonation of "older sister disapproval." I'd spent two years of high school fastidiously keeping them apart, but Rhony's eyes always narrowed when I spoke about Isabella, as if Isabella were a circus tiger that hadn't quite been tamed.

"Don't you want to?"

"No, it's fine — but —" She was watching me with a frown. "But is there anything new to see? We were just there last week."

"Ah." Isabella pressed her lips together to make a chipmunk face. "You spoiled the surprise — this time we get to go inside the building!" She leaped to her feet.

"Oh?" I didn't see what was so exciting about that.

"We can go ghost hunting."

I frowned at her. "Sister Teresa is taking us ghost hunting?"

She rolled her eyes. "Of course not. But while we look around we can keep an eye out for anything spooky to tell the girls about later."

I tried to picture something indistinctly ominous and settled on a silver locket swinging from an iron doorknob.

"Anyway, hurry up — she's waiting for us."

I felt harassed. I hadn't been expecting to leave; she could have given me more notice. I pulled the T-shirts out of my closet and scrabbled among them for my hat. Isabella kept glancing over her shoulder toward the door.

"I'm coming, I'm coming," I said, stepping over the pile of clothes.

Sister Teresa was waiting for us by the side door. She was wearing a long tunic over white pants, and her hair was tied in a white scarf knotted at the back of her head.

"Ready?" she said, smiling.

Isabella and I nodded.

"Follow me," Sister Teresa said. As she turned, I could make out two triangles of her skin at the nape of her neck between the scarf and her tunic. There was something sweet and endearingly clumsy about this wardrobe mishap, like when a schoolgirl's name tag sticks out of the collar of her uniform.

We walked down toward the spa along the shady path under the pines and climbed carefully over the rock ledge. Sister Teresa was walking faster than either of us, and Isabella and I struggled to keep up with her pace. Finally, we approached the gated, overgrown garden at the back of the spa, and Sister Teresa paused while we leaned against the railings and wiped our sweaty faces.

"It is a bit of squeeze," she said, pointing to the gates.

Isabella grinned at me. "Here we go!" She clapped her hands expectantly. Sister Teresa crouched down and slipped through a gap between the railings where the ironwork had buckled. I maneuvered through with as much athletic grace as possible, conscious that Isabella was watching me from behind. I wriggled through the brambles and took a step forward. It was a graveyard. Three rows of white stone crosses marked lumpy hill-ocks in the soil. At the back, closest to the building, were four crumbling headstones sunk and tilted into the earth. I shuddered, then rebuked myself for being so naive. Of course it was a graveyard. I don't know why I hadn't expected it, since I knew it had been a sanitarium and a hospital.

The quality of the light had changed, filtered through the yew trees. The earth was littered with spines from the trees and the scarlet, gummy spittle of crushed yew berries. A sparrow in the hedgerow cocked its head toward us. The back of the spa building was visible behind the trees. In the middle was a ramp leading to a large wooden door. The back wall had six windows with ornamental frames, their glass panes fractured here and there. The south side of the building was shadowed by the aftereffects of the fire, with a trail of blackened bricks that led up to the roof. At the top was a gaping hole where the ceiling had burned away, and for the first time I noticed an empty aperture where a clock must once have been. Sister Teresa was waiting by one of the grave markers with her hands folded.

"Oh," Isabella said from behind me. She stopped short and looked around her. "It's so creepy," she said.

Sister Teresa laughed, and both Isabella and I turned to her in amazement. Her laugh was high and girlish. For the first time, I wondered how old she was.

"You'll grow used to it," she said, smiling.

"Jeez, well, how often do you come here?" Isabella's voice was exceedingly loud in the space, and I thought of how to Sister Teresa's ears, we must sound like a horrible cacophony of jackdaws, jabbering nonsense.

"Quite often," she said.

Noticing the condition of the graves, it was now obvious the sisters must go there regularly. The markers were polished white, and by the corner of the hedge stood a broom. I nudged Isabella and pointed over to where I spied the broom. Behind it, in the shadows, was a scythe.

Isabella snorted with nervous laughter, and we clutched each other, giggling.

Sister Teresa glanced in the direction of the scythe but apparently didn't see the source of our amusement, and instead I saw her eyes follow the lines of the graves. As Isabella and I walked up the central path toward the building, Sister Teresa leaned over one of the older graves and picked a withered bundle of flowers from the stone. She tossed this into the hedge, retrieved a tiny pair of silver scissors from the pocket of her pants, and cut a spray of pink dog roses and placed it on the grave.

"Do you do that for all the graves?" I said, and my voice boomed in the space, growing and stretching out into the garden.

"No," Sister Teresa said. She ran her hand along the top of the stone. "We're not supposed to have favorites, but these are mine. Their names are gone, but we must not forget them."

It was a lovely sentiment, but I suddenly

170

felt queer. Imagine spending so much time with silent women that you have favorite dead people.

Sister Teresa crossed to the back door of the spa. Isabella inched in front of me toward the door, but I looked behind us at the grave markers. Their faces were pitted and crumbling, the etchings worn away to shallow scratches.

"So, you don't get creeped out?" Isabella was saying to Sister Teresa. "Briddie and I found the ossuary at the back of the chapel and we almost lost our minds."

Sister Teresa paused at the door and turned to her. She gave Isabella a thoughtful look. "Perhaps it takes practice to get used to it," she said, opening the door so Isabella could go through.

"Wow." Isabella's voice echoed from inside the building.

The room was large, with pine panels and sprung wooden floors. The wallpaper was a faded fleur-de-lis print in lilac. Above us hung a chandelier, its crystals coated in thick layers of dust. It looked precarious, and I took a cautious step from underneath it. The front windows facing out to the lake were boarded, but even with the paltry light from the back of the building, it was clear it had once been a grand room. On the left-hand side was a huge mirror with a gilded frame. Our three figures wavered in the tarnished glass, obscured by clouds of rust-colored speckles. Underneath the mirror was a monstrously large fireplace, its wooden shelf carved in whorling apples.

"This is the ballroom," Sister Teresa said. "Over there —" She pointed to a wooden staircase that became a gallery. "That is the" — she scrunched up her eyes as she searched for the word — "the balustrade," she said finally, her face relaxing.

I turned to Isabella, and as she caught my eye, a flicker of amusement passed between us.

"We can go up there." Sister Teresa walked toward the staircase, and Isabella drew closer to me, so we processed in single file. I could smell her scent, Soir de Paris, and cigarette smoke.

"The horror flick begins," she whispered. "Virgin sacrifices — get ready." The cool weight of her hair settled on my shoulder.

"Quit it," I said, batting her away. Still, I was pleased she remembered our joke. The afternoon we swam naked in the lake had the shining quality of a dream.

We followed Sister Teresa up the stairs and onto the gallery, where we paused to survey the ballroom.

"Wait," Isabella said, putting her hand on the banister. "Why's there even a ballroom here at all? Did the invalids have parties?"

I pictured a crowd of men wrapped in bandages, like mummies from a bad movie, dancing around the room in a stiff embrace.

"Yes and no," said Sister Teresa. "It was considered good therapy for patients to dance, and both men and women were stationed here."

"Oh," we said in unison.

"But weren't they horribly injured?" I said.

Sister Teresa paused. "No, the sanitarium was quite popular. The patients enjoyed the view and fresh air. To restore their health. Only later was it a hospital for tuberculosis."

"You don't think there's still tuberculosis in here?" Isabella said, wrinkling her nose as if the disease lingered in the wooden panels.

"No." Sister Teresa laughed her schoolgirl laugh again. As she walked along the up-stairs corridor, she opened the doors to reveal the old hotel rooms. They were bare, with black-and-white marble floors and large shuttered windows. "There used to be more furniture here, but it was stolen after the fire. If you look carefully" — she smiled wryly — "you may see ashtrays stamped

'Hotel Reale' in front rooms all around the lake."

"And is it safe? Is the building safe?" I said, placing each foot tentatively on the wood like it might collapse at any moment.

"Quite safe. We often come to sweep here."

"But why?" The question was out of my mouth before I had time to censor myself. It sounded like a terrible waste of time, to be sweeping an empty building.

"The Sisters of Pentila were gifted the building by Signor John Henry. In time we hope to repair the fire damage, but for now we care for its condition."

I nodded. Isabella was biting her thumbnail.

We walked down a narrow back staircase and along the front of the building.

"This was Signor Henry's chamber." Sister Teresa pushed one of the doors open. It was a small room with faded, peeling wallpaper and a set of glass doors that opened onto the patio. The doors were boarded only halfway, and through the gap at the bottom I could see someone had snipped a clearing in the weeds to chalk a gloating message about Arnaldo the cuckold. I tried to imagine the room as it must have been, with wildflowers in a vase on the mantelpiece, a crackling fire in the grate.

"He was brought here in 1917 and stayed for six months."

"Why did he get a private room?" I said.

"I'm not sure," Sister Teresa said. "But perhaps it's fortunate he did."

She allowed the door to swing closed. We went down the corridor and into a marble lobby, where a grand oak staircase led back up onto the landing.

"Do you have any questions?" she said.

"Can we see where the fire started?" Isabella said.

Sister Teresa wrinkled her nose. "Really?"

Isabella nodded. "Please?"

"If you want." Sister Teresa shrugged.

She took us through an arched door under the staircase, then down a few steps and right, along a corridor. I could tell we were approaching the kitchens because over the lingering damp scent there was now a dark, chemical smell, like hot asphalt. Sister Teresa pushed on one of a set of swinging doors and stood aside to let us peer through. There were only narrow windows at the top of the room, and the light was poor, but even so, it was clear the room had been badly scorched. The left wall around the stove and half the ceiling were matte black with starbursts of gray. Twigs of calcified plastic hung from open shelves. The roof of the kitchen had been haphazardly boarded, and a bird's nest was resting in a crook between two planks.

"How sad." I covered my mouth and nose with my sleeve. "And it goes all the way up?"

"Yes, those rooms are quite ruined. Hard to believe this was all because of a steak," Sister Teresa said with the faint trace of a smile. "Perhaps after all, the chef was too good at his flambé."

I watched the expression on her face, unsure if she was joking. She caught my eye and smiled wider. The oversize of her front teeth rather suited her, I thought. A subtle imperfection that somehow made her prettier.

After our tour, Sister Teresa said she was going to stay to tidy the garden, which I supposed meant the graveyard. I hovered, expecting Isabella to offer to wait for her. But to my surprise, she gave her thanks and steered me away from the building.

As she climbed through the gates, she shuddered, like a bird unfolding its wings. "Come on, Briddie, let's get away from here; it's giving me the creeps." She lit a cigarette.

The climb back to the academy was even hotter than earlier in the day. Cicadas rattled in the sun-blanched thistles. I plucked a stem of rosemary from a bush and rubbed the oil between my fingers. At first it had made me queasy to imagine such a beautiful building filled with coughing and sickness. But now I was glad the invalids had been hosted in such gorgeous surroundings. When Rhona was in the hospital, it didn't seem like the kind of place anyone could recuperate. The ward was overheated and it smelled like bleach and sour milk.

I pictured Rhona tucked under a yellow blanket, lying on a deck chair rolled out on the patio overlooking the water. She would drink mineral water and be put on a special float to paddle in the lake. I moved her into John Henry's old room and furnished it with a chaise longue and a writing desk. And I would sneak a pet kitten into her room and she'd have to keep it hidden from the nurses. I would tell the girls I was volunteering, but secretly, I'd come down from the academy in the afternoons to visit her. We'd feed the kitten saucers of milk and sit by the lake and she could read her Civil War textbooks and I would study friezes from my art books.

"So who's that old guy?" Isabella said.

With some effort I broke out of my reverie. "What?"

"Mr. Henry. I stood there quite stupidly

while you and Sister Teresa were talking about him."

I turned to her in disbelief. "But you must know who he is. There's a whole section about him in the welcome file. Didn't you read it?"

"No, Briddie." She stuck out her tongue. "We're not all boring little bookworms."

The insult burned my windpipe, but I kept my voice steady. "He was the patron. Or founder. But I'm sure Sister Teresa would know all the details."

We were quiet for a moment.

"She's so funny," I said, taking a chance.

Isabella watched me expectantly. "What do you mean?"

" 'And there is the — um, I don't know the word — balustrade.' "

Isabella grinned. "And here I can't even order a sandwich."

"Maybe she's trying to use up all the words in the dictionary before her speaking time runs out," I said tentatively. Was I straying too close to sarcasm?

But Isabella hooted with laughter. "Good old Sister Vocabulary."

13.

OCTOBER

Over the course of three days, the sisters picked all the apples in the orchard until the boughs had a naked, startled look. As they worked in the avenues between the trees, snapping apples from the branches, it produced a rustling noise that swished through the corridors of the academy like the train of a wedding dress. Isabella and I watched them from our window and tried to distinguish nun from nun. Occasionally we saw Sister Teresa down in the orchard, smoking on the stone bench with Sister Luisa. Often, though, Sister Teresa's "speaking" status meant she was sent to La Pentola or Brancorsi to stock up on Band-Aids or headache tablets or safety pins or any of the many other things the sisters couldn't make for themselves.

On the Sunday of St. Teresa's festival, the bells began ringing at five a.m. We congregated on the stairs, pale and puffy-faced, our eyes beady with sleep. Donna Maria ushered us into the courtyard, and we stood blinking into the morning. It was a perfect autumn day. The breeze was sharp and the light was thin and golden like weak juice.

As we stood yawning and stretching and adjusting our dresses, there came a strange murmur from the bottom of the hill.

"Look," Nancy said.

A crowd of people from the village was slowly walking up toward the academy, humming a low dirge. At the head was Father Gavanto, holding aloft a cross decorated with paper leaves.

"The Inquisition," Isabella whispered in my ear. "I knew Donna Maria was a secret witch." I snorted.

The sisters filed out of the chapel, led by Sister Luisa. They crossed through the gate and walked through the double doors to join Father Gavanto. With a few words, he handed over the cross and Sister Luisa took it solemnly. I watched her face for any trace of emotion. Was she saying to herself *Don't drop it, don't drop it,* as any normal person would?

Donna Maria appeared, smiling her gummy smile. She gestured for us to back up to the far side of the courtyard, and we pressed against the wall as people from La

Pentola shuffled through. Donna Maria returned, holding a white candle burning inside a metal lantern. Around the base of the candle were twigs of applewood and silk roses. She approached me and, reaching out, tucked my hair behind my ears. I froze, thinking in a wild moment she was about to offer me a benediction. But instead, she handed me the lantern and pointed into the crowd, speaking in Italian.

My hand shook so hard, the flame fluttered. "What do I do with this?" I said stupidly. "Nancy," I hissed. "Nance, help."

After a brief conversation with Donna Maria, Nancy turned to me. "You're supposed to walk at the front of the girls, after the sisters. Then you put the candle on the shrine."

A shiver ran through my jawline. "At the front?"

"Yup." Nancy smiled. "Just go at the front and walk."

I gulped, looking around. "Why me?"

Nancy frowned. "Why not you?"

I searched for Isabella, but she was talking to Sylvia and I couldn't catch her attention. Swallowing, I squeezed through the crowd of girls and villagers from La Pentola, receiving a resplendent smile from Signora Bassi. The courtyard was crammed with people, humming, coughing, bemused-looking kids in their Sunday best. The lantern clattered against elbows and shoulder blades as I picked through the crowd. My stomach roiling, I took a place directly behind the sisters. I looked back for Isabella but instead caught Ruth's eye. She was glowering at me from beside Donna Maria, her arms folded across her chest. In front of me I spotted Sister Teresa somewhere in the middle of the sisters. Like the other nuns, she had her mouth closed, her eyes focused on the ground.

Sister Luisa raised the cross aloft, and our procession began to climb the hillside toward the shrine. The narrow path was choked now with brambles and so we walked in single file, incrementally slowly. The grass was wet underfoot and the earth pearly with dew. The air was spicy with that first scent of autumn — smoke from singed leaves and an inkling of mist. The path was steep but I enjoyed being pulled by the weft of the crowd, as if I were hardly making any effort to walk at all. Hawthorn berries hung so heavy along the path it looked as if red wax had been splattered over the trees.

Father Gavanto began to sing, and the crowd from the village joined in, a low, atonal hymn. I couldn't catch the words.

When Sister Luisa reached the shrine, the father joined her at a dignified, slow pace. He looked through the crowd and motioned for me. I walked around the sisters toward him. Conscious that the eyes of all of La Pentola and all the girls were upon me, I tried to keep my face solemn and stately, but I felt illuminated, like I was floating in a beam of sunlight. The father said a blessing and then fell silent. The silence grew; it became a thing of itself. Birdsong called through the air. Down in La Pentola I could hear the bright strike of a hammer against metal. The sisters knelt in the long grass, staining their habits with green fingers.

The father took the cross from Sister Luisa, and one by one, the sisters approached St. Teresa's shrine, touching their hearts, their mouths, the cross at the top of the alcove. I was strangely moved by the gesture, having not much thought of nuns' hearts until then. They all loved St. Teresa. I pictured her image from the tapestry in the hallway, her tongue and her heart pierced with a quill from heaven. Nuns weren't really supposed to have personalities or opinions; I knew that much. But love was allowed. More than allowed — it was necessary.

■ ■ ■ ■

Our whole procession retreated back along the path, through the academy, down the hill, into the village to the church, where the cross was leaned against the altar. There, I was ushered into a front pew, and Father Gavanto delivered a long speech in Italian. I understood it was something to do with silence, and patience, but the rest was lost to me. In the dim church, the lack of sleep and the incense stung my eyes and brewed into a sludgy headache. I turned to search for Isabella, who was some way toward the back, her posture unusually upright. She was squinting at the father, frowning in such a way that there was a single dash between her brows.

When the bells tolled again, we stretched our stiff necks and joined the queue by the church door. Oak barrels of the convent's hard cider had been rolled into the square, and laid out along two wooden benches were all manner of drinking implements: jelly jars, plastic beakers, even a pair of silver tankards I thought I recognized from the altar. Marco, the market greengrocer, gestured for me and, selecting a large tumbler, filled it to the top with cider. He winked at me. "Bravo," he said, clinking my glass with his, spilling bubbles of amber liquid.

Over the cobbles Signora Bassi pushed a wheelbarrow draped in dishcloths, which she removed with a flourish to reveal "lingua cakes" — essentially apple turnovers baked into a diamond shape. She selected a large one for me and pressed it into my hands. "Beautiful," she said, gesturing over my figure.

Isabella appeared on the other side of Signora Bassi's wheelbarrow as I took a large, ungainly bite of the pastry.

"Hi," I said, swallowing so quickly a chunk of apple caught in my throat. "Where have you been?"

"When?" The tip of her nose twitched.

"Before — this morning. I was looking for you."

Isabella shrugged. "Around. You were probably distracted," she said rather archly.

I opened my mouth and shut it again. My eyes stung.

Kids from La Pentola were pushing pudgy fingers into the cakes, and Signora Bassi chased them away with a volley of remonstrations. Isabella smiled at them deliberately. Indulgently, even. What had prompted her to smile at them but not at me? A flush of shame bristled over me. I'd made a fool

185

out of myself; of course I had. All that attention. I'd overstepped. Embarrassed myself.

Nancy tapped me on the arm, nibbling on a cake. "Good job this morning, Bridge." She nudged me. "You're a natural."

"Thanks," I said, glancing at Isabella, who had been joined by Sylvia. They were kneeling to chat with a little boy dressed in a bow tie and knitted vest.

"So. Was it heavy? The lantern?" Nancy put a hand on my shoulder.

"Not so much," I said, giving her a shallow smile and willing her to stop talking. If I was careful to be quiet, small, I might be able to revert Isabella's mood. Father Gavanto began beating a cider barrel with a stick and Isabella grabbed hold of Sylvia's arm as the little boy in the bow tie raced toward him, cheering.

The father climbed onto one of the rickety benches and gave a speech punctuated with cheers and claps from the crowd. Greta put her arm through Nancy's. "What's he saying, Nance?"

Nancy cocked her ear toward the father. "Something about a bonfire."

"Bridge, you did swell this morning," Greta said, reaching in front of Nancy to grip my hand. "You looked just like Liz Taylor."

"Thanks." I shot a glance at Isabella. She was helping Sylvia to light a cigarette but was laughing too much to keep the lighter steady. There was a grating thump in my chest. Why did she have to be so obtuse? It wasn't fair. It wasn't fair to punish me, when I hadn't even asked to be given that lantern.

"What's that?" Greta pointed toward the hill, where, coming down from the convent, two sisters carried a straw figurine in a white cloak. At first I thought it was a scarecrow, but as the sisters drew close I could see a rosary around its neck. It was meant to be a nun.

"Mother Mary," said Isabella, crossing herself ostentatiously, then burying her face in the crook of Sylvia's shoulder.

I set my teeth.

"They're not going to burn it, are they?" breathed Greta. "Surely they can't burn a fake — a fake sister?"

Nancy grimaced. "We should ask Sister Teresa."

We searched the crowd for her, but she was nowhere to be seen.

"Weird." Nancy frowned. "I'd've thought she would be joining in. It's her saint's day, too, after all."

"Don't sweat it, Nance," Isabella called over the wheelbarrow. "Sister Teresa's got to attend some special prayer anyway back at the convent. Me and Sibbs will smuggle her a cake."

Sylvia screeched with laughter as if it were the most hilarious joke she had ever heard.

I turned away from them both and squeezed past Nancy through the crowd. The straw figurine of the sister was being passed through outstretched arms until Marco grappled with it in the center of the square. He propped it up in a wooden bucket, and as I looked closer I saw that a sprig of silk apple blossom had been set where the mouth should be. I couldn't decide if it was pretty or creepy. Greta and Sally came with a tankard filled to the brim with cider to find me, but it mustn't have been too clean, as the liquor tasted bitter and dank with dust. Marco pulled a cart of wood from behind the chapel and began loading wood around the figure.

Katherine nudged toward us. "Nancy said you were asking about the —" She gestured toward the firewood. She was unsteady on her feet and her breath was sweet.

Greta nodded. "It's spooky. It's so strange they're going to burn it."

Katherine shrugged. "Not so strange. That is how she died, anyway."

We fell quiet. I had forgotten the way in which St. Teresa was martyred. I tried to remember the details from our welcome file, but only settled on the image of her red hair mingling with the flames.

"But — but why would you celebrate it? Someone dying in such a horrible way?" Greta asked, her cheeks going pink. I saw Sally slip her hand into Greta's and give it a reassuring squeeze.

Katherine sighed. "It's not a party or anything. More like a — commen — commem —" She focused hard on the word, and I was embarrassed for her to be so obviously tipsy in public.

"Commemoration," I supplied.

"Yes," Katherine said. "Since she was already supposed to be dead" — she tapped her chest — "you know, inside. A shell. Filled with God." She blinked at us. "You could ask Ruth. She knows even more about it —" She turned to and fro, searching for Ruth in the crowd.

"No, thanks," I said. "We're fine."

After Katherine left us, Greta was pale. "I don't think I could do it," she said quietly.

"Do what, honey?" Sally brushed the hair from Greta's face.

"Stay silent, even while I was being burned." She looked at us seriously. "Even if I was filled with God."

"Course not, honey," Sally said soothingly. "That's why God would never test you like that. He would trial you in a way you could really bear. Like asking you to give up peanut butter." And she tickled her.

Greta broke into a smile, reluctantly at first, and then she began laughing and batted Sally's hand away before leaning over and embracing her.

I took a step away from them and averted my eyes, feeling suddenly like I was intruding.

"What would be your trial, Bridge?" Greta reached out over Sally's shoulder for me.

They shuffled to stand with their arms over each other's shoulders, watching me with identical expressions of cheerful expectation.

"I don't know," I said.

"Giving up your beautiful curls?" Greta lifted her hand to my hair.

"I'd get rid of these in a flash," I said, but they had begun to talk between themselves about the tragedy of a life without dogs, or chocolate, or Christmas.

I watched as Marco and his brother argued about how to build the fire over the figure of the sister. Was it true that all the sisters were being tried by God? It was odd to imagine them as nothing but husks filled with God. Sister Teresa didn't seem especially like an empty shell to me. A bit boring maybe, but not *empty.*

After the firewood had been arranged around the figure, Marco bashed again on the cider barrel until everyone fell quiet. He gestured for me.

"Me? Oh no." I shook my head, clutching the tankard, now slippery with condensation.

"Go on." Sally nudged me forward, seizing the cup from my hand.

Marco handed me a matchbox and pointed toward the bonfire. I tried not to look at the white figure of the sister scarecrow. With clumsy fingers, I struck a match against the box and held it to the crumpled copies of *Il Giorno.* It curled the edges of the paper and then blew out straightaway. I lit another and another, until the paper caught and began to smolder, the young wood popping and bursting. Marco gestured at me and everyone clapped. I gave a theatrical bow, not even caring what Isabella might think. Greta and Sally and I toasted small apples in the flames and rolled them in trays of brown sugar and cinnamon. The kids danced around, poking at the scarecrow until it disintegrated; someone brought out a guitar and Donna Maria and Signora Bassi danced in a circle, arm in arm. We stood out in the square until the sun hung low and orange over the chestnut trees. I didn't even look for Isabella. I was giddy on sugar and cider and damp wood and smoke and the first glittering stars.

That night at dinner the candles were blurring and I wondered if I had taken too much cider. But it made everything soft-centered and hilarious. Unsteadily, I ate my whole bowl of buckwheat noodles and concentrated hard on my lamb cutlet. My hand kept slipping and my knife scratched against the plate. There was a tinny sound in my ears and Greta and Sally's conversation seemed distant and muffled. I glanced up to see Isabella watching me over the other side of the table. Coolly, I blinked at her, twice, and looked away. The side of my face tickled with the awareness that she was still staring at me. I kept my head carefully poised on Sally, miming absorption. Inflated with a strange sense of victory, I marched out of the refectory and straight up to my bedroom after supper, not even bothering to look backward for Isabella. I took off all my clothes except my bra and panties and slipped under the coverlet. I was as warm and floaty as if the bed were drifting on the lake.

And then, sometime in the night, I woke to find Isabella standing by the bedside.

"Move over," she whispered.

I was too surprised to object, and shuffled back against the wall so I was lying in the chilled part of the sheets.

"I'm freezing," she whispered.

I felt her forehead, which was hot and clammy.

"You're sticky," I said, pretending to wipe my palms on the sheet.

"Am not," she said, flicking me the finger. "I swear. I couldn't sleep because my teeth are chattering." Her breath was syrupy on my face.

I hesitated. She was the one who'd been ignoring me. Was I making it too easy for her?

"Briddie, come on, warm me up."

I took her damp hand in mine.

"Where did you go? After the bonfire?" Her eyelashes brushed against the pillow.

"I dressed in Greta's room. She wanted to borrow my blouse."

"Surprised she fit into it," she said with a snort.

I said nothing.

After a moment, she said, "I couldn't find you." Her expression was peculiar, somehow both wounded and predatory.

"Sorry," I muttered.

"I looked everywhere."

"You did?" My heartbeat wobbled against my eardrums.

She nodded, slipping her hands under my arms. She grazed the tip of my breast as she moved, and a ribbon spun through my body and I stiffened, daring myself not to breathe and give away the rippling feeling. Isabella was watching me closely. I was holding myself so tight my stomach was shaking. She wriggled closer to me, and the glint of light from the window shone in her eyes.

She wriggled in closer still.

And then she kissed me.

When I woke the next day I thought I had dreamed it. I was alone in my bed. It was so dark I was disoriented, thinking I had slept until the afternoon. My watch on the bedside table said five thirty. Dazed, I stretched out, trying to make sense of the night before. Perhaps it had been a dream? But there on the floor by the bed was Isabella's green hair tie. It had a tangle of black hair caught into a bobble at the side. I picked it off the tiles and lay back on the pillows, stretching it between my thumbs. I closed my eyes and ran over only an image at a time, like letting drops of scent out of an almost-empty bottle. Isabella's warm, treacly breath against my lips. The weight of her hair as I wrapped it around my wrist, dipping my mouth to her skin. And the unwinding and tickling ran through all the muscles in my body, and my skin felt burnished and glowing like after a hot bath. And the day was rearranged and re-sorted. And I was rearranged and re-sorted, and everything was good.

I ran to the bathroom and stared at my reflection in the mirror, inspecting my mussed-up hair, the rosiness in my cheeks, the round purple bruises on the inside of my arm where her grip had grown stronger and stronger as I kissed her, again and again. Remembering the violence of her grasp shot a throb of desire into my core, so raw it was nearly painful. It strobed through me like the glare from a lighthouse. I splashed water over my face and tried to shake the weakness from my limbs. My fingers were trembling, my pulse veering in unsteady tilts. Everything would be different now.

14.

OCTOBER

That morning was bright and chilly. It was the first day that truly called for sweaters and scarves, and the girls turned up at breakfast bundled up against a cool breeze feathery with bonfire ash and ripe wheat.

Every time someone entered the refectory, my head snapped to the door. I couldn't help myself; I needed to see her face. Last night hardly seemed real. When I saw her expression, I'd know for sure. I lingered until Sister Luisa began clearing the table and mopping under the benches. But Isabella never came. My face was pulpy and tingling as I ran to Italian lessons. What if she was so tight on cider she'd forgotten the whole thing? What if she regretted it and now she was avoiding me deliberately?

But there she was. Sitting at her usual desk. She turned as I entered, and as her eyes lifted to me, a frail smile crossed her face. It was a slender, almost sad smile. A smile I had never seen before. Elena was explaining the past conditional tense, and I gripped my pencil so hard it cut into my thumb. I ached to look at Isabella properly, the edges of my vision burning. When I dared to glance at her, her face was colorless and she was listlessly doodling pansies in the margins of her notebook. I decided to slip her a note, staring so long at the paper, the lines began swimming. In the end I decided on *You OK?* She scrawled back, *Headache.* And then she put her hand over mine, giving it a quick squeeze. I breathed with relief. Just a headache. She really had drunk too much cider.

Isabella went for a nap at lunch, so I sat with Bunny and Mary Babbage and pretended to listen as they chattered about their plans for the Christmas vacation. It was so easy for them. There was something almost unjust in the careless way the other girls began to plan for ski lodges in Sestriere and RSVP to champagne receptions in Vienna.

After lunch, I knocked on Isabella's door but she didn't answer. Back in my room I smoked three cigarettes in a row, then forced myself to write a letter to Rhona. Even I could see it had a febrile, manic quality, with exclamation marks in every sentence and half the words underlined. I bumped into Joan as I went down to leave the letter in Donna Maria's tray. As she blinked politely I told her a long and tedious story about my cousin Rhona and her exploits on an imaginary sailing boat I conjured out of unadulterated panic.

For the afternoon's lecture, I took my place in my usual spot and draped my cardigan over Isabella's seat — although everyone knew she always sat next to me. She came in late, her hair mussed up on one side of her head. She sat down and pulled my sweater around her shoulders.

"Do you mind? I'm frozen."

"Of course not," I said. Although actually I was cold and had to fold my arms over my chest to keep warm.

Half an hour through the lecture, Isabella pinched me on the back of my hand.

"I'm going to split," she said. "I feel like hell."

She did look wan, so I nodded. As she squeezed through the row of students and left the room, I composed my chest into a place of order. There was no reason to be disappointed. Just because she left early didn't mean anything. I marked down the time until the lecture was over, then knocked at her door. There was no answer.

After vespers I sorted through my closet, meticulously polishing all my shoes and stuffing them with tissue paper. Before dinner, I went and knocked again on Isabella's door.

"Hello?"

The room was stuffy and dark. I crept closer to the bed.

"Are you OK?" I said.

"Yes," she said wearily, lifting her head off the pillow. With some alarm, I noticed she was still fully dressed.

"Izzy —" I never called her that. I don't know why it popped into my head. "Don't you want to get your nightdress on?"

"Too tired," she said, pulling the sheets up to her chin. "And I'm cold. Will you get a blanket from the chest?"

I picked up the notebooks and the pair of pumps lying on top of her chest and pulled out a tartan blanket, which I laid over the bed.

"Thanks," she said.

I walked round to her pillow and put my palm against her forehead. "You're hot," I said, trying to keep the concern out of my voice.

"It's fine," she said. "Be better tomorrow." She turned over and lay so still, I figured she had already gone back to sleep.

I filled up the water jug from the bathroom faucet and left it by her bed, then closed the door quietly, smiling to myself. I would have to discourage her from overindulging on hard cider if it disagreed with her so much.

The next day when she didn't appear for breakfast I began to worry. During Italian, I could hardly concentrate. I asked Elena if I could be excused to go to the restroom and ran two stairs at a time to the upstairs corridor.

Isabella didn't answer when I knocked, but I pushed the door open anyway. Piled on the bed was a random assortment of clothes — two of the gray towels, a kilt, her woolen overcoat — as if she had ransacked her closet in a hurry.

"Isabella," I said tentatively, in the singsong voice Mama always used on Christmas mornings.

She murmured.

I brushed the hair back away from her face. She looked dreadful. "Jesus, you're burning up." I pulled some of the bedclothes away to find the sheets soaked in sweat. I heard myself give an intake of breath.

"Isabella," I said, more sternly.

She opened her eyes. "What?" she said crossly.

"You're burning up," I said. "You're sick. You need a doctor."

Her eyes found mine and focused. Her pupils were small and tight. "No way."

"What are you talking about? You have the flu or something. We need to get you cooled down and get you some aspirin." I looked around the room for inspiration.

"No point," she said, turning back into the pillow.

"What?" I was angry at her now. Did she *want* to be sick? The least she could do was cooperate. I yanked on the shutters and they gave way with such a sudden violence I lost balance. I was glad, though, knowing the brightness of the day would hurt her eyes.

She yowled, pressing her face into the pillow. "Bridget, go away."

"No," I said, opening the window so cold air sliced into the room. "I'll get Donna Maria to ring for a doctor." With a last look at the bed, I walked toward the door. "I've got to go. Elena thinks I'm in the restroom."

"Briddie —," she said.

I paused. Her voice was pathetic. I softened and waited.

"Briddie?" she said again, a little desperately.

"I'm here."

"Come over?"

I sat on the end of the bed. She blinked at me from the pillow. Her eyelashes were wet. I touched the shape of her arm under the sheet. She closed her eyes briefly. "Don't get the doctor — I know what it is. It's the malaria again."

"Oh God," I said, glancing at the nightstand for I don't know what.

"No." She shook her head. "It's not like that. It happens sometimes. I get sick for a couple of weeks, and then I'll be fine. I feel like death for a while. But it's OK."

"God, really?" I reached and stroked her hair away from her face.

Two tears rolled down her cheeks. She nuzzled her face against the pillow to disperse them. She smiled, and a web of spittle broke open between her lips. "My doctor gave me pills. They should be in the closet, with my makeup."

I leaped up and yanked open the closet door. I prayed under my breath that the tablets would be in there. What if she had forgotten them? Would Italian doctors know how to treat malaria? I rummaged in between the rolling tubes of lipstick until I saw the carton of pills.

"They're here," I said, holding them aloft,

although my hands were shaking and the pills rattled against the glass.

Isabella wormed a hand through the blankets. "Just one," she said.

I shook a tablet onto her palm and poured her a glass of water, but she had swallowed it dry.

"I should tell Elena or Donna Maria," I said, gripping the water glass with both hands.

"Tell them it's the flu. I don't want the grief. I'll be fine soon, I swear."

"OK," I said, putting the glass down on the edge of the table. I went toward the door but turned back to her. Surely the nuns must know how to nurse? I pictured Sister Teresa sitting at a bedside, spooning pea soup into a baby's mouth. "I'll get Sister Teresa," I said. "She'll know what to do."

Isabella sat up with such sudden energy her face blanched. "No," she said. Her hair was wild. She looked so fierce I was almost afraid of her. "I don't want her here," she said, and slumped back on the bed.

"OK," I said, "I won't tell her."

"Promise?" She blinked.

"I won't say anything, I promise," I said. A strange emotion passed through me. Isabella only wanted me there. She needed me. I was the only person she trusted. I would take care of her, by myself. The responsibility of her care nestled in my arms like a sleeping cat. I would look after Isabella. I would make her well again. I would be her private nurse. She would be so grateful.

"Do you want something to eat?"

"No," Isabella said, rolling away from me.

"Come on, maybe bread and butter?" I wondered if we could get carrots for her.

"Sure," she said, although her voice was flat.

"OK. And anything else?"

"Can you find me a bottle of Coke?" she said, turning into the pillow. "Those pills taste like shit."

"Of course," I said, certainty radiating through me. I would look after her until she was all better.

It took only a few days before Isabella's temperature dropped. I told all the girls Isabella had food poisoning — that prevented any questions, and it meant I had her all to myself. I wiped her brow and sent her nightdress out to the laundry. I taped a bandage to her arm so she wouldn't scratch at a rash in the crook of her elbow. I bought bottles of Coke from the post office in La Pentola and balanced them on the windowsill to keep them cool. Between classes I walked her down the corridor to the bathroom. I braided her hair and piled her with blankets and forced her to drink water and take aspirin. And eventually she was sleeping less and said she felt better.

I was feeling better, too. I made lavish plans for all the things Isabella and I would do together, once she was well. A trip to Pisa! A boat trip on the lake! I murmured suggestions as I wiped her forehead and neck with a wet flannel, as I folded her sweaters and arranged her earrings. I was bribing myself as much as her with the promise of new adventures. Soon it would be Halloween, I told her. We could have a fancy-dress party, hand out candy to the kids in La Pentola.

And true fall had arrived with a sudden flourish of claret and mustard and gold. Swirling mists rose from the lake and got tangled in the orchard so the trees slit the sunlight in columns. I started closing my windows, or else the smoke from burning leaves crept in and left my clothes smelling bitter as embers.

The term had been generous with butter, and I had noticed the waistband of my kilts getting tight. Courtesy of one of Greta's magazines, I was practicing some calisthenic exercises in my bedroom. The maneuvers seemed somehow easier than they ever had been before. My kicks swung in high arcs; I spun around in effortless circles. I bounced on my toes and felt my heart lifting, as if I could bounce out of the window and straight into the sky. As I bent at the waist there was a series of raps on my door. This was Donna Maria's characteristic knock, and I pulled on my robe so she wouldn't be scandalized by my shorts.

"Entra," I said.

Donna Maria peered around the door. "Telephone," she said, miming the receiver. "Telephone, telephone." She looked so frazzled I smiled and put my hand on her birdlike arm.

She shook me off. "Now, now." She pointed down the corridor.

So I ran down the stairs two at a time. Barbie stuck her head out of her room. "Where's the fire?"

As I ran down the steps I thought — *Granny.* What if she'd died? What if she was dying and it was too late? I picked up the phone. It was Granny's voice.

"It's your grandmother," she said, rather formally, as if I wouldn't recognize her unless she used her full title.

"Oh." I was so relieved. "But, Granny, what is it?"

"It's Rhona," she said. "I'm sorry to tell you this, Bridget — but she's had a heart attack."

■ ■ ■ ■

III
CONNECTICUT

■ ■ ■ ■

15.

OCTOBER 1957

On the train to St. Cyrus, I was restless at every grade crossing, uncomfortable in my coat, itchy. Even the idea of going straight to the hospital was making my skin prickle. My mind began to travel down the white corridors to the overheated rooms, the radio tuned so low it was like a humming mosquito. Rhona's room was ahead, doors swinging, an alarm somewhere buzzing. I snapped out of my dream. The zipper of my slacks was digging into my stomach and I discreetly reached down and released it an inch. In the panic of leaving, I'd stuffed my case with an impractical assortment of clothes, some of them not even mine. There hadn't been time to say a proper good-bye to anyone except Isabella, but at least she could cover for me until things were back to normal. Which wouldn't be long. Maybe I'd even be back before Halloween. I readjusted my seat, rubbed the beads of my rosary. A woman in a plum coat sat opposite me, and she glanced at me from behind her novel. I saw myself as she must: a glamorous, melancholy stranger. I felt her eyes working over my outfit and my suitcase, with its stickers from the airport in Milan. I thought, *She must know I've traveled by airplane,* and I sat up straighter. If she spoke to me, I decided I would tell her I'd rushed back from Europe for a family emergency. Her face would wrinkle in concern. "What an ordeal," she'd say. "Your family is lucky to have you." But she didn't speak to me, and I leaned my head against the glass and fell into a half sleep. I decided I would be the one to talk sense into Rhona. I'd be so helpful they would make me an honorary nurse. I would wear a white apron and pin my hair in practical waves. And Rhona would sit up and open her mouth meekly, her eyes lustrous and willing. Dr. Callahan would shake his head. "A miracle." And Mama would rush to me and say, "Thank God you're here," and I would pat her shoulder and say, "It's OK, Mama, I'm here now."

But Mama didn't rush to me. She hugged me loosely and smiled in a fixed sort of way, like she was remembering an old movie. I'd been working myself up over how relieved she would be to have me back home — me, the sensible one.

But she just smiled and said, "Thank you, Rhona."

I flinched and opened my mouth to correct her, but she still had a faraway expression, as if she were peering at the ocean over the railing of a ship. She turned to my father and asked him about some paperwork he had to sign. And as she turned, I swallowed my correction so it landed in my stomach and curdled.

It was peculiar to be suddenly back in St. Cyrus. My bedroom was dusty, airless. The house was so quiet. No girls playing golf along the corridors with umbrellas and crab apples. No rattling pipes, no chapel bells. No Isabella. No Rhona. I kept the door to Rhona's room closed, since the breeze kept clicking the latch and I kept doubting myself, calling out to her. Each morning I almost ran up the drive when Granny's car pulled up. We most often went to the tearoom of the Greene Hotel and drank cocoa. The atmosphere at home was so heavy with misery that we had a tacit sort of understanding we shouldn't make it worse by talking about it. And so Granny and I chatted only about conspicuously bright things.

We made deliberate remarks about the people sitting near us: "Look at that darling dog," and then later, "Wasn't that dog just a darling?" We talked about the beauty of European architecture and the glories of Italian food. I told her all about the academy, about the silent sisters and the old spa, about patronage and sculpture and mosaics. And once I started talking about the academy, I found it hard to stop. It made my life there become alive, luminous, like holding a pebble underwater.

We drove to New Haven and hopped from store to store, buying jars of coffee, tiny sachets of fancy English tea. I asked Granny to take me to an Italian delicatessen, where I bought slices of mortadella and bags of risotto rice. We strolled around department stores sourcing gifts for Mama — peep-toe slippers and face cream and bath oil. We shopped with the frantic concentration of storing up for a long winter, and something about the process lent the season a Christmasy spirit that sugared the edges of the horribleness.

When we had wrung out as much of the day as we could, we went home, exchanging fewer and fewer words as the car rolled closer to the house, until we sat in total silence. When the car pulled up in the front yard, Granny turned to me with an artificially sunny smile.

"OK, Budgie, let's go."

And we struggled in with sacks of groceries, unpacking nets of pumpkins and slices of cheese and decanting flour and arranging gerbera daisies in vases.

Granny and I took care of the house with precise determination. She washed the net curtains and ironed all the bed linens. I scrubbed the upstairs bathroom, cleaning the grout between the tiles with a toothbrush. While Granny arranged Mama's closet, I tipped out the cabinet in the guest bathroom downstairs and wiped the dust from all the half-used bottles of cologne. Under the sink, I found a ball of soap Mama had pressed together from odds and ends to make a monster. I turned the mutant soap over and over, struck with an acute pang that Mama refused herself the pleasure of using the scented soap because it had to be saved for visitors. Granny dusted the trophies in Rhona's room, and I rubbed the two silver coins from her spelling bees to a gleam with a paste of salt and baking powder. Granny wanted to go through Rhona's drawers, but I wouldn't let her open them. Instead we pulled out the bed and vacuumed underneath it, throwing out boxes of tissues, spent ballpoints, gum wrappers.

We didn't know what else to do. We couldn't make Rhona better again.

She looked like a bird. Her skin was a gray-yellow color and under the hospital lights I could see downy hair covering the hollows of her cheeks. She looked so dreadful I was afraid to get too close. Like if I were to touch her, she would be cold and damp and leave an ashy residue on my fingertips. I stood by the edge of the curtain, ashamed. Ashamed of myself and ashamed of Rhona. She had harmed herself, and worse, she had harmed Mama.

Mama had aged since I left for Italy. Her clothes were wrinkled and the skin on her forehead was dry and flaking. Granny routinely marched her to the visitors' restroom and made her apply lipstick that was far too pink and made her sad, creased face look like a horrible worn doll's in a yard sale. Mama barely left the hospital, driving back with Dad late at night when he joined them after work.

The nurses at St. Christopher's were very good with Mama. I guess because Mama had been a nurse too, after all. They sat with her on their breaks and brought her cups of burned coffee from the cafeteria and boxes of saltwater taffy they'd been given by grateful patients.

Sometimes Dr. Callahan visited to check over Rhona's charts and consult with Dr. Porter, who was Rhona's main doctor at St. Christopher's. I was so happy to see Dr. Callahan in the ward, it surprised even me.

"Bridget, you look sensational. Italy's agreeing with you?"

I nodded gratefully. A grubby, lumpy bit of me wanted my normality to be appreciated. As if I could easily be as sick as Rhona if I tried, but instead I was carrying on. I wanted attention for not drawing attention to myself.

When Dr. Callahan came in to talk to the other doctors about Rhona, everyone treated him as if he was a celebrity. It surprised me, because the nurses hadn't made a fuss over Dr. Callahan the last time Rhona was in the hospital. No one had stopped to whisper with him behind the vending machines or trailed him around as he checked Rhona's chart. But then I understood. Rhona was the celebrity. The cardiac ward didn't normally have young women like Rhona there; the other five beds were occupied by overweight older men.

Rhona slept a lot, or else she pretended to

sleep. Lying down so much was rough on her skin, and sometimes when she was awake, Mama would roll her onto her side and rub lotion on her hips and back. It was my job to support Rhona from the other side. Mama showed me how to prop her against a rolled-up towel to help her balance. Lying on her side like that was hard on her lungs, making her breath shallow. I pulled my sleeves over my knuckles so her cold fingers didn't touch mine. As Rhona coughed, her eyes watering, I looked up, away. I stared at the grooves in the vent in the corner of the room. I tried to conjure promises to make her, enticements, like I had done with Isabella. But I had nothing to offer.

On Friday morning, I couldn't bear being witness to another lotioning. When Mama began to turn Rhona, I made an excuse and went to the restroom, even though I didn't need to go. I perched on the lid of the seat and covered my face with my hands, waves of tiredness rolling over me. I flushed the toilet anyway, and washed my hands carefully three times. The mere scent of hospital air gave me a creepy-crawling feeling over my skin, as if I would never scrub it all away. My scalp was raw because I religiously shampooed whenever I came home from visiting Rhona.

I went down to the lobby, where there was a small store. It sold cans of root beer and magazines and sparkly balloons and teddy bears. And also "With Sympathy" cards, which, superstitiously, I tried not to look at. I bought myself a box of Junior Mints, one of the few things I had truly missed in Italy. As I stood by the register I picked up two packets of wintergreen gum for Rhona. Rhona went through gum at a ridiculous rate. I always brought a couple of packs home for her when I went out. Mama and Dad didn't like her to have it because they assumed she chewed it to curb her appetite. But I knew Rhona was self-conscious about her breath, which was sweet and acidic — like pear juice. *I'll leave the gum by her bedside,* I thought. It was the closest I could come to coaxing her recovery.

I stood for the elevator behind two medical students. One was blond, with hair that had gone too long without a cut. The other was a redhead with a pug nose and ginger eyelashes. They filed into the back of the elevator and I stood in front of them, absently reading the tattered poster about early polio detection that I had already read a hundred times.

"What've you got this week?" the redhead said.

The blond one yawned. "Nothing good. Case of the clap."

"Shh," the redhead said, giggling. I heard the rustle of fabric as they jostled each other, and the back of my neck tingled; I knew they had been pointing to me.

"Guess what I have."

"What?"

"Nervosa."

My body tensed.

"No? The cardiac case?"

"Yup. Come up tomorrow before rounds, have a look."

When the door opened I walked straight ahead, although it was the wrong direction. I didn't want to turn my face toward them in case they saw my expression. I felt singed, like they would be able to see through the top layer of my skin.

On Monday, Granny and I drove to the hospital to wait for Dad to arrive. We decided we were going to take Mama to the movies that night. Her misty preoccupation with Rhona made her unusually compliant, so she silently went along with whatever schemes Granny and I cooked up during the day to try to distract her.

When we arrived, Mama was strangely agitated. She gripped Granny's wrist and handed her a sheaf of papers Dr. Porter had given her to sign. Dr. Porter had asked her for permission to write about Rhona's case for a journal. Mama said in a moony voice that Dr. Porter suggested Rhona might have inherited a genetic disorder because of her mixed blood.

"What did you say?" Granny's voice sharpened as she turned the papers over in her hands, scanning the words.

"I told him I would consult with Roger," Mama said.

Something about the way Mama said "Roger" made me feel floaty and incorporeal, like she hadn't noticed me standing there. She hardly ever used Dad's first name, instead saying "your father" or, sometimes, "Daddy-O" if she was teasing him. Clearly, the conversation was far too adult for me, and one of them should have recognized and dismissed me so I wouldn't be exposed to any horrible details. My body was rigid and I tried to hold the strangeness of it away from me so I wouldn't be tainted by it.

"You didn't sign anything, did you?" I had never heard Granny use such a harsh tone with Mama.

Mama shook her head.

"Good girl," Granny said. She took a deep sigh and caught my eye. The look of adult collusion implied in that glance made my insides squirm. I felt hot and itchy and I wanted to cry.

Granny asked Mama to go out to the diner three streets down and pick us up a sandwich. It was clearly a ruse, since she hadn't asked Mama to do a single thing since Rhona went back into the hospital.

But Mama trotted off anyway, saying, "Ham, Budgie?" with a genuine expression of panic on her face. Her anxiety over my sandwich, even a decoy sandwich, was too much to bear, and I nodded and swallowed against the pain in my throat.

Granny and I sat in the greasy chairs in the lobby. She put her glasses on and read through the pages, handing them to me one by one as she finished. I didn't want to read them. I thought, *She can't make me read them.* So I held them in front of my face for what seemed like an appropriate amount of time, then put them down in my lap. When Granny had finished the last page, she handed it to me and I could feel her watching me. I let my eyes trail over the paper, but I wouldn't read a word.

"The sheer cheek of him," she said. Her

face was in high color.

"What will Dad say?"

"You wait," she said, her head twitching. "You wait until your father sees this."

An hour later, after I'd eaten both my and Granny's sandwiches, I saw Dad coming down the corridor. He smiled and put his briefcase down on the floor to give me a hug.

"Hi, sweetheart," he said, pulling back his head and smiling deeper. He was unshaven and his eyes were faintly bloodshot. When he smiled, his face was almost the same as it used to be, but subtly changed, like a sweater that's a bit lopsided after darning.

Was I supposed to tell him about Rhona's doctor? Surely that was something Mama should do. She was hardly able to brush her hair — would she be able to explain it to him?

"Um —," I began, horrified it would, after all, be me having to start a conversation about those papers. I hadn't even read them.

"What is it, sweetheart?" he said, his eyes snapping to focus on mine. "What's wrong? Rhona?"

"Rhona's fine." My Granny's voice. She removed her glasses and let them hang around her neck, offering her cheek for a kiss. "Now, come with me. I have to discuss something with you."

"Everything OK?" Dad looked between us.

"It will be," she said ominously.

I gave him a wan smile.

Granny and I waited for Dad outside Dr. Porter's office. I didn't want to sit there, but Granny had this smug, expectant posture, and I couldn't wriggle away. Her smugness grew palpably stronger as the sound of Dad yelling came through the door. I couldn't hear what he said, only his voice getting strained and ragged, and the monotone of Dr. Porter's voice trying to keep Dad calm.

When he came out, his face was red. "Good Lord. Where's your mom?" He looked at me.

"She's with the nurses," I said. "They took her to see the babies in the maternity ward." It was a little creepy, I thought, peeping in on the babies while they slept. But it made Mama smile, and that was reason enough.

Dad sighed, rubbing his face. "It's probably just as well."

"Roger?" Granny's voice was strangled. "What did he have to say for himself?"

Dad motioned with his head down the corridor and marched us behind a pair of swinging doors.

I kept one eye on the glass windows in the doors, since it was a precarious place to stand.

"That quack," Dad said, gripping his briefcase.

"We should get Dr. Callahan," Granny said.

"Callahan *suggested* it," he said, and Granny took a sharp inhale of breath.

"Do you know what kind of nonsense they're saying?" he said, jostling his brief-case, where, presumably, the papers had been stuffed.

I nodded blankly, since he seemed to want a response. *Don't say it,* I thought. *Don't tell me.*

"These *geniuses* want to make a study of your sister," he said. I didn't know why he was focused on me. Why he wasn't address-ing Granny. "Genetic disorders. Mixed heritage. Oral phobias of impregnation," he spat. His eyes flickered between mine and Granny's, as if challenging us to leap to the doctors' defense.

"But — you — you can't get pregnant by mouth." The words were out before I could stop them. A rush of shame sprang to my head so quickly, I became woozy. But neither of them appeared to be ruffled.

"No, Bridget, you most certainly cannot," Granny said, staring at my father as if he were about to correct her.

He looked at me and shook his head. "No, Bridget."

"And that has nothing to do with your sister's appetite, either." Granny's lips were tight.

"Of course not," my father said. He cleared his throat. "Or blood heritage." He began coughing. "So let's not hear any more about it. Understood?"

"Yes, Daddy," I said. "I understand."

16.

OCTOBER

Three days later, I was sitting cross-legged on the floor, flipping through a biography of Ghiberti and sipping from a glass of defrosted orange juice. Coursework had become a particular kind of bittersweet torture; I yearned for anything that connected me to the academy, but the reminder that I was missing out made my gut tingly. I'd even had to hide my old *Treasures of Italy* book in the closet. I sipped again from my orange juice. Condensation dribbled down the insides of the windows. I doodled in the margins of my notebook, keeping an eye on the drive for the shadow of the mailman's van.

Each morning I went out to check the mailbox for a letter from Isabella, but nothing had arrived yet. Typical of the Italian mail system. Still, I didn't want her to worry, so I'd been writing her daily updates. Mr. Anderson, our old Latin teacher, was now sporting a rather obvious toupee. The Creamery had flooded after a storm and would be shut for six months. The PTA had raised funds to install a statue of John Everett Jr. in Bloomsville Park, except the forklift couldn't fit through the gates so they'd had to chop down a hedge to drive it in. After being away, everyday life in St. Cyrus seemed quaint, almost sweet, a pastel-colored childhood memory. And writing about our hometown made me feel closer to her — it was a special code between us. On the street, a car lumbered past and I sat up on my knees. But it wasn't the mailman. I sighed, rubbing at a sore spot where the cuticle was peeling from my fingernail.

"Do you need a manicure?" Granny said hopefully.

I smiled. Granny was ready to pounce on any excuse to spend money. "I'm OK," I said. Involuntarily, I glanced up toward Rhona's room.

Granny shut her novel with a snap. "Sweetheart." She tipped her head back to look at me over the top of her glasses. "I know you've been worried about Rhona. We all have."

My chest tightened. I thought, *If she starts talking about anything medical, I won't listen. I'll put myself back at the academy, in a rowboat on the lake, feeding birds in La Pentola Square.*

"But she's on the mend now, and there's no point in punishing yourself. Heaven knows there's enough of that going around."

A bubble of self-pity swelled in my chest. It seemed perverse to be anything except glum when all anyone could think about was sickness. Despite all our scrubbing and cleaning, the house maintained the hushed and anticipatory atmosphere of a funeral parlor. The detritus of sickness was strewn about the place: boxes of Kleenex and packets of vitamin powder and lapsed visitor passes and deflating balloons and "Get Well Soon" cards. I looked around the room at all these mundane relics of suffering. How couldn't Granny see I wasn't *allowed* to be happy? I was *forced* to be bored and wretched. To sit at home losing out on my one chance at adventure, at friends. Because after all, it was Rhona's fault I was back, instead of at the academy with the other girls. With Isabella. I wasn't punishing myself; I was punishing Rhona.

"It's not doing you any good to be moping around the house. Aren't any of your high school friends in town?"

"Perhaps." I hesitated. Would it be nice to see girls from school? It might just make me feel worse — flimsy, insubstantial.

"Well, call them and make plans," Granny said, opening her novel. "There must be some kind of" — she scrunched up her nose — "*Halloween* event you can attend."

My mouth fell open. Granny didn't approve of Halloween one bit. I seized my chance. "OK, I'll call around. And maybe we should get some candy in case we get trick-or-treaters here as well?"

"Hmm," Granny said, cracking the spine of her book. I wondered with a pang what the girls would be doing to celebrate, back at the academy. Pumpkin carving probably. And spiderweb decorations in the common room. And pranks: creepy-crawlies made from sugar paper slipped between sheets before bedtime. In all the fun, would they remember to remember me?

I called Flora from the telephone in the hallway, hoping all of a sudden she would be home. I was itching to talk to someone about how rotten everything had been. But Flora's brother Roddy answered and said she was still at college. As I was about to hang up, he said, "Hey, Bridget?"

"Yes?"

"I'm real sorry to hear about your sister. I hope she gets better soon."

"Thanks, Roddy." My ear burned against

the receiver. I held my breath, hoping I had summoned sufficient gratitude.

"She was always so good at school," he said. His voice was loose and nostalgic.

"Yeah." I deliberately left an awkward pause, searching for a way to change the subject. I had forgotten Rhona and Roddy had been at middle school together. "Well —"

"I mean, we could hardly keep up with her." He laughed, a strangled sort of laugh. "Honor roll, history club, president of —"

"I'll be sure to tell her you said hello," I said primly, twirling the cord around my finger until the skin blanched. "Thank you, Roddy."

"Sure thing," he said, then hung up abruptly.

The next afternoon, Granny's driver dropped me off at Sophie LeBaron's house. The drive was littered with leaves and the house appeared even larger than usual now that the banks of roses had died and the full scale of the building was clearer. The length of the porch had been decorated with orange and green squash placed in a pattern of alternate colors.

"Imagine, what a waste. Using vegetables to decorate," Granny muttered. "I hope they'll eat them afterward."

I smiled to myself, since Granny's idea of what constituted waste was variable. "Maybe when you come to pick me up we'll take them home and give them a proper burial in a pie," I said.

Granny laughed — like a firecracker going off. It was a fantastic sound and I congratulated myself for having produced it. "Away with you, child," she said. "Don't fall over in there and come back draped in a tiger skin."

Sarah, Sophie's maid, opened the door. "Hello, Miss Bridget," she said, smiling.

"Hello, Sarah!" I said, as if I was fifteen again and it was another Saturday morning trailing into Sophie's house after Isabella. I handed over my coat and hat, feeling stupid for wrapping up so warm for the short steps up the front porch.

"Mrs. Sophie is in the front room. How nice to have you back. I've missed all the noise in this house," she said, smiling rather wistfully. "It's just you?"

I licked my lips, suddenly nervous. This would be my first time alone in the LeBaron household — it wasn't as if I could sit quietly in the corner if there were only two of us. I pressed my fingernails into my palms and then released them. There was nothing to be nervous about. Now I was Isabella's closest friend, surely Sophie would have to entertain me. And after all, I had just flown back from Europe, and Sophie had been at home the whole time. I didn't need Isabella as our focus; I was the guest star.

The door to the front room was ajar and a fire was crackling in the grate. I looked behind me for a glimpse of the ballroom. No matter how often I had been a visitor at the LeBaron house, I had never managed to get inside there. Sophie had never offered, and it seemed gauche to ask.

"Bridge," Sophie squealed, lifting her arms and flapping them at me so her shawl fell back into her elbows.

"How are you? You look fantastic," I said.

"You mean ginormous!" She gestured to the gentle plumpness in her stomach.

I laughed. "Don't be silly, you can barely tell."

"Thanks, you're a darling," she said, beaming. "*You* look fantastic." Her gaze flitted over my outfit. I had chosen it particularly for her. I was wearing one of Greta's silk scarves and a sweater with bone inlay buttons. I hoped it conjured European chic and approachable girlishness all at the same time.

"Come sit down and tell me everything."

Sophie motioned to an ottoman near the fireplace, then kicked off her slippers, crossed her knee over her other leg, and rubbed the instep of her naked foot. I watched the skin blanching and springing back to pink under her thumbs.

"Sorry," she said, following my gaze. The joviality drained out of her expression. "This week has been murder on my feet." She blushed, then dropped her foot and rested her arm on her belly as if she were covering the ears of her unborn.

"How is Matty?" I said.

"He's well. He's fishing with his brothers this week. They've driven up to some god-forsaken cabin in Maine. Heaven knows what they're doing up there. They go every year and they never come back with any fish."

"I bet it's nice for you to get some time with your mom," I said, trying to gauge if Mrs. LeBaron was in the house. A tidbit I could take back to Rhona — what she was wearing, her choice of perfume. Suddenly now, as I imagined Rhona and me sitting on her bed, gossiping about Mrs. LeBaron's bangles and her bleached hair, my heart throbbed. I put my fingers to the top of my breastbone.

"Mom is so happy to have me here. And I

think Matty's glad to get away too; he's been ever so patient with all the girly business. I swear all I do these days is shop for the nursery." She wriggled down into the armchair. "So, tell me everything about Italy. Everything." She waved her hands and the shawl fluttered. "The food, the art." She smiled at me. "Did I hear you got to travel by plane? I'm *dying* with jealousy."

Inspired by Sophie's relaxedness, I kicked off my shoes and held my stockinged feet toward the fire. Granny had bought me five pairs of new stockings, so I had no need to worry about darns or stitches. "The plane was superb," I said. "You could see right through the clouds," I said, and Sophie gasped. I didn't mention that a spring from the metal seat had cut into my back or that the cabin stank so strongly of oil that it made me light-headed. Or that I chanted Hail Marys for the first half an hour while the cabin thundered and shuddered and tipped to and fro. Or that the man sitting next to me smoked two cigars during the flight and his ash settled in my cream soda. "The art is divine. We have a trip to Rome in the spring."

Sarah knocked at the door carrying a tray and put it down on the footstool. Hot chocolate and sugar cookies in the shape of maple leaves.

"Thank you, Sarah," said Sophie. As Sarah shut the door, she grinned at me conspiratorially. "It's so nice to come home and get spoiled." Her face fell. "Oh, Bridge — I'm so sorry, it must be dreadful for you at home. How is Rhona? Is she home yet?"

"She came home a few days ago," I said. "She's much better now."

Sophie gave me a sympathetic smile. "What a shame," she sighed.

I didn't reply. People often said that in reference to Rhona. As if she were milk that had spoiled and been wasted unnecessarily. I fought the urge to conjure a prickly response about Rhona's future potential.

"You must've been worrying yourself sick," she said. "Such a shame you can't have a break from it, even in Europe! You deserve a breather."

"Oh," I said, walking back my antipathy — she had been feeling sorry for me, not Rhona. "It has been refreshing to have a change of scene," I said. It sounded cool, worldly; I applauded myself.

"Well, I hope she feels better soon," she said.

"Thanks."

We were silent a moment. The carriage clock on the mantelpiece ticked. I considered saying something more. But when I opened my mouth I couldn't think of what.

"And how's Izzy?" she said, smiling. "Has she told her mom about Ralph yet? Or is she getting herself into all kinds of romantic larks?"

I felt shaky. It really *was* true — I was now Isabella's best friend. In the beneficence of my new popularity, I decided I could afford to be generous. "Sophie, don't tell anyone," I said, dusting the crystals of sugar from my fingers.

She nodded greedily.

"But she had a relapse — the malaria."

"No! Is she OK?" She laid a half-eaten cookie down on her stomach as if it were a shelf. The gesture was so odd, my eyes kept traveling from her face to the cookie.

"Yes," I said. "She was almost recovered by the time I left." I stared into the fire to conceal my expression. Truthfully, I didn't actually know she was recovered. She could be ill again, for all I knew. Panic swarmed in my gut. What if she was so sick she couldn't leave her room? She'd had a relapse and she was still in bed. That was why I hadn't heard from her. But then — someone would have gone looking for her. Donna Maria, or one of the other girls. Elena would have sent someone up to collect her if she missed classes. The panic dispersed. I decided I would ask Dad if I could phone the academy in the morning. Perhaps I could make up some lie about an urgent assignment.

"What are the doctors like in Italy?" Sophie was saying. "I remember when Pop went out to France and he fractured his ankle skiing. They just gave him Valium and didn't do anything at all. He had to use his ski poles as crutches. Are they as bad as that?" she said.

I looked at her blankly.

"The doctors?" she prompted.

"Actually —" I paused.

"What?"

"She asked me not to call a doctor," I said, hugging my knees.

She frowned. "Did you take care of her all by yourself?" Crumbs from the cookie fell into the lap of her skirt.

I shrugged. "I didn't know what else to do."

"Oh, Bridge." Sophie gave me a sad smile. "You have had a time of it, haven't you? You poor thing."

I laughed, although my face was tight. "I'm fine," I said. "I can't complain."

"She's lucky to have you, you know," she said, motioning for me to pass her another cookie. She took a bite and closed her eyes. "The best thing about being pregnant is, I don't have to worry about my figure," she mumbled.

I laughed, but I was waiting for her to keep talking about Isabella. So I said nothing until she returned to her thought.

"No, honestly. I mean it," she said through her mouthful. "You must know — she's lucky to have you out there with her. Izzy adores you. And for good reason."

I pretended to take a sip of the hot chocolate. But it was still too hot to drink, so I let it glance against my top lip. "She does?" I said, as nonchalantly as I could manage.

Sophie frowned. "Of course she does — she worships you! You're pretty much soul mates."

"Did she say that?" I said, pretending to study my fingernails.

Sophie laughed. "You know Izzy — she doesn't like people to know she's a human. She didn't need to say it. Anyone could see you two are peas in a pod."

I took another pretend sip of the hot chocolate as the blood rushed to my cheeks. She adored me. Soul mates. I tried to write everything about that moment onto my memory. The way Sophie's eyes widened, the inflection in her voice. I would take it home with me and withdraw it later, to savor. She worshiped me. She adored me.

We spent the rest of the afternoon drinking hot chocolate and chatting about the other girls from high school. Eleanor had gone to do mission work in Uganda. Flora was having a ball at Mount Holyoke. After two hours, the telephone in the back of the house began ringing and we both glanced at the clock on the mantelpiece.

Sarah put her head round the door. "Mrs. Sophie, it's Mr. Matthew for you."

Sophie scrunched up her nose and pulled the arm of her sweater back to look at her slim gold watch. "Already?" she said. "Sarah, could you tell him I'll reach him at the club in an hour or so?"

"No, it's quite all right," I said, hopping as I stood up. My buttocks and thighs were numb. "My grandmom will be coming to collect me soon anyway. Why don't we say our good-byes now? I'll walk around your drive until she's ready to collect me."

"Are you sure?" But even as she demurred, she held out her arms for a farewell hug. "Send my love to Izzy. And tell her to reply to my letters, the silly cow," she called as she walked down the corridor.

I collected my coat and hat from Sarah and waved good-bye as I walked out onto the drive. The cold air was refreshing after the hot stupor of the front room. I was invigorated, more buoyant than I had been in weeks. Rhona was home. Isabella adored me. Anyone could see we were soul mates. Everything was going to be OK.

17.

NOVEMBER

It was Dad, in the end, who decided I should go back to the academy. I'd spent all afternoon making a pot roast, and when he came in from work he stood chatting in the kitchen while I pulled it out of the oven to check on it. But the dishcloth was too flimsy and the tray was too hot and I let it slip. The tin caught in a ridge in the oven door, and the roast was saved, but the juice poured out and dripped over the linoleum.

"Oh nuts!" I jumped out of the way of the pooling liquid.

"You didn't get burned, did you?" he said, pushing me aside as I ran my thumb under the faucet.

"I'm fine, Dad." I sighed. "I'm sorry." I looked up at him.

"Whatever for?" he said, groaning as he knelt to mop up the spill with a dishcloth.

"It'll be all dry now," I said, wrinkling my nose.

He turned and wrung out the cloth in the sink. "It doesn't matter," he said, coming close and unexpectedly kissing the back of my head. I smiled.

"I wanted it to be nice for you."

He was silent, staring vacantly out of the window.

"Daddy, can I get you something?" I said.

He turned to me. The expression was half shy. "Bridget, I've spoken to your grandmother. I think it would be good for you to go back to school soon."

I didn't say anything; the sentiment was too tantalizing. Like when you approach a squirrel in the park — I thought, *If I move too quick, I might spook it.*

"Would you like that?"

"Really?" I said.

He nodded.

I squealed and hugged him.

He chuckled, glanced over at the staircase and back at me. "I booked you a room on the *United States* for next week. I've spoken to your mom. And to Rhona."

"Are you sure, Daddy?" I said, holding my breath.

"Quite sure." He closed his eyes and a net of exhaustion settled over his face and obscured his features. He looked totally unlike himself. Then he opened his eyes and

Dad was back. "I've got enough women cooped up in here." He smiled, although I knew he was not entirely kidding. "Last thing I need is one more captive."

"But who —" I was going to say, "Who will take care of you?" but I didn't finish my thought. I couldn't admit Mama wasn't doing anything.

"Don't worry about us," he said. "You'll be home in May anyway." My spirits dropped. I knew it was true, but I didn't want him to spoil my joy by acknowledging the end of it.

"We'll get a girl to come in until your sister is better," he said.

I nodded, knowing the "girl" could hardly be his idea. Granny must have fixed the whole thing up. She was probably paying for it, too. An improbable series of events flew through my brain, ways I could repay Granny for the plane ticket, the nurse — I would write an art history book and dedicate it to her. I would graduate top of my class and have the certificate framed. And on the wood, engrave: "All because of you."

I went up to knock on Rhona's door. She was lying on her bed with a blanket tucked between her knees, reading a novel with a picture of a sphinx on the cover.

"Any good?" I said.

"It's OK." She put the book down and placed her finger in between the pages instead of finding a bookmark. The temporariness of the placeholder was as far as Rhona would ever go to demonstrate she didn't want to be disturbed.

"Actually," she said, turning the book over, "it's a bit saucy, this book. Christ knows where Granny found it."

I laughed, sitting on the end of the bed. Rhona shuffled her legs over to make room for me.

"Did Dad talk to you about me going back?"

She nodded. A cloud outside the window shifted and a square pane of sunlight fell across the bedspread, illuminating specks of dust in the air.

"Will you be OK? If I go?"

Rhona leaned over and for a moment I thought she was going to hug me, but she only smacked me on the arm with the book. "Stop it," she said. I smiled but my smile was stiff. "I already told Daddy it's not fair to keep you here."

I bristled. "I'm not a pet."

"Well, I'm the one who's stuck here," she said, leaning back against the headboard. "No reason you have to live *your* life like a nun."

I laughed. "We come pretty close at the academy."

Rhona frowned. "Please tell me you're not in chapel when you could be zooming around the countryside on a scooter."

"I swear."

"From your letters it sounds like you spend all your time gossiping with Isabella."

I winced. I thought my letters had been sweet, considerate; that gossip was what she wanted, not descriptions of places she couldn't go to, things she would never see. "There's plenty to do," I said tersely, to my knees.

When I looked up she was watching me. "You are making other friends, aren't you? Not just hanging around like Miss Crowley's handmaiden?"

I pressed my hands between my knees. "Don't lecture," I said.

"What else are older sisters for?" she said ironically.

The question hung. I chewed the inside of my cheek against the ugly urge to say something I wouldn't be able to take back. That she wasn't behaving like much of an older sister anyway. That as far as anyone at the academy knew, I didn't even *have* a sister. That I had barely missed her snippy observations and sardonic commentary.

Eventually I let out a breath. "And you'll be OK when I'm gone?"

She rolled her eyes. "I wish everyone would stop asking me that. I feel miles better. Granny has promised all kinds of wild things. And she wants to pay for some special nurse to come and give me vitamin shots and exercises."

It was unlikely any nurse would encourage her to exercise. But I let the comment go, since it seemed to have cheered her up.

"She even brought me a pamphlet with the different nurses, to choose from. Like a mail-order catalog."

"What if the nurse is a witch?"

"You know how Granny positively loves firing the help," she said. "I'll tell her the nurse gave me a copy of *The Watchtower,* and she'll be gone in a snap." She grinned.

"As long as you're having fun," I said weakly.

"Oh," she said, wriggling off the bed. She opened her closet door, parted the rack of clothes, and peered into the back. The walls were hung with ribbons and scarves, and plastic bead necklaces clattered against the wood. I grasped the opportunity to take stock of Rhona's clothes, recognizing them as old friends. Her calfskin boots filled with tissue paper to keep the shape, her green peacoat with the satin lining. The familiar sight of all her beautiful clothes suddenly pierced me in an unguarded place. Rhona was wearing faded gray riding pants that drooped low over her butt, a jagged tear at the back of her left knee.

She tugged at a suitcase on the top shelf. "I looked up La Pentola in the atlas," she said, her voice straining. "And — it'll be cold, right?" The suitcase fell on the floor and she staggered back to keep her toes from being battered. "Right?" She turned her face to me and it was flushed.

I was still reeling from the odd emotion her clothes and purses had provoked. I nodded without saying anything.

"So — ah, here!" She unlocked the suitcase and snapped the lid off a brown hatbox. She pulled her fur coat from the box, shaking it so a cast of dust rose and thickened the pane of sunlight. "Take it," she said, smiling.

I rubbed the oil-rich fur, relishing its musty smell. I loved that coat with a delirious jealousy. It had been Great-Aunt Mary's, given to Rhona when she died because Granny said I was too young for fur.

"You're always so cold," I said. "You'll need it when it gets brisk." I folded it over my arm and tried to hand it back to her.

Rhona laughed, a sharp, almost cruel laugh. "I don't go outside, Bridget. When would I need it?"

I kissed her papery cheek. "Thank you," I said. "It'll be perfect. I'll take good care of it."

Rhona clambered onto the bed and put one hand on her novel. I knew it was a sign I should leave, but I lingered.

"Don't get sick again," I said, all in one breath.

Rhona gave me a tight smile. "I'll try."

I rubbed my hand over the fur, watching the shine on its skein. "I don't want to be an only child," I said. I had meant it as a joke. But as I spoke them, the words felt truer than anything I'd said since I'd left for Italy. Rhona's room, empty. Her magazines in boxes in the basement. Her clothes, her necklaces, left behind — just a horrible shadow of her life. My Rhony. I swallowed against the tightness in my throat, crossing my fingers under the fur. What would Rhona think if she knew I'd practically disowned her? The tears rose in my eyes and I blinked to keep them away.

"You'd turn into an awful brat," she said, covering for me. "Granny would have to buy you a pony."

I laughed with the relieved, wet crack of someone who is half crying.

"You'd have to get a special lecture at school about sharing, like Helen Malone," she continued as I wiped the corners of my eyes.

"My birthday parties would be fabulous, though," I said.

"You could have lobster delivered from Maine."

We continued like this for five more minutes, each pulling on the joke until it was thin like taffy. The more terrible the joke became, the more it stretched away from the truth at its core.

IV
ITALY

18.

NOVEMBER

When I left the train at La Pentola, I dragged my case uphill so quickly it juddered over the gravel and shook the joint in my shoulder. And although the day was cool, I was sweating and red-faced by the time I arrived at the academy.

Donna Maria rushed out before I rang the bell and gripped me in a tight hug. She was babbling in Italian and I barely caught her words. She seized my case and with alarming strength hoisted it up the remaining steps and into the lobby. I could have cried, it was all so familiar, down to the ugly clock and the battered chairs.

I followed her upstairs, the weak light throwing late-afternoon shadows into the courtyard. As my suitcase clattered along the corridor, Sylvia stuck her head out of the bathroom.

"Bridget!" she yelled. "Hey, Bridget's back!" Bunny and Barbie came out of their bedroom.

"What's the yelling about?"

"Oh, Bridge!"

And a pile of girls fell upon me in the corridor, hugging and pinching and squealing as if we'd just won a football game. My eyes smarted and I was exhausted and deliriously happy all at the same time. I hugged each of the girls in turn, feeling perilously close to tears. Nancy approached from the common room with a pencil stuck behind her ear. When everyone else had picked themselves off me, she came forward and gave me a stiff, formal embrace, as if she'd been forced to greet the ambassador of a hostile foreign nation.

"Is everything OK?" said Nancy, pulling the pencil from behind her ear and chewing on it. "At home?"

"It's fine, thanks."

Nancy's face relaxed. "Good. I was worried. Izzy said she didn't know what was going on."

"She didn't tell you anything at all?" I crossed my fingers under my elbows.

Nancy shook her head. "She said she was totally in the dark. But then Sally insisted you had some fancy ball to go to."

As I unlocked my room, the girls hung back and I opened the door to see paper streamers hung with BENTORNATA written on the bunting. Milk bottles filled with physalis stems decorated the bedside table and windowsill.

"Oh, girls," I said, turning back to the small crowd. Their faces were identically pink and smiling. "I'm so touched," I said. They had gone through all this trouble, just for me! As I entered the room I didn't know how to demonstrate my gratitude. I went around putting my hands on the physalis and the bunting, nodding and grinning.

"Do you like it?" said Greta.

"You're A-plus." I hugged her and she nestled her head in the crook of my neck.

I sat on the mattress and it creaked in such a familiar way I couldn't help but grin. I sighed and bounced and looked around my room. It smelled like vinegar and beeswax and I knew one of the sisters must have been in to mop the floor while I was gone. It seemed so odd, not that I was back, but that I had ever been away in the first place.

"And you're OK?" Greta said, watching my face.

I nodded. "Yes, a bit of fuss over nothing."

She glanced nervously at Patricia. "We figured it must have been serious if they sent you an airplane ticket."

I looked away from her. "Oh, my grand-mom had a turn, but she's fine now."

Sylvia tucked her hair behind her ears. "Tell us about the plane! What were the air hostesses like? Did you see the pilot?"

I laughed. "Yes, they're terribly glamorous. I got to shake the pilot's hand."

Sylvia sighed. "How dreamy. I've been begging Mom to let me take a plane trip, but she says maybe for my twenty-first birthday."

Everyone crowded onto the other bed. They squeezed in, arms over each other's shoulders, knees crossed over legs, eyes expectant. There was a fierce clench of joy in my stomach and I felt myself drifting backward, up, until the moment was granted the soft, oval framing of a greeting card. The girls were laughing, gum chewing, hair twirling, brimming with gossip and compliments. It was like being lowered into a warm bubble bath. This was what real people must feel like all the time. Talking over each other, they filled me in. Betty got homesick and returned to Texas a week after I left. Bunny's grandfather had died, but her family didn't want her to go all the way for the funeral, so the girls sat and cried with her and Father Gavanto said a special Mass. Katherine and Mary Leonard had fallen out and everyone had been forced to take sides until they called a truce. Two boys from La Pentola had followed Sylvia up the hill and Donna Maria had gone out with a broom to chase them away.

I nodded along to the rabble of good-natured interruptions and bickering, although the journey was catching up with me and I began to feel unkempt and woozy, my eyes detached from the rest of my face. To give myself something to focus on, I unpacked the bags of Hershey's and candy corn from my luggage.

"I brought these for everyone," I said, scoring the Saran Wrap with my room key, now embarrassed by the gesture. Should I have brought fancier treats? Perhaps it was transparently desperate to return with gifts of candy, as if I were trying to bribe an underpaid babysitter. But I needn't have worried; the girls fell on the softened chocolate bars, giggling.

Greta cheered. "Oh, Bridge, I *knew* you wouldn't forget us."

I laughed, delighted. Was that my reputation? Someone who didn't forget. Someone thoughtful, generous.

"How I wish we'd had a proper Halloween," Greta said. "I tried to carve a squash but just ended up with a mess."

"She cried," Sylvia said.

"And why did you come back now?" Patricia said. Mary Babbage elbowed her in the ribs. "No, no." Patricia blushed. "I didn't mean like that. I mean, why not wait until after Thanksgiving?"

"That's *ages* away," Mary gasped.

"But she's missing out on the party," Patricia said to Mary with some truculence.

I frowned.

Patricia looked at me. "Your mom's Thanksgiving party," she prompted.

"Oh." I pretended to scratch an itch under my sleeve.

Greta leaned forward to address Mary. "It's why they had to let go of the summerhouse — too much work."

"Oh." Mary nodded sympathetically.

I blinked. Had I said that? I'd have to check with Isabella. "Well." I rubbed my face. "I don't want to miss any more school."

"You're such a good student," Greta said mournfully. "I'm simply *dying* to get dressed up and go to a proper party."

"Yes, Bridge, do tell us about the parties! Did you meet any boys?" Mary batted her eyelashes.

"She's not allowed any boys, are you, Bridge?" Sylvia said. "Remember? She's locked away like a good Catholic girl."

I smiled. "No boys. But look." And I pulled the fur out of my suitcase.

Sylvia swooped upon it. "Glorious! Can I try it on?"

"Of course."

She shrugged it over her shoulders and examined herself in the closet mirror.

"It looks spectacular on you," I said. And it did. The color brought out the gold in her eyes. "Borrow it anytime you like," I said, flushed with philanthropy. Sylvia beamed. She plunged her hands into the pockets and twirled in front of the mirror.

She withdrew a folded piece of green paper from the pocket and examined it. "Gosh, Bridge, you're just as forgetful as me." She winked, handing over the paper, which I now saw was a fifty-dollar bill. Blood roared to my cheeks. Where had that come from? Had Rhona left it there deliberately? Or had it been lingering in the coat since Aunt Mary died?

"You should get a lockbox, you know," Sylvia said, arching her eyebrows in the mirror. "Or you can share mine if you like."

My mortification receded. "Thanks," I said.

The door to my room had been left ajar, and I kept one eye on the corridor as we spoke. But as the sun set, the girls peeled off to pin their hair and change their outfits until it was only me and Greta.

"So have you seen Isabella?" I said, pretending to search in my nightstand drawer. "I have some mail for her from her mom."

Greta yawned. "I think she's in the chapel."

"Oh?" I tried to sound casual. I pulled the sweaters from my case and shook the wrinkles out. They still had the stale, cabbagy smell of the boat about them.

"I'll go fetch her," she said. "She must not even know you're back — she'll be so surprised!"

"No, don't worry." I yawned as well, catching it from Greta.

"I'm so stupid," Greta said, jumping off the bed. "Here I am banging on and you're probably dying for a nap." She looked down at the candy wrappers that tumbled onto the bedspread from her lap. "Golly, now I don't even need supper." She snatched them up and ironed them out with her fingers. She paused. "Can I take a couple for Sally?"

"Help yourself."

Greta smiled. "I'm going to hide them in her pillowcase for a surprise when she gets into bed." She crinkled the wrappers in her fists. "For sweet dreams — get it?"

Her expression was so eager, I felt the urge to congratulate her. "It's adorable. She'll love it."

Greta cocked her head to one side. "Bridge, can you keep a secret?"

I tried to smother the indecent curiosity I could feel brewing on my face. "Of course."

"My mom's writing to Sally's mom to see if she can come with us to France after graduation!"

"Oh?"

"But it's a surprise and she doesn't know yet. She'll think she's got her place on the *United States* booked, but really she'll be coming with us!"

"How lovely!" I gave her my most congratulatory smile. But there was a strange ache in my throat. A disappointment that she hadn't asked me and a shame at my meanness of spirit.

"I've been *dying* keeping it a secret. You have to swear not to tell."

"I swear."

Greta squealed and planted a sticky kiss on my cheek. "I was desperate, waiting for you to come back — I thought I was going to burst."

The sour feeling in my throat relaxed and I realized how ridiculous it had been. I hugged her with one arm. "You're a doll. Well, I'm here now. You can talk to me about it whenever you like."

Isabella still hadn't appeared before dinner, so I dressed with extra effort. I chose a peach cashmere sweater from Granny and a new scarf with iridescent blues and purples in it like a peacock's feather. It was a little dressy, so I left my face bare, with only a touch of lipstick. Greta and Sally knocked on my door after the bells and we walked down to dinner together. As soon as Sally descended the staircase, Greta turned and wriggled her eyebrows at me, radiant with mischief, as if she thought me so overwhelmed by her secret that I might take to the chapel roof and begin chanting it for the whole convent to hear.

In the hall, I sat on the other side of Sally and spread out my knees to keep the place next to me free for Isabella. But then Patricia approached. "Bridge," she said, "can I sit here?"

Nancy strode over. "Oh no, it's my turn," she said.

Patricia pouted. "But she's been away for so long. I need to talk to her about something."

I stared at the table, not wanting to seem like I was gloating over the luxury of friends.

And strategically, it was a good thing. Isabella would come in to find me in conversation with the others. In demand. I thought about trying to say something funny, but I searched for a joke and came up empty.

Nancy lifted her long legs and folded them under the table. "Yes, well, you had her all afternoon. Slide up, will you, Bridge?"

I shot Patricia an apologetic look.

"Later, then," Patricia said. "I'll come by your room?"

I blew her a kiss. It was breezy, fun. Isabella wasn't there to see it.

"So. How's your folks?" Nancy said, filling our glasses with cider.

"Everyone's fine. But I'm glad to be back. I'm so behind."

Nancy took a gulp of cider and I watched the liquid travel down her throat. I felt dislocated from everything, the benches lurching and the girls' faces moving in the dim light with stuttering trails.

"I can talk you through what you've missed, if you want?"

I snapped back to attention. "Would you really? I could use the help."

"Sure." Nancy shrugged. "Tomorrow, before breakfast?"

"*Before* breakfast?"

Nancy nodded.

"You're worse than the nuns," I said, although her enthusiasm was reassuring. At least I'd get caught up quickly.

Then Isabella came through the door, and my heart snagged. She was wearing her hair loose — I'd forgotten how long it had grown. She had rolled the cuffs of her shirt, and something about her air of scruffy sophistication made her look like a sculptor or an experimental painter. I felt suddenly fussy and prim in my sweater and silk scarf.

She came behind me and hugged me. I leaned my head back under her chin. My chest pulsed.

"Briddie," she said, her hair falling on my shoulders. She planted a kiss on the top of my head. "So glad you're home!"

"Bella," Sylvia called from across the table, gesturing to a place next to her.

"Don't go anywhere," Isabella said, keeping hold of my hand, bowing over it and kissing the back.

Dinner that night was buttered pasta with sage and thin shavings of white truffle. Nancy took her offer of tutoring quite seriously and launched into a detailed presentation of the lectures Signor Patrizi had given in my absence. I twirled the slippery noodles and said, "Uh-huh" and "OK" and "Yes," as she talked. But I didn't hear any of it.

Down the table, I watched the candlelight shine on Isabella's profile. The way she ran her fingers through her hair, tossing it behind her shoulder, leaning in to Sylvia. She licked her finger, stuck it to a shard of truffle on Katherine's plate, and ate it. She glanced over her shoulder and caught me looking at her. And in the same moment, I realized I had been staring. I lifted my gormless, fixed stare into a grin, and her eyes lit up. She raised her glass of cider to me in a salute, breaking into a bright smile.

She adores me, I thought.

19.

NOVEMBER

Nancy was true to her word and arrived at my door the next morning with two cups of Nescafé she'd made with a heating coil in her bedroom. She sat on the bed and talked again about the syllabus they had covered. I made hasty notes in my notebook and was dismayed to learn I'd already missed a large section on the Baroque, which I hoped was going to be the subject of my special essay in the spring.

"Do you think Patrizi will give me a catch-up session?" I said, a headache beginning at the corner of my right eye.

"Maybe," Nancy said. She raised her eyebrows. "But when would you do it?"

"Jeez," I said. "I don't know. Weekends?"

Nancy looked solemn. "That's probably a good idea."

I threw myself back on the coverlet. "This is awful," I whined. "I'm going to be the stupidest alumni in the history of the academy."

Nancy touched my leg. "Well, there's always Bunny."

I laughed, although I didn't feel any better.

I went early to the Italian classroom to find Elena before our lesson. She had a smudge of lipstick on her teeth I couldn't stop looking at. I made vague allusions to my family emergency, but I think she already knew and was pretending ignorance for the sake of discretion. She said she'd be available to me for extra tutoring on Saturdays if I wanted. Which sounded horribly depressing, but I was grateful anyway.

As usual, Isabella was late to class. She came in rubbing a pink line on her face where the contour of her pillowcase was imprinted.

"Hello." She slipped in next to me.

I smiled, but I was annoyed at her. She hadn't been in her room the night before. Or in the common room. I'd stayed up, waiting, while Ruth insisted on showing me photos of her niece's christening. After Ruth left, Mary Babbage came in with a pair of tap shoes she'd had sent in the mail from Milan. And then she put them on and tapped about until Nancy came by and begged her to stop. I ended up falling asleep upright in the armchair, groggily starting every time the corridor floorboards creaked. And then she hadn't been at breakfast either. Neither had I, but that wasn't the point. Isabella should have been at breakfast looking for me. Waiting for me.

She wrote a note on the margin of her book and slid it over. *Miss me?* it said.

I stared at the note. Was it a test? Should I say yes or pretend I hadn't missed her? Which would she find more interesting? *Course!* I wrote. I examined it again before I slid the book back over. That was the right tone. Cheery but not needy. Then I wrote next to it, *Miss me??*

She scribbled for ages on the paper, and my pulse raced. Why was she taking so long? Could she have missed me all that much? When she passed back the book, I pinned it under my elbow. I was desperate to read the note straightaway, but Elena was looking at me.

"Don't worry, Bridget," she said in English. "You won't understand this yet, but try to follow along and I'll talk to you about it on the weekend."

I nodded. The paper was burning under my elbow. Patricia began to read aloud from the textbook.

When I looked down at Isabella's note, it was a paragraph of tight writing. I scanned it for important words. "Missed you," "thinking of you," "adore you." But there weren't any words like that. I had to read it twice to squeeze any sense out of it.

SO much has happened! Betty was boo-hooing all night because she was homesick and she left practically in the middle of the night. Also Patricia has a very unfortunate-looking twin. And the academy has its own rowboat — the sisters have to row over to Brancorsi sometimes and it's the funniest thing I ever saw. Rosaria fell in and I almost split a gut! Katherine isn't talking to Mary L. anymore.

Betty had been homesick and gone home — I already knew. Katherine and Mary L. weren't talking — I already knew. How like her to assume nobody else would have told me. What did she think I'd been doing since I arrived? Sitting alone in my room? And Patricia's unfortunate-looking twin — well, she *knew* I knew about that because we'd talked about it at length! How could she have forgotten? And the rest of it made no sense to me at all. I couldn't even place

Sister Rosaria. I decided not to ask her, as a matter of pride. I scanned the note again. There was another thing — she hadn't asked me a single question. Had she even received my letters? My chest prickled. Rhona could have died for all she knew. Rhona could be dead and buried and she hadn't even bothered to check.

She yawned dramatically, and Elena looked up.

"*Sei annoiata?*" she said archly.

"No," said Isabella.

"*Continuare da questa pagina,* Bella," Elena said.

Isabella picked up the textbook and began to read. At one point everyone tittered and I searched the page for the joke, but I didn't know what they were laughing at.

At lunch I decided to ignore Isabella, but she wasn't there. Instead, I saw her loping across the courtyard, eating her sandwich from a paper napkin. All my determination to ignore her vanished, and I hurried from the refectory to follow her. Halfway across the courtyard I called out.

She turned and saw me. "Hi," she said, although her smile was not entirely genuine.

"Sneaking off to smoke?" I said. It came out false and overly jovial.

"I was going round the back." She pointed

vaguely to the convent gate.

I stood and waited.

"Want to come with?" she said.

As we walked, I cleared my throat. "Did you get my letters? I know how bad the mail is." I tried to keep my voice neutral.

"Oh yeah, they were hilarious." Isabella stuck her tongue out. "St. Cyrus is just the most tedious place on the planet."

I nodded, fixing my face into a smile. But the letters weren't supposed to be funny. Despite all her protests, I thought Isabella would enjoy having updates about our town, our teachers, our old friends.

Sister Teresa appeared at the gate. She squinted as she saw me, then broke into a smile. "Bridget," she said. "Welcome back." She crossed to take my hand and held it between her own. Her fingers were rough and calloused on mine. She looked carefully at my face and I willed myself not to blush.

"Thanks," I said.

She bounced my hand up and down. "I've been praying for you."

"Thanks." I focused on the flagstones under my feet.

"And your family?" She was still holding my hand. I was conscious she'd feel my sweaty palm in her dry one.

"Yes, thanks. Everything is fine."

Isabella was growing restless; I saw her walking deliberately within our periphery, kicking a loose stone at the edge of the courtyard.

Sister Teresa released my hand. "So, have you come to see the garden?"

I glanced at Isabella. Had she been going to the *garden*? "Sure," I said uncertainly.

We passed left of the bell tower, then around the back of the convent. I tried to snoop through the windows into the cells, but the glass was thick and mottled. The earth behind the convent building was muddy, and the grass had been trampled bare. As we wove past the laundry room, the scent of warm soap floated in a damp gust of air. All the while, Sister Teresa chatted about the garden and what a great help Isabella had been with the planting and weeding.

I glanced at Isabella over my shoulder. "Weeding?" I said, expecting her to grin, that we would pull faces at each other.

"Yes," she said, shrugging. As if she had always taken a great interest in gardening. The closest I'd seen her come to horticulture was clipping her split ends.

Sister Teresa dodged another shed and we approached an allotment hidden from the orchard by a waist-high hedge. She pushed open a squeaky gate with patchy chicken wire wound between the bars. I didn't know how to react appropriately. Was the yard dying? Wilted flowers tangled with mushy, browning leaves. The gaps in the wire fence shone with spiderwebs.

"Has Bella shown you before?" Sister Teresa asked.

I shook my head.

"Here, for example, are herbs for cooking. We have rosemary and oregano and fennel and basil and thyme. Isabella has been helping me to dig here," she said, walking to a rectangular patch of crumbly soil. The hem of her skirt dragged in the mud and I winced. She must have to scrub her skirt every single day to get the spots of earth out. "We've been planting garlic and winter lettuce," she said.

Even as I smiled and nodded at the indistinguishable lumps in the earth, I struggled to keep my amusement in check. I watched the focus on Isabella's face as Sister Teresa pointed to furrows in the dirt. Had she really been so lonely without me that she was digging lettuce with a bunch of silent nuns? There I had been worrying about what a jolly time she was having, and instead she was acting like an old lady. Worse. Even Granny didn't dig in her own backyard.

"Isn't this kind of a waste of your time?" I said.

"Bridget!" Isabella snapped.

Sister Teresa blinked at me.

"I don't mean it in a bad way." I felt the heat rise to my cheeks. "Just — since you're the only speaking nun, isn't it kind of wasteful that you're planting cabbage, instead of —" I hesitated. What was it Sister Teresa did exactly? I cleared my throat. "Conducting convent business?"

Sister Teresa cricked her neck. "Ah. I understand."

"Growing food is still important work," Isabella said defensively.

"What work have you seen us conduct?" Sister Teresa said, watching me with the sharp, encouraging eye of a teacher.

"The sisters?"

"Yes."

"Um." I thought of the bags of our laundered clothes, which appeared weekly in our rooms. The plates whisked away after every meal. The perpetual sound of brooms swishing against marble. "Sort of — housework," I muttered.

Isabella was shaking her head. "I'm sorry," she said to Sister Teresa, shooting me a contemptuous look.

"No." Sister Teresa nodded. "She's quite correct. Menial labor — is that what you mean?"

"Um, yes," I said in a quiet voice.

"There's a reason for this." Sister Teresa rummaged in her apron and lit a cigarette, offering us the pack. "Do you know the meaning of 'kenosis'?"

Next to me, I felt Isabella shaking her head, so I joined in.

"It means something like death of the self."

Isabella caught my eye. We exchanged a grimace, and my mind settled on the scythe in the spa graveyard. "I thought that was a sin," I whispered, finally.

Sister Teresa laughed. "No. In this sense, it is beautiful. It means to empty yourself of yourself. To practice death of the self, so God can fill in all the empty space."

I remembered Katherine's comment about St. Teresa — how when she died she was nothing but a shell, filled up with God. But if St. Teresa was tried by fire, then what was Sister Teresa's trial — gardening? I pointed at the bumps in the earth. "I don't understand, though. What does that have to do with lettuce?"

"Repetitive work is a way of teaching discipline," she said. "Weeding. Sweeping."

I thought now of the strange calm that comes with erasing a whole page of notes, the pencil marks obliterated into scraps of hot putty.

"Our humble acts are a form of mortification," Sister Teresa continued. "They help us to die."

I shivered. All around us were moldering leaves and white pebbles glinting through the dirt. I looked more closely at Sister Teresa. Was she really slowly trying to die? The smoke was putrid in my mouth. I wanted to be away from the garden and Sister Teresa's uncanny calm. "No offense," I said, trying to lighten the mood, "but that sounds sort of creepy." I laughed and looked at Isabella, but she was pale.

"I know it sounds unappealing," Sister Teresa said, "but it is meant to aid concentration." Her tone was obliging; I recognized it as a storytelling voice. She must have had the same conversation many times with many other nosy academy girls.

Isabella turned and stubbed her cigarette out on the gate, and without looking at her, Sister Teresa held her palm out. Isabella placed the crumpled butt on Sister Teresa's outstretched palm; then Sister Teresa shook open her packet and slid the two burned ends back into the packet. It was such a natural, synchronized gesture that a circle of complicity was cast between them and shut me on the other side. My chest squeezed. I ground my cigarette butt under my heel, not wanting to test if Sister Teresa would also hold her hand out for mine.

"Mortification is a form of devotion," Sister Teresa was saying. "And silence, also. It brings its own blessings."

"The quickenings? Yeah, I read about —," I said.

Isabella frowned at me. I stopped talking.

"Exactly," Sister Teresa said, with no trace of a smile. "Silence allows us to hear the voice of God. It's hard," she said. "But it's supposed to be hard."

While she spoke, I imagined yellow sand draining through the throat of an hourglass and gathering in the empty bulb below. I was struck by how strange it was. That her concept of fullness was my idea of lack. I looked around the shabby allotment of straggly herbs. This was what she did all day. Sweeping and weeding and snipping apple leaves and pulling worms from the earth.

"Well, I'm glad," Isabella said, swallowing. "I mean, it's a good thing we're here now. Since your time is short. Your speaking time, I mean."

Sister Teresa smiled at her. "I'm glad too."

It occurred to me with a tilting lurch that Isabella and Sister Teresa had become friends. And why not? She was beautiful, otherworldly, with her white cloak and meditative calm. I was a sort of gargoyle next to her. My stomach gave a despairing twinge.

"I should probably head in," I said to Isabella, putting my hands in my pockets. "You coming? I could use some help with my grammar."

Isabella stuck her tongue out. "Grammar? No, thanks. I'll take my chances with the lettuce."

That evening it began to hail. Hard, sharp little teeth of ice that skittered against the window frames. I was in the common room when it began, copying the notes Patricia had made of Patrizi's lectures. Barbie had raised the window, and the clattering sound of hail filled the room. Chips of ice were bouncing off the floorboards, and Joan caught a little rubble of hail in her palm. "It stings," she said.

"Taste it," Bunny said. "I dare you."

Joan balked. "You taste it."

And before I knew what I was doing, I'd scooped the shards of ice from Joan's hand

into my mouth, where they dissolved. "Delicious," I said. "Just like ice cream." Truthfully, it tasted like rainwater, slightly metal-
lic.

"Bridge, no!" shrieked Bunny, as if it were
the most hilarious thing she'd ever seen.

"Oh, I miss ice cream," Barbie said
mournfully.

I yawned and stretched and went to stand
up. "You're not going to bed, are you?" Joan
said, wiping her hands on her jeans.

"Maybe not quite yet," I said, collecting
my papers.

"I need to ask you something," Joan said.
She looked pointedly at the corridor. "But
not here."

"OK." I walked down to my room, Joan
following at my heels.

Joan took a seat on the second bed, pulling out a book lying on the blanket. "Your
—" She began to hand it to me, then
frowned at the cover.

"Oh." I reached for it. It was a German
recipe booklet I'd found jammed into the
magazine stand in the common room. It was
old and grimy, and I didn't understand the
words, but I found it soothing to look at the
photos of neat little pies tucked into their
trays, glossy and plump. "It's just some
magazine," I said, casually sliding it onto

my nightstand. Isabella teased me for looking at pictures of German pies in the middle of the night, and I wasn't keen for the others to begin, too.

But Joan had a glazed, distant expression. "Bridge, your family is Catholic, right?"

I started. "Of course. Everyone is, aren't they, other than Nancy, but —"

"Yes, but I mean *Catholic* Catholic."

I slipped my hands under my legs. "Yes," I said, a little stiffly.

Joan's shoulders relaxed. "It's just — the other girls can be so —" She twirled her fingers. "And Ruth is so —" She grimaced.

I laughed.

Joan gave me a weak smile. "Listen, don't tell anyone, will you — but — it's my sister."

"Oh?" My ears tingled. I hated talking about sisters. It made me feel like I was standing at the edge of a deep pool.

Joan swallowed. "She wrote me and —" She looked over at the door. "She thinks she might be" — she licked her lips — "in — in the family way. But — but she's not married."

"Oh." I tried to keep my expression neutral, not to look too shocked, too sorry. After a moment, I said, "Does your mom know?"

Joan shook her head. "And I just don't

know how to help." Her eyes filled with tears.

I stood to embrace her but she waved me away. I sat back down, impressed by her self-containedness, that she wasn't using the moment to snare attention for herself. I passed her a box of tissues instead. Joan dabbed at her eyes.

"And her beau — is he —"

Joan sniffed. "Oh, he's all right. He works for the postal service."

"Ah. Good." I took a moment to imagine what a *Catholic* Catholic might say to sound reassuring. "So, I suppose, isn't this a happy thing?" I said. "A baby?"

Joan cocked her head to one side.

"I mean, no one's sick or dying. It's a good thing, surely," I said. "That is, if they get married right away," I added.

Joan rubbed her eyes with the tissue. "I guess."

"I bet your sister is scared, but perhaps she needs someone to remind her what a blessing this is."

Joan licked her lips. "I hadn't thought about it like that. But I guess it will be a blessing in the end."

"My mom always says" — I hesitated — "she always says, God doesn't make mistakes."

Joan took a deep breath. "Right."

"So it can't be a mistake," I said, gaining confidence now.

Joan nodded slowly. "I guess you're right. And it sounds like your mom is just as strict as mine. No boys and all that."

I pretended to adjust the hem of my skirt instead of answering.

Joan reached for another tissue. "I suppose my mom —"

There was a soft knock on my bedroom door, and Joan shot me a terrified look.

"I won't say a word," I whispered. "I swear."

Joan nodded.

"Come in," I called.

Katherine poked her face around the door. "Did you see it's hailing?"

"Yes," I said.

"Wild, huh?" Katherine lingered. "Wonder how long it will last." She twisted the door handle. Her excuse for loitering was so feeble that it became awkward.

I grimaced apologetically at Joan. "Did you want to come in?"

"Yes, please! So, what are we talking about?" Katherine settled on the bed, kicking off her slippers and folding her legs under her.

"Nothing," Joan said abruptly.

Katherine smiled. "Ah, Bridge confession."

"What?"

Katherine tucked part of the blanket over her knees. "You know, like confession. But with St. Bridget."

There was a bright sting in my chest, like a knitting needle. I tried to control my expression. Was she being cruel or was it a joke? "Don't be an idiot," I said eventually.

"Oh, Bridge, I didn't mean it like that," Katherine said, her forehead pinched.

I forced a laugh. "I know." I pretended to plump my pillow.

"You're just so patient with us," Katherine said. "You're never in a mood or anything."

Joan was nodding. "Like Old Faithful."

Despite myself, I couldn't help but laugh. I was so relieved, my eyes began watering, but I passed it off as mirth.

Katherine was staring at Joan. "What's Old Faithful got to do with saintliness, you goose?"

"I just mean it's steady, you know." Joan's cheeks were going red.

Katherine laughed and they began to talk about national parks and bears and camping stoves and poison ivy.

While they talked, I pulled out a bag of

biscotti cookies and a bottle of wine, which I poured into the toothbrush glasses I now strategically kept washed and ready for visitors.

There was another knock on the door. "Oh, I thought I heard a party," Bunny said. She called behind her, "Barbs, come — party in Bridge's room."

Then we were six, then eight, and everyone was lounging across the two beds, laughing, drinking, squabbling over whose turn it was to try on Rhona's fur, to fluff up my curls. I marveled at the magic of the cookies.

"Would someone knock on Isabella's door?" I said. I could have gone myself, but it was better that one of the girls collect her — that way she could see me nonchalantly at the center of the fun.

"Tried," Sylvia said, her mouth full of crumbs. "Her door's locked."

"It's locked?"

"She always locks her door when she gets one of those headaches."

"She does?" This worried me. What if she was ill again? And she was in there, coughing, turning, flushed, restless.

As discreetly as I could, I untangled myself from Sally's knitting and went down to Isabella's door. I knocked. There was no answer.

"Isabella?" I said, knocking again. "It's just me." Nothing. I tried to jiggle the door handle, but Sylvia was right; it had been locked.

I stooped and looked through the keyhole. The room was dark, the curtains closed. I couldn't make anything out except for a clothes hanger lying on the floor. I came away feeling uneasy. It was one thing to lock the door by turning the key in a moment of pique. It was quite another to lock the door, take out the key, and place the key on the dresser. That was a truly locked door.

I went back to my room and stood for a moment in the doorway to appreciate the view. The hail was still falling, catching sparks of light. The girls were lounging on the beds, on the floor, thumbing through the German recipe magazine, tossing around my green beret, passing the bag of cookies, clinking glasses, dropping crumbs on the bedspread. Making a mess, a glorious mess.

20.

NOVEMBER

Over the next couple of weeks, Isabella spent a lot of time in the garden. She said being cooped up with the academy girls aggravated her headaches. But I much preferred to be indoors with the other girls. And also, I didn't have a choice. I had assignments to finish and comprehension exercises to catch up on, so I bound myself to the common room. After Signor Patrizi's lectures we all crowded in there. Joan took territorial responsibility for stoking the fire; Katherine sat in the armchair and knitted in companionable silence. Nancy helped correct my copybook. Greta and Sally decided it was the right place to learn handstands, and my pen wobbled every time the floor shook. In the evenings I hosted girls in my bedroom, sharing cookies and wine. And at night, carefully bathed, wearing my new nightgown, my hair unbraided, I sat in bed, waiting. I waited as long as I could, just in case, struggling against sleep until my head knocked against the iron headboard.

Weekends weren't much different from school days. I spent Saturday mornings with Elena and Saturday afternoons with Nancy. I learned Nancy had a fiancé, and when she showed me a picture of him, I was surprised to see he was strong-jawed and extremely handsome. I'd figured her as a spinstery sort who would go back to California and adopt three Great Danes and play the cello to them every morning and go protesting the atomic bomb with her knitting circle.

After my sessions with Nancy, I studied in the common room or sat by the fire while girls took turns to perform dramatic readings from care-package magazines. The engagement notices were most popular, followed by ruthlessly specific advertisements for home help. We had to place a ban on anything to do with Laika or else Greta cried. When I could escape, I went down to the garden to visit Isabella and Sister Teresa. Usually Sister Luisa was also there, picking vegetables or digging. If Sister Luisa was there, then I waved and smiled and walked on, as if I'd only happened to be passing. I don't know how they could bear to exchange words while other sisters worked in silence beside them, listening. Something about seeing Sister Teresa speak in front of the other nuns made me more aware of their presence in the academy. I watched the sisters more carefully now. The slow, gliding way of walking that they shared. The downward tilt to their gaze. Perhaps because I had been away, or because of Sister Teresa, I noticed the nuns in all the places where I hadn't before: trimming trees in the orchard, hanging bedsheets to dry on the lines behind the bell tower. When I watched Sister Benedict sweeping the steps with a fixed expression, or Sister Maria mopping the refectory floors, I wondered if they, too, were wearing away at themselves. If they were practicing their own numbing paths to oblivion.

If Isabella and Sister Teresa were alone in the yard, then I'd stop and ask them inane questions about herbs and vegetables. Isabella would come over and kneel on a sackcloth bag while I rubbed the stiffness out of her shoulders.

When it was the three of us, Isabella insisted on calling her Rosaria. But I couldn't get used to the idea that she had another name. I thought Teresa *was* her name. It was so odd, to look at Sister Luisa and think she might really be Giulia or

Holly or Delphine or Bridget.

"How do you pick your nun name?" I asked Sister Teresa finally, one Thursday afternoon. Why would anyone pick a name as ordinary as Teresa, if they had anything to choose from? I would have selected something delicate and classy. Sister Anastasia, perhaps, or Sister Hyacinth.

"It is personal choice," she said. "But also, we must be able to sign for it."

"What?" My mouth dropped open. I looked to Isabella and she was nodding. Clearly they'd already had this discussion.

Sister Teresa laughed. "How did you think we communicated?"

"I don't know." It had never occurred to me that the sisters would communicate with each other. I'd never seen two of them exchanging as much as eye contact. With the routine of the place, I figured everyone just knew their positions, their routines, their duties, and slid along as if on grooves inside a cuckoo clock.

"They have all sorts of symbols," Isabella said excitedly.

"Oh yeah?"

"Like if they get sick or something."

"Right," I said, looking at Sister Teresa. But I was losing interest. It seemed prurient and unsettling to be privy to the intimacy of the sisters' private customs, like spotting a teacher on the weekend, grocery shopping with her own kids. I would rather the sisters stayed part of the scenery of the academy, drifting peacefully in the background. Not miming to one another about their period cramps.

"Neat," I said.

"Honestly," Sister Teresa said to Isabella, "I shouldn't have told you my birth name."

"Yeah," I said. "You're not meant to be fixated on personal things, are you?" Wasn't she supposed to be trying to kill her personality?

"I regret it," Sister Teresa said.

Isabella grinned. "She didn't want to say, but I got it out of her. I just *knew* she wasn't a Teresa. Are you, Rosie?"

" 'Rosie' is awful," she said, wrinkling her forehead. The expression was so un-nunlike, so like a normal girl, it transformed her. She could have been one of our classmates.

"No, it's not! What does old William say? Rose by any other name smelling sweet?" Isabella pouted.

"But that means despite my name I would be the same person."

"Oh yeah?" Isabella bit her nail. I thought of the earth on her fingers and suppressed a shiver. "You think that can really be true?"

She licked the corner of her thumb where she had chewed the nail away. "I think I'd be totally different with a different name. If I was, I don't know, Cookie instead of Isabella."

Sister Teresa frowned. "Cookie? That's not a real name."

"It is too," said Isabella. "In my middle school class there was a girl called Cookie. And another called Muffin."

"Those were their actual names?" Sister Teresa said.

"Well, no, nicknames."

"Like Rosie?" she said, raising an eyebrow. "I think Teresa suits me much better than my birth name."

I winced. The phrase "birth name" was horrible.

"Don't you mean your christened name?" I said. I knew I was being a know-it-all but, spitefully, I wanted to puncture their little moment of banter.

"No." Sister Teresa held my gaze. "That's very astute of you."

I glanced at Isabella, expecting her to catch my eye. Astute. What a word. I waited for the spell of our joke about Sister Vocabulary to be cast, to link us back together. But she was watching Sister Teresa.

"Actually, my birth name is different from

my christened name. The politics are complicated. In Ethiopia."

"Don't you miss Africa?" I said, not knowing I would ask that until I heard myself voice the question.

She stretched her neck. "Sometimes I miss my family, that's true."

"You have a family?" My mouth fell open.

She laughed at my incredulity. "My mother and my siblings are all living in my hometown," she said. "And my brothers and sister are all married now. With their own families."

"And your father?" I said.

"My father moved back to Italy."

I stared at her, astounded. I looked at Isabella, who was wriggling her eyebrow at me meaningfully.

"Your father's here?" My voice was stringy.

"In the south." She pushed the rake over to the fence. I thought for a moment I had offended her and she was walking away to end the conversation. But instead she turned and pulled out a pack of cigarettes from the pocket of her tunic. She took off her gloves with her teeth, pinned them under her elbow, and shook the packet, offering it to Isabella and to me. We all shared a match. She blew it out and threw it carelessly toward the fence. It fell only a yard away and I watched the stalk still smoking in the earth.

Sister Teresa leaned back on the railing, hooking her elbows over with un-nunlike casualness. Isabella and I stood on either side of her against the fence.

"Do you see him?" I said. "Your father, I mean."

She shook her head. "I don't have contact. My mother did for a while."

"But —" My mouth wouldn't shut.

Isabella leaned forward and caught my eye. "Leave it, Briddie. She doesn't want to talk about it."

Sister Teresa shook her head. "Really, it's fine."

My mind was crowded with questions. I took another two drags before speaking, trying to measure my words. "He's here, in Italy?"

She nodded.

"You could find him."

"That assumes I want to find him," she said. A wry smile appeared on her face. Again, I was unsettled by the transformation from nun to girl. I thought suddenly how Isabella had been right to uncover her other name. And how in disclosing her name, her other identity, Isabella had allowed me to trace how she shifted from

Sister Teresa to Rosaria and back again.

"But —" I cleared my throat. "You only have two years, don't you? Until another sister has her turn speaking."

"She only has one year of speaking left, actually," Isabella said.

"Is that true?"

"Yes. Ten months have already elapsed."

"But then, time is running out!" It sounded terribly overdramatic, but my heart began to beat quicker, for it was quite romantic. A young, beautiful nun, cloistered away, with only months to find her long-lost father. What if he was dying? I saw Sister Teresa approaching the deathbed of her father. The sheet was tucked over his belly, his face gleaming with sweat in the murky light of a single candle. "My daughter," he would say, "forgive me." The scene had raced in front of me so vividly my expression must have been hectic.

Sister Teresa sighed and rubbed her neck. "I think there has been plenty of time," she said, "and if God means it to be, then it will." She stabbed her cigarette on the post with unnecessary force.

"How wild," I said, breathing out. "I never would have guessed."

"You know what's really wild?" Isabella said, her eyes shining. I recognized the expression. She was desperate to tell me something. I looked between the two of them.

"What?"

Isabella glanced around us, but there was no one in sight. The day was overcast and breezy; a paper bag had become snared in one of the apple trees and was crackling in the air. "She's mixed, just like you," she whispered.

I didn't understand her meaning at first. "Mixed?" I pictured blue and white paint, swirling together. Isabella's brows were raised. She was breathing shallowly. Then I understood.

"Oh," I said.

The ground slanted. I swallowed.

"Isn't that a kick?" she said.

I caught Sister Teresa's eye, and I must have blinked or twitched, because she said softly, looking to Isabella, "Maybe you should talk about this privately."

"You told her?" My palms began to sweat.

Isabella's eyelids fluttered. "I wasn't going to *lie* to Rosie."

I opened my mouth and shut it again.

"I'll leave you alone," Sister Teresa said.

Isabella frowned. "No. Why — what's the big deal?"

"I can't believe you told her," I said.

Something inside my chest was wobbling.

"I thought it was neat." Isabella shrugged defensively. "You're both mixed African and European. It's neat."

I pressed my fingernails into my palms. I could feel Sister Teresa watching me. "It's not the same at all," I said.

"But don't you get it? Isn't that a kick?" Isabella said again, louder. "That you should both be here at the same time?"

My lips were numb.

"It's cool, right?" Isabella prompted. "For there to be two of you here at the same time —"

"Two of us?" I repeated woodenly. Me and Sister Teresa weren't "two of us." The shells of my ears tingled. "What did you say to her?"

"I just . . . just about your family and stuff —" Isabella frowned at me as if I were an imbecile. "You know — how your mom . . . and your sister . . ." She trailed off.

The loose, cracked thing in my chest swerved to and fro. "Who else have you told?" I said.

"Nobody. Just Rosie here." Isabella tried to smile, but I stared at her until the corners of her mouth dropped.

Icy tingles of shame thrummed over my skin. After how nice it had been, how easy.

Now everything was ruined. Why would she do this to me? For what? For the sake of idle gossip with a nun? And how long before everyone in the academy knew? Before all the girls were asking me dumb questions about pharaohs and snake charming. Trying to draw me into dinner-table debates about Suez. Interrogations about the Labor Day parties and Christmas parties and skiing holidays. My palms were slick, my scalp buzzing. After everything I'd said. About Connecticut. About why I'd gone home. About being an only child.

I walked off toward the gate.

"Bridget!" Isabella called.

I didn't turn around.

I let the gate slam behind me and strode through the bare orchard. As I stamped through the fallen leaves and the wet grass, I realized what I should have said. I should have said that just because Mama is from Egypt, it's not the same kind of Africa. That it doesn't make me and Sister Teresa part of the same club. I should have said how I didn't even look mixed. Not like Sister Teresa — no one would have guessed she was mixed. We used to call her the *African* nun. That's what we called her, and Sister Benedict. The *African nuns.* Because they were obviously from Africa. Mama wasn't even obvious, hardly even that different at all. I kicked a tiny apple lying in the grass until it spun over the hill. Isabella was sneaky and selfish and stupid. She was so stupid she didn't even understand how basic geography worked. My throat tightened. Isabella was supposed to look out for me. She was supposed to help me. And instead she'd broken everything.

21.

NOVEMBER

That evening I didn't go down to dinner. I paced my room, shaking out the bedspread, lining up my grammar books. My anger at Isabella had brewed into resentment and a slimy, creeping fear. She *said* she hadn't told anyone. But surely it was only a matter of time. Who would she tell first — Sylvia? I pulled open my drawers and individually rolled each stocking. I wiped my earrings with a damp cloth. Difference was borderline forgivable. But phonies stood no chance. How could I begin to explain myself? Joan's face when she thought I couldn't be trusted. Greta, closing her door quietly as I approached. My chest was tight with a sickening, shimmying heartbeat. I smoothed the bedspread again. Would I have to wait for the whispers and the looks? Or perhaps someone would come to me first — Nancy, probably. She'd knock at my door, tentative, concerned. "Can I talk to you for a moment?" she'd say.

There was a knock at the door. A bird flapped in my stomach.

Greta peered around the door. "You weren't at dinner." She tossed me a bread roll.

"No." I squeezed the roll so hard I punctured the crust.

"What's going on?" Greta frowned. I evaluated her expression. Had she heard? Had it begun already?

"I'm not speaking to Isabella," I said tersely.

"Oh no! But you and Izzy are so close." Greta bounced on the other bed.

I watched her, the back of my neck brisk with frosty shivers. Was she trying to trap me? Did she already know? After a moment, I said, "She spread a rumor."

Greta's eyes flew open. "No way."

Her expression was so stricken, it was clear she had no idea. "You didn't hear anything?"

"Of course not, my goodness." She shook her head. "Izzy? Really? How horrible!"

"She *can* be horrible, you know," I said, the vindication growing. "But no one ever seems to see it." My voice cracked and I gulped back the wobble in my throat.

"Well." Greta crossed her arms. "You

should just stay away from her." Her eyes flashed. "Keep your distance from her and I'll make sure no one listens to any vile rumors."

Her defiance tickled me. She looked like a little frog that had puffed up its mouth with air. "Thank you." I squeezed her hand.

The next morning, I sat with Greta and Sally and drank my coffee quickly, hoping to finish breakfast before she came down. When Isabella appeared in the refectory, her face was puffy and red — she'd clearly been crying. She conspicuously looked away from me.

"Bella, what is it?" asked Sylvia with horror, holding out her arms.

"Nothing," Isabella muttered, sitting on the bench. Sylvia hugged her. Katherine stroked her hair. Over Isabella's shoulder, Sylvia gazed at me in disbelief. They began to whisper and Katherine glared at me contemptuously. I think Isabella was crying, because Sylvia took a napkin off the table and dabbed Isabella's face, then embraced her again.

"Just ignore them," Sally said. "And the *second* they start spreading stories, me and Gigi will give them a piece of our minds."

"Thanks," I said weakly. My guts were swarming. I stared around the refectory, interrogating every glance. Once I had been found out, Katherine and Sylvia were sure to take Isabella's side. Mealtimes would be insufferable. The whispering. Sitting by myself at the end of the table. Sideways looks, graceful disdain. I'd have to sit alone in my room after dinner instead of going to the common room. I drank the rest of my coffee so quickly it scalded my tongue. As I stood up to leave the refectory, I gripped Greta by the arm.

"Tell Elena I'm sick," I whispered. "I'm not in the mood for Italian today," I said.

"Of course." She patted my shoulder.

I waited until ten minutes after the start of class and slipped out across the courtyard, through the gate, and toward the allotment. As I approached the yard, I could see Sister Teresa was working in the garden alone. She was wearing men's black gloves and it made her costume look unwieldy and comical.

I walked toward her, wrapping my coat about myself.

"Hello," she said.

I nodded, not trusting myself to speak.

"I'm checking on the vegetables," she said.

"Sure." My jaw was tight.

"Isabella's not here," she said.

I let myself in through the gate. The

ground was glittering with crystals of ice. What was she even doing out there? Maybe she was just wasting time, knowing that none of the other nuns could admonish her. "Do you even have work to do?" I said, sniffing. "Since it's actually winter?"

"Some vegetables — carrots, leeks — they taste sweeter after the first frost," she said.

"Oh. Right."

"You don't have lessons now?" She leaned on the rake, her weight probing divots in the earth. "Or have you caught up with your studies?"

My cheeks flared. Isabella wasn't content gossiping with her about my family; they'd been talking about my schoolwork too? "My studies are great, actually," I said. "But anyway — I need to speak to you about something else."

"Oh?"

"It's about what Isabella said yesterday — about my family."

Sister Teresa nodded. "I'm sorry for your unhappiness. I've felt very contrite."

A flutter of the old quip about her vocabulary bubbled up, then subsided. For a reason I couldn't place, I knew Isabella and I would never be able to summon that joke again. Sister Teresa had sailed past it. I felt foolish and ashamed we had ever employed it in the first place. The shame bundled up with my resentment and lay heavy in my stomach. I concentrated on my mission — there was no point in feeling sorry. Sister Teresa could spoil everything for me now. I needed to focus on securing her silence.

I pushed my hands into the pockets of my coat. In the bottom of my right pocket was the hard nugget of an old register receipt and I dug my fingernail into it. "I just —"

She watched me, pushing the handle of the rake out to the side and balancing it in the center of her palm. How could I justify the lies about my family? It probably seemed as if I was an untrustworthy sneak, when really, Isabella was the untrustworthy one. I bet she was whispering to Sister Teresa minutes after I left for the States. I bet she was gossiping about me even while I was on the plane. For all she knew, Rhona could have been on her deathbed even while she blabbed.

"Please don't say anything to the other girls about my family."

Sister Teresa looked into the dirt, where the tines of her rake were tapping crumbs of soil. "I'm sure Isabella didn't mean to break your confidence. She has a very big heart," she said.

"Hmm," I said, just to say something.

Now that I considered the idea, it didn't sound right. Rather, I thought of Isabella's heart as a puckered little pouch, one that swells when love is tucked into it and shrivels without nourishment.

Then a strange moment of understanding crossed over me, and I looked at Sister Teresa there scraping the earth with her rake. Not only did Sister Teresa know the truth about my family, but Isabella had chosen her as a confidante. Deliberately. It was one thing to be friendly with a nun, but I was Isabella's closest friend. Her best friend. The most important one. The unfairness of it singed my lungs.

"I need you to keep it a secret, what she told you — about everything. My mom or my sister or —" I pulled the sleeves of my sweater into my fists. My eyes stung. Sister Teresa was hardly even a real girl. She wouldn't understand what it would mean for me. The prickly kind of embarrassment, the genteel, self-righteous snubbing I would have to live with for the rest of the year.

Sister Teresa licked her lips. "Of course. And I don't carry any judgment —" She paused.

"But?"

"But you might find that if you give them a chance, people are more accommodating

305

than you expect." She smiled a soft sort of smile, assuming the dreamy eyes of a kitten crawling into a warm blanket.

Her expression rankled me. Was it Isabella who she considered so "accommodating"? A pang of anger flickered under my rib cage. I chewed the inside of my cheek.

"You wouldn't understand," I said. "It's hard not fitting in."

Sister Teresa's eyebrows twitched. "I have some experience," she said mildly.

"It's different for me." I swallowed. "You and me have really different backgrounds."

She laughed, but it was hollow. "Yes, Bridget, that's quite true."

I yanked the sleeves of my sweater tighter in my fists. "You're wrong, about the girls being accommodating. Isabella doesn't know what it's like." It was oddly exhilarating, talking back to a nun like that.

Sister Teresa gave me a half smile. "She might not understand now, but you could try explaining it to her."

Irritation blistered in my gut. "Explain to Isabella that it's hard work just being normal? Isabella is pretty shortsighted about what it's like." I paused, evaluating Sister Teresa's expression. I needed her to understand. To coax her into even a reluctant alliance. After a moment, I added, "And she's often judgmental."

Sister Teresa's eyes softened. "I'm sure that's not true."

But she had no idea about Isabella. How unpredictable she was. How unreliable. My lower lip wobbled. "No insult intended," I said. "But we've been close for a long time. And she can be pretty brutal. In private."

Sister Teresa gave the most minute of shrugs, as if she had never seen evidence of this prejudice. My earlier admiration for Sister Teresa splintered. She was so meek. So placid. It was maddening. All that stuff about the death of the self. She was mild as unflavored toothpaste. How could Isabella bear to hang out with her? If anything, Sister Teresa should be siding with me. She should recognize Isabella was wrong for gossiping behind my back.

"You've never heard the things she says," I said, pressing my fingernails into my palms. "About —" I had a sudden flash of inspiration. "About people like us."

Sister Teresa opened her mouth, but I continued.

"She couldn't keep my confidence, even though I begged her. And you shouldn't trust her either. You — it would be better if you kept your distance from her."

"Bridget, would you like to sit down?"

Sister Teresa said.

But I was distracted by flickery premonitions. Sister Teresa might easily reveal my falsehoods to the other girls if she thought it was the right thing to do. She'd probably even believe she was helping. And once the girls realized I had defrauded them, I'd be poisoned. Abandoned. Isabella wouldn't dare to come near me. And then there would be questions about why I had gone home. About Rhona. About phobias of oral impregnation.

"I *had* to keep it a secret," I said, my pulse lurching. "But Isabella would never understand." What proof did I need? How could I bind her to silence and ensure her distance from Isabella all at once?

"Bridget." She was watching me. "We don't have to talk about this anymore —"

"My sister died."

Her mouth opened. "Bridget —" She put her hand out and touched my arm. Her fingers were cold.

I was reeling. It had dropped from my tongue unplanned. There was time — I could yet pull it back. I could say "for a moment" or "that's what I thought." But instead, I heard myself seize on it.

"She died when I went home and that's why you can't tell anyone about my family."

I began to cry.

All the long hours at the hospital, pulling tufts of Rhona's hair from the shower drain, rubbing her swollen knuckles, the waiting. All of the awfulness of it came out in an unwinding roll of sobs that clattered from my chest in painful twists. I leaned against the fence, my fists at my face, and wept.

Slowly, Sister Teresa patted my back. "Oh," she said. "Oh."

I gulped. "I've always been afraid she — Rhona — that she would die." Sister Teresa rummaged in her tunic and pulled out a handkerchief. "She gets this empty look — you talk to her but she's not even there. But even so, she's walking around in the middle of the night, like a robot." I shivered, remembering how Mama had to hold her down in the hospital bed to keep her from exercising. Even though it was untrue, it felt extremely true. I had an alternate life where Rhona *had* died. Where she would die. Where everything I was saying was real. I was squeezed by a slippery sort of relief. Finally, I was admitting it out loud. "It's like, like she doesn't want to get better. I can't bear to talk about it."

"Oh, Bridget, I'm so sorry." She continued patting me.

"You must think — think — I'm a terrible

person," I said.

"No, of course not."

"Rhona's been sick for a while." I sniveled into her handkerchief. "And that's why I don't like to talk about my family. Because then I'd have to explain why — why —" I sobbed into the handkerchief. "And I'd have to explain her soul is probably in purgatory."

"Bridget —" She rubbed my shoulder. "I am so sorry for your loss."

I nodded.

"Have you talked to anyone? Father Gavanto?"

I shook my head. "No, I can't." I looked at her. "I have to pray. For her soul."

Sister Teresa bit her lip. "Of course —"

"And Isabella doesn't know."

"She —"

"You can't tell Isabella about Rhona." My breaths were coming in ragged, wet heaves. I felt wild, unshackled, like I had leaped off a diving board. "You mustn't tell her about my sister dying."

"I don't — But why not try and talk to her?"

It took several moments before I steadied myself. "Isabella can't know. She would judge. She said — she says — she thinks Rhona's only sick because of my mom —

my family. That it's hereditary. Because we're mixed."

Sister Teresa took a sharp inhale of breath.

I waited a moment for Sister Teresa to absorb this. Her forehead scrunched in fine fractures. "You have to keep this all secret. Like confession. Right? I need time to pray for her soul. My sister's soul."

"Bridget." She swallowed. "I am so sorry." She hugged me. "I can't imagine how you are suffering."

"But you won't say, will you? To anyone? About anything?"

"Not if you don't wish —"

"I don't wish."

Sister Teresa nodded. Her eyes roved over my face, her own eyelashes wet. "I will pray for your sister," she said, grasping my hand. "Shall we pray together now?"

"And you especially can't tell Isabella. You have to promise."

"I promise."

"On the Holy Bible. A holy promise."

Her pupils flickered in a strange way. But dutifully she crossed herself, slowly. "A holy promise."

22.

DECEMBER

That evening I sat alone in my room instead of going down for dinner. I felt like a cushion that has had its stuffing pulled out. Every time I thought of my conversation with Sister Teresa, my body rattled. I sat on the tiles, put my fists to my face, and rocked back and forth. I pressed my forehead into the coverlet and prayed for Rhona in earnest. What if my lie was a jinx — and God would now punish me by making it true? I whimpered into the bedclothes. I began with prayers for Rhona, and then for Mama, and Granny and Dad. Reluctantly, I included Isabella.

There was a knock at the door and Sally stuck her head around. "Bridge? Oh —" She saw me on my knees. "Sorry," she whispered, closing the door.

I crawled into bed and lay awake, jittering and fretful. I heard the girls come back from dinner, smelled the wood smoke of the common room grate. I tossed and turned and quailed until the girls retired, the bathrooms gurgled water, owls began to call from the orchard. Finally, long after midnight, I slept.

The next day, white clouds rolled over the lake, threatening snow. I joined the girls in the common room with a heavy ache in my muscles. Isabella wasn't there. Joan, Barbie, and I bundled around the fire in sweaters and blankets, drinking cocoa made with Nancy's heating coil, listening to the draft surging through the floorboards. Katherine, Sylvia, and Isabella kept to Sylvia's room all weekend, and occasionally I caught the muffled sound of Isabella's voice from outside the door. I set my nerves. It was only a matter of time until Isabella realized how much she had hurt me. How wrong she had been to betray me. And until then I had to be alert to rumors. And to focus, carefully, on protecting my reputation.

A strange listlessness spread over the academy with the change in weather. The wind was sharp and sought out vulnerable skin to slice, slamming unseen doors, whistling frosty arias in the courtyard. Apart from Nancy, the rest of us barely left the upper corridor. Instead, we entertained ourselves by watching from the common room windows as the sisters shoveled grit on the pathways around the building. Growing contemptuous of each other's opinions, we stopped setting our hair or wearing lipstick and dressed in old shirts and boyfriends' sweaters and went about with holes in our socks. If I happened to come across Isabella in the queue for the telephone I turned pointedly and went back to my bedroom.

Over the next week, I nodded obediently as Nancy delivered tedious lectures about regional dialects while her dirty hiking boots dried out by the fire. I painted Patricia's nails. I held Greta's yarn as she knitted and unpicked a sweater for Bobby, never tutting when she dropped a stitch, never complaining when she made me count for her. When Sally wanted to compare dress sizes, I let her try on my skirts and provided deferential compliments about the slack material of my gowns around her waist. I helped Joan paste the photos from her sister's wedding into a scrapbook, supplied her with tissues as she mourned not being a bridesmaid. I loaned homework assignments and searched for lost earrings. I rescued spiders and shared cigarettes. I was the perfect companion.

Sometimes I caught Isabella looking over at me in the refectory and felt a sting of bitter victory. It was only a matter of time before she apologized, begged for my forgiveness. It was clear she missed me. Of course she missed me. She had said it herself — I was her favorite.

The meals grew heavier and heartier: quail with polenta, tiny ravioli filled with pumpkin and sage, slippery saffron risotto. And hazelnut cake with fresh cream, and trembling egg yolks whipped with sweet wine. I retreated straight to my bedroom after supper and lay on my bed, gratefully stunned with food and clumsy with cider.

One evening for dessert we were served cups of crispy fried pastry filled with semi-sweet ricotta. I ate two, one after the other, showering myself with powdered sugar.

Sally poked one of the shells suspiciously with her fork. "Is it Bridge-approved?" She'd never quite recovered from the treachery of a seemingly chocolate bun that turned out to be marzipan.

I lifted my third pastry and contemplated it. "It's so good I want to salt it with my tears," I said.

The table fell silent. A row of faces was staring at me. I reeled with shame. Where had that sentiment come from? It had flown from somewhere uncensored inside me. I was mortified. It had eased out so quickly I hadn't had time to catch it.

"Bridge," Sally gasped. "You're like a poet."

"So passionate," Greta said to Sally.

"Is that from the Bible?" Bunny squinted at Barbie, who shrugged, staring at me wide-eyed.

I wiped my mouth with my napkin. "It's nice, is all I mean," I said, and took a long sip of cider.

"Well, we figured that," Sally said, laughing. The girls were smiling at me, at each other. Sally picked up her pastry and tapped it against Greta's. "Cheers."

I felt almost giggly with relief. "Cheers," I said.

Although I searched for her, Sister Teresa was no longer working in the yard. Instead she was often down in the spa, where the sisters took turns chasing out roosting birds and lighting the ancient furnace to keep the pipes from freezing and shattering. I watched her and Sister Luisa walking back and forth between the cypress trees with a flounce of shallow triumph. I didn't see her and Isabella together anymore.

On Friday night after dinner, I returned to my room to find Isabella sitting on the right-hand bed. She was turning a soft pack of Lucky Strikes over and over in her hands.

"Oh," I said, almost tripping over the threshold.

"Will you shut the door?" Her voice was hoarse.

I closed the door and took an awkward seat on my own bed. I slipped my hands under my thighs.

She put the cigarette pack down on the coverlet. "I feel like everyone hates me," she said.

I said nothing. Her face was drawn, exhausted.

Isabella cleared her throat. "Even Rosie — Sister Teresa is hardly speaking to me."

A soft warmth illuminated in my chest, slight as a birthday candle. After a moment, I said, "I don't hate you." As I said it, I tried to gauge if I was truly ready to forgive her.

"Sorry," she said finally. "For telling Sister Teresa about your family." Her lips were chapped, her face blotchy. "I know it's kind of — sensitive." She looked disheveled, almost pitiful. I shouldn't have punished her for so long. I held my arms out and she crossed the room to hug me.

I closed my eyes, squeezing her as hard as I dared. She nudged her head into the crook of my shoulder, and I buried my face in her neck, taking deep, damp breaths.

"I missed you," I said. My heartbeat skittered into the arches of my feet. I flashed back to the last time we had fought, the last time she had come to me.

"So we're OK, right?" she said, pulling back. A strand of my hair snagged on her lips.

"You swear you're done gossiping?" I said, my voice wobbling.

She almost smiled. "I swear."

"Nothing to no one."

She crossed herself. "Double swear. I'll be as silent as the nuns."

"The *real* nuns."

The almost smile became a hollow laugh. "The real ones, yeah."

I leaned forward and kissed her on the forehead, lightly. As I pulled back, her breath was heavy between us. My stomach tightened, my fingers trembling. She was so close I could see the flecks of green in her irises. She glanced down at my mouth, only for a second.

I kissed her.

Her lips were rough against mine, her tongue hot and sour from cigarettes. I leaned into the kiss, tight with an unbounding ache that throbbed through the core of my body. Shakily, I reached for her neck, her shoulders, her hair.

Gently, she closed her lips against mine,

easing herself away.

I swallowed wildly.

She ran the back of her wrist over her mouth, tucking her hair behind her ears. "Friends again?" she said. The skin around her lips was swollen from the force of my kiss.

I nodded, my pulse stuttering.

With a sigh, she slumped forward, resting her head against my collarbone. I wrapped my hands around the back of her head, trying to steady my heartbeat. Every muscle was jolting, my skin burbling with hectic shimmers.

With a groan, Isabella flung herself aside onto the bed, bouncing on her back. "God, it was boring when you were away," she said loudly.

I laughed, but I was delighted.

"Briddie, let's never fall out again." She held her hand up and I pressed my palm against hers. We clasped fingers and she shook our joined hands from side to side roughly. "I was going out of my mind without anyone to talk to."

23.

DECEMBER

It was the final week of term, and oyster-colored clouds released flurries of snow over the academy. The powder settled over the hills, frosting the rocks around the lake, sliding from the branches of the apple trees with sudden sighs. The last day of term fell on the feast day of St. Allegra, and Father Gavanto announced he would be leading a special prayer service each afternoon of the preceding week. I began wearing earplugs while studying; else it seemed like the chapel bells never stopped ringing. Each day after lunch, Isabella went to chapel for the special services, while I stayed behind to work on my Bernini essay. I waited in the upstairs corridor until she crossed the courtyard, stopping to turn and blow me a kiss, crystals of snow in her hair.

The girls began packing their cases for the Christmas vacation. We drew our own Christmas cards and made trips down to

La Pentola to buy plum wine and splintery icons of St. Teresa from the market. We constructed paper garlands to hang from the lampshades and cut holly sprigs to put in jelly jars. The girls who were packing recklessly donated barely worn stockings and sweaters and tubes of lipstick, confident they'd be getting replacements at home anyway.

Since I was the only one with work left to do, the girls became my cheerleaders. Nancy sat next to me in the common room, offering assistance from her thesaurus as I scribbled and cursed. Bunny provided me with two packs of oatmeal cookies. In the spirit of true camaraderie, Mary L. drew me a picture of the Quattro Fiumi fountain to attach to my essay. It was lopsided and kind of smudged, but I pretended to be grateful anyway. Ruth, meanwhile, was going on a special trip to the Holy Land over vacation and became even more insufferable than usual. In preparation for her visit to the Church of the Holy Sepulchre, she was conspicuously fasting between sunrise and sunset, clicking her rosary while she sat by the fireside, solemn-faced and weary, as if she were personally atoning for all of our sins.

And gradually the girls peeled off one by

one. Greta left on Thursday morning, grinning and waving from the front step like Mamie Eisenhower boarding a plane. Afterward I had to spend an hour consoling Sally, who was sobbing on my bedspread.

By the Sunday of St. Allegra's feast, there were only five girls and the sisters left at the academy. The feast-day service was held so early I could smell the starch on the sisters' tunics as I entered the chapel. Isabella was already seated between Katherine and Mary B., so I sat with Joan across the aisle. During Mass there was a loud clatter from the sacristy as a mousetrap snapped, but Father Gavanto carried on, pretending to be oblivious to the piteous squeals. Next to me Joan's body was shaking with stifled laughter, but when I tried to catch Isabella's eye, her head was dropped. Maybe Ruth had been rubbing off on her.

Breakfast was truly depressing: water and St. Allegra crackers with salt. The sisters then led a procession down to La Pentola. I squeezed in next to Isabella and kept my eyes on where Sister Luisa's boots marked the slush so I wouldn't slip and fall.

Whoops and cheers echoed from the lake as we approached; village kids were already on the ice, leaping about and scraping pearly foam from the surface and flicking it at each other. My gut twinged — even if the lake was truly frozen, surely it wasn't a great idea to be *jumping* on it? But as we reached the harbor I could see the ice was thick and clear, spangled with frozen bubbles fixed in silver. The five of us students stood on the pier, jiggling our weight to keep warm while the sisters tied on their skates. One by one, they launched off onto the ice, smacking and sliding into each other. As Sister Bernard began to effortlessly glide backward with a sweeping stride, Katherine shook her head. "This is nuts. Why didn't we bring a camera? My mom will never believe me."

Sister Teresa was hanging on to Sister Luisa, and they were staggering in sudden jerks to avoid the rubble of twigs and pebbles that had been thrown to test the ice.

"I think I've seen enough," Joan said. "What do you think, Bridge? Shall we go back? I can't feel my toes."

I glanced at Isabella, but when I turned, all the girls were looking at me.

"Um." I put my arm through Isabella's. "Are you bored?"

Isabella shook her head. Her scarf was covering her mouth, her eyes bright with amusement.

"Let's stay for a bit longer, then," I said.

"We don't get to watch the nun Olympics every day."

Everyone laughed, their breath white in the air.

Joan shivered. "Bridge, you must have a furnace in your belly. I'm freezing."

"Oh, come here," Katherine said, embracing her, and then me and Mary and Isabella. As we stood bundled up together watching the sisters, I felt a strange rush of emotion, like I might be about to start crying.

Tentatively, I slipped my hand into Isabella's pocket and squeezed her fingers.

She looked right into my eyes and smiled.

24.

DECEMBER

Christmas was a strangely somber affair. Father Gavanto held a long Mass in La Pentola, the church full of wheezing old people I hadn't seen before. Signora Bassi was wearing a curious black hat and rocking a mewling baby I supposed must be hers, although I didn't ask after its parentage. Back at the academy, we ate a plain lunch of boiled-chicken-and-dumpling stew followed by strips of candied orange peel. To the sound of jangling bells from the chapel, the five of us gathered in the common room and opened our gifts. Isabella gave me a pair of earrings wrapped in a copy of *Il Giorno*. They were button-size cloudy amber studs, and I immediately wished I had somewhere nice to keep them, rather than in an Altoids tin with the rest of my jewelry. I had knitted her a red cap, and she put it on and posed in a range of serious stances, as if she were a girl in a pattern magazine.

We toasted each other with plum wine and dozed companionably in front of the fire.

But in the days following Christmas, the academy felt hollow and strange. The sisters appeared often in the upper corridor, sweeping and dusting, changing the bed linen even in the empty rooms. I watched them leaving the chapel, shoveling snow in the courtyard, or Sister Teresa and Sister Luisa sheltering in the orchard to smoke. Occasionally I saw Sister Teresa by herself, walking down toward the spa to light the furnace and keep the pipes from cracking. Isabella, meanwhile, was complaining of a cold and spent most afternoons locked in her room, scribbling lists of people to invite to her wedding. Her notes were extensive, and many of the guests were Ralph's friends from Yale — men called Badger or Tibbs. She began going down regularly to La Pentola and visiting Signora Bassi at the *enoteca* to quiz her about different wines and different foods and how they were meant to be paired. I nodded along to her menu conversation about dessert wines and champagnes, but I don't suppose I was much of an audience, for she quickly gave up trying to get me interested. Katherine and I made a nest in the common room with a blanket and a bag of walnuts. When Isabella came to join us in the evenings she climbed into my armchair and slipped her cold feet under mine and I read out loud to her from one of her Georgette Heyer novels.

At night I lay in bed listening to the pipes sighing, the floorboards creaking, as wind swelled through the cracks. The falling snow muffled the sounds from outside, so the corridors of the academy felt charged with static. I kept my bedroom door closed now, since the windows overlooking the courtyard were badly fitting in their frames and let through keyholes of icy air that pierced my nightdress. But often I lay awake long into the night, hoping Isabella might grow cold and slip in beside me.

New Year's Eve was another snowy evening. We gathered in the common room and counted down until midnight, wearing paper hats and eating chocolate cookies that had grown soft in the mail. At the stroke of midnight we cheered and hugged. We exchanged good-luck kisses, and as Isabella's face came close to mine, a thrill passed through me at the smell of plum wine on her breath, the weight of her hair, cool upon my cheek. Joan began singing "Auld Lang Syne," but we didn't know the words, so we hummed the tune with our arms over each other's shoulders. When we'd drunk the last of the wine, we said good night and "Happy 1958" and went to our beds. Isabella followed as I entered my room, and I deliberately turned off the lamp so it would be darker, more intimate. We stood by the window, watching the dim moonlight catching on flakes of snow. An icy breeze was skirling through the chinks in the window frame, and Isabella shivered. I yanked the blanket off my bed and tucked it over her shoulders. She smiled absently. I was conscious of the join between our bodies, my arm against her shoulder. I thought again of the night when she had climbed in beside me. When I had kissed her pulse, my tongue against the warm beat of her heart. We stood in silence until the silence stretched out and became meaningful. My heart was blinking rapidly. I thought, *Maybe, maybe it will happen. If I creep ever so softly.* I inched closer to her, tiny, incremental movements, hardly daring to breathe, until the whole of my arm was pressed against hers.

We stood like that for two minutes, and then Isabella twitched and covered her mouth, yawning.

"I'm beat," she said.

"Want to sleep here?" I looked pointedly out at the snow. "It'll be warmer."

"No, thanks," she said in a chirpy tone, unwrapping herself from the blanket. "I'm snoring something awful these days with this cold."

She folded the blanket over her arm and held the bundle toward me. Stretching, she called, "Good night!" before turning the handle with a wave. I busied myself spreading and straightening the blanket. But as soon as she closed the door I let it fall and leaned forward until I could feel the warmth of her body still lingering on the blanket.

25.

The days after New Year's were long and tiresome. Joan and Katherine quarreled over the atomic power station in Pennsylvania, and I had to spend an hour with Katherine in her room, listening to her complain about Joan's politics. I was almost jealous of her, that their quarrel was so straightforward. It was like a piece of broken pottery, with real, sharp edges to it.

Isabella was down in La Pentola, learning about port wine, and I was growing bored and restless from sitting indoors. After a heavy lunch of mutton and carrot stew, and a disorienting nap, I sat in the common room and stared idly out at the thin line of smoke coming from the spa chimney. I leafed again through the magazines in the basket, even though I was sure I'd read them all. Sluggish and irritable, I decided to walk down to the spa and see if it was Sister Teresa stoking the pipes.

I wrapped myself up in my coat and hat and scarf and two pairs of socks and left the academy. The air was so cold it made me gasp, but it was instantly refreshing, like a shot of peppermint schnapps through my veins. I crunched down the slope toward the spa, quickly growing too warm in my layers. Glazed footprints marked the path where the nuns' boots had tramped down the ice, then frozen over to leave imprints as slippery as glass. I descended carefully, sticking my tongue out of the corner of my mouth as I clambered over the rock.

When I approached the spa garden, I was so bundled up I had to turn myself and squeeze sideways through the gates. The graveyard was quite beautiful in the snow. Sister Teresa had obviously been working on it a great deal. The hedges were trimmed into neat blocks and at the back was a new wooden crate storing stripped foliage for mulch.

The ramp had frozen into an icy sheet, and so cautiously I put my foot over and yanked open the doors into the ballroom. The white snow light bleached some of the beauty out of the room. I had remembered it as grand, but it was clear where the paper had runched and buckled. Thin crusts of hoary mud were smeared over the wooden floorboards where the sisters had walked to and fro over the threshold. It was much warmer than outside and I pulled off my hat, running my palms over my hair to disperse the static. With the building warmed up, I could smell the sour, grassy smell of the old wood and the sweet stink of a dead mouse.

"Hello?" I called, and my voice echoed. But I remembered it might not even be Sister Teresa feeding the stove. I went through the double doors and into the downstairs corridor toward John Henry's room, running my gloves along the wood paneling. Since I'd last been to John Henry's room, it had featured often in my day-dreams, where Rhona had acquired a cozy fireplace and her own TV.

And as I came up to the door, I heard a cough from inside the room, followed by a murmur and giggle. The sisters were *talking*! My heart hammered. What a victory this would be to take back to Isabella! I had caught the sisters talking to each other when they thought they were alone! They must come here to whisper, away from the nosy ears of the academy girls. I put my face to the keyhole and my lashes scuffed against the wood, the heat of my own breath reflecting back on my face.

Through the rotting keyhole I clearly saw two figures lying side by side on a mattress. Isabella and Sister Teresa, touching.

26.

JANUARY

There was Isabella's bare foot, jiggling at the end of the mattress. There was the red hat I had knitted for her under the window. There were the convent-issue boots, the wimple cap and scarf, thrown on the floor, lying in the dust. I realized suddenly that Sister Teresa was uncloaked, and crouched down further to look at her. She was still dressed, but without her cap, she seemed so naked. Her hair was dark and shorn so short it barely covered her ears. Isabella picked up her arm, and Rosaria rested her head on Isabella's chest. Isabella absently worked at Rosaria's scalp while they muttered quietly. Rosaria laughed. For Sister Teresa was quite scrubbed away.

I was standing on a high ledge. My mouth went dry and a sour taste filled it from the back, silty like the dregs in the bottom of a cider glass.

Isabella stretched out, yawned, and, taking Rosaria's hand, kissed it lightly upon the inside of the wrist. I pressed my head closer to the keyhole and my eyelashes brushed against the wood. The casualness of it was awful. More awful, maybe, than any other part of it. This was no frantic moment of solace. This was the companionable time wasting of two people already intimate with each other.

The longer I looked, the more I understood. There on the mattress was an orange coverlet, one from the academy. They must have brought the blanket there deliberately. The mattress itself must have been brought there deliberately. So they could lie upon it.

I pulled my head away from the keyhole and crouched down in a squat, pressing my face into my knees. Had Isabella ever gone to the *enoteca*? She must have been meeting with her for weeks. My neck was pinched by the angle, my vision speckled. I put my face back to the keyhole. Rosaria's head was still on Isabella's chest, and Isabella's fingers were still kneading her scalp. Both had their eyes closed, and they were murmuring about something. Isabella's face broke into a slight smile that fluttered over her eyelids, as if she were dreaming.

I pulled my head back again, straightening my right leg. It bumped against the wooden door. Panic surged into my throat. I froze. Their murmuring stopped. There was the startled, static charge of silence as they listened. I stood as quickly as I could, my legs stiff, and hobbled down the corridor, back the way I had come. Stumbling through the ballroom, I nearly slipped on the ramp, catching my hand across a nail in the bricks and cutting the heel of my palm through the glove. I crunched down the path, holding the graze to my mouth, hearing distantly the muffled sound of my own wails.

I trudged through the graveyard, through the railings, scrambled up the rock and along the path as quickly as I could manage. All I could think about was getting back to the academy, to be safe, away from them. I ran through the side door, along the downstairs corridor, praying nobody would see me, that Joan and Katherine wouldn't appear and ask what was wrong. I ran to my room and, slumping by the bed, pushed my face into the bedding and sobbed, my ears still smarting from the cold.

I cried into the blanket until my throat was aching and I thought I would be sick. Then I bunched my knees up to my chest, yanking the blanket down and pulling it over me. My face was swollen and tender. I remembered how I had thrown the blanket over Isabella on New Year's Eve and how she had flinched away from me. How in the moment when I was looking over the snow and thinking of her, she must have been thinking of Rosaria. With a feeble moan I threw the blanket on the floor and climbed onto the bed, kicking off my boots and wriggling under the comforter, still in my outdoor clothes. My coat was damp from drops of melted snow, and the graze across my palm stung. I was far too warm, the scarf chafing at my neck, and the tips of my ears were burning, but it was satisfying, to be so uncomfortable. Another crying jag came over me and I sobbed into the pillow.

All this time, I'd been so careful, so patient. And for what? The lie I had told Sister Teresa — for what? It was supposed to protect me. And it had been for nothing. And Sister Teresa — what had possessed her? She was a nun! Her vows — her promises. And after what I had told her about Isabella — how had she forgiven her so easily? She was so weak. Weaker even than me. All the efforts I had made. Pointless. Humiliating. Waiting for Isabella. When I kissed her, after our fight, the tension in her lips I had taken for shyness. How gently she had pulled back from me, how subtly she had eased us apart. I cringed and covered my head with my arms, waiting for the surge of shame to pass. I saw her face as she looked at me on New Year's, and twitched, and moved away from me. It was so awful.

I thought of the time when Sister Teresa first took us to the spa — was that when it had begun? I pulled a pillow into my stomach and held it there against the hollowness. Had they been selecting the right place for their rendezvous? Absurdly, I thought, it was the room I had chosen for Rhona, and they had sullied it. I cried into my pillow until it grew dark and I fell into something like sleep, then woke up, fretful, overheated, needing the bathroom.

I waited behind my door with one ear to the wood, listening for any sounds in the corridor. But it was silent, so I pulled the door open, ran down the corridor as quickly as I could, rushed into the bathroom, and peed. When I washed my hands in the basin, my eyes were bloodshot, and the skin around my nose was raw from rubbing it on tissues. I looked awful. I tucked the hair behind my ears. I was glad I looked awful. It was proof of how unhappy I was. What she had done to me.

I raced down the corridor and into my room, locking the door. I hadn't drawn the shutters and the night was blue with a scattering of wan stars. A headache began, pulling from behind at the muscles in the back of my neck. I grabbed one of the bottles of plum wine from my trunk, and tugging the comforter around me, I swigged the liquor straight from the bottle. There was a perverse kind of satisfaction in feeling so terrible, in the exhausted bruise in my throat. I swigged and cried again, in little blurts that dried up in seconds.

I thought over and over of the night when Isabella had come to me, after the festival. How I had kissed her neck, felt the bead of her nipple under my fingers. And as I sat there, I imagined pushing open the door to John Henry's room, slamming it so hard that dust fell from the roof, and they would've looked up at me, mouths open, horrified, humiliated, exposed. I wondered then why I *hadn't* just swung open the door. Perhaps because the moment I had witnessed was so intimate, so domestic, it had felt, at the time, that I shouldn't have been spying. As if *I* were in the wrong. Maybe I would've been bolder if they'd been lying there naked. A wriggle of odd desire squirmed through me and I shook myself to dislodge it. Perhaps — I thought — perhaps I hadn't opened the door because I wasn't sure what I had seen. I put the wine bottle down on the tiles and licked the sticky crud from my bottom lip. Maybe I'd overreacted. What had I really seen after all? Maybe I'd let my imagination run away with me.

Relief bubbled up to the top of my head and popped like a bottle of champagne. What a fool I had been! So what if they were sitting together, lying on each other? It didn't mean anything at all. Why, half the girls in the academy lay mingled on the sofa, rubbed each other's shoulders, walked around the grounds arm in arm. And after all, Sister Teresa was a nun. An actual nun.

I stood up, giddy, close to giggles. How stupid I'd been! I paced up and down the room, inspired almost to skip and jump. Imagine if I *had* burst into the room, making accusations. How embarrassing! My cheeks grew hot and I congratulated myself for creeping away, for not saying anything. I took another celebratory swig of the plum wine. I could go to Isabella — find her, tell her about it, and laugh. But I touched my face; it was still sensitive, aching. She would know I'd been crying. Better, I thought, to wait until the next day.

I climbed into bed, smearing cold cream across my face to try to salve the blotchiness. I resolved to concentrate. Isabella and

Sister Teresa — their friendship — it was just a blip. A freak of circumstance. I would have to work harder; that was all. Go along with them when they went gardening. Pretend to care about apples. I'd have to be more interesting, more delightful. What was it that Isabella liked about her? Her hair? Her laugh? Her wholesomeness? The other girls already called me St. Bridget. I could be better. I could read more poetry, cultivate an air of wisdom. It was going to be fine. The bed tilted. Strangely, I felt much better for my outburst. As if I'd been trying to gulp down a pill that had finally settled. How could I ever have been worried about it? Isabella and Sister Teresa. Stupid.

27.

JANUARY

___

When I woke my head was throbbing and the room was a mess. I'd trudged muddy snow over the tiles, and there lay a half empty box of saltines I had risen and eaten in the night, crouched over the packet like a skunk in garbage. My suffering, which had seemed so dramatic the night before, now seemed banal and almost sordid against the dusty bottle of wine and crumpled tissues. I could smell my own sweat, acidic and flowery under my sweater. I remembered my victorious jig around the room when I realized I'd mistaken Isabella's embrace. I was just as embarrassed as if I'd been standing outside myself, witnessing my own foolishness.

It was only half past five, so I went to the bathroom, my body aching, my shoulders taut from crying. I let the bath run, then climbed into the water and soaped my belly and thighs, thinking over the night before. I resolved to get better control of myself. Anyone could have seen me stumbling around the corridor. One of the sisters. Katherine, Joan, Isabella herself. No wonder she was now friends with Sister Teresa — my poor decisions spoke for themselves. I scoured my face with a washcloth, trying to scrub the poison out of my skin.

The door opened, and as I turned I twisted at the stiff muscles in my neck.

"Morning," said Isabella, yawning. She had a pillow crease across her forehead and her hair was tied in bunches. "You're up early."

"Hi." I began shampooing my hair, wishing I could cover my own nudity. As if she might see all the hysteria and shame written on my body.

"Turn the faucet on, will you?" she said, opening the stall. I heard the echo of her peeing.

I leaned across to the other tub and turned the faucet, dripping sudsy water on the tiles as I put in the stopper.

The toilet flushed, and Isabella came out and rinsed her hands, then stuck out her tongue and examined it.

"Actually, to hell with it." She caught my eye in the mirror. "Can I jump in?"

"With me?" I both wanted her and didn't

want her. I wanted her to be close to me, but I felt self-conscious — my breasts heavy, my body puffy, spoiled.

"If you don't want?" She looked amused.

"No, it's just, I've got the curse," I lied.

"OK, cellmates, then."

She sat on the edge of the other tub and dangled her dirty feet in the rising water. I rubbed shampoo into my scalp, deliberately not looking at her. I lay back and rinsed my hair, the drip of the faucet loud over the sound of my own body swirling.

"It's so nice, filling it right up to the top," she said, pulling off her nightdress and throwing it onto the tiles. She climbed into the tub with a sigh. "I'll hate it when the others get back."

I squeezed the shampoo out of my hair. The water turned cloudy. "I hadn't thought of it."

Isabella laughed, dipping her bar of soap in the water and rubbing it under her arms. "God, Briddie. You're as bad as the nuns."

I smiled, unnerved. Was that a compliment now? Since she was back to being friendly with Sister Teresa? Or was she mocking nuns? Was it an insult?

"What's up with you?" She reached over and pointedly turned on the faucet in my own bath.

"Nothing," I said, but my voice sounded flimsy.

"Cramps? I have some of Barbie's painkillers. The strong ones."

"No, I'm fine." I drew my knees to my chest.

"What shall we do today?" she said. "We should make the best of it while the others are gone."

"You're not going to the yard? Or the spa?" I couldn't bring myself to say Sister Teresa's name.

Isabella lifted one foot out of the water and rubbed a scratch on her shin. "I'd rather enjoy having the run of the place while we can."

"Mmm."

"Briddie —" She splashed me. "What is it?"

"Cramps," I said.

"At least you're not pregnant." She was teasing me, but I wasn't in the mood to play along.

"Sure."

Isabella sat up. "Let's do something fun today. We'll climb the bell tower."

I winced. Although I had lied about the cramps, I now felt the tenderness that did come with my period. I wondered if I was getting it after all.

"OK," she said. "We'll go into the cider cellar."

"Sure," I said, with the doleful reluctance of someone being treated after a trip to the dentist. *At least,* I thought, *at least she wants to spend time with me.*

"Breakfast first." She leaped out of the bathtub and I turned to watch the drops gleaming on the dimples at the backs of her thighs.

"You stay in there and soak," she said, tucking her towel under her arms. "I'll go find us something to do."

"OK," I said. I lay weakly in the bath, overcome with tiredness, fixing on the spot where an empty hook hung from the heart of a ceiling rosette.

When my hair was dry, I went down to meet Isabella. She was on her way back up the stairs, holding a cup of coffee and a brioche roll. I took the coffee from her and she held out the roll, then pulled out a Hershey's bar from her pocket and broke off a shard. "Wait." She pulled open the bread and closed it on the Hershey's. "Now it's a *pain au chocolat*," she said, holding it out to me.

I smiled, but it was pinched. I ate the chocolate bun in miserable, small bites. I tried to talk myself into being cheerful. But it was like someone had pulled my plug out and all my insides had swirled away, and now I was hollow.

Isabella stretched. "I'm dying for a smoke. You want one?"

I nodded.

"Drink up, and I'll go grab our coats. Wait down at the bottom for me." She disappeared up the stairs and I stood woodenly sipping my coffee.

She came back with our coats, took my coffee mug, and put it on a side table in the hallway. "Let's go," she said. I didn't protest at leaving mess for a sister to clean up. I didn't much care about the sisters' workload at that moment.

We went out into the courtyard. A fresh powder of snow must have fallen overnight, as the courtyard was a flawless, paper white. I followed her around the left side of the building, where we usually didn't walk. I searched for the path leading up to the shrine, but it was buried in snow. It seemed like a hundred years ago we had gone up there with Nancy and Greta and Sister Teresa.

We came to the grated door of the convent, and Isabella looked around, then slid her hands through the bars and unsnipped the lock.

"Don't," I said.

She shook me off. "Shh, it's fine. No one's even here." She pulled the grate and it swung with a screech.

I peered down the dark corridor. And then someone came out of a room on the left. I yelped. I heard Isabella behind me laughing, and her hand rested on my shoulder. But my senses were all going at once. Behind the grate was Sister Teresa in her tunic and head scarf.

"I thought it was just you and me today," I said, turning around to Isabella, unable to keep the accusation out of my voice.

Isabella frowned. "We're going to tour the convent — isn't that a scream?"

I looked back toward Sister Teresa. I nodded and tried to smile. The pleasure of having Isabella to myself was gone, but so was my numbness. My pulse quickened, and all the heaviness of moments before broke off like a plaster cast. Now that they were together, I would be able to observe them. I would have to pay careful attention to Sister Teresa, to find out what it was that Isabella liked so much — why she chose to spend time with her. Over me.

Sister Teresa grinned and waved us through, miming that Isabella should shut the door behind her.

"We'll have to be super quiet," Isabella whispered in my ear.

My blood washed against my eardrums. How did Isabella know we had to be quiet? Had they been there often, together?

We went down the corridor in single file. Unlike the academy, this building was made from whitewashed rough stone. I could see the texture on the walls where the brush had missed pores in the rock. The corridor was gloomy, and it gave me the distinct impression of traveling to the bottom of a shaft. As we passed the cells, I glanced through the doorways. From the brief glimpses, they looked cramped and austere, with a bed and a cross on the eastern wall. The air was icy, and I shivered.

"Sorry about the cold," Sister Teresa said.

"It's OK." My voice was hoarse. I turned to Isabella. "Are we allowed to be in here?" I whispered.

Isabella wrinkled her nose. "It's not *forbidden* or anything."

That didn't reassure me much. Especially as I could see the back of Sister Teresa's head jolting from side to side as she peeked about us. There came the sound of boots across the tiles, and Sister Teresa ushered us through a doorway and onto a narrow ledge, where we all pressed together, shuffling to make room for each other while Sister Teresa groped in the air for a light pull. It swung against my head, and as her hand brushed my cheek I felt the dryness of her skin, the calluses on the pads of her fingers. With a click she turned on a naked bulb overhead, the filament glowing in wiggles on the inside of my eyelids.

We were standing above a set of steep wooden stairs with gaps between the treads, like a ladder. Sister Teresa went first and I followed her, allowing each foot to dangle and make contact with the next step before transferring my weight. I had a childish fear my foot would get snared in the space between the steps, and I would fall headfirst.

"Here we are. This is the apple store," Sister Teresa said.

It smelled sweet and grassy, like a barn. A wooden crate filled with straw was standing on the right-hand side, apples gleaming in the straw like Christmas ornaments. Sister Teresa picked out three apples, throwing one to me and one to Isabella. Isabella caught hers, but mine slipped from my hand. I rolled it under my fingers, probing the flesh where it had grown loose and wrinkly. I was unsettled by the way she had lobbed it across the room, the swift athleticism of her arm. The Rosaria-ness of it. She crossed to a set of round metal disks on a sort of press, with a long lever.

"After the harvest, we put the cider apples into this. It crushes the fruit. Then the fiber comes out of the bottom. We pile up the crush into the circles."

"They're called cheeses," said Isabella proudly.

"When they get this high" — Sister Teresa held out her palm — "we wrap it in cloth, and repeat until we have a cake. Perhaps eight cheeses."

"When the cake's made —," prompted Isabella.

"We squeeze it with these bricks." She gestured to a huge brick in the shape of an old-fashioned iron. "Then we squeeze out all the juice."

But I didn't care about the apples or the juice or the squeezing. I hated how Isabella already knew the script.

Sister Teresa walked over to place her hand on one of the huge wooden barrels. "The cider is stored in these, and we leave it here in the shed for a year or more."

"Show her the bottles," Isabella said, and crunched into her apple.

I glanced at her, feeling vindicated, as if she had just trapped herself in a lie. So she *had* been there before. Maybe many times.

Why had they never invited me? I wanted to throw my squishy, sagging apple at the wall and splatter it against the bricks.

Sister Teresa went over to a wooden door on the left and it opened with a squeak. Inside were hundreds of misshapen green glass bottles along two shelves. "We only use these when we sell the cider." She smiled at me. "You may have seen them in Milan?"

I wasn't sure if it was really a question, so I gave her a noncommittal shrug.

"Can we show her the music thing?" Isabella said.

Sister Teresa smiled indulgently, a sort of child's-birthday-party smile.

From a rusty faucet in the wall, she filled three of the green bottles with small amounts of liquid, gauging each one by stooping and squinting at the water. She settled on the floor and knelt in front of the bottles. She licked her index finger and traced the tip over and over the top of the middle bottle until it began to hum. Then she brought her other index finger over the far bottle and rubbed it until the glass was warm and singing.

Isabella laughed, and Sister Teresa hushed her.

"I can't," said Isabella helplessly, tears

streaking down her cheeks.

"Quiet or you won't hear," Sister Teresa said.

Isabella wiped her eyes and crawled forward to join her, tracing circles on the lip of the third bottle until a strange chord rang in the air.

I watched them giggle, running their fingers along the mouths of the bottles. I wished with all my heart that they would both shut up.

28.

JANUARY

Term began again and the girls came back from their vacations. They were tan from skiing and plump from Christmas. They had new haircuts and new gloves, and new furs and new engagement rings. Patricia had gotten engaged to Charles, and Sylvia was now engaged to Patrick. The academy was overstuffed. Shampoo bottles bubbled stickily onto the tiles and stockings trailed over the bathtubs. Grammar books lay facedown on the floor, and pens were abandoned without their caps, and brassieres hung by pegs from the fireplace, and the place was soupy with hairspray and cigarette smoke and Chanel and face powder and damp wool. I felt strangely disoriented by the intruders in what I had begun to think of as my space. But my grumpiness soon wore off as girls stopped by my room to drop off magazines and melted packets of Junior Mints. The girls were glossy with time off studying;

brimming with stories of flirtatious ski instructors and reunions with beloved pets. Greta even gave me a Christmas gift: a pair of truly ugly gold earrings in the shape of rabbits. I was so touched I almost cried. I was happy to see everyone, except Ruth perhaps. She was fresh from her pilgrimage and particularly intolerable. She'd brought back a bag of rosaries purchased in Jerusalem and went around giving them to each of the sisters with an obsequious note. I squirmed even harder to learn she had traveled back via a one-week detour in Egypt, to visit St. Catherine's Monastery in the Sinai.

"And did you have to wear a turban?" Bunny said.

"Don't be dumb — only the men wear turbans," said Barbie. "Right, Ruth?"

Ruth simpered. "No turbans. Though, of course, I had to wrap my hair, to be modest," she said, gesturing to the collection of photos of her at various crumbling walls and dusty gates wearing a head scarf so tight she was bundled like a dowdy little grandma.

"And did you ride a camel?" Sally said, chewing a toffee so loudly each smack of her lips came with a great kiss.

"No," Ruth sniffed. "That's only for the

tourists."

As they spoke, I sat on my hands, allowing the conversation to pass above my head. I focused so intently on the rug I grew cross-eyed and woozy.

"They don't actually ride camels," Ruth continued. "Honestly, Arabia is really quite civilized. Especially Jerusalem."

My cheeks prickled. I knew from Mama's box of photos that she had spent her childhood riding a tricycle around the suburbs, eating ice cream, visiting zoos. I'd seen the evidence that she'd worn white gloves to church and had a pet dachshund and that her cousins had dressed in straw boaters for picnics. But somehow, I still harbored a slender fantasy in which one day, I would descend from the stairway of the Orient Express and slink into a welcoming gauze of dust. Where I would mount a fierce stallion and canter across a landscape of coral sand, jewels glittering on my fingers, a silk shroud rippling back to reveal my ivory-handled pistol.

"I'm going to the library," I heard myself say, standing up. No one took any notice of me. Sally and Bunny were bickering about the Mohammedan tradition of harem dancers. I left the common room as quickly as possible and went to the library, where I took a seat at the table with a slump of immediate relief. At least we were forced to be silent there. The potbellied coke heater on the right wall smelled like warm chemicals, and the stuffiness of the room was soporific and comforting. I opened my textbook.

In the new term, I was determined to prove to Elena and to Signor Patrizi that I had caught up with my studies, and to dazzle Nancy with my new skills. I would not be left behind again, stuck indoors on Saturdays. With the trip to Rome coming up, I wanted there to be no excuse for me to be excluded on account of schoolwork.

And there was a different reason. The more I thought over the night I had seen Isabella and Sister Teresa in the spa, the more I was sure I'd overreacted. When I tried to recall the details in my mind, they became hazy and clouded, like looking at something from the bottom of a tumbler. I was deeply embarrassed by my hysteria, but also protective of myself, as if there were a small wound now in my chest, a cigarette burn, that I had to defend at all costs. And the way to defend it was to be prepared. Watchful.

I took to knocking on Isabella's door after lunch, to check she was inside. And when she said she was off to the *enoteca* in La

Pentola, I let myself into the spa and slammed the door hard enough to make the chandelier shake, so if Isabella was there, she would know I was also there. And when Sister Teresa appeared, looking harried, her cap tied on at the side, I was glad.

One day after lunch when Isabella wasn't in her room as she was supposed to be, I realized she must have slipped off without telling me. I rifled through her bag and took her green notebook back to my room. I only meant to flip through it, to check for clues, scribbles, messages from Sister Teresa. But she came into my bedroom after dinner, half in tears, for her book had gone missing, and with it, all her notes. And so as she went through the common room, desperately turning over cushions and looking behind chairs, I tucked it away. And together we went from room to room, asking girls if they had seen it, and could they just check their bags anyway. And with sympathetic eyes, the girls pretended to search their bags, knowing it wasn't in there, and I pretended to wait hopefully, knowing it wasn't in there. But I told her not to worry. That she could copy from my own notes, themselves copied from Nancy's. That she could sit with me in the library, and together we would make a fresh set. I would help her, I said. She could rely on me.

29.

FEBRUARY

With the beginning of February, all we talked about was our trip to Rome. Girls pulled down books about the Vatican and the Borgheses and discussed what they would wear and speculated about how cold it would be and debated if spring would have begun by then. I was nervously thrilled about the trip, since it would be a whole week away from the academy. And the sisters didn't come with us, not even Sister Teresa. Instead, Elena and her husband, Signor Moretti, were leading the trip. It would be a proper vacation, with no one to get in between me and Isabella.

With Valentine's Day approaching, many of the girls were expecting to receive parcels from their beaus. They crowded in the staircase, bugging Donna Maria about letters twice a day. And so, while Isabella was in the bathroom, I opened her bag and slipped in my own Valentine's note. I had drawn it myself — it was a picture of a swimming pool in the shape of a heart, and I had written *Dive in* across the top. It was a reference to the day we had gone swimming in the lake, but also somehow the day we had crawled into that bathtub. It was a code between us, I decided.

As I tucked the note in her bag, I took a moment to flick through the pages of her new notebook. It was becoming a habit — flipping through whenever I had the opportunity. Just to check. And stuck in the middle was an envelope with Ralph's handwriting on it, with a card shoved halfway back into it. My pulse racing, I slid it from the paper. It had a heart on the front, and Ralph had scribbled a line drawing of the Eiffel Tower through it.

Dear Izzles, I miss you terribly. It's awful cold here and I can't wait for you to get back and keep things warm for me! I miss you babe. Happy Valentino's Day as they call it in Italy.

Love from your Ralphy.

I replaced the card inside her new notebook and sat for a moment with a strange tumbling feeling in my stomach, like my belly was a raffle drum with bits of paper churning in it.

Ralph. I had forgotten about Ralph. I mean, I hadn't *forgotten* him. He came up occasionally in conversation. Isabella had a pile of papers about the wedding, a brochure for his club, a bridal magazine she had ordered in the mail from Milan. But I had forgotten about the meaning of him. I felt a surge of gratitude to Ralph. To his bouncy brown hair and his pug nose and the robust way he always clapped me on the back. *God bless Ralph,* I thought. *God bless his stupid ring and all the stupid promises that came with it.*

When Valentine's Day came, I asked Isabella if she'd received anything, and she said, "Oh yeah, I got a note from Ralph," and then she smiled. "And yours, of course, Briddie," she added, and blew me a kiss. And never said anything more about it. But it had been a sort of test. For surely she wouldn't have mentioned Ralph so easily if Sister Teresa meant anything more to her.

I received a shiny card from Mama with a cartoon elephant holding out a box of chocolates. She'd written a distracted note inside, sending me kisses and asking if the Leaning Tower of Pisa truly leaned. I read it twice, confused. She evidently thought, for some reason, I was going to Pisa. I had a separate card from Rhona. Even the envelope was in her own handwriting, which was a good sign, because it meant Mama wouldn't have had a chance to peek in before mailing it. I had sent "Cousin" Rhona a long, self-pitying letter during a moment of depression after the New Year's fiasco, and I'd been dreading her response. I wished I could have unsent my original letter to her — I had no idea what I'd said.

Rhona had written an acerbic yet encouraging note, including bombastic quotes from Virgil annotated with actual footnotes. She said, *Quit moping, would you?* And *Why not try to learn some German?* And so on. Thankfully, I had obviously not gone into much detail about my despair. The caustic way she tried to pep up my spirits made me chuckle, and I put it with Mama's card on my bedside table.

We were leaving on the trip the next day, so we were excused from classes while everyone packed. There were lost bags and loose buttons and rips in seams and moths in the closets. Donna Maria ran around from room to room, handing out tags for our luggage, and Elena appeared to remind us we were permitted only one suitcase each.

The next day, Donna Maria woke us by walking through the corridors ringing a brass handbell. The bus had pulled up outside, its engine running white steam in the cold air. We lugged our suitcases down the academy steps, where the driver, a mustachioed man wearing a navy dinner jacket, hauled them into the luggage compartment. We stood outside the bus, patting our furs and stamping our feet and smoking cigarettes and rubbing our hands together. I looked around for any sign Sister Teresa had come to say good-bye, but she wasn't there.

We piled into the bus and I took a window seat so Isabella could sit across from Sylvia. The metal seat was icy even through my skirt, and we practiced blowing vapor into the frigid air.

The trip to Rome was to take at least five hours, so we settled in with a thermos of tea and a paper bag filled with brioche rolls. And as the bus started, we turned and waved at Donna Maria on the steps of the academy. Joan began singing "You Send Me" and we all joined in, even Ruth. As we drove down the hill we passed the train coming the other way from Switzerland, and it released a feather of smoke that shot straight into the still, cold air. As we followed the lake and drove through La Pentola and past the square and down the narrow little streets, we cried out to each other.

"Oh, that's where Sally cut her foot."

"Look, Katherine — didn't that old man try to grab a feel?"

And as the bus pulled farther away from La Pentola, we drove through winding lanes, bouncing over the uneven roadway, past tilting slate walls, through rows of plum trees, and then Nancy's voice was the only one to call out.

"There's a great farm back there," she said, pointing through a line of chestnut trees to a white building. "And there, there's a Baroque fountain; it's beautiful." And on she went, until she was no longer speaking, and we sat in silence, the tiredness ringing in our ears, and girls rested their heads on their neighbors' shoulders and dozed.

When we finally arrived in Rome, we were all cranky and saddle-sore. I had a headache, and Patricia had come down with a cold that made her sniffle every two seconds, which was infuriating to listen to. We were to be housed in a Pentilan convent, and everyone groaned as they climbed out of the coach. We'd all had enough of nuns by then. Me especially.

I looked around our surroundings without much enthusiasm. My thighs were numb and my breath was sour from all the cigarettes I had smoked on the bus. Wet snow in the roads had been churned into a gray slurry, and melting frost from the eaves of buildings dripped grimy water onto the sidewalks. The whole city smelled of burned chicory and engine oil and had the dank, cool humidity of a train station.

I was put into a narrow coffin of a room with a pipe behind the wall that ticked through the night, but in the morning it gurgled and pinged and became warm, and I squirmed around in bed until I could press my cold feet against the warm spot on the plaster. Lucky nun, I thought, who'd been allocated that room.

Our first day in Rome was a free day for exploration. Isabella and I went down to breakfast late, since I had taken my time getting dressed and putting on lipstick. We drank weak coffee in the Pentilan refectory, with crescent-shaped hazelnut pastries that had been delivered in white cardboard boxes. Along with Sylvia and Katherine, we walked to the Spanish Steps. I still hadn't shaken off my headache and wasn't in the mood to run up and down the stairs, so I took pictures with Katherine's camera while the girls posed like movie stars.

We marched through the streets arm in arm, dodging glamorous women swathed in mink, children kicking soccer balls, drips of icy water falling from window ledges.

"We're in Rome, girls!" shouted Katherine as we entered Piazza Barberini, and we cheered. A man sweeping trash on the other side of the square cheered back, then ran across, broom in hand, to jig across our path, and Katherine broke out of line to dance with him.

For lunch we drank seltzer water and ate cheese and tomato pizza, toasting each other with all manner of silly and improbable toasts: "To Modess"; "To Elena's earrings." After lunch, Katherine found a blind cat sleeping outside on the still-warm saddle of a scooter, and we stood about and stroked it until Sylvia spied a flea.

My headache was getting worse, and it now felt like there was a boiled egg pressing behind my left eye. "You know, I think I might give the Trevi Fountain a miss," I said, as Isabella stopped at a kiosk to buy cigarettes. I tried to sound bright, uncomplaining. "I can feel a headache coming on."

"Oh no, really?" Sylvia pulled off one of her gloves and pressed her hand to my forehead. She laughed. "My hands are too cold to tell if you're sick!"

"I'm fine," I said, smiling. "I have some aspirin in my room." I crossed my fingers and hoped nobody would volunteer headache pills from their own purse. Now I'd said it out loud, I desperately wanted to be lying down somewhere dark and warm.

"OK, darling." Katherine leaned in and kissed my cheek. "We'll miss you. Feel better soon."

Isabella hugged me, a lit cigarette between her teeth. I waved good-bye as cheerily as I could. As soon as I turned away from them, it was a relief to let myself wallow in the headache. I walked back to the convent feeling sluggish and miserable. Despite all the glories we'd been promised, Rome wasn't so different from Milan. There were newspapers soaking ink into the gutters, and mounds of dirty snow on street corners. Men on scooters drove over the edges of the sidewalks and called after me. I stepped into a puddle and icy, filthy water leaked through the lining of my boot and into my sock. I peered into store windows through foggy glass and watched black-haired women in turtlenecks laughing, a barber snipping a toddler's hair as his father yawned on a bench. And as I watched the warm happiness of these Italians, tucked indoors with their families, having lunch, children chasing each other under table legs, I felt keenly their coziness, and, out-doors in the cold, my own uncoziness. I wondered if there had ever been a time when I'd been indoors, sipping cocoa with Granny, or laughing with Isabella, and there had been others passing by the window, marveling at my air of easy belonging.

I arrived back at the convent, stiff and miserable with the sort of wet cold that creeps into your bones and makes your jaw ache. I took two aspirin, wiped off my lipstick, and crawled into bed to warm up. The blankets were flimsy and the mattress hard. For the first time, I wished I was back in Connecticut. I wanted to be in my own bed with a hot-water bottle. And then I would be allowed downstairs wrapped in my comforter to watch TV while Mama made chicken noodle soup.

I allowed myself a few doleful tears. I was longing for home. For snowball fights with Flora in Bloomsville Park, and browsing department stores with Granny. For Mama's Nat King Cole records, and the sound of the washing machine running, and getting into the bath, my own bath, with the ceramic fish still stuck on the tiles.

■ ■ ■ ■

The next morning I felt stiff and sickly, and it was Greta, in the end, who came to find me. She brought me the blanket from her own bed, and although I wasn't much warmer, the extra weight was reassuring. I slept, and woke later when Sally and Greta sat on the edge of the mattress, rustling paper shopping bags.

"Bridge, are you OK?"

I murmured something, but my tongue was thick and hot.

"Should we get Izzy?" Greta said, touching my forehead.

"Is she here?" I said with some effort.

Sally shot Greta a look. "Uh, no, honey. She's with Katherine and Sylvia, trying on bridesmaid dresses."

I pictured the three of them lined up on a wedding cake, adorned with swirls of fondant icing. "Oh, I didn't know." My voice sounded mournful, even to me.

Sally patted my hand. "We'll leave a note under her door."

Greta rooted around in one of her paper bags and pulled out a glass jar of fresh orange juice, which she handed to me. My wrist was floppy and weak and I struggled to hold the bottle. I drank half the orange juice in one go, thinking as the pulp stuck between my teeth that there had never been anything more delicious ever created in the world.

I slept fitfully again through the whole day, tossing with a fretful, looping dream in which I had to drive to a grocery store before it closed, only my keys were missing. The following morning, I woke as the pipe next to the bed gurgled and, carefully minding my aching bones, crept to the bathroom and lay in a hot tub until the water went chill, then filled it up again and again, not caring at all about the others. Rather, I thought of my bathroom at home, and the little ceramic fish, and felt I was somehow owed all the hot water, since my own bathroom was so far away.

Back in bed I had another hectic dream where I was eating layers of white fondant, forcing it into my mouth, where it stuck, heaving and cloying in my throat like I was swallowing gauze. I sweated and shivered in the thin convent sheets, thinking of Isabella as Sylvia's bridesmaid. Wouldn't Sylvia be worried about Katherine and Isabella as her bridesmaids? With both of them flanking her, she would look like the ugly stepsister. Perhaps this meant Isabella would have to extend the same invitation and ask Katherine to be her bridesmaid? Absurdly, I thought, I wouldn't show her up. With my thick ankles and frizzy hair, Sylvia should choose me as a bridesmaid, and I would let her shine like I was a dumpling in white crepe.

At six I made my way out of the bed, sitting on the edge of the frame for five minutes before dressing slowly, my fingers numb and clumsy. The convent bathroom had no mirror on the wall, but one of the girls had set up her makeup mirror on a wooden sideboard. In the lipstick mirror my eyes were bright, my cheeks pink. I took a seat on one of the bucket chairs in the lobby and waited for the girls to arrive and change for dinner. I stared into the distance for some time, transfixed by the velvet of a small moth on the edge of the visitors' book. The girls came bustling through the door of the convent a little before seven, bringing a great blast of icy, wet air. One by one, the girls embraced me, their cold cheeks pressed against my hot ones.

"Darling, are you feeling better?"

"We missed you today!"

"Do you want some Tylenol?"

"I have Alka-Seltzer."

"That's not going to help her!"

Isabella came in behind the others. "Briddie!" she said, waving. "Oh, you missed the Vatican! I can't believe what bad luck it is for you!"

I couldn't help it at all but began to cry right there in the lobby.

"Briddie, shit, I'm sorry — that was so tactless of me." She grimaced, putting the damp wool arm of her overcoat around my shoulders.

"It's OK," I said, snuffling and thinking it was the worst tragedy to ever befall anyone.

"Well, we can go again, can't we?" Greta slipped her arm through mine on the other side. She was looking around as if for someone to confirm with her.

"Sure we can," crooned Sally. "We'll ask Elena. I'm sure it'll be fine."

"And you didn't miss much anyway," Katherine said. "Tourists — so many tourists everywhere. Joan fell on the stairs and grazed her knee and it was wretched. And you could hardly see anything. You know — you can see everything better in the catalog."

"When we get back, we'll make it up to you," Isabella said. "Right, Sylvia?"

"Of course, darling," Sylvia said.

"Come, let's get you washed up." Isabella pulled me along the hallway to her room.

"How was the bridesmaid dress fitting?" I

said bitterly, trying not to trip on the uneven flagstones that lined the corridors.

"What?" Isabella looked surprised. "Oh." She gripped my wrist right over my pulse. "Briddie, the dresses were *divine.* Silk organza. Of course, Sylvia's not going to order it from here." She unlocked her room, turned on the spare bulb, and tossed her coat carelessly onto the floor. With a groan, she threw herself on the bed, which squeaked dangerously. She slipped her shoes off her heels and dangled them from her toes over the edge of the bed. "I'm going to write to Ralphy about that organza — it was like being wrapped in a cloud."

I blinked at her. "Will you invite Katherine?" I said.

"Hmm?" Isabella was examining her nails.

"Will you invite Katherine to be your bridesmaid, do you think?"

Isabella blinked up at me. "Briddie." She grinned. "You're a genius!" She sat up on the bed. "That's a marvelous idea. Oh, won't she scream when she finds out I've been engaged all along?" She laughed.

I was happy that she had declared me a genius; my body was strumming feverish and frosty.

"I suppose you'll be practicing together for Sylvia's wedding. You'll have to attend rehearsals and fittings and stuff."

Isabella shrugged. "I guess."

Suddenly I was desperate. "In that case —" I stopped.

"What?" She pulled her sweater over her head, and the static trailed her hair in spikes.

"Nothing."

Isabella began to unbutton her blouse. "Oh, come on, Briddie, don't tease me."

I opened my mouth again and shut it, running my hand along the door.

"You are a queer color," Isabella said. "Maybe you oughta go back to bed."

I shook my head. "It's just — I heard Katherine and Sylvia."

Isabella draped her blouse over the bed frame and pulled a woolen dress from a hanger she had slung over an icon of St. Teresa.

"I heard them — and — well, I probably shouldn't say."

That made Isabella snap back toward me. "What? Did they say something about me?"

I shook my head. "Not about you." I folded my arms under my chest. "I really shouldn't've said anything."

Isabella sat down on the bed, laying the dress over her knees. "Well, about who, then? You?"

"It's more —" I licked my lips, which were

dry and scabby. "They were being cruel, about Sister Teresa."

Isabella's head jolted. "What?"

"I don't think they knew I was there," I said hastily. "They didn't know I was listening."

"What did they say?" Isabella's voice was different, deeper. I could see the fluttering of her pulse at the top of her collarbone.

I cast about for something suitably appalling to report. "I can't repeat it," I said primly, in an ominous tone.

Isabella looked at the floor. "I can't believe it. Even Katherine?"

"Well, no, it was mostly Sylvia."

Isabella chewed on her fingernail.

"But also Katherine," I added.

Isabella stood up and pulled the dress over her head. Her jaw was set. "Those bitches. How could anyone have anything —"

"I know," I said, sagely.

She looked at me out of the corner of her eye. "Was it really bad? What they said?"

I nodded. "But — but they didn't know I was there. They'd only deny it, if you asked them." My head grew light. "They wouldn't admit to what they said about her."

She shook her head. "God, Briddie. People make me sick." She turned, and I helped draw the zipper up along the top of her dress, my hands shaking. She swept her hair away from her neck. "Not you, of course."

I laughed weakly.

She turned and faced me. "You really are an odd color. Give tonight a miss, eh? I can scoop some penne into my pocketbook."

I nodded glumly, the sore spot still throbbing in my throat.

Isabella regarded me and sighed. "Well, at least we've got each other." She was smiling, but there was a flat sort of resignation in her voice, as if she had been assigned a task.

"You always have me," I said, the blood running to my cheeks.

"Great," Isabella said, patting my cold hand. "You're a doll, Briddie."

30.

FEBRUARY

When we arrived back at the academy, I felt the same dislocation as when I'd returned from Connecticut. I stretched out on my own bed blissfully, scratching my scalp, rolling my ankles. A delayed Christmas card had arrived from Mama, along with a photograph of her, Dad, Rhona, and Granny by the fireplace at Granny's house. Underneath she had written *Ryan Family Greetings* in a looping hand. I held the photo up to the light. Rhona was wearing a velvet dress that draped in a forgiving way, and I scrutinized her figure. Was it a trick of the costume or was she truly healthier? She had certainly lost the glassy look in her eyes. The photo had caught her off guard and her mouth was poised on the brink of opening. Mama, on the other hand, had silver running through her hair I hadn't noticed before. Her expression was one of terrified relief, as if she had just swerved to miss a deer. The photo made me edgy. It wasn't fair for Mama to look so happy when I wasn't there. I slid the picture into the drawer of my nightstand.

When I went to find Isabella, she wasn't in her bedroom or in the common room. I knocked on Greta's door with the pretense of asking if she'd seen my gray gloves. Really, I wanted to be able to see out her window toward the convent, to make sure Isabella hadn't gone straight to visit Sister Teresa. I kept one eye on the window, distracted, as Greta showed me the photos of her horse Bobby had sent while we were away. When she caught me glancing toward the view, I told her I had seen a bird, an injured bird flying, and couldn't stop wondering about it.

"Oh," she cried, getting up at once and crossing to the window. She pressed her nose against the glass. "Poor thing. I don't see it. Do you?"

I joined her and pretended to look in earnest, although I was peering down into the remains of the slushy snow to see if I could trace footprints leading to the back gate. Might they have gone down to the apple store?

"What kind of bird was it?" Greta said, her breath clouding the windowpane.

"A robin, I think," I said, suddenly depressed. If only my best friend was a girl like Greta. Her face was tight with anxiety as she searched the tree line for an injured bird. And not even a real bird. How easy it was to hold her attention. How carelessly she offered her energy to me.

"If I see it, I'll tell Donna Maria," she said, the pinch in her brow deepening. I suppose she saw the strange expression on my face and thought me terribly disturbed by the little broken robin.

At once, I decided to tell her about Isabella and Sister Teresa. "Greta," I began, and my heart raced. But what would I even say? I was put out because Isabella was friends with Sister Teresa? That was ridiculous.

She was watching me. "Everything OK, Bridget?" she said in a soft voice.

"It's, well —" I recalled the image of them together, embracing. And even as I thought of it, the uneasy, squeamish, butter-churn feeling pounded in my stomach and groin. But then, what had I seen, really? Two friends lying together? Greta and Sally were always sharing beds and tickling each other. They doodled love hearts on each other's bedroom mirrors and soaped each other's hair in the bathroom. Sister Teresa and Isabella sitting on a mattress together would hardly sound worth getting worked up about.

Greta was struggling to compose her face. I recognized the deliberate settling of her expression as one of someone who is frightened and doesn't want you to know it. "Bridget," she said seriously. "What's wrong?" She took a step toward me.

I opened my mouth and shut it again. It suddenly seemed absurd to tell her what a goose I was being, and I laughed, so abruptly that Greta flinched. "Nothing at all. I was going to ask if you have any napkins, that's all."

"Oh." Greta smiled, a narrow keyhole smile that was part relief and part annoyance. "Of course." She went over to her closet and pulled out a box. "Have as many as you like," she said. I took three and hid them under my sweater.

"You're a doll," I said.

It was March, and we had two more months of lessons and lectures. With weeks ahead of us with no vacations or feast days, our final term at the academy was deliciously boring. The weather dissolved into spring, with sweet-smelling white narcissus and pale yellow primroses blooming in the meadow at the front of the academy.

Girls switched to Italian during mealtimes, calling performatively to each other across the table, thrilled with their own cleverness. We sat outside at the *enoteca,* our eyes watering from brisk wind still bitten with snow from the mountains. I lay awake at night, trying different phrases out loud, imagining scenarios where Rhona would be home from college for the weekend and she'd call me in from the next room. "I can't make sense of it," she would say, pointing to a line of Dante, her shell earrings bobbing against her black turtleneck. "Don't worry." I would laugh. "It's complicated at first." And she would frown. "Thank goodness you're around to help me."

As the weather grew warmer, the fruit trees in the orchard began to sprout tight little buds. Then the plum trees sprang into blossom. The hills around the lake were a mantle of pink and white, a flurry of pastels and silk that flew in the air and settled on the water. I had not quite realized the number of plum trees around the lake, which was silly, considering how much plum wine we drank. Only now they were illuminated was it possible to see how many fruit trees there were, tucked behind the church in La Pentola, growing from the bottom of an old well near the shrine, shrouding the hills behind Brancorsi. The petals fluttered on the breeze and collected in downy mounds in gutters, sticking to the glass of the common room windows, piling in the academy courtyard, and flitting in between the cracks in our bedroom window frames like ash from some gauzy volcano. Bees buzzed in drowsy diadems through the orchard, and buttercups blazed in the clover. I took to walking underneath a parade of plum trees at the bottom of the orchard and lying wrapped in my coverlet on the grass so I could look up at a cloud of coral and apricot and lose myself in the great cathedral of whirling sugary loveliness.

One Sunday afternoon, two weeks before Easter, I walked down to the orchard and sat under the trees, catching the odd petal in my hand. Sugar-deprived from Lent and not able to resist, I kept putting the petals to my mouth, where they were inevitably wet and plantlike between my teeth, not at all like the confectionary they promised. On the way back, I walked by the path to the spa and decided at the last moment to climb down and see if Sister Teresa was there. I'd been going there regularly, just to check.

Sometimes I met Sister Luisa smoking in the graveyard, and then I would wave to her and leave again through the railings.

But Sister Luisa was nowhere in sight, so I let myself in quietly through the back door. I crept along the corridor to John Henry's old room, but even as I approached, I could hear quiet murmuring. My heart pounded against my ribs. I bent down, tucking the blanket between my knees, and put my eye to the keyhole.

There they were.

Rosaria was lying on the bed, facedown, and Isabella was sitting on her buttocks. Isabella had a jar of lotion in her hands and she scooped out a coin of cream and rubbed it into Rosaria's naked back. The lotion melted into her skin until it glowed. Although I couldn't see much of her body, she looked so terribly naked. Isabella leaned forward, her hair falling over Rosaria's back and onto the greasy trails of cream. She made some kind of joke, and then bit her playfully on the shoulder. She paused and, wiping a gleam of spit from her mouth, leaned further and kissed Rosaria gently on the mouth.

I waited for the wave of grief to hit me, the surf to drag me under. But as I paused, willing it to come, it didn't gather. Rather, I was angry. Acid boiled at the top of my gut.

How could they be so stupid? To return to the same place where they'd already been caught? How could they be so reckless? I watched as Isabella kneaded underneath Rosaria's shoulder blade. But then I remembered — they didn't know they had been caught. They were completely ignorant. I turned away in disgust at their stupidity. I walked back down the corridor and into the ballroom. The petals flew in a scatter of sprinkles through the open door, but all the magic had gone.

They had returned to that room again, without worrying who might see them. Without even thinking about who they might hurt. Only thinking of themselves. They were *laughing.* As if this was a joke. Some kind of silly caper. They were careless. Beyond careless — reckless even. I had hardly even been *trying* and I had caught them. A sly bitterness coiled in my throat.

I waited until later in the day, when Isabella came to her room. I heard her steps on the stairs and stood deliberately in the doorway while she stretched out on her bed. I couldn't stop looking at her hands, wondering if they were still slippery from the lotion.

"How was your walk?" I said.

"Nice. It's lovely outside. You should go before it gets dark."

Of course, I thought, *she assumes I'm so meek and homely that I would've been indoors all day.* As if I needed her permission to go out and enjoy the sunshine. "And Sister Teresa? How is she?"

Isabella yawned. "Fine."

"Is she making the best of her last months of freedom?" I said bitterly. "Getting all her words out while she still can?"

But she didn't notice my tone, or else she didn't care to comment on it. She started massaging her temples. "Damn, I forgot about the reading. Who's got the book?"

"Patricia," I said. "Maybe you should go find her."

"I will," Isabella said quizzically. She brushed past me and walked down to the common room.

I put on my peacoat and went down into the courtyard and through the gate. I figured they were so stupid they probably didn't even wait to come back separately, caring so little for who noticed them together.

I didn't see her at first, so I walked up the hill toward the shrine. The day was growing colder and my nose began to run. I didn't notice the flowers or the clover or the buds on the trees, just counted my steps, to fifty and back. Until I thought enough time had passed and I could check again. I was prepared to pace and wait all afternoon if I needed to. But I didn't need to, since Sister Teresa was standing in her usual place, smoking.

"Hello," I called, walking toward her, warming my thumbs between my palms.

"Good afternoon, Bridget." She smiled. Smiled as if she was pleased to see me. As if there was no reason for her to be ashamed. The churning, coiling feeling grew thicker.

"Would you mind terribly if I had one of your smokes?" I said.

"Please." She handed me her pack and I took one, then lit it from a matchbook she'd slipped inside the packet.

"Thanks, you're a doll." I gave it back to her and sat on the step, not even looking to see where the muddy boot prints were. "Gosh, it's such a nice day."

"It is," she said.

"I went down to the orchard today, to enjoy the blossoms."

"It's very beautiful this time of year."

"Yes, quite lovely." I breathed out a lungful of smoke. "How long does the season last?"

"It depends. But not more than a few weeks."

"What a shame."

"It's more beautiful, though, because it's so temporary."

I wasn't in the mood for any of her nunnish contemplation. Her innocent platitudes about time and silence and the death of the self. I shook my head, hating myself for ever believing her, being taken in by her gentle voice and storytelling rhythm. Now I could see it for what it was. A sham. She was a fraud. An arrogant fraud who thought me so naive I would still gobble up her lies like little sugared pills.

"Mmm, how true. I was thinking, I might cut some branches and press them for Isabella's wedding. Do you suppose it would work?" I leaned back against the stone buttress and it nestled hard and cold between my shoulder blades.

"Sorry?" she said.

I glanced up at her. She was poised to laugh, ready to humor whatever silly joke I was about to make.

"Well, I thought it would be a nice gift. I could press them and frame them. Or would daylight bleach out the color?"

"The color of the blossom?" I watched the clockwork of her expression changing as she mulled over my words.

"Well, from the sun. If I frame it and give it to Isabella. I mean, as a wedding gift — wouldn't the colors have faded by November?"

She was silent. Her eyes grew watchful, but they were absently scanning the scene in front of us. I looked at it too. The muddy, threadbare grass, the thin stream of smoke from the common room chimney.

"This November?"

"Yes," I said. "I'd simply hate for it to be all ruined by the time of her wedding. What do you think?" I turned now to face her, pulling my eyebrows up in an exaggerated question.

She finally laughed, a relieved little tinkle like that of a Christmas tree ornament. "Sorry — *my* Isabella?"

I took a deep drag on the cigarette, feeling my teeth catch on my bottom lip.

"Yes," I said sweetly. "Isabella Crowley. Who else?"

She blinked, again and again, and crossed her arms in front of her chest. She squeezed her arms hard enough that the outline of her breasts pressed through her tunic.

"She's so difficult to buy for. And Ralph *does* spoil her. I mean, you've probably seen the size of that ring. You know — the one she keeps in her nightstand? I'll get her a real gift, too, but it might be nice for her to have something from the academy. Something to remember this year by, once she's gone. As a memento. For her new home, with Ralph." I knew I was overacting. I thought, *Surely she'll realize what I'm doing.* But I couldn't stop myself.

"Ralph," she said, and drew from her cigarette. But her voice was loose, as if she was trying out his name.

"Ralphy's a sweetheart," I said brightly. "And thank *goodness* he's finally let Isabella get her way with the wedding. She's been going on and on about that blasted clubhouse." I tried for a bright, chirpy laugh.

She was still staring ahead.

"But I expect you're sick of it too?" I watched her.

She turned to me. Her expression was dreadful, her lips pale. She made a noise, a mumble.

"I honestly can't take any more of it," I said. "All this silly nonsense about the wedding. But one can't exactly blame her for being excited. I mean, childhood sweethearts — it's quite romantic, really."

While I spoke, her eyelids dropped and fluttered, and she squeezed her arms harder.

"Are you all right?" I said, as if I had just

noticed her distress.

She nodded and swallowed. "I'm — I've — I've forgotten something inside. Do you mind if I go fetch it?"

"No, of course," I said, grinding out the last of my cigarette. "So sorry for keeping you."

31.

MARCH

Monday and Tuesday it rained, hard, icy rain that needled the earth into loose mud. The cold snap prompted a surprise leak in the bathroom ceiling, and everyone was sulking on account of the pans of gritty drip water in the bathtubs. But for me, it was a gift. Two days with Isabella's full attention. I entreated Donna Maria for a couple of eggs and persuaded Isabella into painting them with yellow flowers. We left them to dry on the common room mantelpiece, even though Ruth complained they weren't appropriate paschal decorations. I tried my best to distract Isabella. I plied her with cookies and wine, borrowed Nancy's radio, read aloud to her from the back catalog of *Life* magazines in Katherine's care package. But every time she stopped to chew her nails or look out the window or sigh, my gut wrenched. Was she thinking of her? Was she missing her? What would she say when she found out I'd blabbed about her engage-ment? I wrestled my disquiet into the pit of my stomach. Sure, she might be mad for a while, but she'd forgive me. After all, it was for her own good.

On Wednesday, I woke early and drank a Nescafé in the common room. The rain clouds had dispersed, and with the first rays of sun, the water in the earth rose in a mist. I sipped my coffee and flicked through a five-day-old copy of *Il Giorno,* feeling alert in the way that only early risers do. I heard soft footfalls behind me and saw Nancy rummaging in the shelves by the door. When I said good morning, she jumped and glanced her head off the top of the cup-board.

"I didn't see you in here," she said accus-ingly, as if it were my fault. She rubbed the crown of her head. "What are you doing up so early?"

I folded the paper. "The first bells woke me. I couldn't get back to sleep."

She paused, unrolling a pair of gloves. "I'm going for a walk before breakfast. Do you want to join?"

I heard myself agreeing before I had time to formulate an excuse. Nancy lent me one of her waxed jackets, and I put on Sally's walking boots. We left by the side exit, and our breath rose in waves and mingled with the swirling mist. It was a pale lemon morning, the air so cold it felt like you could crunch it. The grass was crispy with sparkling frost, and the blossoms trembled with drops of dew that caught the sunlight and quivered. As we walked down to La Pentola, I looked back. The hill at the front of the building dissolved in the mist so the academy appeared to rise from layers of foam.

Nancy and I walked through La Pentola, where birds were chirping in the market square, picking in between the cobblestones. In an open window someone was gargling water; we heard them spit and turned to each other, miming disgust. We passed out of La Pentola and walked down the winding little road that went to Prugnati and led, eventually, to Borgomanero. We stuck to the sides of the road, walking in the steep grass banks. The sudden cold after days of rain had frosted a crust over inches of slippery mud.

Eventually, Nancy gestured to a gate at the top of one of the mounds, and we walked up to it, our feet cracking through shards of ice and sinking into the earth.

"What is it?" I said.

"Look —" She pointed at the field, where

black-faced sheep nestled lambs so tiny their legs could barely hold them up.

"They're so cute!" I squealed.

Nancy wiped a drip from the bottom of her nose. "Aren't they? They're pretty much fresh out of the oven."

"Really?"

"Brand-new."

We stood and watched the lambs. I tried to coax one to come over with a branch, but although it turned its head in my direction, it was unmoved.

"Strange. Cute as they are, we're still going to chop them up and put them in a pot with rosemary," Nancy said in a deadpan way.

"Don't!" I pushed her, and the wax on her jacket crumpled where I had hit loose fabric instead of arm.

"But they don't eat them this young, do they?"

Nancy rolled her eyes. "No, Bridget," she said, louder than she needed to. "The 'lamb' in 'lamb chop' is nothing more than a figure of speech."

As we walked back to the academy, the smoke from the common room chimney puffed in a thick swirl, and I smiled, recognizing Joan's vigorous handiwork with the poker. When we came in through the side door, Nancy went to find Donna Maria, and I climbed the stairs, feeling the chill evaporating out of my hair into the warmth of the building. I was considering how I would describe my walk. I'd talk about the beautiful sunlight and the baby lambs. Or would I tell them? I wondered — surely they'd see my rosy cheeks and know I'd already been outside while they were still sleeping.

As I approached the common room, I could see there were at least six girls in the room already, huddled in the way of deliberate discussions. Patricia was wringing a dry tissue in her hands, shredding bits of paper onto the carpet.

"What's up?" I said.

"Bridget —," Joan said, getting up and coming over to me.

"What is it?" I gripped the back of the chair. My heart was already quicker from coming up the steps, but now it came in half beats. I thought, *Rhona. Rhona's dead.* And the obviousness of it overcame me and I thought, *I knew this morning — I knew — something was wrong.*

"It's Sister Teresa," Joan said. "She's missing."

32.

The last anyone had seen of Sister Teresa was three days before, on Sunday, when Bunny had met her and Isabella as they were coming back from the spa. Bunny's shoelace was undone, trailing in the mud, and Sister Teresa had pointed it out. Isabella had walked on ahead while Bunny and Sister Teresa stopped to talk.

"We spoke about walking boots," Bunny said. Her face was pale. "It was so normal. Not anything unusual at all." She looked frightened, as if the banality of the conversation was ominous in and of itself.

"We're making a timeline," said Ruth. There was a notebook open on her lap.

I wrinkled my nose. "Of what?"

"Of where we last saw her," Ruth said. She cleared her throat. "Joan said she might've seen her going into Compline on Sunday evening. But she's not sure. It may have been Sister Benedict." She looked at

Joan, and Joan nodded, her eyes downcast.

I yanked off my hat; my ears and cheeks were blazing. "No," I said. "She definitely wasn't in chapel on Sunday." I pulled my hat through my hand and seized it at the end so the fluff of the bobble rested in my fist. "I was looking for her —" The girls looked at me, then quickly among themselves.

"You're sure?" said Ruth.

"I'm certain," I said. "I'd hoped to ask her a question. About gardening."

Ruth held my gaze, pursing her lips and nodding.

I had been looking for Sister Teresa because of Isabella. I'd wanted to inspect her expression. Would she be mad? Upset? I was sure I'd know when I saw her face. But she never turned up. I'd been relieved. I thought it meant she was sulking in the convent, that she wouldn't be likely to confront Isabella straightaway.

Ruth was still scribbling. I tried to read her handwriting upside down. What was she writing? Why had I said that, about the gardening? I tried desperately to think of a gardening question, in case one of the girls quizzed me. About roots? About root vegetables?

"Is Isabella awake?" Ruth looked up from

her notebook.

On the page, I saw now, was a list of names. They weren't in any discernible order, but I could see my own name and Isabella's name near the bottom.

"I don't know," I said. "I was out." I shook my hat in my hands. It now seemed a disadvantage that I'd been out, that I was late to join the investigation.

"You've been out already?" Joan glanced toward the clock on the mantelpiece.

"Yes, me and Nancy. She's downstairs." I was happy to turn the attention over to Nancy and give me time to rouse Isabella. I took a step backward toward the door. "I should go and fetch Isabella. Tell her."

Ruth gave me a sympathetic smile. "Of course — go ahead, Bridget."

She was so clearly enjoying this. Sitting up all primly with her list and her pencil, like the official academy notary. As if I needed her dispensation to talk to my best friend. I didn't acknowledge her smile; instead I turned and went quickly down the corridor to Isabella's room. A sliver of light shone under her door, so I knocked and she said, "Yes?" in a gravelly early-morning voice.

Isabella was propped up on her pillows reading a Georgette Heyer novel. She was wearing her glasses, her hair tied up roughly at the top of her head so a few rogue strands flopped over the side of her face. She looked so silly and ruffled, I smiled despite myself.

"Hey," she said, putting her book down. "So what's all the fuss about? I've been listening to tramping and coming and going and whispering for hours. Is someone finally knocked up?"

I stepped closer to the end of the bed and wrung my hat. The muscles in my stomach clenched. Isabella was only going to get worked up. Maybe even worried. And I'd have to talk to her about Sister Teresa. I'd have to hear her talking about Sister Teresa.

"Well?"

"No, it's just —"

"Why are you dressed?" She took off her glasses and yawned.

"I was out," I said. "Anyway, listen — there's something I need to tell you."

She frowned, sliding the book onto her nightstand.

"Sister Teresa — no one can find her."

Her head tilted back, giving her a slight double chin. "What do you mean, no one can find her?"

"She's — well, she wasn't in chapel on Sunday, and no one has seen her since then." I stared at a darn in her sheets. "Do you know where she is?"

Isabella glanced at her watch. "She'll be at the laundry by now, surely?"

"So you *have* seen her?" I felt strangely triumphant, like I'd caught her in a lie.

"No, I mean, not today. But this is ridiculous." She swung her legs over the side of the bed. Pulling the tie out of her hair, she shook it down and ran her fingers through the kink it had left.

"Why?" I said. "When did you last see her?" Conflicting emotions tugged at me. I wanted Isabella to have seen Sister Teresa, because then we could all stop talking about her. But I also hoped they hadn't spoken yet. I needed more time to prepare an excuse for mentioning her engagement.

"I guess I last saw her Sunday afternoon."

An acrid sort of triumph gurgled in my stomach. I knew all about Sunday afternoon. And they were both too stupid to even know they'd been caught. "And not since then?"

Isabella shrugged. "Sometimes she's busy for a couple of days, Briddie. She has things to do, you know."

"It seems Ruth —"

"Ruth? What's she got to do with anything?" Isabella stood up and pulled her robe from behind the door. As she came closer to me I could smell the warm, musty sleepiness of her body.

"She's trying to figure out — Look, shall we go to the common room? The others know more than I do."

"But this is stupid," she said as she opened the door, tiptoeing down the corridor since the floors were cold. She minced to the edge of the common room carpet. "So, what's going on?" she said, tapping Joan on her hip until she shuffled off and gave Isabella the seat. I followed, lingering by the doorway.

"It's Sister Teresa," said Joan, talking over Ruth and winning by force of volume. "She's gone."

"What's that supposed to mean?" Isabella said irritably.

"No one has seen her since Sunday. Donna Maria said she didn't go to chapel this morning."

Donna Maria's name made things crystallize. Suddenly, it was more serious than a common room game. The back of my neck prickled. Could something truly have happened to her?

Isabella licked her lips. "Has anyone checked her room?"

"Donna Maria went. She said the bed wasn't slept in."

Isabella opened her mouth and closed it again. She started chewing her thumbnail. "But she probably just left really early?"

"Donna —"

"This is ridiculous," said Katherine, interrupting. "Let's just get Donna Maria up here and ask her ourselves."

Isabella looked at me. Then the others were looking at me.

"Me?" I said, affronted I'd been designated the errand girl. And yet, there I was, standing by the doorway.

"Would you mind?" said Ruth.

"And get Nancy, too, while you're at it," said Isabella.

"And some coffee," said Katherine. Joan laughed, and although I knew it to be a joke I shot them both a frigid look.

Nancy was talking with Donna Maria on the threadbare chairs in the lobby. From the staircase, I caught the words "Father Gavanto," "hospital." I hovered until Donna Maria noticed me and her expression shifted from concern to a tired pretense of cheerfulness. Like I was a kid, bugging them in the middle of an adult discussion to show off a finger painting.

"Do you think — the others have asked — could we check with Donna Maria about Sister Teresa? It would help, maybe, if we got everyone together," I said to Nancy, blushing and feeling ashamed of my meekness.

Nancy turned to Donna Maria and asked her in Italian, and Donna Maria nodded.

"Are the girls up in the common room?"

"Yes." I smiled weakly. "There's a sort of summit meeting going on. It would help, maybe, if we could get everyone together to answer questions."

"I suppose you're right. Good thought," she said.

And my blush faded, because now it was my idea to collect everyone together.

Donna Maria and Nancy followed me up the dingy staircase to the common room. Mary B. rose from her chair and gestured for Donna Maria to take it. Nancy stood on the other side of her.

"Thanks — oh, thank you, Bridget," Ruth said, turning to me with a grateful smile. I suppose she was smart enough to know her moment of power would only hold up for as long as we tolerated her being in charge. I went to stand by the fire even though I was already too warm dressed in Nancy's jacket.

"What does Donna Maria think?" said Isabella, looking at Nancy rather than

Donna Maria.

"Why don't you ask her yourself?" Nancy said pointedly.

"Please, Nance," Greta said softly. "None of us are as good at Italian as you. And we don't want to misunderstand something."

"Fine," Nancy said. "Donna Maria is a bit concerned."

At her name, Donna Maria tipped her face up to look at Nancy.

"She says no one has seen Sister Teresa since Sunday afternoon. She was definitely in the convent then, but she didn't come to chapel on Monday or Tuesday. And Donna Maria says she hasn't been to her room today either."

There was a moment of silence. We all looked at each other. Now that an adult, a real adult, had confirmed it, the room was bristling with nerves.

"She's really missing?" I said.

"Yes, Bridget," Ruth said with some astonishment.

I dug my fingernails into my palms. The girls were always launching inquisitions about lost earrings and mislaid fountain pens. How was I supposed to know when it was something really real? My stomach scrunched and tumbled, and an acid taste rose at the back of my throat.

"But — but maybe she's been going out early and coming back late?" Isabella asked. She had taken a pillow from the armchair and was holding it against her stomach.

Nancy shook her head. "Apparently she should've collected the garbage pails yesterday evening, but they haven't been emptied. Donna Maria says Sister Teresa would never have forgotten."

The room fell silent again as we all assimilated this.

"You don't think" — Isabella swallowed — "she could have had an accident or something? She's always walking around by herself."

I pictured Sister Teresa trapped in a pile of rubble. A part of the ceiling in the spa fallen through, and she lay crushed under the bricks. Her cap fallen off, exposing her as Rosaria. Isabella, kneeling by her side, wailing with grief. Sweat began to trickle under my collar and I edged away from the fireplace.

Nancy sighed. "Look, let's get Elena and Signor Moretti, and I'll ring Signor Patrizi. We won't get carried away."

"Signor Moretti and Elena went to Terrato for the Easter festival," said Barbie. Her face was ashen.

Nancy chewed her lip. "Well, we can get

Signor Patrizi at least."

"And we should ask the sisters," said Ruth.

"But. They. Can't. Talk," said Katherine.

"If ever there's a time to start speaking —," Sylvia was saying.

"OK," said Nancy, and since everyone just kept bickering, she said it again. "OK. I'll call Signor Patrizi, and I'll ask Donna Maria to speak to the sisters. They *can* write, you know, girls. They'd have written a note if something was up." She offered her hand to Donna Maria, who blinked at the hand and then around the room.

"And," Nancy continued as we began to talk over each other. "And someone should go to La Pentola and get Father Gavanto."

"I'll go," said Mary B. and Joan at the same time.

I looked at Isabella. She was picking at the button in the center of the cushion. I went and touched her arm. She stood but shrugged me off, keeping hold of the pillow.

"Are you OK?" I said, following as she walked back to her room.

She shut her door and threw the pillow on the bed. "I don't get it," she said. "Why has nobody noticed until now? What have they all been doing?" She ripped off her robe and dropped it on the floor and turned away from me. I averted my eyes as she pulled on a pair of jeans and grabbed her orange sweater from the chair.

"Where are you going?" I said as she unrolled a pair of woolen socks.

"To find her."

"But where?"

She whisked her coat off the peg in her closet, catching the edge of her book on the bedside table so it toppled onto the floor. "Out. Around." She leaned against the door and pulled on her boots.

"She's not at the spa. They already checked," I said.

She grabbed her red hat from under the bed. "Well, then I'll check the orchard or the shrine."

"OK." I followed her out.

She turned around. "Bridget," she said, pausing. "You're not coming."

"Oh." I felt as if she had slapped me.

"I'll be quicker by myself. I know where she goes."

"But —" I swallowed. "I can help. It might be better with two of us. What if —" Isabella was walking away, and I trotted to keep up with her. "But what if she's hurt, or bleeding or injured?" I said, not liking the way it sounded at all, since I had to almost shout as we went down the stairs.

At the bottom of the staircase Isabella

stopped and turned to me. "Bridget. Seriously. Don't come. I don't want you."

I stopped. I stood in the dark staircase and watched the door swinging.

Back in my room I sat on the bed, willing myself not to cry. I bunched my hands into fists and worked them across the threads in the coverlet. The others were calling to each other, making plans. Who was ringing whom, who was going where. Footsteps clattered on the stairs, and girls ran up and down the corridor. I heard Mary L.'s groggy voice — "What's going on?" — and Bunny whispering, "No one can find Sister Teresa."

My throat was aching. I *wanted* Sister Teresa to be gone, didn't I? Not injured or anything, but certainly away from the academy. Like maybe if she had to be in Brancorsi until the end of term. Had I wished for it too hard? Had I prayed for it, and now God was punishing me by making it true in the worst way? Isabella's anguished face sliced my insides. I pictured Sister Teresa taking my hands in hers. What if she really was in danger? And then an oozing kind of jealousy crept over my gut. Everyone was so worried about Sister Teresa, and all she did was go missing. I could easily have gone missing if I'd wanted to. She was practically being rewarded for being so careless as to go missing. I pictured Isabella's face as she snatched up her hat. If I helped find Sister Teresa, everyone would be so pleased with me. Isabella would have to be grateful then, if I was helping.

I went down the stairs and out by the side gate, but I couldn't see Isabella. I pictured her turning to me: *"I don't want you."* My eyes stung. She didn't realize how harsh she sounded, that was all. I walked up toward the shrine path, trying to spot Isabella ahead of me. I imagined finding Sister Teresa lying beside the shrine, shivering in the cold, her lips trembling. She'd fallen, twisted her ankle. She'd been lying there all night. "You found her just in time," the doctor would say. "Thank heavens you were there." Sister Teresa would take my hand over the hospital linens. "God bless you, Bridget," she would say.

I picked up my pace, hoping to catch up with Isabella. By the time I reached the top of the hill, I had to unzip Nancy's jacket and let the cold air circulate over my chest. I stumbled toward the shrine. There was nobody there. "Isabella?" I called out, walking in a circle around the shrine and looking tentatively over the edge of the hill and down toward the fruit trees below. I pictured stumbling across Isabella's body lying there. Her dark hair beneath a pile of stones. I shuddered.

I followed the hilltop toward the spring. On the other side of the spring, a row of cypress trees marked the edge of the hill, plunging down to meet a scrubby patch of woodland and the Blue Mountains beyond. To the left was a field with yet more sheep. "Isabella?" I shouted. "Sister Teresa?" My voice rolled down the hill and was swallowed by the trees. Then, after some time, I called again. "Rosaria?"

On the way down the hill, I decided that it was probably better if Father Gavanto found her so he could scold her for getting everyone worried. Everyone might even be mad at her. And this whole charade would prove just how thoughtless Sister Teresa could be. Probably she'd been in the bath this morning. Or wringing out the laundry. Or out for a walk. What a lot of fuss! Isabella might end up being annoyed at her. "What a drama queen," she would say, rolling her eyes. I took a right at the stile and walked through the pear trees on the other side to prolong my journey. Maybe, I wondered — if I stayed out long enough, someone would worry about me for a change. I pulled a branch from a tree and yanked it until it yielded, and began shredding the leaves. Donna Maria had only known Sister Teresa was missing when the garbage hadn't been emptied. What a sad reason to be discovered missing.

It started to get colder, and I became aware of a hard ache in my stomach. I pressed my hand against my belly and the ache didn't go away. An icy breeze ruffled my hair and plunged down the back of my collar. What if she'd been out in the cold all night? And now she was hurt and afraid? A lump rose into my throat. Sister Teresa had always tried to be nice to me. It wasn't her fault she was boring and weak. Hastily I took back all the terrible things I'd ever thought about her. She was a nun, after all. Surely God would protect her? My mind cycled through all the awful things that could have happened to her. Crushed under a cider barrel in the apple cellar. Or drowned in the lake, her wimple floating to the surface. Or snared in a rabbit trap in one of the fields. As I thought through each calamity, it made it safer somehow, as if cataloging all the ways she could be injured would neutralize it, make it less likely to happen. A new thought struck me: what if this was divine retribution for all those games of Dead Nun? Our punishment had been brewing all this time and now Sister Teresa was suffering on our account. My throat tightened. I made a bargain with God. The longer I took to get back to the academy, the more likely it was that Sister Teresa would be found. I would go to chapel twice a day. Isabella, too.

I began to get truly cold, my fingers stiff, my toes numb. I tucked my hair into the collar of Nancy's jacket as a kind of insulation, but I could still feel the chill stabbing at my ears. As I approached the academy building, I spotted Greta's face in her window. She waved at me, then opened the window and shouted something, but I couldn't hear. She beckoned, so I ran. They had found her! She was back! I was so relieved my whole body felt light, even as the hard ground jolted through my ankles and knees. I ran as fast as I could, holding my breasts in place with my forearms. Thank God it was over! Greta had come down to the courtyard door to wait for me, and as I ran up, she unlocked the door and stood aside.

"Anything?" she said, wrapping her cardigan tighter around her.

I closed the door, gasping. "What do you mean? Weren't you calling me?"

"No, I was just hoping —" She dropped

her eyes. She glanced back into the building toward nothing. "Father Gavanto rang the cops," she whispered. "They're in the library."

I felt dizzy. "Why'd he do that? There's no crime, is there?"

"I don't know." Greta rubbed the hem of her cardigan between her thumb and index finger. "Sally and I were wondering if maybe somebody hurt her."

"Oh God," I said, a shiver creeping over my scalp, lifting all the roots of my hair. "Like, a murder?"

Greta bit her lip, her cheeks shaking as she smothered a nervous smile. "Gosh, I'm so sorry. I know it's not funny."

"So there are clues in the library?" I looked toward the door, picturing spots of blood over the mantelpiece, a reporter taking photographs of a chalk outline. I felt the vulnerability of all of us now, as if we were naked in a field.

Greta cocked her head. "No, it's just warm in there."

"Oh." I smiled too, and we caught each other's eye.

We went back up to the common room, where the chairs and ottomans were still arranged in a rough circle. Katherine was feeding the fire, huddled under a tartan blanket. Someone had pulled a card table into the middle of the circle and it was piled with homemade cookies and Life Savers candy that girls had brought from their rooms as offerings, all our Lenten promises forsaken. Bunny made me a cup of coffee in a Girl Scouts mug and tucked a brown knitted blanket over my knees. Joan offered me a tin of Anzac cookies and I ate six, until my head was ringing with the sugar. My clothes were damp and my forehead tight. It seemed like a thousand years since Nancy and I had gone to see the lambs. I fell into something like sleep against the headrest of the armchair, jolting myself awake every so often when my chin dropped. I was aware of people coming and going, but the sounds had a hollow quality to them, as if I were at the bottom of a well. Then someone shook my shoulder, and I started. Sally was peering at me.

"Come on, sleepyhead, look sharp!"

I was groggy and grumpy, chilled and yet sticky, and felt far worse than I had first thing in the morning. My head was aching and my mouth dry. Nancy was standing by the door with Isabella. I wondered how long Isabella had been there, and why she hadn't woken me.

"Is she found?" I said.

Sally shook her head.

My tongue was so papery it was hard to speak. I reached for the cup of coffee. The mug was horribly cold, with an oily patch on the top. But I drank it all the way to the bottom, wincing and not breathing through my nose.

"OK," said Nancy, rubbing her face vigorously all over, like she was trying to rearrange her features. "Listen up —" Bunny and Barbie were muttering to each other by the window and Nancy cleared her throat. "Seriously, listen up," she said, rather desperately.

"Shut up!" Sylvia shouted over to the window, and Bunny snapped her mouth closed.

"Father Gavanto called the municipal police. They're going to do a search of the convent. But first Donna Maria has to get the sisters out. So they'll all wait here, and the cops will go in."

"What are they looking for?" asked Sylvia.

"They're just checking." Nancy reached out her hand and I watched, amazed, as Isabella took it in hers and squeezed it. "They want to search the buildings. In case of an accident."

"But we already searched," said Bunny.

"We checked all over the academy. Every room."

"Even the classrooms," Joan added.

Nancy nodded impatiently. "I know, I know. Still, they want to check."

Barbie began to cry and we all looked at her. Bunny took her by the shoulder, sympathetic tears wobbling in her own eyes.

"Also," Nancy said, "we have to stay here, in the common room."

"What? Here?"

"Why?"

"Look, it's only for a while. They'll search the convent and the academy. We have to stay here. So we don't mess anything up or confuse anyone."

"How are *we* going to confuse them?" Katherine said. "We know this place; it's our home."

"Listen. We just have to put up with it. The main thing is to find Sister Teresa. She might be absolutely fine — gone out for a hike and now resting in a villager's house." Something about her tone of voice made it clear that was Nancy's personal theory. "Or she could be hurt. We have to keep still and let them search."

Barbie sniffed. "What if she's dead?" she said, her voice breaking.

"No, no, honey. She'll be fine." Bunny

stroked her shoulder again and again; it looked too aggressive a movement to be comforting.

"But what if she isn't? What if she's been murdered? And there's some creep going to murder us all?" Barbie wailed.

"You don't think we're in danger, do you?"

"What if there's some murderer hiding out in the spa?"

"Shut up," said Isabella. She had her arms folded over her chest. She licked her lips. "She's not murdered. Don't be a fool."

Bunny glared distastefully at Isabella. "We're all spooked, Bella. Give her a break."

Nancy put her hand out again on Isabella's arm.

Isabella let out a ragged breath. "This is fucking ridiculous." She sat heavily on an ottoman and put her head in her hands. "It's fucking ridiculous," she was saying.

The girls broke into fractured conversations. Barbie was still crying, and Greta went over to pat her head while Bunny murmured into her ear. I rose stiffly from the chair and walked to Isabella. I didn't say anything. I just put my hand on her back. She glanced up at me, and her face was awful. Pinched, the corners of her lips turned down. I kept my hand there.

"Wait, wait, everyone," Katherine said,

kneeling on the seat of an armchair and peering over the back to address us. "If the cops are going in our rooms, does that mean *I* can't go in there first?"

There was some debate about this. Bunny said no, we shouldn't risk getting in trouble with the cops. Joan said we had rights as American citizens.

"It's just — I don't want a cop nosing around in my room." Uncharacteristically, Katherine blushed.

We looked among ourselves, each compiling a mental catalog of shame awaiting the Italian cops. The panties on the floor, the bras hanging over the closet door handles, saucy letters from boyfriends in the top drawers, the empty bottles of plum wine, cigarettes stubbed out in saucers of cold cream.

"Oh God." Mary B. put her hands over her face. "I've got a box of Modess on the dresser," she gasped through her fingers.

A nervous laugh broke through the room until Sylvia and Katherine were giggling and wiping their eyes.

"To hell with it," said Katherine, getting up off the chair and tiptoeing to the door. She opened it and peeked out. "I don't see anyone. I'm making a dash for it."

"Don't," said Ruth. "It might seem suspicious."

Katherine turned and stood up to her full height. "*I* didn't kidnap Sister Teresa. Did any of you gals?"

"Kitty, don't," said Bunny, looking pointedly at Barbie.

"Sorry, Barbs," Katherine said. I wondered how Barbie had ended up as the injured party. I squeezed Isabella's shoulder tighter.

"But it's not as if I'm about to go bury her body. I only want to put my dang panties away." Katherine ran down the corridor, still on the tips of her toes.

Sylvia followed her, then Sally. After a moment, Greta went too. "I'm desperate for the bathroom. Sorry, Barbie."

Ruth shook her head.

I tried to remember the state of my room that morning. It had been a tad messy, but nothing truly shameful. I'd even made the bed, I recalled with a certain smugness.

"Shit," Isabella said, her eyes snapping into focus. She stood up and, almost knocking over the ottoman, flew down the corridor to her room.

I trotted to keep up with her, my knees stiff. "What's wrong?"

Isabella glanced behind her as I came

through her bedroom door. "Oh. Bridget. Nothing. I forgot something," she said. She began rummaging through the drawer of her bedside table, then pulled open her Bible and took out a piece of lined paper. I watched her body grow lax with relief. She lifted up the corner of her mattress by her pillow but then let it drop.

"What did you forget?" I said. I could hear the whine in my voice. What was on that paper? Since when did she keep her Bible in her nightstand anyway?

"Bridget." She looked over her shoulder. "Why are you just standing there?"

"Um —"

"Grab my chloroquine pills," she said, tipping envelopes and notepads and pamphlets from her desk drawer onto the tiles.

"Bridget!"

I fetched the pills from her closet and held the bottle out to her.

"Take this" — she shoved a box of aspirin at me — "and switch them."

"What?"

"Sit there and switch the damn pills, will you?" She gestured to her chair.

I sat down, unscrewed the lid of the bottle, and tipped her pills onto my lap. I poured the aspirin into the bottle, then put the pills in the aspirin packet. I brushed the crushed powder from Nancy's jacket. Over my shoulder I saw Isabella pulling a sheaf of pale blue paper from behind her mirror, folding it in half, and stuffing it in the waistband of her jeans.

"What do you want to do with them?" I held out the packet and the bottle.

She yanked the packet from me and threw it in her brown purse at the end of the bed.

"Leave that wherever," she said, turning around and adjusting the mirror. I tucked the bottle under a pair of stockings in the top drawer of her dresser. She caught my eye in the reflection. "Don't you have anything you need to sort out?" she said meaningfully.

My mouth was dry. "Not really."

"No love letters of your own, huh?" There was a cruel slant to her voice. "No trinkets stashed away?"

"I have fifty dollars in Rhona's fur," I said, knowing that wasn't what she meant.

There were voices on the stairs — Donna Maria and the low baritone of a man coughing.

"Damn," she said. "Come on."

We waited by the door until Donna Maria went into the common room, then crept out and back the other way around the corridor, into the bathroom. Isabella pulled the chains on two of the toilets. I stood watching her, confused. I thought perhaps she was going to flush the notes.

"Jesus, Bridget. What's wrong with you?" She ran the faucet over her hands and pushed past me, opening the bathroom door with a loud bang. I followed her down the corridor to the common room. There were two men there, both quite old and ropy-looking.

They nodded at us.

Nancy frowned. "Where were you?"

"Restroom," Isabella said, shaking her wet hands and gesturing down the corridor, where it was possible to hear the last of the water in the toilet draining away.

Nancy sighed. "You can't leave the room anymore. No more bathroom trips, OK? For at least an hour. You'll have to hold it."

We nodded dutifully. Isabella slipped through the doorway and crouched by the fire. She began tearing up pieces of newspaper and twisting them into little ribbons. I couldn't believe the nerve of her. She was going to burn her love tokens now, right in front of the cops.

I took a seat in one of the chairs and watched Isabella ripping and tucking, poking scraps into the fire. I tried not to think about what was on the papers, about the kind of notes they sent each other. Maybe some of them were about me. Maybe that was why she was burning them now — to make sure I never saw them. Isabella's hair was still frizzed from the pillow, and it needed to be combed. Her sweater was bunched up at her wrist, where it had snagged on itself.

Isabella caught my eye, and my face must have been strange, for she gave me a queer look. As if we were speaking two different languages at the same time. I couldn't tell what she was thinking. She had a sort of restless, hungry expression. I looked away, back at the detectives.

They were still conferring with Nancy, nodding and pointing out the window toward the convent. I tried to focus on their conversation, but the harder I listened, the more it slid into nonsense. The two cops were speaking in an odd sort of Italian, chewing on the words, adding breathy sounds between syllables so I could hear Nancy's accent contextualized against theirs.

Father Gavanto's head appeared at the top of the stairwell and both of the cops started fidgeting in the loose way that indicated they were ready to leave, jingling change in their pockets. The older man patted Nancy on the arm and must have complimented her, because her concentrated expression broke and she smiled self-consciously. Both cops stepped out into the corridor and pulled the door closed behind them. We heard the scratch of metal on wood, then a key turning in the common room door.

Nancy covered her face and groaned.

"You OK, Nance?"

"Did they lock us in?"

"Come have a cup of coffee."

Nancy went to sit by Sally, rubbing her neck. Her eyes were small and puffy, as if she'd just woken from a nap. She rummaged in the tin for a cookie.

"They won't forget about us, will they?" Sally giggled, although there was a tightness in her voice.

No one answered. We were conspicuously waiting for Nancy to be ready to tell us what was happening. Patricia brought out a pack of cigarettes and we passed it freely among ourselves, muttering thanks to Patricia.

"What happens now?" said Katherine.

"Well." Nancy sighed, leaning back. "Those two cops are from Brancorsi. I guess we couldn't get the state police yet. They have to do paperwork and stuff first. They'll go and check out the academy, the convent, Sister Teresa's room."

"So where are the sisters?" said Mary B.

Nancy took a bite of the cookie. "Donna Maria went to get them. They're in the refectory."

There was something ominous about the idea of all the sisters gathered up in the refectory, corralled like animals.

"And when do the cops come back?" Greta said, looking reflexively in the direction of the convent.

Nancy shrugged. "I don't know. Father Gavanto called for a doctor to come too, as a precaution." She put the rest of the cookie on the table. "Ruth, can I borrow your notebook?"

Ruth handed it over and searched in the cushions for a pen.

"Thanks." Nancy opened it and, propping it awkwardly against her knees, began scribbling. We watched her writing, waited for her to finish and tell us more details. But her pen kept scratching away. So eventually we started whispering among ourselves, then murmuring; then girls were hanging out of the window to see if they could spot anything, and other girls were shouting for the window to be closed because it was freezing.

Isabella sat by the fire, feeding it scraps of newspaper and letting them curl in flashes of green. I went to sit next to her.

"Sorry I yelled at you," she said in a hollow voice, gazing into the back of the fireplace.

"It's OK." I paused, not knowing what else to say. She must not realize I knew about Sister Teresa, or else she wouldn't have tried to distract me with her pills. I wondered if I should pull her aside, tell her I'd found out. But the situation had slipped away from me. The focus was no longer on me, betrayed by lying, sneaking Isabella. Now Sister Teresa was lost, maybe hurt, maybe dead. I imagined Isabella's disgust: "You think I care about *your* feelings right now?" *If only,* I thought, *if only I* had *pushed the door open on them in the spa.* Isabella would have had to chase after me, apologize. Now Sister Teresa was the victim. And we all had to be sorry. I heard the liquid sound of Isabella swallowing.

"I don't know what to do," she said, her voice shaking. She turned her face to me and tears were rolling over her cheeks, landing on the wooden floorboards with an audible tap.

"Oh." I leaned on my knees and reached to hug her. She pushed her head into my neck and her tears ran down into the collar of my sweater. "It's OK. They'll find her.

Don't worry. She can't have gone far." I said boring, soothing things like that until she sniffed and pulled back, rubbing her face.

"Do you really think she's OK?" she said. Her expression was so vulnerable, a pull of pain yanked at the bottom of my heart. I wished there was anything in the world I could do to make that look on her face go away. I hugged her to me again, harder.

"Yes." I tucked her hair behind her ear, although it didn't need tucking. "I'm sure she'll be fine. You worrying isn't going to help."

"I guess." Isabella looked back toward the fire. I was disappointed her attention had slipped from me already. "I just have this feeling something's wrong. It doesn't seem like her, does it?" She looked at me, imploring. I realized now she was inviting me to comfort her. Who else did she have to talk to about Sister Teresa?

"Well, she's very independent," I said.

Isabella nodded.

"And she does go for lots of hikes."

"That's true." Isabella smiled a sad, tight-lipped smile. Her eyes moved over my face, looking from mouth to cheek, and her wet lashes flickered.

"And she's good with plants, isn't she?"

Isabella laughed weakly.

"So, if she got stuck out walking, she'd find herbs or berries; she'd know which plants to eat." Isabella rested her head on my shoulder, and so I carried on. "And she'll have matches on her. So she'd be able to light a fire. Keep nice and warm."

"That's true," Isabella said, delighted, lifting her head. A lock of her hair caught in the teeth of Nancy's jacket.

I congratulated myself on having thought of that fact, which, now said out loud, made me feel better, too. I nodded as if the idea had come to me hours ago. "Uh-huh," I said, "so she can make a fire and send out a smoke signal, too — so we can find her."

Isabella searched out my hand and squeezed it. I let our fingers interlace and took a deep breath. I rubbed my fingers over the tips of hers.

"And she has those heavy boots. Good for walking," I said. "And those habits look nice and warm."

"Yes," Isabella said. "They are. There's three layers to them."

I paused for a moment, letting the skewer pass through me. How could she know how many layers they had? I forced myself to keep talking.

"And she's the speaking nun. So she won't be shy about calling out."

"Gosh, yeah." I felt the movement on her brow as Isabella frowned. "What do you suppose the others would do? If they fell over and broke their leg? Just lay there quietly?"

"I don't know," I said. "Sister Teresa — didn't she say the silence was a choice? That they choose it — you know, even after the Holy Father lifted the rule."

Isabella looked up, her frown still in place. "Did she say that?"

"Yes, one time, when we were in the garden. Remember?"

Isabella's face twitched; then she sighed. "I don't remember." She bunched her sweater into her fists.

"Oh!" Nancy stood from the chair, the notebook slipping halfway down her thigh so she fumbled to catch it. There was the distinct clunk of a key turning in the lock, and the door opened to Donna Maria's face.

We all cheered to see her, as if she'd been gone for days instead of hours. Isabella let go of my hand and swiveled around on her knees to face the door.

"Nancy —" Donna Maria gestured to her.

Nancy walked to the doorway, tucking the notebook under her arm.

We looked between each other.

Isabella sat back on her heels. "I feel sick,"

she said, more to herself than to me. I felt queasy too, with a sudden rise of pressure to my head.

Nancy and Donna Maria whispered, and Nancy was nodding seriously. I watched her, a loop of hair caught in her earring. Absently I thought, the accidental authority she'd acquired over the course of the day would never wear off. We were bound to think of her differently from now on, defer to her, wait for her to leave Mass first, to stand dumbly next to her while she haggled on our behalf in the market. I wondered if it would make her more popular or more aloof. We'd start keeping our jokes clean around her, not let her see us copying from each other's exercise books. She'd be more like a teacher now than a classmate. Poor Nancy. She was too straight for her own good.

Nancy closed the door enough to obscure her face, so the notebook jostling up and down was all we could see. Then the door was shut completely, and Sylvia said, "Shh," and we all kept quiet, to hear footsteps traveling down the stairs.

There was a horrible silence.

"You don't think they found something?" said Bunny.

Isabella put her head forward, clutching

her stomach.

"You're OK?"

She sat up, slowly. "I think I'm going to throw up."

I knelt into a half crouch. "Shall we go to the restroom?"

She shook her head, but her lips were gray and her forehead gleamed with sweat.

I ran to the garbage pail and turned it over, tipping out the crumpled tissues and cigarette packets onto the floorboards. "Let's go to the restroom —"

As she stood, I put my arm under her elbow, holding the garbage pail within a strategic distance.

Then Nancy's voice came up the stairs. "Still there?" she yelled.

"We're here," said Katherine, too loudly.

Nancy stood in the doorway, catching her breath. I grabbed Isabella's arm.

"So. Here's the deal," she said. "They checked the place. Sister Teresa's not missing. She ran away."

33.

MARCH

"What do you mean, she's run away?"

"She did what?"

"No!"

The girls were out of their chairs, standing on the furniture. Bunny stopped crying. In moments it had gone from tragedy to scandal. Isabella's eyes were glassy.

"Excuse me, coming through," I said, loud as I could over the clamor. I barged Joan out of the way and rushed down the corridor with Isabella clutching my side.

I pushed open the restroom door and Isabella dashed into the bathroom. I stood by the door, holding the pail in front of my knees.

"Shall I get you some water?" I said.

Isabella didn't reply. I put the pail down and went into my room anyway. It was exactly the way I'd left it that morning. The bed was made and one stray gray glove lay on the coverlet. It didn't look like anyone had been through my stuff. I unzipped my suitcase to check on Isabella's notebook. It was there. The fifty-dollar bill was still in the pocket of Rhona's fur. I wasn't interesting enough to have any other secrets.

I took a glass from the dresser; it had a dried residue at the bottom that could have been cola or wine. I couldn't remember what I had last used it for. I sat on the unsteady springs. Run away? Disappointment wasn't the right emotion, but it was close — it was almost anticlimactic. She wasn't dead — that was a relief. She'd run away. On purpose. From us. From all of us.

And then I realized. I stared at the empty glass with its sticky purple rim.

She ran away because of me.

Who had even seen her, after me? I turned the glass over in my hands. She wasn't at supper on Sunday, and no one had seen her the following day.

The blood drained from my head and pooled in my stomach. I thought suddenly I might faint. I slithered off the bed and leaned back over it, pressing my forehead into the mouth of the cup.

She hadn't gone missing. She had run away. Because of me. I pulled the glass from my skin and it peeled off with a sucking sound. A thrill squirmed down my spine and lodged at the tops of my thighs. I caused this. Not just by hoping or praying or wishing. But by doing. My skull felt empty, my fingers prickling. It was all my fault. That expression on Isabella's face, her shaking hands — I had caused that. A stab of pain jabbed under my ribs so hard I flinched. "Oh God," I said, so loud I startled myself. A drop of sweat trickled between my breasts. I had caused the cops to come. A police investigation! I sat up, reeling, strangely in awe at my own power, as if I'd be suddenly able to lift furniture with my mind. I squeezed my eyes shut and prayed for God to understand. I didn't *make* her run away. She was a nun! God should be angry at Sister Teresa, not at me. And then my eyes flashed open. What if Isabella found out?

Sweating, weak-kneed, I stumbled down the corridor to the common room, where Bunny and Barbie and Ruth were still talking.

"Where are the others?" I said.

"Gone to see if there's any food."

"Can you tell me what happened?" I directed the question at Ruth, knowing she would be the most desperate to spill the details.

"Well." She took a great breath, like she

435

was about to do the breaststroke. "The cops go in her room. And it's all tidy. They search around. Turns out her coat is gone, and clothes and her Bible."

"Was there a note?" Isabella's voice came from behind us. She looked awful. The capillaries around her eyes had burst, marking her brow with scarlet stars. I put my hand out to touch her and realized I was still holding the glass.

"No," said Ruth. "But here's the thing. Her papers are gone from Donna Maria's desk."

"What?"

"Her travel papers," Ruth said. "They're gone too."

Isabella made a sound, a whine mixed with a cough. We all stared at her. She covered her face. "She can't be gone," she said, pulling her hands away. "There has to be a mistake."

"Father said so," Ruth said, her tone chastened. She looked from Isabella to me, as if I was going to account for her distress.

Isabella turned and walked down the corridor toward her room. Even from behind I could see her shoulders working. I stepped toward her and heard her crying, in a wail, like the whistle on a boat.

"Isabella?" I said.

But she went into her room and closed the door. I could hear the muffled sound of her crying into something soft. My eyes were stinging.

"Is she all right?" Ruth was standing against the window, her arms folded.

I was shaken by Isabella's grief. My heart was rattling around in my body. "They're friends. They were friends." I swallowed. "I suppose she's worried."

Ruth looked skeptical. "You'd think she'd be relieved. Surely, run away is better than dead?" Her mouth twisted to one side and I followed the line of her lip. Quite clearly, the voice in my own head said, *Bitch,* and it was so loud and certain that for a second I thought Ruth must have heard it.

"She's made her choice. And now she has to live with it. If you ask me, it's selfish of her," Ruth said.

"What?"

"A vow is for life. For more than life; it's for eternity," she said, rather priggishly. I realized she was talking about Sister Teresa, not Isabella, and my anger throbbed and pulled back.

"You don't feel sorry for her?" I said, making my face solemn.

"No, I don't," she said, tipping her chin up. "It's extremely serious. She absconded

on her vows — she can't ever come back.
Her very soul is in danger." Ruth rubbed
the cross around her neck.

I didn't care to hear much about Sister
Teresa's soul. "She can't ever come back?" I
said. Then I wondered if I had misstepped;
perhaps I should have asked about her soul.
Isn't that what a real person would do?
Worry about her salvation?

"No," Ruth said, her eyelids fluttering.
"Not ever. When you renounce your vows,
you can never return to the order."

"Never?"

Ruth shook her head. "Not ever."

After Ruth went back to the common room,
I put my head against the wood of Isabella's
door, not sure even what I was listening for.
I tried to open the door, but she had locked
it. I looked through the keyhole and could
just about make out her shape on the bed,
the sad flutter of her wheezing breath.

I went back to my own room and put the
glass back on the bedside table. I pulled off
Nancy's jacket and then all the rest of my
clothes. I climbed under the blanket and,
within moments, fell into a numb half sleep,
dreaming that someone was knocking on
my door, over and over.

When I woke it was light, and I sat up,

not knowing where I was. I could see the shapes of the beams, the furniture, but I couldn't make any sense of them, thinking for a few moments I must have stayed at Flora's house. Then I remembered and pulled the comforter back over my body. The room was cold, but under the blankets I was warm and damp with sweat. The chapel bell tolled. I lay still for what seemed like hours after that, perfectly still, and I thought over everything. Sister Teresa was really gone, and she really couldn't come back. Now they knew she left of her own choice, the cops would go back to Brancorsi, and we'd all go back to normal. It must happen all the time, a sister deciding to leave. Father Gavanto would choose a new speaking liaison. My heart raced, a dry tapping against my ribs.

I would have Isabella to myself again.

The faint smell of coffee floated under the door and I sniffed it eagerly. I climbed stiffly out of bed; my calves and knees were aching. Wrapping my bathrobe around me, I went to the common room. Katherine had lit the fire and was knitting a snood from pale yellow wool. Next to her on the floorboards was a cup of coffee.

"Hi," I said, my voice frayed with sleep.

She smiled at me over her shoulder.

"Couldn't sleep?"

I shook my head, although it wasn't true.

"Me neither." She looked back at the fire. "I keep thinking about Sister Teresa out there."

I went to sit by her. "I'm sure she knows what she's doing."

She smiled weakly. "I guess. Though as soon as it was light, I went walking around, unlocking all the doors. I keep thinking — what if she tries to come home and the door is locked . . ." She trailed off.

"But she can't, can she? Come back?"

"That's what Nancy said."

We sat in silence while the wood popped.

"Seems cruel, doesn't it?" she asked. But before I could answer, she seemed to change her mind. "She must be brave, though. To leave it all behind, her whole life. She must have been planning it for months."

"Yeah," I said, although an uneasy, slithery feeling was crawling in my gut. What would happen when the cops went through her cell and realized she wasn't planning for months? Wouldn't they ask questions about it? Wouldn't they want to know why she'd split? I had the image of Sister Teresa being brought back to the convent under the flashing lights of a police escort. Would they make her confess? My stomach scrunched.

Would she be forced to tell about Isabella? I squeezed my nails into my palms.

"Morning," said Nancy. She was standing in the doorway, her jeans spotted with mud.

"Have you heard anything?" Katherine said, half rising out of her chair.

Nancy shook her head. "The officers will be asking questions."

My pulse picked up.

"Questions about what?" Katherine frowned.

I cleared my throat. "Nance," I said deliberately. "I still have your jacket. Will you please come with me so I can give it back to you?"

Nancy looked startled. "Sure."

In my room I climbed onto the left bed while she took the wicker chair. I lit a cigarette and offered her the pack. She shook her head without even looking at it.

"Nance, I'm sorry. This has been crummy for you."

She rubbed her eyebrows with the back of her sleeve. "I'm not the one in trouble."

For a moment I thought she meant me, and my vision squeezed. Nancy took off one of her earrings and massaged the lobe.

"So, the police, what kind of questions —," I began, but Isabella's elbow knock came at the door and I shut my mouth.

Isabella was wrapped in a blanket over the same orange sweater from the day before. Her eyes were swollen and her nose pink. "Oh. Nancy, hi," she said.

I shuffled over on the bed and patted it. She came and sat down next to me. Her hair was greasy at the roots.

"Are you OK?" I said, reaching over to hug her with one arm.

She blinked. "I couldn't sleep."

I offered her the cigarette, and she took a pull and handed it back to me.

Nancy rose from the chair with a groan and sat on the other side of Isabella, the bed lurching. She put her arm round Isabella, underneath mine. "Yesterday was horrible. I know. But at least you don't have to worry anymore."

"What?" Isabella stood up. She took a step away from us. "Of course I'm worried. She's *gone missing*. Who knows what might've happened to her? She *disappeared* in the middle of the night!"

Nancy froze. "Izzy —," she started.

I stabbed out the cigarette in an espresso cup.

"Something awful has happened, I know it." Isabella clutched the blanket tighter in front of her chest. "She wouldn't leave like that, there's no way. I've been thinking about it. And I'm sure something happened to her. I think —" She pointed in the direction of the convent. "I think someone came in and took her. And they took her stuff, too, so it would look like she left deliberately. And that's why there's no note — because some stranger came and took her away, and they couldn't leave a note because that's how we'd know it wasn't her and it wasn't in her handwriting." Her words came quickly; then she began crying and rubbed the sides of her face roughly with the blanket.

Nancy took a deep breath and glanced quickly at me. It was the same worried, collusive look as the one from Granny, in the hospital. I felt like I might cry myself, I was so exhausted by being implicated by that tired, responsible look.

"Izzy." Nancy stood up and took a step toward her.

Isabella flinched away before she had a chance to touch her.

Nancy let her hand drop. "I'm sorry you're so upset. But —" Nancy looked at me and I deliberately kept my eyes blank. "There's no doubt Sister Teresa left of her own accord. The boat — the rowboat? It's missing too. She was the only one with the key to the padlock on the gate. Other than

Donna Maria. But, look — clearly, she decided to go out and live her own life. Be independent. Can't say I blame her either," Nancy said.

"No," said Isabella, sobbing in hard, wet fractures. "She wouldn't've gone, not without saying good-bye."

Nancy softened, putting her hand gently on Isabella's shoulder. "Maybe she thought we might tell the father? But what's important is that this was her decision. She'll be OK. And she's very smart, and she'll take care of herself."

Isabella gripped the blanket. "But why wouldn't they just *check*?"

Nancy grimaced. "Um, well, now we know there's no crime — I doubt the cops are going to pursue this. Her."

"Why not?" Isabella stared fiercely at Nancy. Then at me, and back at Nancy. "She's all by herself. She could be in trouble!"

"Honestly, because —" Nancy looked at me again.

"*I* don't know," I said defensively.

"Because she's not a high priority, Izzy."

"*You* mean, because she's black," Isabella said, taking a step back again, so she was pressed against the window. "That's what you mean, isn't it? Because she's black, so nobody cares."

Nancy opened her mouth.

"Nobody cares," Isabella said, her voice dropping. "Nobody cares. Except for me."

"Look, that's not fair," Nancy said, her mouth twitching. Isabella's face was pinched with disgust. "She's not a fugitive from the law, Izzy. She's an adult."

"Ugh." Isabella wrenched herself away from Nancy. The edge of her blanket knocked over the glass from my bedside table so it rolled and dropped onto the bed, and Rhona's Valentine's Day card fell onto its face.

"It's disgusting. This is — this is — prejudice. This is *disgusting.*" She strode out of the room, her blanket billowing behind her like a cape, making the dramatic exit slightly comical.

Nancy groaned and rubbed her face. "You know that's not what I meant," she said to me. "Why *would* they go looking for her? She doesn't want to be here."

"I know. Listen, I'll deal with her," I said as I went after Isabella.

I approached Isabella's door and pushed against it, but it was locked.

"Isabella?" I said, knocking on the wood. "It's me."

"Go away!" she yelled. "I can't bear to

talk to any of you." The pitch of her voice was verging on hysterical, and it irked me. I chewed the inside of my mouth.

"Fine," I said, as obligingly as I could manage. "Come and find me when you're ready to calm down."

When I went down to breakfast, there were a few bleary-eyed faces. No one had put on makeup or pinned up their hair. To my surprise, the two cops and Father Gavanto were sitting at the end of the table, their hats lying next to their plates. I squeezed in beside Katherine and Greta, and we ate three rolls each, cramming them into our mouths, pressing our shoulders into each other in mute solidarity.

Father Gavanto came behind us. "Ladies," he said, dipping his head. Then in Italian, he said they would be waiting in the library to interview us in turn.

We nodded, and then, as they walked away, looked between each other.

"Oh jeez, what now?" said Katherine. I started laughing — I couldn't help it — and Greta caught the giggles bad and choked on a mouthful of bread so we had to tap her on the back while she coughed, her eyes streaming.

Katherine went first. Greta and I stood by

the door into the courtyard smoking.

After the library door closed, Greta sighed. Finally she said, "Do you think they'll let me call Bobby?"

"Whyever not?"

"It's just" — Greta grimaced — "this is so bad of me. His dog, Buster, is really sick. I want to see if he's all right. Is that terrible of me?"

I shook my head at her, not understanding.

"To care about a dog with cancer when" — she waved her cigarette — "all this is going on? But Buster was sick before Sister Teresa left, so —" She wrinkled up her nose as if she were balancing the two incidents on a scale.

I understood then how little Greta cared about Sister Teresa; it was a disconcerting itch at the back of my ribs. It made me envious of her and feel distanced from her, too.

"I'm sure they'll let you," I said. "Try at lunch."

Greta let out a breath. "OK."

When Katherine came out of the library, she crept over to us and asked for a cigarette.

"Well?" Greta whispered.

"They want to see if there's any funny business going on."

My skin flared hot and cold at the same time. "Like what?"

Katherine shrugged. "Search me. Nancy's there, though, and Donna Maria. It's not so bad."

"Jeez." Greta jiggled another cigarette out of her pack. "It's like I'm back in high school, getting in trouble for skipping lacrosse."

Katherine pointed her cigarette at Greta and laughed. "Exactly! I kept waiting to have my hall pass revoked."

Greta grimaced at me. "Who should go next?"

"It's OK, I'll go," I said, desperate to get it over with. I pressed my fingernails into my palms. What if they could tell it was my fault? The dread was so hard in my stomach it was like I had gobbled down a sack of marbles.

I knocked on the door, and Father Gavanto's voice called out, *"Entra."*

Two of the tables had been pulled into the center of the room, and the stove was blazing. Nancy and Donna Maria were sitting on the left side of the table. Nancy's hair was escaping from her bun and her shirt was stained with drops of coffee. Donna Maria had put on a blue blouse I had never seen before and had tied a long navy scarf around her neck. The idea she'd made an effort to look nice for such a macabre occasion was heartbreaking.

On the far side of the table were the two detectives, their shirtsleeves rolled up. The younger man had strangely hairless fore-arms. Father Gavanto was sitting on the right, and there were two chairs by the door.

I took a seat.

Father Gavanto cleared his throat. "Bridget Ryan," he said, and one of the cops looked down a list of names and crossed mine off.

The cops introduced themselves. The younger was Vigile Roberto and the older man Vigile Mario.

"What's this about?" I said, turning to Nancy. My mouth was dry.

"They want to get a sense of why Sister Teresa left. To make sure she wasn't under pressure," Nancy said.

"Do they know something? Has something happened?"

She translated my question. The cops began smiling even before Nancy had fin-ished speaking.

Vigile Mario said, "No crime. Don't worry," and shrugged as if it were a joke I didn't understand.

Then Father Gavanto said, "The agents

will check why the sister left."

"Sister Teresa?" I asked.

"Of course," Father Gavanto said, bemused.

"Father Gavanto is helping us," Vigile Roberto said.

The father gave him a bow of the head.

Then I understood. This was all for the benefit of the cops. Imagine how it must look to have a runaway sister. Father Gavanto couldn't risk any scent of a convent scandal getting back to the families of prospective academy girls. Mrs. Fortescue must be frothing at the mouth. I looked again at the way Father Gavanto's hands were neatly folded over the table. I felt sorry for him.

The detectives began speaking to Nancy. I waited, glancing politely between them.

Nancy cleared her throat. "They are asking if Sister Teresa ever discussed being unhappy with the academy, and if she ever discussed her plans to leave. They want me to reassure you that everything you say in here is confidential. I've been sworn to silence." She gave me her best attempt at a smile.

I licked my lips. "Should I tell them?" I gestured toward the cops. "Or?"

"You can say it to me. I'll translate."

"I often spoke to Sister Teresa," I said. Nancy nodded. "Occasionally we spent time in the garden together." I pressed my thumbs into the groove in the wooden table, simply to keep them occupied. I worked the tips of my thumbs back and forward over the lip in the wood. "She is very smart and kind," I said. I felt a surge of tearfulness and swallowed against it.

Nancy nodded patiently.

I licked my lips again. "But —" I paused, working my thumbs back into the groove.

Nancy stopped translating and stared at me, surprised. "Go on."

"She has family here, in Italy. I don't know if the officers —" I looked at them, and they turned to Nancy, their eyes expectant.

"Family?" Nancy said. Vigile Roberto began to ask her something, but she raised her hand to indicate that he should wait. I was shocked by the casualness of the gesture, her total confidence. He glared at me as if I'd encouraged her impertinence.

"Yes," I said, looking between Nancy and the cops. "Her father. Her dad — he lives in the south, she told me."

The cops asked Nancy questions. Her answers went on for a great deal longer than I'd expected. Vigile Roberto was making

451

notes in a book; then he addressed Father Gavanto, who spoke to Nancy; then Donna Maria was speaking.

I focused on a crack in the top of the table where the light was pooling.

"Bridget," Nancy said. I could feel all their eyes on me. "Did she say where her father lived? Anything about going to see him or reconnecting with him?"

"She said he was in the south," I said, trying to recall the details. Bari popped into my head, but I couldn't remember if she'd mentioned it or if I had made an independent connection. "Maybe Bari?" I said. "But I'm not sure."

Vigile Mario asked Nancy another question.

"What does he do for a living? Work in a fishing boat?" she said.

"I really don't know." I said. Then I realized why they automatically assumed he would work on a boat. "But he wasn't — He's not from Africa; he's Italian."

"An Italian citizen?" Nancy asked.

I nodded.

She translated again, then asked, "Was he a soldier?"

"I don't know," I said.

After a minute of conferring, Nancy said, "What were you discussing, when her father came up? Maybe her father is taking her back to Africa?"

"No," I said. "Her father isn't African; that's what I'm saying. He's Italian. He lives here, in Italy. We were speaking about it because she's mixed." Nancy's eyes were focused on mine. I felt myself blush to the roots of my hair. "I really don't know anything about his profession."

Nancy translated for the cops. My heart lurched against the front of my body.

"They weren't aware of that, apparently," Nancy said. "I suppose it's in her papers, but — are you absolutely sure?"

"I'm sure."

"Maybe she meant —"

"Look, I'm sure." My chest squeezed, and a thrill of adrenaline curdled in the drum of my stomach. I cleared my throat. "I'm sure. Because I'm mixed too. That's why she told me."

Nancy opened her mouth, blinked, shut it again.

I swallowed. "I am also of mixed heritage, and we discussed it often. I was of the understanding that her Italian father lives in the south and she wished to see him."

"Right," said Nancy. "Right." She blinked down at the table. And then back at me. "Right."

"My mother is also from Africa," I said, releasing my thumbs from the groove in the table. A strange calm had settled over me. "And so Sister Teresa and I had a special connection. That is why . . ." I sat up straight. "That is why I can reassure the officers they don't need to waste any resources searching for Sister Teresa or bringing her back."

Nancy took a long drink from her glass of water and then turned to the detectives. Their heads snapped to me. I kept my posture straight as the two officers began a deliberate, evaluative look over my face, my figure. Nancy's cheeks were flushed, her eyes fixed on the corner of the room. Donna Maria frowned, her face focused on mine.

After an exchange of queries, Nancy turned toward me but didn't catch my eye. "They have questions," she said in a tight voice. "But they're not exactly relevant." She took another sip of water.

I let a long breath of air out of my nose. Just as I'd thought. Good old Nancy.

"And as you promised — this information is confidential?" I said, batting my eyelashes. Nancy held my gaze and nodded seriously. "Of course. This interview is strictly confidential."

"So . . ." I trailed off.

Nancy scratched the back of her head. "So, I don't think they'll need anything else. Hang around for a few minutes, though, anyway."

The cops scribbled notes and talked between themselves, and Father Gavanto joined in. Vigile Roberto made a joke, and the father laughed.

"Thank you, Bridget," the father said at last. "Very helpful."

"You're welcome," I said stiffly.

The two cops stretched. Vigile Mario lit a cigarette, offering the pack to Nancy and to me. We both shook our heads.

"Bridget, you are free to leave," the father said.

I stood up slowly, trying not to seem too eager. "Should I send in Greta?"

The cops looked between themselves; Vigile Roberto folded his arms behind his head and rubbed the back of his ear. "No," he said, smiling.

When I left the library, I could smell my own sweat, a sweet, faintly tomato smell on my clothes. Greta was in the same spot where I had left her, still smoking.

"How was it?" She stabbed out the cigarette in an ashtray.

"Fine," I said. "I think it's all over now anyway."

I opened the door to the courtyard, and a gust of cold air mixed with the sweat under my arms. I longed for a bath. The wind stirred petals in the courtyard, gathering them in silky whirls. A cigarette carton wheeled under the gate and tumbled around the paving stones. I wondered if Isabella was awake.

The door to the library opened and Nancy appeared, followed by the father. He nodded to us and crossed through the courtyard doors.

"What's happening?" Greta said.

"It's all fine. Over," Nancy said, leaning against the doorframe and rubbing her eyes.

"Oh." Greta's shoulders dropped. "What a relief." She turned to me. "I'm going to call Bobby." Greta put her hand on my arm. "Thanks, Bridge. For the advice." And she half skipped along the corridor after Donna Maria.

"What was that about?" Nancy said.

"Nothing, trust me."

Nancy smiled weakly. "You're all right?" she said, squinting at me in an anxious way.

"Of course," I said, as somberly as I could. "Thank you for being discreet."

Nancy blinked. "Bridget —" She looked around us. "Thank *you*. For being so brave."

■ ■ ■ ■

Two steps at a time, I ran up to Isabella's room. My limbs were tingling, my body light. First, Isabella needed a decent meal. And a proper night's sleep. She'd probably sulk for a while. And it might take a few days for her to feel better, but then we could forget all about the fuss Sister Teresa had caused. The weather would soon be hot again. We would sunbathe by the lake and sit outside the *enoteca* late into the evening, drinking red wine. We would get up early to go to the market together, crunch through bags of almond biscotti sitting at the Brancorsi pier. I felt as bright and peppy as if I were floating in ginger beer. I was safe — *we* were safe! Graduation was approaching, and the long vacation beyond. And the last few weeks of term would be for us alone. I reached the landing with a jump and only just restrained myself from doing a jig. If Isabella saw I was so cheery, she might not take it kindly. I composed my face.

As I walked along the corridor to her room, there was a sudden flash of orange in the courtyard. I stopped and glanced out. It was Isabella. What was she doing? I knocked on the window, but the sound was swallowed by the glass. With a creak, I yanked the window and opened my mouth to call for her, then stopped myself. Isabella was running. Running with a lilt to her stride, like she was preparing to jump on a carousel. I stood by the window and watched as she passed through the courtyard gate. The breeze cast a velvet flutter of petals against my neck. It took me a moment before I understood why she looked so suddenly strange. She was happy.

Without thinking, I ran to the end of the corridor and down the back staircase, then out by the side door. Over the top of the hill I spotted her orange sweater behind a cloud of blossoms. She was winding through the back of the orchard. I picked up my pace and jogged up the hill to see her disappear behind the cypress trees on the path that led toward the lake. I ran after her, my heartbeat lodging somewhere in my throat. The day was cooler than I had realized at first, and I was unpleasantly sticky, like a thawing piece of meat. I crossed my arms over my chest. A ticking began in my temples, a clutch of dread in my gut. Why was she so happy? She was almost skipping. What could she even have to do down at the lake? Then it came to me — she was going to the spa.

34.

MARCH

I entered the spa as quietly as I could, straining to detect any sound. First I went to John Henry's room. The door was open, and I crept toward it, my breath catching. But the room was empty. Even the mattress had gone. I slumped against the doorway. Isabella was in the building, I was sure of it. Unless she had run through and crossed out the other side? I peered through the window onto the front patio, where white butterflies were flickering among the weeds. Maybe I had misunderstood? Maybe she wasn't cheerful after all. She might have just been running off somewhere to cry. Somewhere that reminded her of Sister Teresa. I dragged my knuckles over the wooden paneling. I was so sure she would be here. Walking back along the corridor, I opened each door in turn. Eventually I arrived at the ballroom and caught sight of my dim reflection in the rust-spotted mirror. When

Sister Teresa worked here, she'd often had to light the furnace to keep the pipes from freezing and bursting. Maybe Isabella had gone to the boiler room. The room was barely more than a cupboard behind the central staircase, and when I pulled the door open, the room contained nothing but the furnace and a pair of heavy gloves. I put my hand toward the copper pipes. They were warm. Why were they on? Surely it was far too late in the year to risk freezing pipes now. I was closing the door when I heard the half squeak of a footstep. I stood still and listened. The kitchen. Someone was in the kitchen. I ran through the arched door, down the stairs, and along the hallway, catching a gust of bitter charcoal even before I swung open the kitchen door.

There in the middle of the room was Isabella. And standing on her left was Sister Teresa.

They both turned to look at me.

"Oh," I said. My pulse rippled through my eyeballs. I steadied myself on the doorframe. I thought I might be sick.

"Bridget," Isabella gasped, a hand at her chest. Then she broke into a smile, as if she'd been expecting me. "Oh, Briddie, thank God."

"What?" I stared at her, and then at Sister

Teresa, who was wearing a pair of men's trousers, a knitted blue sweater, and a woolen cap. The outfit made her look so unlike herself it was like seeing an actor auditioning to perform her in a play.

Isabella wiped her face on her sleeve. "What a relief it's only you . . ." She trailed off. She had clearly been crying, but her eyes were bright.

Although they were standing apart, their bodies were angled toward each other. There was intention in the space between them. As if they had been poised on the brink of embracing, or as if they had only just pulled themselves apart.

My vision was churning with glitter. I rubbed my tongue around my mouth.

"I thought you ran away," I said eventually. I couldn't bear to look Sister Teresa in the face, staring somewhere in the direction of her collarbone.

"I did," she said with a smile in her voice. "I suppose."

"It's not funny," I snapped, catching her eye now. "The cops are here. Donna Maria was crying."

Her face fell.

"And what are *you* doing?" I turned to Isabella. "You know everyone is looking for her."

"Why are you mad?" Isabella frowned.

"Mad? The whole academy has been searching for her! All anyone has talked about is Sister Teresa for days."

"She's not a sister anymore," Isabella said. "It's Rosaria now. Right?" she said to Rosaria, and although I felt her nod in the corner of my vision, I didn't turn to look at her.

"Did you know?" I said to Isabella. "Did you know she was here the whole time?"

"Bridget —," Rosaria began, but I ignored her.

"Well, did you?"

Isabella smiled, a tear running down the side of her nose. "No." She shook her head. "I only just found her note." They exchanged a look of such saccharine intimacy, my stomach swirled.

I turned to Rosaria. "You should probably hurry up if you're running away," I said, crossing my arms. "Since the cops are looking for you and everything."

"Briddie, it's OK," Isabella said. "You heard what Nancy said. They're not going to chase after her."

"Well." I straightened my shoulders. "We can't be so sure about that. I had a meeting with them this morning, and they are seriously concerned." I swallowed. "And anyway, it's not going to help if they find you here." I motioned to the room, looking for evidence of a tent or a mattress. Had she been hiding out here the whole time? Had anyone even thought to check the kitchen? "Let's go," I said to Isabella. "Before they catch us and start asking more questions," I said pointedly.

"Briddie —" Isabella licked her lips. "Wait."

"For what? Let's not waste any more time," I said, heading toward the door.

"Bridget — wait."

I paused, my hand on the doorframe.

"I'm going with her."

The floor seemed to roll under my feet.

"Rosie knows some people," Isabella continued. "They can put us up for a while."

"Don't be stupid," I snapped, turning back to face her.

Isabella was chewing her lips. "I just — the last few days have been like — like — hell." Her face was flushed, tears glittering on her eyelashes. "I was already wondering, thinking about it" — she sniffed — "and now —"

I gritted my teeth. "What are you talking about?"

"I've decided," she said. "I want to go. To leave with Rosie. We'll stay out of the way until this has all blown over."

I heard a hollow bubble of laughter rise from my throat. "And then what? Don't be ridiculous. What about Ralph? Your family? Remember? In St. Cyrus. In *our* hometown, back at home."

Isabella swallowed. "I'll write Ralph a letter," she muttered. "And my mom."

"Saying what?" I spat. " 'Dear Ralph. Sorry I broke your heart but I've spontaneously decided to go on vacation with a runaway nun'?"

Isabella licked her lips. "I'll tell them the truth." She hesitated. "Nearly." She shifted her weight. "The academy is making me crazy. I need a break. And term ends in a couple of weeks anyway."

I pinched my fingernails into my palms. I could feel the situation sliding beyond me. "Listen," I said quietly. "Do you honestly think Ralph won't ask questions? That your mom won't call up Mrs. Fortescue in hysterics? For what? A whim?"

She licked her lips. "It's not — it's not." She held her hand out, and after a moment, Rosaria reached out, and they clasped hands once and let go. My heart pulsed so painfully it throbbed in my jawbone.

"And your vows," I said, turning to Rosaria now.

Rosaria's lip twitched.

"You turned your back on your vows. You made a promise," I said. "A holy promise to God."

Rosaria's eyes flickered. "I did. And then —" She swallowed.

"Well?" I said. "Is it so easy for you to break promises to God?"

"Bridget!" Isabella gasped.

"She's not the victim here." I pointed at Rosaria. "Why does everyone act like she's the victim? Like she's perfect. Like she never makes mistakes. She ran away! And now she's trying to convince you to do the same! She acts so wise and holy — but she's been lying —"

"You're right," Rosaria said.

I stared at her, nonplussed.

"I am a liar," she said, crossing her hands over her chest. "I've been lying to myself and to the father." She took a deep, steadying breath. "And to my sisters, and to you."

I bit the inside of my cheek. "Oh brother," I said. "You really expect me to feel sorry for you when you're forsaking God?"

Rosaria swallowed. "A novice must make a pledge," she said. "To empty themselves. It means to commit to death of the self —"

"Yeah, you already told us all about that."

"But I can't." Her voice cracked. "I've

failed. I've prayed and prayed but I can't make myself die."

I rolled my eyes. "You don't *actually* die," I said.

She grimaced. "It feels like it sometimes." She rubbed her face. "And when you told me about the wedding —"

My gaze flew to Isabella, but she was watching Rosaria with wet eyes.

"I realized the extent of my hypocrisy. Failing before God in my vows. Trying to empty myself, but — but — myself keeps fighting back. And to feel —" She glanced at Isabella. "To feel pain over such human things —" She began half laughing. "Jealousy. Regret."

"Jealousy?" I said woodenly.

Isabella took a step toward her, and without looking at each other, their hands found each other and intertwined. "Briddie, me — Rosie and me, we trust each other — we —" She wiped her face with the inside crook of her elbow.

"Don't," I said tersely. I couldn't bear to hear it. "Don't. I don't want to know."

Isabella released Rosaria's hand and rushed toward me. She wrapped her arms around my shoulders. "What will I do without you?"

I stood rigid. Her tears fell against my

neck. Over her shoulder I stared at the drops of melted plastic hanging from the shelves. Without me?

"I can't bear to go back to it, Briddie. Being Mrs. Wifey. Becoming my mom. Waiting around at the club, bored out of my mind, eating scallops."

"But you love scallops," I said into her hair. I seized on the image of Isabella, mournfully gazing into the salty liquor of a scallop shell.

She laughed ruefully. "It's not about the seafood."

"No, wait —" I was gulping for breath. "You can't." I gripped her to me, bracing her by the elbows. My ears were thick. "I don't understand. This is a mistake." I must have misunderstood, misheard. We were a pair. We were a set.

Isabella sniffed and pulled back, looking over at Rosaria. Her eyes were swollen and her lips mottled. "It's not a mistake, Briddie."

My body filled with heavy, wet sand. I was sinking through the floorboards. I put a hand on my chest. My ribs were cracking together and pressing into my lungs. She was leaving. She was truly leaving. She had finally seen that I had nothing to give her. I could stop trying. I could become nothing.

An empty room, unobserved.

"We can write?" Isabella said.

I pictured her letters arriving in the mailbox while I sat at home, waiting. Dull postcard reproductions of famous paintings, starchy, polite messages. "The weather is fine," she would say. "I had a cold but it's better now." It was too awful.

My ears popped; my limbs grew light. "But I could come with you," I said breathlessly. "I'll come too."

"What?" Isabella stared at me. A strand of hair fell into her mouth and she yanked it out.

It flashed before me. Me and Isabella standing at the window of a clapboard summerhouse. Isabella might yet become ill again, feverish, yielding. I would wipe her brow. She would gaze up at me, limpid, grateful. If I had just a bit more time, she might snap out of it. The whole thing would all be over by September.

"I don't want it either," I said. "The club. St. Cyrus." Even as I said it, it didn't feel true. But I continued. "The girls here — they don't understand me. My background," I said.

Over Isabella's shoulder, Rosaria's eyes focused on mine.

"I'll be back in half an hour. I'll pack a

bag. I can meet you back here."

Isabella spluttered. "I'm not leaving right this exact second. Tonight maybe."

"OK. Tonight, then." I would have to write to Granny immediately. I'd tell her I was touring art galleries. She'd send me an allowance, I was sure of it. Which bag would I use? "Tonight's perfect," I said. "Should I bring Rhona's fur, do you think? Will it get cold at night?"

Isabella was frowning. "No, but — but — you can't."

Rosaria tapped Isabella aside. "Bridget, are you sure you want to?" she said. Her eyes were willing. "Why not wait until after graduation? We could write with an address —"

"Oh, I don't need to wait," I said wildly. "It's like you said — when you know you're not happy, you have to make a decision." Had she said that?

Rosaria smiled. "You'd have to leave a note, explaining. And talk to Donna Maria —"

"I will," I said.

"But your mom," Isabella said woozily, and chewed on her lips. "Your grandmom."

"Don't worry about them," I said. "This is about me, not anyone else."

"Bridget's right," Rosaria said. "She has

the right to determine her own future." She folded her hands in a reflexive, nunlike way. "Yes. Of course. Yes — come with us!"

"But — what about — what about Rhona?" Isabella said. She crossed her arms and tugged at a lock of her hair, looping it around her finger.

"Oh," I said. "That's not important. I'll talk to you about Rhona later. That doesn't matter now."

Rosaria stepped forward and took my elbow in her hand. "Bridget," she said quietly. I could smell something sugary and medicinal on her breath, like licorice. "You should tell her."

I shook my head. "There's nothing to tell."

"Please. I know what you thought." She glanced at Isabella. "But you were mistaken. I assure you. Now is the time. You can trust her with the truth," Rosaria said. "We all need to be honest with each other."

"Trust who?" Isabella said. "Me? What?"

"Nothing," I said. "Nothing."

Isabella paled. "Has something happened?"

"No," I said. "Nothing."

Rosaria gave me a pitying look. She put one hand on Isabella's arm. "Rhona passed," she said gently. "Before Christmas."

Isabella gasped, then pulled away. "Wait,

what?" She frowned. "No, she didn't. I got a Valentine from her. Ralphy is tutoring her for her Wellesley exams."

Rosaria turned to me.

I opened my mouth. "It's not — it's complicated," I began.

Rosaria's eyes twitched and glazed over. "She's alive?" she said in a hollow voice.

"Yeah, she's fine," Isabella said, airily. "Briddie's grandmom wrote and asked me about sending her for a graduation surprise." She looked at me. "Sorry. Spoiled it now." She turned back to Rosaria. "Anyway, where'd you get that idea?"

"It's not — it's not like you think," I said. My throat was so tight I could hardly get the words out.

Rosaria said nothing. She put her hands in her pockets, and her eyes traveled over me slowly, a careful assessment. My stomach coiled into a rope.

"Rhona's coming all this way — she's been looking forward to it," said Isabella, turning to me. "You can't just jet off."

I shook my head. "I didn't know — anyway it's not — no, it's not —"

Isabella squeezed my hand. My palm was slick with sweat. "You're lucky, Briddie. You have Rhona. But there's no one that really needs me. Apart from Rosie."

"I need you," I said, trying to catch her fingers. She pulled away.

Rosaria cleared her throat. "You know, Bridget," she said, slinging her arm over Isabella's shoulders, "I believe you can take care of yourself."

"But —"

"I don't think you will be joining us," Rosaria said.

"No, I need you," I said to Isabella. "I need you."

"I'll miss you, Briddie," Isabella sighed with a reluctant grimace, as if she had mislaid an expensive sweater. "But I know you'll be fine. All the girls love you. You really don't need me."

"You can't," I said, my voice squeaking.

"We already are," Rosaria said. Her posture was rigid. As if she were up on a balcony looking down at me.

"But I can come with; it'll be easy. What do you need? I can help. I'll help."

"I don't think so, Bridget," Rosaria said. Her eyes flickered; she looked harassed, almost embarrassed. "That is not going to happen."

"Rosie's right," Isabella said, twirling her hair into a knot that immediately unraveled. "We kind of have our own thing planned," she said. "And it'll be cramped as it is, even with just the two of us. Won't it?"

Rosaria nodded. "Yes."

"But —"

Isabella chewed her fingernail. "Sorry, Briddie. But we already decided. And it won't work with three people anyway. Right?" She looked at Rosaria.

Rosaria shook her head. "No, that's right. Just the two of us."

TWO MONTHS LATER

The morning of graduation, bottle green dragonflies descended on the academy. I woke early and watched from my window as the bugs browsed the white grass, whispering in the leaves of the orchard. Donna Maria was sweeping outside, humming tunelessly under her breath. Someone was nailing a wooden dais in the courtyard, and the knell of a hammer echoed through the building.

"Make it stop." Rhona stirred in the next bed, putting her hands over her ears.

I ignored her.

"What time is it?" she groaned.

"A quarter of six."

"Damn it, I've been bitten again." She held up her arm and inspected the swelling.

I rummaged through my bedside drawer and tossed a tube of lotion on the bed. "Quit pouting," I said. "And if I were you, I'd get up now so you have a chance at hot water."

Slowly, Rhona sat up, combing her hair with her fingers. She rubbed a smudge of lotion on her forearms and, grumbling, climbed out of the sheets. As she stood, I evaluated her figure with forensic watchfulness for any indication that she had lost weight since arriving in Italy. She caught my eye, and her expression pinched as she took in my slack mouth and narrowed eyes. Hastily, I looked away. She said nothing.

Rhona and I had exchanged two terse phone calls after Isabella left, during which I'd frantically tried to preempt her appearance as "Cousin" Rhona. Wound with frenzied nerves, I'd pleaded with her to play along with my lark, my elaborate prank, my good-natured hijinks. It was a spoof, I said, a gag, a bit. All the girls did it. It was normal. It was so funny. Hilarious. She'd been out of school so long, I said, she'd forgotten what kind of antics were normal. Remember, I had told her, remember to bring her chicest clothes, her boar-bristle hairbrush, her ruby earrings. Remember, I had said, to be nice.

But now she was finally at the academy, I felt a queasy detachment, as if I were watching everything through the porthole of a boat. She might play along, or expose my lies. It both mattered more than anything and didn't matter at all. Rhona was brushing her hair in front of the mirror, and as it grew fluffy, she frowned at her reflection, smoothing it down with her palms. I sat on my bed and watched her combing and combing.

"Aren't you finished yet?" I said after some minutes. "I wasn't kidding about the hot water."

Rhona caught my eye in the mirror and slowly put the brush down. "I'm trying to look nice," she said. "For you."

My throat burned. I wished, suddenly, I could flip myself inside out, like a magician's hat. When she took her toiletry bag to the bathroom I knelt heavily on the floor by my bed and counted off my rosary, praying for nothing, for everything.

We joined the other girls for breakfast in the refectory. Everyone was wearing the required white day dresses, and alongside the sisters, everyone looked fluttering and tranquil as a flock of nesting birds. A few of the girls' family members had joined us for graduation — Patricia's parents had been vacationing in Spain and were gloriously tanned in the varnished way of people accustomed to traveling by yacht. Ruth had an incongruously bubbly and curvaceous older sister. Greta's mother was entertaining a group of students with a story of how Greta's brothers had returned from a camping trip infested with ticks.

Rhona and I sat at the end of the far table, away from all the hubbub. I positioned myself as a buffer between her and the rest of the girls, so no one would scrutinize how impossibly slowly she ate her roll. Across from me Sally tried to start up a conversation about our plans for Rome. I smiled at her and made what seemed like the right noises. Since Isabella left, I'd been pitied and petted and pampered and pitied again. But though I was aware of the girls' kindness, I couldn't feel it. Like I was watching their ministrations through a Perspex box. Sally made what I gathered from her expression was a joke. I laughed. Around us girls were brimming with summer. With weddings and family reunions, with Fourth of July galas and trips to London and Paris. I looked at Rhona, who was deliberately working her way through her butter roll with a knife and fork. My daydreams about Rhona smuggled away at the spa felt like the delusions of a stupid, childish version of myself. We weren't peacefully reading by the lake or petting kittens. Rather we were bickering about leaving the windows open, and Rhona was demanding archeological provenance for every blade of grass.

Farther down the table, Katherine leaned forward. She motioned for me to shuffle toward her. "Bridge —" She grabbed hold of my hand.

I looked down at it.

"You're not at the summerhouse this year, are you?"

I stiffened. Could Rhona hear?

Katherine's face fell. "Oh, sorry — you don't have it anymore, right?"

I shook my head.

She squeezed my fingers. "Will you come, though? For the cup match? It's the end of June so there's still plenty of time. My mom is dying to meet you."

I watched her carefully. Was this a prank? "What do you mean?" My voice was croaky, as if I hadn't used it in a while. "What about Sylvia?"

Katherine sighed. "Sibbs is at Lake Michigan 'til August. But please say you can come? We'll have a scream. Or — you're not going to be in Italy all summer, are you?"

"No." I swallowed. "But —" I stared at her, not wanting to say the words aloud. "It might just be me," I said finally.

Katherine frowned. "I know."

I pictured myself on a leafy patio surrounded by Katherine's family, wide-mouthed cousins in tennis whites, all bony elbows and inside jokes. "Are you sure?"

I suppose she must have taken it as a yes, because she hugged me. "Oh, Bridge, I can't wait. You can have Marion's room. And Mom says Princess is about to have puppies, so . . ."

As she talked, I was aware of Rhona behind me. She had put down her knife and fork and was sitting silently, her hands pressed between her knees. I had a sudden image of all the times she must have sat like that, clenched, silent, in her bedroom, at our dining table. All the times that I hadn't been there.

"Can I let you know later? For sure?"

Katherine beamed. "Of course. Write me from Rome when you know your plans."

The way she said it: *Write me from Rome.* The carelessness of it, the usualness. As if writing from Rome was an indelible part of my life now. I knew it should have bewitched me, but it just made me feel strange. Like there was a scent in the air everyone could smell but me. I shuffled back up the bench to Rhona.

"Ready?"

She nodded, then tipped her head over my shoulder. "That redhead has been trying to get your attention."

On the other side of the room, Nancy was staring at us. As she caught my eye, she began walking purposefully across the refectory. I gripped the underside of the bench, my neck prickling. I'd been dreading Nancy meeting Rhona. She was so earnest; it would be like trying to deceive a Girl Scout. I picked up my water glass and pretended to drink from it, but it was empty.

"How do you do?" she said to Rhona. "I meant to come introduce myself earlier." She held out her hand. "I'm Nancy."

The bench shuddered underneath me as Rhona inched her legs over and stood up.

"Bridge, I didn't know you were expecting a visitor," Nancy said to the back of my head.

I turned around so I was facing them. "Yeah."

Rhona shook Nancy's hand. "I'm Rhona. How do you do?" A fizzy swell of hysteria surged in my chest to see these two incongruous parts of my life colliding — like mingling sausages and cherries.

"Ah . . ." Nancy tipped back her head. "Bridge has told us all about your adventures in Capri," she said.

Rhona cleared her throat.

A heavy, leaden thump flung itself against

my rib cage.

"I'm sure," Rhona said in a deadpan way. She nudged her handbag into the crook of her elbow.

I poured myself a glass of water, but my hand was unsteady. Water spilled over the rim and onto the bench, pooling in the grain of the wood.

"I wish my cousins cared enough to visit for graduation," Nancy said, laughing with a snort. "At Christmas they thought Milan was a type of cookie."

Rhona adjusted the handle of the bag again on her elbow. "Well," she said. "Well. Yes. We — we don't have much family," she said at last. "So we have to stick together."

My skin flushed with relief, gratitude, shame. My eardrums were ringing.

"And how is your grandmother's health, if I may ask?" Nancy frowned. "I suppose she's your grandmother too?"

Rhona's lower lip twitched. "She's —" She stared at me, a question mark wobbling on her face.

My stomach pounded. Rhona was checking with me. Checking to make sure that Granny was OK, in this version of my life. I wished again I could knock myself inside out, that I could nullify myself utterly. I gave her an almost imperceptible nod.

"She's — she's fine," Rhona said, her face relaxing. "Thank you for asking."

Nancy folded her arms across her chest. "You know, I'm glad you're here," she said abruptly.

"You are?" Rhona's face tightened.

"Well —" Nancy shot me the fraction of a look. "It's good, I mean. For Bridge. That someone could be here."

I squeezed my palms between my legs. Now Isabella was gone. That's what she meant. There was a torpid crumpling inside my chest, a scrunching.

"You're probably right," Rhona said sharply.

After breakfast, we congregated in the courtyard. Everyone was wearing their Sunday best, Donna Maria in a blue dress and matching hat, Elena in an astonishingly stylish white linen suit. Mrs. Fortescue took to the dais and spoke about the virtues of the Pentilan scholars and then made a discreet allusion to contributing to the alumni fund. She then awarded Nancy a prize for best academic achievement, and in lieu of a speech, Nancy read a long Clemente Rebora poem in Italian, which made Signor Patrizi wipe his eyes while the rest of us examined our cuticles and nervously swatted away curious bees. Then Mrs. Fortescue handed out our graduation certificates, announcing our names one by one. Mary Babbage was first, then Sylvia. I waited for what was coming next. My heart thrummed.

"Isabella Crowley?"

Desperately, I looked through the crowd of girls. I searched through the convent gate, scanning the doorway to the nuns' cells, toward the shrine, behind us, into the open doors of the building. There was a chance, wasn't there? There was still a chance. But after a moment, Mrs. Fortescue cleared her throat. "Granted in absentia," she said.

Katherine applauded. "Hooray for Izzy," she shouted. Nancy frowned at her and then looked at me. Greta was looking at me too. I pretended to be adjusting my gloves. Sweat ran down the back of my neck and into the collar of my dress. I had been so sure. Something in the pit of my stomach cracked in half.

After the final certificate had been handed out, we climbed the dais and posed for a group photograph. I kept my eye on the corner of the courtyard by the convent gate, feeling the camera flash against the side of my cheek.

After the photograph, Rhona and I took

shelter in the meager shade on the stone bench by the palm tree, cradling warm glasses of prosecco.

"Listen," she said, shifting her sunglasses onto her head with such determination I knew she was about to pass some sisterly judgment. "You do know she's not coming back?"

I didn't answer her. I took a long sip from my glass.

"You understand that, don't you?"

I shrugged. "She's unpredictable," I muttered. "You never know what she's going to do."

"I think that's part of the problem," Rhona said, rolling up her sleeves and cautiously scratching a circle around one of her mosquito bites.

I chewed the inside of my cheek.

"It's weird," Rhona said with a sigh. "I'm proud of you — but . . ."

I looked at her. "But what?"

"All of you girls . . ." She gestured to the mountains rising above the convent. "What an amazing experience you've had. It feels pretty wretched, sitting on the sidelines."

I was stung. "It's my graduation," I said. "What did you expect?"

She rummaged in her purse and lit a cigarette. I had never seen Rhona smoke before Italy, and it still looked alien on her, like a pair of shoes that hadn't been worn in. "Not the graduation, dum-dum. This whole year of living abroad, studying."

I shrugged. "You have Wellesley."

"That's true." She blew out a thin stream of smoke. "But it doesn't erase the past year. Sitting at home playing Go Fish with Granny."

I looked down at my knees.

Rhona tapped her ash onto the base of the palm tree. "It's no fun being the accessory to someone else's adventure."

She was watching me shrewdly. My heart squeezed. The disappearance of Sister Teresa had set everyone gossiping, but Isabella's early departure had been shrugged off as bratty eagerness for a month of sunbathing in Monaco. What had Rhona guessed?

"I'm not her accessory," I said sullenly.

"I wasn't talking about you," Rhona said, replacing her sunglasses.

"Oh." My cheeks burned. A skewer of guilt probed me under the ribs. Rhona was conspicuously not looking at me, but at the convent gates where Sister Luisa, the new speaking liaison, was intently concentrating on one of Sylvia's meandering stories.

"I'm really sorry, Rhona," I said.

She said nothing.

"I wasn't trying to upset you."

"Hmm."

"It's funny," I said, conjuring a desperate laugh. "The Dalmatian, the sailing boat. I thought you'd enjoy it."

"I'm not enjoying it," she said, pinching the end of her cigarette.

I swallowed. I was so exhausted from being sorry it felt like grains of sand were embedded under my skin.

"I am sorry," I said again.

She flicked her ash toward the tree. Then she sighed. "Does Cousin Rhona at least have a glamorous background? Black widow?"

"Knock yourself out," I said wearily, laying my head back against the trunk of the palm tree. It was straggly and coarse, but my head was heavy for my body.

"And can you get them to stop asking me about sailing? Say I have amnesia or something — I can't fake any more enthusiasm about boats."

"Sure," I said. I should have been grateful she was helping me. That she was even still talking to me. That she hadn't told Mama or Granny. I tried to summon a flicker of gratitude. "Thanks," I said eventually.

Rhona began talking about the logistics of

traveling to Rome, and the map of the catacombs she had picked up from the tourist office in Milan. I allowed myself the daydream that at any moment, I would see Isabella's dark hair flashing through the blousy trees in the orchard. "Didn't think I'd miss out, Briddie, did you?" she'd say. Across the courtyard, Greta and Sally tipped their heads back and laughed at a shared joke.

"Well?" Rhona was saying, watching me.

"Whatever you think makes the most sense," I said meekly.

Greta's mother delivered a card to Sally with a shy underhand, and after Sally opened the envelope, there was more laughter and hugging.

Greta peeled away from the embrace and caught my eye across the courtyard. She raised her hands and yelled, "Secret's out!"

Sally turned her tearful face toward me. She mouthed, "Thank you." Her happiness, her gratitude for the nothing I had done, was sharp on my tongue. I nodded at them.

Rhona stabbed the cigarette out on the bench. "Between you and Ralphy I don't know who's more heartbroken."

"Ralph?" My stomach jittered. "What about him? Has he heard from her?"

Rhona tutted to mean "no." It was such a

Mama gesture that for a moment it disarmed me. There, somewhere in the corner of her mouth, was the faintest trace of Mama. How had I not seen it until now?

"I forgot he was tutoring you," I said. In fact I hadn't known at all until Isabella had told me. "Isn't he at Yale Law, anyhow? What could he possibly teach *you,* Miss 4.0?"

"Greek," she said.

"What does Ralph know about Greek? Other than Greek drinking societies."

She folded the cigarette butt neatly in a napkin and stowed it in her handbag. I opened my mouth to tease her about it and stopped myself. I had lost all rights to poke fun at anything.

"Once you get to know Ralph, he's not so bad. Sort of sweet, really. A goofball."

I watched the defensive line of her nostril, the guarded way she snapped her jaw. "Jeez. Not you too with that guy? I'll never understand the appeal."

She raised her eyebrows at me. She had lined them, and the angle made her look unusually haughty. "I could ask you the same question."

I stared off into the corner of the courtyard. Katherine was gesturing for me to join a photo with Sylvia. I shook my head, trying to smile and failing.

Rhona sat upright on the bench. "I think Ralph's got the right idea, actually," she said meaningfully.

"Oh?" I said, anticipating a trap.

"Well, for one thing, he's not wasting his time longing for Isabella."

"Don't," I said.

"*He's* not lying awake, mourning."

"Don't," I said again. And all at once I began to cry. It was a slow, bitter cry, as if the tears were made from sludgy ice. It hurt me to cry like this, like walking across splinters of glass in bare feet. I didn't even care that across the courtyard, Sally looked over, and Ruth, and Ruth's sister, and Patricia, and Patricia's parents. "Please don't."

"OK," Rhona said, embracing me. "Shit, I'm sorry. I'm sorry. Truce?"

"Truce," I said, wiping my eyes. I put my head limply on her shoulder.

She patted the side of my face. "Now let's get drunk and go sunbathing. I need to work on my tan before fall."

I laughed, wiping a dribble of tears from my top lip. "Ease up about the tan, will you?"

"You can't talk — you're a milk pudding." She pinched my arm, quite hard.

I swatted her away, but a rush of affection

for her swirled through my insides like a stream of amber.

After three glasses of prosecco, Rhona became dizzy and demanded a siesta. She dozed off straightaway, one arm over her eyes. I was restless and uncomfortable. The sugar from the wine had given me a headache, and after twenty minutes, I left Rhona to sleep and paced aimlessly into the common room. Since Isabella had gone, it had surprised even me, the extent of my banal catalog of our time in the academy. I kept snagging on memories too trivial to share: when Isabella dropped her pen down the back of the armchair, when she stubbed her toe on the corner of the rug. I found a soft packet of Pall Malls abandoned on the fireplace, which I claimed for my own. I smoked one sitting on the windowsill overlooking the hill down to La Pentola. I couldn't bear to look at the spa.

I spotted the corner of a familiar brochure lying facedown underneath one of the armchairs. I climbed down from the sill and pulled out the German recipe booklet. It had evidently been lying there for some time, since it left a trail in the dust. Had I dropped it there so carelessly? It was more likely that one of the girls had tossed it aside after leafing through it in my room. I looked at it for a long time, hardly daring to open it, to see if the illustrations would bring me peace as they once had done. I perched back on the windowsill and wiped the cover on my sleeve. I flicked open the booklet and there they were. Cozy little pies, stout and round. And something that I'd thought was lost fluttered back to life. I wished that I could jump through the page and live in the picture. I saw myself making the pies, standing at a marble counter, tucking and folding and clipping and crimping. But that wasn't enough. Somehow I also wanted to *be* one of the pies, actually inside one, nestled and snug. It was so ridiculous I heard myself laughing, and the ache in my chest relaxed, just a bit. I clasped the booklet closer to me.

That evening Rhona and I lay on the twin beds in my room, sweating into the sheets. The evening had grown even warmer, a quaggy, humid heat with the coppery taint of anticipated thunder. Cicadas quavered in the hills. An owl called out from the orchard.

"Isabella," Rhona said, out of nowhere.

My pulse shot into my temples. For a wild moment I thought she had been reading my thoughts. I cleared my throat. "What about her?"

"Do you think she's made a mistake?"

I pictured the space between Isabella and Rosaria the last time I saw them in the spa. How they were standing, apart, but oriented toward each other. All the carefulness and potential of that empty space, the risks they were taking to cross it. I pressed my fingernails into my palms and then released them.

"No," I said at last.

"Good," Rhona said pointedly. "It's good that she's happy."

My temples throbbed. Isabella was happy. Without me. With Rosaria. Their happiness was so unfair I felt quivering in every muscle. Like I had built a house that someone else had come to live in. Their happiness was just beginning. And I had nothing. It was the same sunken feeling from the trip to Rome, the day I had watched smiling families eating pasta and I had stood on the street, unnoticed.

"And in the fall. What will you do?" Rhona said.

"What do you mean?"

"When I'm at Wellesley. You don't want to study anymore, do you?"

"No."

"So what's next, then?"

My eyes prickled. "I don't know," I said. I searched myself for a grain of promise, but I was empty. My soul was too limp to even cry properly. "I don't care about anything."

Rhona reached across in the dark and took my hand. Her grip was weak, her skin cold. "Bridget," she said, "that's the dumbest thing I ever heard."

Despite myself, I smiled. Tears rolled along my cheeks and into the bedding.

"Let's just focus on having a good summer," she said. "You can do that at least?"

I pictured us on the porch of a summerhouse. Sitting side by side on matching Adirondack chairs, a salty breeze ruffling the pages of our magazines. Rhona passing me a pack of cigarettes. It was peaceful, kind. It was safe. "OK," I said.

"This might be my last vacation for a while," she said, as if the thought pleased her. "I'll have to work really hard next semester."

I recognized that she was trying to talk about herself. Maybe even to confess her nerves about school or studying. But I wasn't ready to relinquish the conversation to her hopes or dreams. "I worked hard," I said churlishly.

"Well, I'm sure you did," she said.

"I tried really hard," I said, my throat aching. "This year."

"At school?" she said, turning onto her side and searching my face. "Oh," she said. She put her other hand over mine as well. Her fingers were still cold, but I gripped them gratefully.

"I tried really hard," I said again.

"With Isabella?" she said quietly.

I nodded, wiping my cheeks with the sheets.

"Oh, Budgie," Rhona exhaled. She squeezed my hand. "Setting your heart on something doesn't mean it's a good idea. No matter how much you want it."

"But —" I swallowed. "What more could I have done?" I braced myself for an acerbic analysis of my faults. I was ready for her criticism. Whatever she said, I deserved it.

"I don't know," Rhona said. I felt her shrugging. "Maybe you should have used your time together better. Talked to her about — about things."

I bit the inside of my cheek.

"Did you?" she said. "Talk to her, I mean. Did you make plans?"

"No," I said. "Not exactly. But we did have plans. We had — There were plans. I had ideas. I have so much to offer."

"Do you?" Rhona said, so doubtfully the comment flew at me like a dart. "What?"

The barb landed in my throat, hard and sour as a bee sting. I swallowed against it. "Love," I said.

After a moment, Rhona said, "Sometimes love isn't enough."

"That can't be true," I said. What did she know? I thought bitterly. What did she know about love? About wanting and waiting and trying and loving? "That can't be true. What else is there? After love?"

Rhona sighed. "Bridget, if you have so much love to offer, you need to be more responsible about who you give it to." I opened my mouth to protest, but she cut me off. "Make sure at least they know how to receive it."

"I do. She —"

"And love doesn't automatically make someone a good person. Lover or —" She broke off. "What's the opposite of 'lover'?"

" 'Beloved.' "

"Lover or beloved," she said. "And —"

"She *is* a good person," I interrupted. After a moment I said, "And so am I," even though that didn't feel true anymore. "I am a good person." My voice was hollow and shaky.

"Are you going to let me finish?" Rhona said tartly.

"Sorry."

Rhona took a deep breath. Along the hallway, I could hear the swirl of water, the bathroom door swinging. Greta and Sally were whispering in the corridor, laughing. Someone creaked open a window overlooking the courtyard, and the whir of cicadas grew louder.

"I'm sorry," I said again. "Keep going."

Rhona pressed her palm against mine. "Bridget, you'll just have to trust me on this. It's totally possible to keep on loving someone" — she squeezed my hand — "even if you don't like them very much."

ACKNOWLEDGMENTS

First, to my agent, Hattie, thank you for your boundless confidence and camaraderie. Thank you for your tireless support of this book during the long process of adjusting the recipe for uncooked cake mix.

Turning a manuscript into a book is the work of so many people, and I want to thank everyone on the team at Blake Friedmann for all the behind-the-scenes support it took to get to the finish line. Thank you also to the team at my new home at The Blair Partnership.

Thank you to my editor Juliet Annan for your wisdom and wit. I'm so grateful for your encouragement and confidence; it's genuinely an honor to be part of Fig Tree. A huge thank-you also to Assallah — your input has been essential at every step.

A big thank-you to Shân Morley Jones for your copyediting skills, and to Holly Ovenden for the beautiful UK cover.

To Catherine Drayton at InkWell Management, so many thanks for believing in *Belladonna* and finding it a home in the US.

Thank you to my editor Amanda Bergeron at Berkley. Our editorial meetings have been a true pleasure and challenged me in the most unexpected ways. Thank you for your insights and your trust. I am so lucky.

For my gorgeous US cover, thank you to Emily Osborne. Thank you also to Sareer Khader and to Eileen Chetti for my copyedits.

Thank you to my first reader, Maria, my incredible partner-in-pd.

Thank you to my family: my parents, Marion and Ahmad, and to Walid, Hussein, Alya, and Yasmin.

To Struan — you've been living with this book since the beginning, and your support, kindness, love, and patience have made it possible. I can't thank you enough.

ABOUT THE AUTHOR

Anbara Salam is a research associate at the University of Oxford and has a PhD in theology. She is named after her great-grandmother Anbara Salam Khalidi, a feminist translator and writer who was the first Lebanese woman to remove her hijab in public. She's half-Palestinian and half-Scottish, and lived in Lebanon for a year and traveled extensively around the Middle East, Asia, and Europe.